Born in Manchester in 1960, R. N. Morris now lives in North London with his wife and two children. *The Cleansing Flames* follows *A Razor Wrapped in Silk*, *A Vengeful Longing* and *A Gentle Axe* in a series of St Petersburg novels featuring Porfiry Petrovich, the character created by Fyodor Dostoevsky in *Crime and Punishment*. *Taking Comfort* was published by Macmillan under the name Roger Morris in 2006. He has written the libretto for Ed Hughes's opera *Cocteau in the Underworld* and his novella *The Exsanguinist* was published in 2010 by Didier.

The Cleansing Flames

R. N. MORRIS

faber and faber

First published in 2011
by Faber and Faber Ltd
Bloomsbury House
74–77 Great Russell Street
London WC1B 3DA

Typeset by Faber and Faber Ltd
Printed in England by CPI Boookmarque, Croydon

A CIP record for this book
is available from the British Library

ISBN 978–0–571–25915–1

2 4 6 8 10 9 7 5 3 1

For Nigel and Jeni

'Some were especially intrigued by the possibility that a fateful secret lay hidden in his soul; others positively liked the fact that he was a murderer.'

The Devils, Fyodor Dostoevsky

St Petersburg

April 1872

1

An idea made manifest

The arsonists had chosen their target well. The warehouse was wooden and it contained barrels of vodka, produced at the nearby distillery on the small island in the Malaya Neva.

Pavel Pavlovich Virginsky stood on Alexandrovsky Prospect, looking up at the burning building. Brilliant orange tongues licked out from the windows, questing the black night. Virginsky could sense the fire gorging itself on this plentiful fuel. More than that, he could hear its savage, drunken roar, as it grew in force and intensity. A series of booming explosions, like gigantic belches, resonated within. So far the structure was holding out, but its collapse was surely imminent. The smoke was thick with the stench of burning resin from the timbers as they started to catch. Weightless seeds of fire swirled in the hot eddies above and around the building, an aura of destruction. It was in the fire's nature to spread itself, consuming and converting everything in its path. These sparks were the emissaries of that intent. The surrounding apartment buildings, exposed in a tremulous glow, seemed to shiver as they awaited its approach.

The choice of location had a symbolic resonance, as the avenue had only recently been named in honour of the Tsar.

They had chosen their day carefully too. Easter Sunday night. Even Virginsky had been shocked by this. He considered himself an exemplary freethinker and indeed was not afraid to call himself an atheist, at least not in the privacy of his own conscience. But even he, that day, had paid a seasonal visit on his departmental head, Prokuror Liputin, to declare Christ risen and exchange kisses with his colleagues.

Virginsky thought now of the extended embrace in which Porfiry Petrovich had held him, as if peculiarly unwilling to let him go. After the kiss, the older man had looked searchingly into his eyes. His look held a challenge, and seemed to sense Virginsky's unease. Certainly, Virginsky had attended largely as a matter of form, for reasons of professional prudence. It would not do for a magistrate to absent himself from the Departmental Head's home on Easter Sunday. It would certainly be noted, and a black mark placed against his name. The question asked by Porfiry's glance seemed to be: *Can you really not believe?* Perhaps for that day, he did. He at least saw the wisdom of pretending to. The unease that Porfiry's gaze identified was the spiritual imbalance caused by hypocrisy.

Perhaps that was why he had rushed out to see the fires. He was in awe of those who had started them. By adding blasphemy to the crime of arson, they proved that they were not afraid of the old superstitions; by bearing witness, Virginsky could perhaps expiate some of his earlier pusillanimity.

One thing was for sure, Virginsky was not there in his capacity as a magistrate. He was not wearing his civil-service uniform and was dressed instead in an old overcoat from his student days that he hoped would not draw undue attention. Had he been observed by anyone from the department, or by a spy working for other departments, he would have been able to argue that it was within his remit to familiarise himself with the nature of the criminal damage being perpetrated. Should any fatalities result, he and his superior – Porfiry Petrovich – may well have been called upon to lead an investigation. He was simply acquainting himself with the scene of a crime on his own initiative.

Except, as Virginsky knew, there was a little more to it than that.

The fire drew him elementally.

The splendour of it gripped his heart. This was an idea, a terrible, wonderful, ineluctable idea, made manifest. A radical fervour lived in the restless twists of the flames, in their eager stabs and sallies. It was an idea that towered over him, that threatened to destroy him, even though it was – at that moment – an idea he believed in, an idea he hungered for.

He welcomed its heat on his face, almost as if he was welcoming the prospect of his own annihilation. If he must become nothing for the sake of the all-conquering fire, then so be it.

Virginsky was not alone. A crowd of mostly students – the fire was not far from the university district – together with some lowly looking clerks, and even a number of junior army officers, was gathered there. Like the fire, the mood was constantly fluctuating. At times, a wild elation spread through them. Their shouts rode on the crack and hiss of the flames. Then, suddenly, it was as if they were cowed by what they were witnessing. They knew that something had been unleashed. Perhaps among them were the individuals who had unleashed it. Just as suddenly, the memory of the grievances they held, on their own and others' behalf, shook them out of this muted depression. They spat and fumed. Anti-tsarist slogans jostled with calls for universal destruction.

Virginsky felt his heart enlarged by the transgressive spirit of those around him, though he was careful not to join in the shouting.

5

But more than anything, the dramatic tension of the building's fate held them. This was more than spectacle, it was theatre. They could hear the clanging bells of the approaching fire carts, close now, very close. But still, would the engines arrive in time to save the warehouse? Surely not. At any moment the fire would take hold of the building's shell in earnest. Conflagration and collapse were only moments away.

The first of the fire carts thundered into the avenue, pulled by a team of two horses. It seemed to be heading straight for the crowd, which scattered at its approach. The men of the St Petersburg City Fire Company were standing on running boards either side of the steam pump engine. They rode the jounces of speed skilfully, ducking and rising on their knees, their Achilles helmets bobbing like puppets' oversized heads. But as the cart banked to pull up, the firemen swayed precariously. One man fell from the cart. He toppled like a surprised acrobat. His helmet somehow came off in the fall. The speed of it all made it difficult to be certain but he must have hit the ground with his head, because Virginsky saw immediately that he was not going to get up.

The cheers of some of the students shocked him. But when the second fire cart came on the scene, and the fallen fireman was trampled under the horses' hooves, they were silenced. They turned away from his mangled body as if from a distasteful outburst.

And then, at almost the same moment, there was another sequence of explosions from the warehouse and the roof was suddenly no longer there. Huge orange waves burst out, a sea of fire lashing the night sky. The fallen fireman was forgotten.

The crews were too late. In almost the same instant, the walls of the warehouse fell in with a low, grumbling crash. The building was no more. There was only fire.

The horses, though blinkered, were naturally uneasy; they whinnied as they strained their heads away from the heat, shifting their hooves in agitation. The men, though, were too intent on the task in hand to pay any heed to the animals. As they jumped down from the carts, they seemed pathetically tiny in comparison to the vaunting flames. They set to with a grim energy, trailing draw-hoses into the river. (Fortunately, the warehouse was situated within pumping distance of the Malaya Neva, at the point where the Alexandrovsky Prospect joined the recently constructed embankment at the southern tip of the Petersburg Quarter.)

The steam engines began pumping, pistons heaving and sliding with mesmerising monotony. Two white jets shot high into the air, breaking up and vaporising before they reached their target, puny and ineffectual for all the red gleam and glissando power of the fire engine. The crackle of the fire was like laughter on a vast, inhuman scale.

All they could hope to do now was contain it.

More fire carts arrived on the scene, smaller ones, some drawn by just one horse, others pulled by men. These pumps were manually operated, and the jets they produced were weaker than the steam-driven ones.

It seemed to Virginsky that all this was a waste of energy and, in light of the fallen fireman, of life. The fire would prevail. There was nothing men could do. They must give it its head, let it have its way. They could empty the Neva onto it and it would do no good. The fire would stop only when it was ready to. And even if they succeeded in putting this fire out, another one would be lit somewhere else.

The arrival of the firemen embarrassed him. They reminded him that he was a government official. What was he doing standing and watching while they risked everything to fight the fire? The fact that one of them had died made matters even worse. Besides, the police had turned up now. The crowd was thinning. It was time to make his exit.

He fell into step beside a tall, rather shabbily dressed man with a high narrow face that was somehow reminiscent of a bespectacled axe head. The man wore a workman's cap pushed back to his crown and an old service greatcoat with the insignia stripped off. The two regarded one another warily. It seemed to Virginsky that the other man was keener to get into conversation than he himself was. Virginsky's overriding instinct was to keep his own counsel.

'It is unfortunate about the fireman,' said the man.

Virginsky nodded minimally.

'Still and all,' continued the other, his voice brimming with daring, 'there must be sacrifices.'

This rankled with Virginsky. 'It's easy to call for others to sacrifice themselves. And cowardly.'

'I quite agree. I was not calling for sacrifices. Merely observing their inevitability. If only the Tsar would abdicate voluntarily, in order to hand power over to a socialist central committee.' His mouth hiked up on one side sarcastically. 'If such deaths occur,' he continued, his voice serious again, almost icily so, 'it is not the fault of those who wish to overthrow the unjust regime. You would do better to lay the blame at the feet of the regime itself. It has made such acts necessary by clinging on to power.'

Virginsky said nothing. He puckered his lips disapprovingly.

'You were there, watching the red rooster rampage, I saw you,' commented the other man.

Virginsky shot him a questioning glance.

'Yes, I saw you. Indeed, I was watching you. Your face. You want . . . this.' His eyes slid shyly back towards the fire. 'As much as any of the others, though perhaps you were not as . . . vociferous. Still and all . . .'

'One may approve the aims of those who wish to change society so that it functions along more just lines, without approving their methods. I cannot condone the loss of life.'

'But was he killed by those who started the fire or was he killed by the St Petersburg City Fire Company who failed to ensure his safety as he travelled on the cart? Or indeed by the Governor of St Petersburg, who has failed to introduce statutory regulation to improve the safety record of fire engines? He is not the first fire-man to take a tumble from a galloping fire cart. He was a work-er – my comrade, my brother. I do not exult at his death. Unlike some of those . . . heartless . . . bastards. Still and all, I am not sure I must hold the fire-starters responsible. You will admit that they were scrupulous in attacking property – government property at that. The risk to life was minimal.'

'This was not the only fire set tonight. His may not be the only death. And I doubt the people will thank them for burning the vodka.'

The same one-sided sarcastic smile returned to the man's face. 'As I said before, there must be sacrifices.'

Virginsky felt the man's hand on his arm, pulling him to a halt; he glared resentfully at the presumption.

'My friend, there is something I would like you to read.' The man's smile now was entirely lacking in sarcasm. It was strangely

9

sweet and ingratiating, almost vulnerable. But he continued to hold on to Virginsky's arm tightly, as though he would not release him until he had responded to the challenge in his last statement.

'Kindly let go of my arm.'

'Will you read it?'

'I cannot say. I don't know what it is.'

'Do you realise what a risk I have exposed myself to in asking this of you?' There was a strange glint in the man's eye.

'You have put me at risk too.'

'No. The risk is greater to me. You may be an agent provocateur.'

'And so might you.'

The man began to laugh. His laughter was like an axe hacking into soft wood. 'We may both be. And we may unwittingly entrap one another.'

'I do not find the prospect amusing.'

'Permit me to assure you, I am not an agent provocateur.'

'It matters nothing to me. And besides, you would say that, even if you were,' observed Virginsky.

The other man smiled. 'I am a sincere and well-intentioned citizen. I consider myself to be a patriot.'

'Of course.'

'And you?'

Virginsky shrugged. 'This is ridiculous. I have nothing to say to you.'

'If I release your arm, what will you do?'

'Go about my business.'

'That would be a shame. For you. And perhaps for us.'

'Who is this *us*?'

'A small group of people who think as you do.'

'You do not know how I think.'

'I saw your face!' The stranger's insistent cry sounded like a denouncement.

Virginsky cast a nervous glance over his shoulder; at the same time, he tried to pull away, though without conviction. The man tightened his grip. Virginsky clicked his tongue impatiently. 'Why do you hold on to me?'

'I told you, I have something I want you to read.' The man's voice was hushed again. 'If you will agree to read it, I'll let you go.'

'Why are you so concerned with having me read this manifesto of yours?'

'I didn't say it was a manifesto.'

'What else would it be?'

'It might be a poem.'

'You mean a manifesto in the form of a poem. I've seen enough of those.'

'So, it is not without precedent. That you would read a poem.'

'Then it is a poem? I'm afraid I do not have an ear for poetry.'

'That's not true now, is it? You were very moved by the poetry of fire. Back there.'

'Unhand me.'

The man released his hold. 'You are free to go. Of course.'

But Virginsky did not move away. 'Very well. I will read your damnable poem.'

The man produced a bundle of handbills from inside his greatcoat. He held one out to Virginsky. 'Take it quickly,' he hissed.

Virginsky obeyed.

'Now put it away. Read it when you are alone.'

'So,' said Virginsky. 'Our business is concluded.'

11

The man smiled. 'I was not wrong about you, was I? You won't let me down.'

'I've no idea what you are talking about.'

'You will read it. And perhaps afterwards, you will seek me out to discuss it.'

'Seek you out? How am I to do that?'

'You will invariably find me at moments such as this.' The man gave a strange smile. 'Do you realise what a risk I am taking telling you this?'

'Then why tell me?'

'Because I saw your face,' insisted the stranger. 'I saw your face when the flames were reflected in it.'

'What's your name?'

'You don't need to know my name. Not yet. Perhaps one day.'

'But if I am to seek you out, I will need your name.'

'If you cannot find me, I will find you.'

'This is ridiculous!' exclaimed Virginsky. 'Mystification. You must give me more to go on.'

The man's expression darkened. 'You ask questions like a magistrate.'

'I am a magistrate,' confessed Virginsky, to his own surprise.

The other man's laughter was so soft it was almost silent. 'That makes you either a very dangerous man, or an exceptionally useful one.'

'I needn't have told you,' Virginsky pointed out.

'And so I should trust you?'

'Sir, permit me to remind you: you initiated this conversation. You held on to my arm. You forced your manifesto on me. I asked nothing of you, least of all that you should trust me.'

The other man smiled and nodded approvingly. 'I chose you not just because of your hunger –'

'My *hunger*?'

'For the flames,' explained the stranger. 'I chose you also for your intelligence.'

'I do not appreciate being chosen.'

'Of course you don't. Which is another reason why I chose you!' The man was delighted at his paradoxical remark.

Virginsky gave an exasperated sigh.

The man seemed to relent. 'If you were to look for me in a tavern, you would do well to start in Haymarket Square.'

Suddenly, the night seemed to cry out in protest. It was a bestial sound, a baying, looping roar, vibrating with panic and wild fury, a hundred contorted throats stretched in the darkness. For a moment, Virginsky could not explain it, and it frightened him for that reason: it was as if pure irrationality had been given voice. Was this what the great idea released? You started from reason and rationality and ended with this: the sound of animal terror in the night.

It frightened him too because it was so close.

He looked towards the source of the noise. It was coming from the Zoological Gardens, he realised with relief. The animals were jittery at the unnatural brightness that seemed to surround them, and at the whiff of fire in their nostrils.

When he looked back, he saw that his companion had gone. Virginsky thought he detected a lingering smell of something pungent and combustible where the man had been.

Ahead of him he could see the contained flickering of the beacons at the top of the twin rostral towers on the Strelka. The ceremonial lights seemed feeble in comparison to the destructive

13

wildness of the fire he had just come from. A plank walkway led across the ice towards the tip of Vasilevsky Island; in a day or so, it would be replaced with a pontoon bridge.

The walkway was clear. Wherever his companion had gone, he had not crossed the river there.

The boards creaked and dropped dangerously as Virginsky stepped onto them. His heart lurched. He took two steps and the boards sank sharply. His arms windmilled as he struggled to keep his balance.

Virginsky swore under his breath, suddenly unsure that he would make it to the other side. The walkway had felt more solid when he had crossed it earlier that evening. All the comings and goings to and from the fires must have weakened the ice beneath it. In many ways it was the worst possible place to cross the river, now that the river was so close to thawing.

But he did not want to get caught on the Petersburg side.

He took slow, shuffling steps, his arms extended either side of him, a tightrope walker suspended over the icy depths of the Neva. He counted his steps. It was an old habit, from his student days, when he had wandered the streets of the city, often in a semi-starved trance.

By the time he got to the other side, he had counted eight hundred and twelve. His calves were aching with tension, almost locked solid. But as soon as he set foot on the Strelka, and felt the firm kick of the ground beneath him, his legs turned to jelly.

There were scattered groups of drunkards wandering over the Strelka, shouting raucously and passing bottles around. Virginsky hurried quickly on.

He crossed the Bolshaya Neva by the Isaakievsky Bridge and soon found himself in Admiralty Square. The square was filled

14

with looming shapes, monstrous silhouettes stalking the night. It took a moment for Virginsky to understand what he was seeing. These were the temporary constructions of the fair, the *balagany* – great square booths for street theatre and puppet shows; he could also make out two towering ice mountains, a dormant carousel and a row of swingboats idling in their frame. It had all been thrown up in the days before Easter. The square was almost empty now, just a few drunken revellers staggering bewildered between the closed-up booths. It made an eerie impression on Virginsky's nerves. The ghosts seemed to be waiting for him to leave so that they could continue their revelry. At one moment he thought he could hear the echoing din of the clashing sounds that would fill the square tomorrow. It was as if something violent and yet vital was about to be unleashed on the city.

He realised it was just the cries of the roaming drunks.

*

Back in his rented room on Gorokhovaya Street, Virginsky lit a tallow candle and set it on the small desk beside his bed. His bottle-green civil-service uniform was hanging on the back of his door. It seemed to look down on him disapprovingly.

Virginsky shook his head at the notion. He was simply projecting his own self-disapproval onto the uniform, turning a set of clothes into a conscience. Wasn't this how man created God in the first place? If it wasn't a set of clothes it was an idolatrous object, or some more sophisticated refinement of that – a symbol or a set of stories.

At any rate, the uniform was nothing more than the extern-

15

alisation of his conscience. Still, it made him uncomfortable. He turned his back on it deliberately.

He wanted tea, but it was too late to disturb Anya, his landlady's servant.

One day I will have my own samovar, he decided. *Then I can drink tea whenever I want.*

Virginsky imagined the axe-headed man's sarcastic smile, as though he had overheard his thoughts and was mocking their pseudo-revolutionary tenor. *Samovars for all!*

He sat at the desk and took out the handbill. What he read chimed strangely with his own recent sentiments

God the Nihilist

I do not say that God is dead,
Nor deny that God exist.
But this I affirm instead:
God is a Nihilist.

God is man-made, but no less real;
Of man's fears, does he consist.
Stitched from such stern material,
No wonder God's a Nihilist.

The only Truth is human reason.
God knows this and does not resist.
Religion is a dog with fleas on,
So says God the Nihilist.

Thus God assents to his own undoing,
And ushers in the realists.
Faith's a juice for slaves to stew in,
Now all our Gods are Nihilists.

For every nation creates its own God,
And on its God, it does insist.
Which I think you'll agree is odd,
Knowing God's a Nihilist.

Human conscience governs all.
The one true Law is humanist.
There was no apple and no fall,
And the only God, a Nihilist.

Virginsky couldn't resist a smile. It was undoubtedly nonsense, and would not stand up to scrutiny, but still there was a certain originality to the central idea. God a nihilist, indeed! He would have to remember that for Porfiry Petrovich. He dared say it would succeed in provoking the old man.

But really, what was the point of it all? What did the author hope to achieve?

In truth, the poem struck him as quite tame and harmless, even with the added call to arms that was printed beneath in bolder typeface:

Christ the enslaver, Not the saviour.
Pull down the icons! Steal the precious stones!
Set fire to the crosses! Desecrate the churches!

**A church is itself a desecration of the one Truth
– Human reason.**

He would add it to his collection, but he had to confess he was disappointed.

2

Petersburg burns

Demyan Antonovich Kozodavlev chose to remain at his apartment, watching the orange glow that was visible from his fifth-storey room. But he was a journalist, for God's sake! Wasn't it his duty to get out there and report what was happening? For, undeniably, momentously, something was happening.

A year ago, Paris had burnt. Now it was St Petersburg's turn.

As his eyes widened to drink in the flaring glow, Kozodavlev bit down on the nail of his right thumb. He glanced over his shoulder nervously. But there was no one there to witness his reactions. Even so, he felt acutely self-conscious. No, it was more than self-consciousness, it was an unshakable sense that there was someone with him, there in the room and always, watching his every move. Was it *her* presence? But she had left him a lifetime ago, and he did not believe in ghosts. Besides, if she were to come back from the dead, he would be the last person she would choose to haunt, unless the dead were moved by regret in ways the living were not.

He turned back to the window, towards the lambent pulse that fringed the sky. The fire flashed and rose, reaching a startling height in the surrounding darkness.

An apartment building, most likely.

Kozodavlev winced and bit harder on his nail. Was he imagining the roar of the people? Was it a roar of approval or rage at what had been unleashed in their name? Or was it the dying roar of those trapped in the flames?

He could hear the tocsins of the fire carts and imagined himself among the crews, handing grateful residents from the burning ruins. After all, property was the target of the attacks, not people. He had always been clear about that.

The consoling fantasy did not last. It was replaced by a cold certainty, more frightening than dread. If he was right and it was an apartment building, people would certainly die. Some of them would be workers.

That was bad, very bad.

These were the people on whose behalf these acts were committed. Or so he had always supposed.

Again he looked over his shoulder and again reassured himself that he was alone.

He had heard the arguments before, made them himself on many occasions, in print as well as at meetings. Sacrifices were necessary. Whoever was called upon should consider it an honour to give himself to the cause.

Besides, the people had brought this all on themselves. If only they had taken up the call when the time was right, none of this would be necessary. But you couldn't trust the people to act in their own interests. Really, the bovine passivity of the Russian peasant beggared belief! Even when the Tsar had cheated them out of what was due to them with that sleight of hand known as the Great Reforms, they were too stupid to see the fraud that had been perpetrated on them.

No, you couldn't leave anything to the people. You had to take up the cudgels on their behalf, even if it meant a few hundred of them were incinerated in the process.

The fires seemed to be spreading.

Had it indeed begun?

All that they had planned for?

Kozodavlev did not sleep at all that night, didn't even retire to his bed. Even after the last throb of amber had died from the sky, he continued to stand at the window, straining the darkness for sight of fresh fires. A nerve sprang into frantic, flickering life beneath his left eye. The end of his thumb was wrinkled from sucking, though he had still not bitten through the nail.

At last the true dawn broke. Slow, celestial flames stretched languidly across the full extent of the sky, dwarfing the bonfires of the previous night.

Not God – no, not God. Never!

Even he admitted that there was something suspect about the fact that he had to remind himself of this truth. It was nature, science, the position of the earth in relation to the sun, atmospheric conditions – that was all. This rosy grandeur had nothing at all to do with any divinity. It intimated nothing more than another warm day ahead, and the promise of a thaw.

Kozodavlev turned away from the window and threw himself down onto his bed. He was surprised to discover that where his face touched the pillow, there were traces of dampness. He wiped the rim of one eye with the knuckle of a finger, lay down his head again, and slept.

*

His dreams were disturbed, but not broken, by the pounding rumble of cannon fire. He knew in the depths of his sleeping Russian soul that they were the cannons of the Peter and Paul fortress, signalling the breaking of the ice and the start of spring. And so the commander of that fortress entered his dream, in all his finery, offering him a crystal glass of pure Neva water, as if he, Kozodavlev, were the Tsar. But it was his hunger that finally woke him.

By the time he put on his coat to go out, a bright spring day was well under way.

There was still snow underfoot, hard-packed and obdurate after the long winter. Lattices of frost clung defiantly to the bases of walls and parapets. But the sun was crisp and businesslike in a clear sky. He felt its warmth on his face, the rays of the new season burning down destructively on the remnants of the old. As he walked, he was aware of the thin layer of greasy slush forming.

He came to the Moika river, heart quickening. The proximity of any large body of water did this to him now. Instinctively, before looking down at the surface of the river, Kozodavlev checked behind him, as if he believed that whoever was spying on him would have noticed this change in his physiology.

Which of these harmless-looking citizens, apparently going about their business without paying him any heed, was the Third Section spy assigned to watch him? He avoided looking too inquiringly into any of the faces that passed him by. But none of them jumped out. He was almost reassured.

At last he peered down, over the balustrade. He knew that he had been delaying this moment, and knew precisely why. It was as he had feared. The surface of the river was mottled with grey slabs of ice, edged in frothy white. Around the slabs, the black water seethed and lapped.

The thaw had begun.

Kozodavlev resumed walking along the Moika embankment, towards the Winter Canal. As he turned the corner, he glanced up along the length of the narrow canal, spanned by a series of bridges, and squeezed between two sheer faces of palace buildings. Ahead of him was the Hermitage Bridge and beyond that the full expanse of the river Neva.

He could hear strange clashing sounds, almost music; rather, what music would sound like if it were at war with itself.

The water of the canal, visible between the series of bridges that spanned it, was flecked with more of the same fragments of ice. The effect reminded Kozodavlev of psoriatic flakes lying loosely on the skin.

The sense of someone watching him was stronger than ever now. Indeed, he had come back to the place where he could confront the one who would never leave him. The one he had sensed standing behind him all through the preceding night.

It was idiotic. Why had he come here? In the hope of attaining some kind of release, or even redemption? Unnecessary. Irrelevant. The idea of redemption did not conform to a rationalistic outlook, which was the only kind of outlook possible. There was no need for redemption, there was nothing for which to be redeemed. Most importantly of all, there was no one to redeem him.

Everything that had happened, everything that he had played a part in – it had all occurred for the very best, the most rational, of reasons. More than that, it was necessary that it happened. He could have no qualms on that front. He should have no qualms at all.

And yet, he had to admit, some of the risks they had taken were not rational. He had made his point at the time. There were aspects of the incident that were coloured by a lurid spirit of recklessness. That was nothing to do with him. He had not approved of it. He had objected to it. They should limit themselves to what

23

was called for by the logic of social and political science. That was what he had said at the time. He had accepted that the deed was necessary on *scientific* principles; therefore it should have been executed scientifically too. But it was almost as if Dyavol had taken pleasure from it.

Dyavol. How appropriate the man's nickname was. The gleam in his eye when he had pulled the trigger was the Devil's own. He had seen it in *her* eye when she had made her choice and gone to him, as if the gleam was what drew them together.

In all conscience, Kozodavlev had nothing to reproach himself with. Indeed, had he not long ago successfully argued away the very existence of conscience, at least as something pertaining to a man such as himself?

All that was true enough. What was also true was that he had come back to the Winter Canal and was now scanning the surface of the water as if he expected to receive from it some kind of . . .

At last the word came to him. *Absolution.*

Kozodavlev was suddenly aware that he was not alone. His thoughts had been so isolating that he had failed to register even the group of young sailors who were running boisterously along the embankment towards the far end of the canal. But now their sharp, joyful cries spiralling in the clear spring air drew him out of his reverie.

As they ran and yelped, they shed their clothes.

One by one, whooping and goading each other wildly, the now naked sailors clambered onto the balustrade and threw themselves howling into the water. Eventually only one man was left, clinging hesitantly to the wrong side of the balustrade, laughing and shaking his head defiantly in the face of his companions' jeers.

24

And then even he let go.

Kozodavlev felt the apprehension tighten inside him as he watched this sailor disappear beneath the ice-capped water. He had a bad feeling about the boy – for he was little more than a boy. The chances were, he couldn't swim, which was why he had been so reluctant to take the plunge. Kozodavlev hoped that the other sailors would look out for him. If the boy drowned, it would be a tragedy. Such a death – an unnecessary death – was unpardonable.

If they must die, let them die for a reason. For the cause.

Thus Kozodavlev reassured himself that he was not a monster.

Then, at last the boy re-emerged, and Kozodavlev saw that he could swim as well as his fellows, despite being somewhat slighter in build. His reluctance perhaps had been feigned, or it was simply the prospect of the icy shock that had put him off.

There was something about this sailor's face that attracted Kozodavlev's attention. Broad-nosed and narrow-eyed, he was from peasant stock, undoubtedly, but his expression was intelligent, and therefore vulnerable. To think – to think deeply and honestly and freely – was to make yourself vulnerable. It involved cutting yourself loose from the security of received ideas and laying yourself open to new ones. It was an unsettling activity. Eventually, if one persevered, it led to greater strength. But first there was a period of uncertainty and anxiety to endure, from which some never emerged. They would spend their whole lives in a state of crippling doubt, cowering beneath a shell of cynicism.

Hence the wariness behind the young sailor's hesitancy. The quick darting glance of his eyes was questioning and slightly remote. He was less spontaneous, less natural. Happiest when he was swimming away from the ugly braying of his fellows. But still, not wholly content alone. Always he would come back to the group, to make himself again the butt of their stupid jokes.

He was a potential revolutionary, judged Kozodavlev. They needed young peasants like this, who could think for themselves – up to a point, it always had to be up to a point – and then take the word back to their villages. Loyalty to the cause is always stronger when the individual believes he has come to his convictions himself.

The young sailor executed an untidy but efficient duck dive, his two pale legs splayed as they kicked against the air.

Kozodavlev's apprehension returned. But this time he was not anxious about the swimmer's abilities.

It was there, just there, where the boy was diving that . . .

The boy's head broke the surface of the river, pushing aside two bobbing slabs of ice with a fierce shake of denial. A circle of spray shot out from his drenched hair. Immediately, he began shouting and gesticulating urgently to his comrades, his finger repeatedly stabbing downwards towards the bottom of the canal.

Kozodavlev bit down on his thumbnail, finally severing it, so sharply that the clash of his incisors scratched the enamel.

He took a step back from the balustrade but did not move away.

The nail fragment caught in the back of his throat, setting him coughing. Eventually, he was able to spit out the nail.

Kozodavlev now watched in horror as the mood of the other sailors changed gradually from hilarity to confusion, and then to a kind of hyper-alert tension. With varying levels of skill, they duck-dived beneath the broken ice.

The moment seemed longer than humanly possible: all the sailors gone from sight, the canal unnaturally quiet in their absence. If Kozodavlev was going to run, now would be the time to do it.

Then, one by one, they broke the surface, with huge, life-swallowing gasps, their lungs strained to the edge of endurance. The young boy who had caught Kozodavlev's eye was the last to emerge, his skin now turning blue with the cold.

Now, almost immediately, there was something else there with them, another presence, or almost a presence, not quite. A smooth, black, glistening mound nudged aside the suddenly agitated chunks of ice.

The sailors shouted excitedly amongst themselves. Then one of them, Kozodavlev's boy in fact, noticed Kozodavlev on the embankment watching them. Treading water, he waved his hands and called out to Kozodavlev.

'Hey, you! Mister! Find a policeman, will you? Or the City Guard.'

Kozodavlev frowned, as if he couldn't understand Russian, or had never heard it spoken with a Volga accent.

'What's the matter with you? Get the police, for Christ's sake!'

'The police?' Kozodavlev's voice had never sounded more false to his ears.

'There's a dead body here. It was tied to some rocks. We got it free. Someone must have dumped it in the canal. Before the water froze over.'

'A dead body, you say? Are you sure? My goodness, a dead body! Who would have thought it? And with all the fires last night.'

Now all the sailors were watching Kozodavlev, their faces dumbfounded. 'He's some kind of . . . madman,' pronounced one of them, a man with an unruly moustache that stuck out at right angles before him.

'Who is it?' said Kozodavlev, brightly. Even he knew it was a stupid thing to say, possibly the most stupid thing he could have said in the circumstances.

'Who is it?' exploded the sailor with the bristling moustache. 'How the fuck should we know?'

'Turn him over, I mean,' answered Kozodavlev. 'Let's have a look at his face.' The truth was, he was simply incapable of tearing himself away from that spot until he knew for sure.

The sailors exchanged consultative glances and decided, wordlessly, that there was some merit in the suggestion, even if it had come from a madman.

They clustered around the low cylindrical form that barely broke the surface of the water.

Like flies, thought Kozodavlev. *Around the proverbial.*

The slabs of ice seemed to shun the alien matter in their midst. Kozodavlev could now see it was the back of a frock coat, taut and filled with bloated mass.

At a signal from the sailor with the bristling moustache, the men gripped and heaved. It was clear they were used to working together. Kozodavlev felt a momentary pang of envy, the envy of the intellectual for the common man, always excluded. At the same time, he envied them their co-operative ease. What he could do with such men, if only he could recruit them to the cause!

He allowed his mind to run on like this only for as long as it took them to turn the sodden trunk, its limbs flailing in protest at the disturbance.

The sailors backed away, to lay bare the strange doll-like face for the madman on the embankment to see. But when they looked up, they saw that he had already gone.

3

A strange-looking fellow

'Do we have any idea who he is?' asked Porfiry Petrovich with a grunt. The granite pavement pressed sharply against his tender knees: he was crouched on all fours on the embankment of the Winter Canal, beside a mound of sodden matter that had once been a man. Additional stabs of pain danced along his spine, spreading out across his lower back. The smell from the body was unusually foul and fetid. Porfiry felt like he was diving into the heart of a rotting swamp.

The Easter fair in Admiralty Square was in full swing. Porfiry could hear the clash of competing barrel organs, and the roar of the crowd. The sounds were close enough to be distracting.

'According to *Ptitsyn*,' Virginsky enunciated the name distastefully, almost spitting it out, 'no means of identification were found on the body.' Virginsky looked down at the corpse with a recriminatory glance, as if he held the dead man to blame for this oversight.

Sergeant Ptitsyn clicked his heels in confirmation. The young policeman had been recently promoted to this rank, and, evidently, transferred to the Admiralty District Police Bureau, which was how he came to be on the scene. He seemed to have grown in confidence with his new position, though he gave the impression of being as eager to please as ever. He was still capable of showing due deference to his superiors.

Porfiry squinted into a blasted hole in the side of the man's head. 'It appears that he was shot. In the head. Therefore it is reasonable to assume that he was dead before he entered the water.'

'Of course, we will need a medical examination to confirm that,' Virginsky reminded his superior.

'That goes without saying, Pavel Pavlovich,' agreed Porfiry, without removing his eye from the side of the man's head. 'Which is why I did not trouble myself to say it.'

'He must have been there all winter,' said Ptitsyn. 'Beneath the ice.' His tone was pitying. He narrowed his eyes compassionately.

'It surely made no difference to him,' said Virginsky. 'He was dead, after all.'

The young police officer's brows dipped reproachfully.

Virginsky was unrepentant. 'At least he is well preserved.'

Porfiry Petrovich straightened himself up with a grunt. He held a hand out to Virginsky to steady him as he got to his feet. The lumbar pains stayed with him. In fact, they had been with him for months now, settling themselves in over the winter. He had hoped that the warmer weather would see them off. But they gave no indication of going anywhere.

Porfiry was long past the age when he welcomed each new spring with unequivocal enthusiasm. Granted it was the return of life to the natural world. Rivers began to flow again. Trembling buds forced their way through the dwindling layers of snow to bask in the warmth of the waxing sun. According to conventional wisdom, the sap was rising in the boughs. But the truth was, Porfiry no longer believed in this rising sap. For him personally, each new spring marked only the passing of another year, and consequently the shortening of his remaining portion. And now it seemed he could not even count on it to dispel his aches and pains. The long winters, that in his youth had seemed to be endless, went by in the blink of an eye. He looked back on the winter just gone as he looked back on every moment of his life so far, with a pang of nostalgia.

He kept his eyes fixed on the man at his feet, as if he found the sight consoling. 'I want a photograph taken. We will publicise the man's face.'

'Strange-looking fellow,' adjudged Virginsky. 'The white on his face, at his cheeks ... he doesn't look quite human. More like a doll, or a mannequin.'

'Adipocere,' said Porfiry.

'What?'

'Adipocere. Or grave wax. It occurs in bodies that are exposed to moisture. The fatty tissues convert to ... well, basically, soap. The medical examiner may be able to calculate how long he has been in there based on the degree of conversion.'

'But it makes identification difficult.'

'Yes. However, there may be enough of the original form of his face remaining to prompt someone into coming forward. You will notice that in the areas that have not converted, the skin is disfigured by severe pockmarking. Furthermore, his eyes appear disproportionately small, do they not? Distinctively so, we might say. We can only hope that someone will be able to piece together these distinctive features, prompted perhaps by the disappearance of a friend or loved one.'

'It would be difficult to love that,' commented Virginsky.

'Show some respect, Pavel Pavlovich. You will be dead yourself one day. I doubt it will be a pretty sight.' The heat of Porfiry's ill temper was genuine.

He turned away from the corpse and looked up. The sky was

31

cornflower blue, an effortless, meaningless expanse of breathtaking colour. He sniffed the vernal air savagely. Spring changed the scent of the city; the thaw released the moisture from the waterways, and the breezes carried wafts of lilacs and bird cherry. But today it was all overpowered by the swampy smell emanating from the corpse. It brought to mind another powerful stench that would soon overwhelm the city. Porfiry wrinkled his nose and settled his gaze on Virginsky. 'Dear God, it will soon be summer.'

'But Porfiry Petrovich, the ice has only just begun to melt.'

'Today the ice melts. Tomorrow the drains are stinking and the flies are back. You know how it is. It all comes around too quickly these days. A sign of getting old, I know. You don't need to say it.'

'I wasn't going to.'

'So the ice melted and the body floated to the top? Is that how it was, Sergeant Ptitsyn?' Porfiry demanded sharply.

'Not exactly, your Excellency. A group of sailors swimming –'

'*Swimming?*' Porfiry stared down at the water, which was still dotted with slabs of ice. 'In that?' He glanced incredulously over at a handful of men in naval uniforms, who were standing watchfully at a short distance. He was sensitive to their proprietorial manner, as if they considered their claim over the body greater than his.

'Is it so different from you taking a cold plunge at the *banya*?' wondered Virginsky.

Porfiry did not deign to answer, except to blink rapidly, as if the question was a piece of grit in his eye.

'I have taken statements from the sailors,' said Ptitsyn. 'But I ordered them to remain, in case you wished to speak to them yourself.'

'You did well,' sighed Porfiry, as if it pained him to pay a compliment. 'You men,' he called out to the sailors. 'Which of you discovered the body?'

The men scowled back, little inclined to answer. Then the youngest of them nodded hesitantly and broke away to approach Porfiry.

'That would be me.' He was glum but not hostile, but neither was he particularly respectful.

'And you are?'

'Apprentice Seaman Anatoly Ordynov.'

Porfiry took out an enamelled cigarette case and flicked it open towards Ordynov. The young sailor took a cigarette and allowed Porfiry to light it for him. Porfiry then lit his own and the two men smoked in silence for a while.

'A nasty shock, I imagine, on a fine spring day?' Porfiry ventured, conversationally.

The young sailor nodded, *Right enough*.

Porfiry read the name on the sailor's cap tally. 'You serve on the *Peter the Great*? A fine ship.'

The junior sailor gave the most minimal of nods as he inhaled.

'The most modern ship in the Baltic fleet,' remarked Porfiry.

'The most modern ship in the world,' corrected Ordynov. His pride was a fierce glimmer in his eye.

'When do you have to be back on board?'

'We have a couple more days in the capital while she undergoes repairs. But now that the ice is melting, we are clear to sail.'

'Two days? Then I am truly sorry we have had to detain you. You will naturally want to make the most of every hour, every minute you are here. You will be off to the fair, I shouldn't wonder.'

The boy gave a shrug, non-committal.

'Still, you have time to smoke a cigarette with me, I dare say. And if I ask you a few questions while we smoke . . .'

Another shrug. 'It's all the same to me.'

'Just tell me how you found the body, in your own words.'

'I was swimming with my mates. I dived down to the bottom and there he was. At first I didn't know what to make of it. Couldn't tell what it was. It was pretty dark down there, you see. But I felt his hair brush against my fingers as I swam. I thought, *Hello, what's this?*'

'So the body was at the bottom of the canal? What prevented it from floating to the top, I wonder?'

'Rocks. It was tied to some rocks that were keeping it down.'

'I see.'

'Me and my mates went back down to loosen it. Then it came up.'

'And so you raised the alarm immediately?'

The young sailor glared at Porfiry. 'Well, yes, but . . .' He broke off.

'But?'

'Well, there was this fellow. We sent him off to get a policeman. But he never came back.'

'I see. One of your mates?'

'No!' Ordynov was indignant at the suggestion. 'Just some fellow. He was watching us, while we were swimming. There was something fishy about him. Not right in the head, if you ask me.'

'Why do you say that?'

'He asked us who it was! As if we should know. I mean to say!'

'That is odd.'

'It was almost like . . .'

'Go on,' encouraged Porfiry.

'Almost like he had half an idea who it might be.'

'That's very interesting. And perceptive, if you don't mind me saying.'

'We thought he was mad, the way he kept gabbling on. And then he made us turn that one over in the water, so that we could see his face.'

'The body was floating face down, of course.'

'Yes. That's right.' Apprentice Seaman Ordynov squinted narrowly at Porfiry. 'I mean why was he so interested in seeing its face?'

'A perfectly reasonable question, my friend. In fact, I would go further than that. A very astute question.'

'And then he ran off. We thought he was going to get the police, but he never came back. So we had to send someone else.'

'Could you give a description this mysterious individual?'

'He was a gent. But like one of them new types of gents.'

'Yes, I know exactly what you mean.'

'You could tell he was educated, but he didn't bother to keep himself as smart as he might.'

'Long hair?'

'That's it. Long hair. All over the place. His face was very . . .'

'Pale?'

'Aye, with dark rings around his eyes as if he had been up all night.'

'Beard?'

'He did have a beard.'

'Not a civil servant then. I take it he was not in any kind of uniform?'

Ordynov shook his head tersely as he blew out his last lungful of smoke. He threw the stub down and ground it under his heel. 'Finished my smoke.'

'Thank you, my friend. You have been most helpful. If we need to contact you again, we can reach you through your ship. You are in Petersburg for two days, you say?'

'We sail on Wednesday morning. Leastways that's what they say. I wouldn't be surprised if it takes longer.'

'And where are you bound once the repairs are completed?'

'Arkhangelsk.'

'How long is the voyage?'

'We are at sea for thirty days. We can't put in to Arkhangelsk before May, on account of the ice.'

'Do you put in anywhere along the way?'

'For sure.'

Porfiry waited expectantly. When nothing was forthcoming, he prompted, 'We may need to get in touch with you.'

'Our first port of call is Helsingfors. After that, Reval, then Riga, then Libau.'

'It is a veritable cruise!' cried Porfiry.

'His Imperial Majesty likes to show his finest ship off at every opportunity,' said the young sailor wryly. 'There are other ports after that. Do you want them all?'

'I do not think that will be necessary. I wonder, did anyone who is not going to Arkhangelsk see this man?'

Ordynov shook his head.

Porfiry gave a silent chuckle and nodded to release the sailor.

Ordynov twisted his lower lip hesitantly. He looked over to his shipmates but did not rush to join them. 'Do you think he had anything to do with . . . you know . . . that fellow in the water?'

Porfiry smiled but said nothing. The roar of the nearby fair seemed to answer the question for him.

*

An hour later, they were back in Porfiry's chambers in the Department for the Investigation of Criminal Causes. The department was attached to the Haymarket District Police Bureau on Stolyarny Lane, though the cases they investigated were not limited to that district. At his desk, Porfiry was bent over Sergeant Ptitsyn's report, which was already written up and filed. Virginsky, who was seated on the cracked artificial-leather sofa, was treated to a view of the top of his superior's close-cropped, bulbous head. The soft light from the window caught the almost transparent hairs in a phosphorescent flash. Virginsky had the impression that if he struck Porfiry on the back, a cloud of dust would rise to join the other fine motes swirling in the luminous corridor of the beam. He had no idea why the idea of striking Porfiry in this way came to him just then. Except for the fact that Porfiry's frockcoat was stretched as tight as an overstuffed armchair and Virginsky had once had a habit of thumping armchairs. But that was a long time ago.

'A fine officer, young Ptitsyn,' said Porifry. 'We are indeed fortunate that he was the first on the scene. This is an exemplary report.'

'The spelling's atrocious,' commented Virginsky. It did not please him to hear other men praised, especially Ptitsyn, and especially by Porfiry Petrovich. Virginsky knew precisely where his dislike for Ptitsyn originated. He had once been assigned to search a crime scene with the young policeman, and it was Ptitsyn

37

who had made the significant discovery. In his defence, Virginsky could say that he had not long been in the job. But still, he had underestimated Ptitsyn, deceived by the young man's good-natured willingness to please, taking that for simple-mindedness. Virginsky could not forgive Ptitsyn for the fact that he – Virginsky – had all the advantages, and yet it was Ptitsyn who had proven himself more able. He knew that it was undemocratic to harbour such resentments, which only made him hate Ptitsyn all the more.

All that had happened several years ago, and Virginsky should have been able to put his antipathy towards his social, intellectual and professional inferior behind him. But the fellow haunted him like a demon. He had an uncanny knack for turning up, like a counterfeit five-kopek coin.

Porfiry Petrovich looked up, his face open in reproachful surprise. 'The spelling is beside the point. He has recorded the exchange between the sailors and the mysterious onlooker practically verbatim. The art of investigation is all in the detail, you know.'

'So you *do* think he had something to do with it? The man the sailors saw.'

'It is certainly possible. It's not so easy as these new men think to shake off such a deed. Murder, I'm talking about. However rational, useful and even necessary the death of this or that individual may seem in advance – after the event, it's a different matter. So yes, I find it psychologically plausible that the murderer is drawn back to the place where he discarded his victim, especially at a time when there is a chance the body may come to light. That is to say, when the frozen canal begins to thaw.'

'But the fact is, we do not know who this onlooker is – and we may never. Indeed, we don't even know who the dead man is.'

'Please don't take this amiss, Pavel Pavlovich,' began Porfiry in-auspiciously. 'But I find your attitude today strangely negative.'

Virginsky felt himself flush.

'It's not helpful, you know, to have this constant carping and criticism to contend with. You could be more encouraging.'

'I am only being realistic. If I may say so, you are not normally so easily discouraged, Porfiry Petrovich. Indeed, usually, you take such challenges as a spur to do your greatest work.'

'Flattery. You can't fool me, Pavel Pavlovich. I have never heard you sound so insincere.' Porfiry rapped Ptitsyn's report impa-tiently with his knuckles. 'What singular feature most strikes you about this case?' he almost barked.

Virginsky widened his eyes as he considered the unexpected question. 'That . . . the body was dumped in the Winter Canal?' he suggested tentatively.

'Good! Yes! Now you're beginning to be useful to me! The body was indubitably dumped, as you so eloquently put it. Quite de-liberately. Brought, by some conveyance, to the Winter Canal and deposited in it. It is inconceivable that he was shot and weighted with rocks in such a public location, immediately prior to dispos-al. No – all that took place elsewhere, we can be certain. But why then bring him to the Winter Canal? That's the question. Why go to all that trouble when there are countless other, more isolated spots in the city where one could far more conveniently dispose of a corpse?'

'Because the killer –'

'Killer? You think this is the work of one man? Could one man contrive this? Would it not be more reasonable to assume some kind of conspiracy? The Winter Canal is a popular spot. A favour-ite haunt of lovers and suicides. People pass along it at all hours of the day and night. Would it not require some organisation, some small infrastructure, to ensure that this dumping of the body was not witnessed? A lookout positioned at either end of the canal, for example. We might also posit the existence of a driver, whip in hand, ready and waiting, should the need for a hasty retreat arise. And two individuals, at least, to manhandle the weighted body from the vehicle to the edge of the embankment. I picture it as a closed carriage.'

Virginsky nodded in agreement. 'A plausible reconstruction.'

'The question remains. Why?'

'By the way you are asking the question, Porfiry Petrovich, I suspect you already have an answer in mind.'

'Where is the Winter Canal?'

'Between the Winter Palace and the Hermitage.'

'In other words, right under the nose of the Tsar.'

'What are you saying, Porfiry Petrovich? What's this man to the Tsar?'

'Nothing – personally. But politically. Symbolically. It's a gesture. One that I believe is known as making a fig.'

'You think it is a political crime?'

'I think it may have a political aspect.'

'Therefore, we should alert the Third Section.'

'Ooh, I don't think there's any need for that. Not yet, at least. This is simply a speculative conversation between ourselves. We have no proof of anything, yet. As you yourself said, we do not even have a positive identification of the body.' Porfiry angled his head to appraise his junior colleague. 'I know what it is about you today, Pavel Pavlovich. You are evincing an unwonted scrupulosity.'

'I beg your pardon!'

'First you remind me of the need for a medical examination. Then you insist on the involvement of the Third Section. An unwonted scrupulosity. With regard to form.'

'I am a magistrate. I must uphold the correct procedure.'

'An *unwonted* scrupulosity,' repeated Porfiry, with energetic emphasis. 'I can't help thinking that you must have done something exceptionally naughty last night.'

Virginsky felt the heat in his face once again, even fiercer this time. 'But Porfiry Petrovich, that doesn't –'

'It is because you were naughty last night that you wish to compensate by being unusually correct today. Am I right?'

'I don't know what you're talking about,' said Virginsky coldly.

'But did you hear about the fires last night? My God, the fools! What do they hope to achieve by such acts? Can you tell me that, Pavel Pavlovich?'

'I am not a spokesman for the arsonists.'

'Five dead.'

'Five?'

'Yes, a fireman, a nightwatchman and some down-and-outs who were kipping on a straw barge that was torched. How can you justify their deaths?'

'I am not required to, as I did not cause them, and I do not defend those who did.'

'What? Quite right. I'm sorry. I am simply venting steam. Sometimes, I mistake you – because of your youth – for someone you are not.'

Neither spoke for some time, each considering privately the implications of Porfiry's last remark.

It was a relief to them both when the door leading to the

41

Haymarket District Police Bureau opened and the head clerk Zamyotov burst in.

He thrust some papers in front of Porfiry. 'Sign this. And this.' After a moment, he added, 'And this.'

'Begging your pardon, Alexander Grigorevich, but what exactly am I signing?'

'You want a poster printing up, don't you? That's what I understood you to say.'

'Yes, of course.'

'Then you have to sign the necessary chit. Even you are not exempt from that, Porfiry Petrovich,' added the clerk sarcastically.

'I appreciate that, naturally,' said Porfiry, signing his name on the first of the sheets. 'And this one?'

'For a statement to be released to the newspapers. And this one is for an advertisement to be placed, calling for witnesses to come forward.'

'There you are.'

'You haven't filled them in.'

'Can't you fill them in? I'm rather busy. I have signed them, as you requested.'

'I don't know the details,' objected Zamyotov.

Porfiry's face sagged with despondency.

'I'll fill them in, if you wish,' volunteered Virginsky.

'Thank you, Pavel Pavlovich. That would indeed be a great help.'

Zamyotov stomped from the room as if he had been cheated of something.

4

Yarilo

That night there were more fires. However, Virginsky did not venture out to view them.

On the way home from the department, he had called in at Gostinny Dvor and purchased the samovar he had promised himself. And so he sat up drinking strong tea into the early hours.

He found it hard to sleep, once he had turned in, and sweated more than usual in the night. Perhaps it was the constant ringing of the fire alarms, or perhaps it was the tea. He thought a lot about what Porfiry Petrovich had said to him: 'Sometimes, I mistake you for someone you are not.' What on earth had the old man meant by the remark?

And yet, Virginsky did not need to ask the question.

Sometimes, he mistook himself for someone he was not.

As soon as he admitted this, he was able to drift off. He fell immediately into an overwrought dream: he was running through St Petersburg away from a fire. Suddenly, he felt his progress impeded. Something was dragging at his feet. He looked down to see that the pavement was carpeted with a thick layer of handbills printed with various manifestos. With each step he took, the paper carpet increased in thickness, rising first past his ankles, then up to his knees, and rapidly reaching his waist. It was no longer a paper carpet, but a paper quagmire. He could hardly move at all now. Looking behind him, he saw that the swamp of manifestos stretched away into the distance. He saw too that it was on fire, and that the fire was racing towards him. He turned to flee the approaching flames, but became distracted by the words of a manifesto right beneath his nose. That was how high the layer of handbills had reached now.

The manifesto that caught his attention was entitled 'Samovars for All.' Now he was floating in a sea of lukewarm tea, and all the anxiety that the earlier phase of the dream had induced in him evaporated. He knew that he was no longer threatened by fire, but he was hot and thirsty. Whenever he wanted a drink, all he had to do was incline his head and lap from the sea of lukewarm tea.

Somehow the reality of his situation, independent of his dream, forced itself on him. It was simply that he was once again bathed in sweat. He woke.

The darkness of the room seemed to squat upon him, pinning him to the bed. There were matches and a candle on the desk, but he couldn't bring himself to grope for them. He felt that if he concentrated hard enough, the vague mood of the dream would form itself into a resolution that he could act upon. At the same time, he half-suspected that he knew already what the dream was trying to tell him. He knew too that he did not like its message, even though he had not consciously articulated it. And so the dream still held him; he was as incapable of movement now that it was over as he had been during it.

As he lay there, he felt his muscles and joints lock. There was a sense of surrendering to his immobility, of conspiring in it, even. This strange paralysis, he suddenly realised, was the product of his own will.

Life was so much simpler when you were incapable of taking part in it.

It occurred to him that in none of the manifestos he had read, and in none of the books on Socialism and Social Utilitarianism from which they were derived, had there ever been any allowance made for dreams.

*

The morning's newspapers were spread out on Porfiry Petrovich's desk. The magistrate's face was hidden by a copy of the *St Petersburg Gazette* and so he could not have seen Virginsky enter his chambers. This did not prevent him from observing, 'You look terrible, Pavel Pavlovich.'

'But you –'

'That is to say, judging by your shuffling step, and the fact that you walked into the door frame as you entered, I imagine that you must look terrible.' Porfiry at last laid down the paper and looked at his junior colleague. 'I see I am not mistaken. A bad night?'

Virginsky ran a hand over his face, as if to wipe away whatever ravages were evident there. 'I didn't sleep well.'

'No? Well, that is to be expected.'

'Why do you say that?'

'The fires, of course.'

'I had nothing to do with the fires,' protested Virginsky indignantly.

'I'm not suggesting that you did. I am merely stating that it is not easy for any of us to sleep easy while such atrocities are perpetrated around us. They set fire to an apartment building last night, I see.'

'An apartment building?'

'Yes. Not far from you. Bolshaya Morskaya Street. So far the number of dead is estimated to be . . .' Porfiry consulted the newspaper. 'Six. Five of whom were children. The sixth was an adult male. There are no further details of the victims given.'

'No,' said Virginsky quietly. The word was as much a protest as a denial.

'I'm afraid so. In fact, it is a miracle that so many were able to escape unharmed. It seems someone raised the alarm before the fire had taken hold in earnest. The devastation was largely confined to one floor. The fifth. Those living below that were evacuated safely. A blessed miracle, I say.'

'But do we know for certain that this was the act of arsonists?'

'There will have to be an enquiry, of course. And you are right to ask the question. It is easy to assume, in a spate of arson attacks, that every fire is deliberately started. In any individual case, there may be another explanation.'

'Indeed. And if you extend that logic, then it is possible to say that perhaps none of the fires have been started deliberately. The frequency of their occurrence may owe more to unsatisfactory building materials and dangerous living conditions.'

'It is simply that we are living in an exceptionally combustible city, is that what you are saying?' Porfiry smiled ironically.

'We are living in a city where men habitually drink themselves into a stupor and then reach for their pipes. I should add that it is invariably by gorging on cheap vodka, brought about by the Tsar's reform of alcohol taxation, that they attain this dangerous intoxication.'

'So it is the Tsar's fault? I thought it might be.'

'It is only the conservative newspapers, so far, who are laying the blame at the door of the students and radicals. And yet the idea seems to have caught hold. Everyone accepts it as the truth.

Even you, Porfiry Petrovich. But you have to ask yourself, what could the radicals hope to achieve by these tactics?'

'There are some men who are, undoubtedly, motivated by a universal love of mankind.' Porfiry leant back in his chair as he warmed to his theme. 'But they find that the mankind they love does not correspond exactly to the sordid, ungrateful, greedy men and women they see around them. Those individuals, they do not love. In fact, they hate them, for they only get in the way. While continuing to nurture a deeply felt love of mankind in general, and pursuing aims that owe their origin to this love, they find themselves acting in a manner that is consistent with their hatred for men and women as they actually are.'

Virginsky exhaled loudly through his nose.

'You don't agree?'

'I wonder from where you derive such sentiments. From the editorials of *The Russian Soil*?' Virginsky picked up the newspaper in question from the desk and held it out accusingly. 'Or from the lurid serials they publish?'

'You forget, Pavel Pavlovich, I have observed such men at first hand.' Porfiry fixed Virginsky with an especially provoking gaze.

'You mean me?'

'I was not thinking of you.' Porfiry's expression softened. He regarded Virginsky solicitously. 'Please, sit down. You really do look dreadful. Would you like some tea?'

'No! No tea. I already feel rather bilious from drinking too much tea last night.'

Porfiry picked up the newspaper that Virginsky had just dropped on his desk. '*The Russian Soil* has at least carried a piece about our body fished out of the Winter Canal. They have also published our announcement calling for witnesses to come forward.'

'I trust that the information is satisfactory in both cases?'

'Yes, thank you. I am grateful for your help with the requisite paperwork. Do you know when we might expect to take delivery of the posters?'

'With luck, we should see something later today, or perhaps tomorrow morning. I emphasised the urgency of the material in my application to the Imperial State Printing Works.'

Porfiry turned the pages of the paper. His eye was caught by an article headed 'The Devil's Professor'. 'Tatiscev, Professor Tatiscev. He must have taught you at the University, did he not?'

'Yes. What of it?'

'There is a piece about him. They call him "The Devil's Professor".'

'There you are! That proves my point.'

'It seems you are a rare exception, Pavel Pavlovich,' said Porfiry as he scanned the article. 'By far the majority of his former students have gone on to be defence attorneys. And very successful ones, it seems, with extraordinarily high rates of acquittal for their clients. *The Russian Soil* links this to the demise of law and order, and the general decline of society.'

'Preposterous.'

'It makes the point that the state is being undermined in its own law courts.'

'Please, Porfiry Petrovich. I can well imagine what those reactionaries have to say about him. I do not need to hear you recite it.'

'In short, they lay all the evils of the present day at Professor Tatiscev's door.'

'It really does pain me to hear you parrot their venomous lies. It's almost as if you believe them.'

'I wonder what prompted them to write this article though.'

'They are his enemies. They print lies about him in almost every issue.'

'What is behind it though?' wondered Porfiry as he folded the newspaper carefully and placed it thoughtfully on his desk.

'Nothing is behind it. Or will you arrest people on the basis of libellous newspaper articles?'

'Not at all. You misunderstand me, Pavel Pavlovich. I rather wondered if they had not been put up to it. Perhaps by our old friends from the Third Section. Such tactics are not without precedent.' Porfiry consulted his pocket watch. 'My goodness, is it that time already?' He rose sharply from his seat.

'Where are you going?'

'Admiralty District. The medical examination is scheduled to take place there this morning.'

'Do you wish me to accompany you?'

'Unless you have something better to do?' Porfiry looked meaningfully at the sofa. 'Such as catch up on your sleep.'

'Would that be permitted?'

'Most certainly not, Pavel Pavlovich. Really, do you not know when I am teasing you, even after all this time?'

*

The gilt dome of St Isaac's Cathedral caught fire in a blaze of easy splendour. A roar of approval greeted the effect, although the stone angels on the cathedral roof seemed about to take wing in panic. The sudden flare gave them a weightless, flighty vivacity.

Porfiry imagined the boundless blue around the cathedral filled with the celestial beings, swooping and flapping as they sought a safe alighting place in the godless city, like seagulls swarming a fishing boat. Of course, the appearance of combustion had been caused by a shift in the sun's position in relation to the one, wispy cloud in the sky. The angels remained attached to the roof, steadfastly static.

Below, under the gaze of the stone angels, crowds of people were streaming around the cathedral on every side, all heading in one direction: north, drawn by the noise and bustle that possessed Admiralty Square. One corner of the fair was visible from where Porfiry and Virginsky were standing, at the end of Malaya Morskaya Street where it joined St Isaac's Square. The carnival colours and teeming movement held their gaze.

There was an undeniably savage edge to the rumble of the crowd, a ferocious hunger for something other than the simple pleasures of the fairground. No doubt many of them were already drunk. The mood seemed fractious, rather than celebratory, bordering on nasty. The grating whine of the barrel organs, incessantly churning out fragments of melody, repeated and overlapping, unmusical, meaningless and quite unpleasant, did nothing to lighten it.

'Yarilo,' murmured Porfiry.

'I beg your pardon?'

'They greet the ancient deity of spring. Yarilo. Sometimes I wonder if we are a Christian nation at all.'

Virginsky offered no reply.

'Those who wish to remove the deity from men's affairs would do well to stand here and watch the crowds assemble at the coming of spring. It is an old, elemental instinct, and it cannot be denied.' Porfiry turned to Virginsky and met his gaze without speaking for several moments. 'Only delayed.'

'You talk as though you wish to join them.'

'Oh but I do, Pavel Pavlovich. I would far rather go with them to the fair than go where we must go.'

With a dip of his head, Porfiry indicated a pair of high double doors standing open. Wide enough to admit a carriage, this was the entrance to the building used by the Admiralty District Police Bureau as stables and storeroom. All the various carriages and wagons belonging to the bureau were housed here, together with the horses required to pull them.

From time to time, an area of the storeroom was put aside for an altogether different purpose.

A distinguished-looking elderly gentleman, wearing the red and black ribbon of the order of St Vladimir, was seated on a stool that had been placed for him on the wooden pavement, to one side of the entrance. He was propping himself up with both hands on his knees, his face an unhealthy shade of grey, eyes standing out from his face in startled horror. He directed this alarming expression towards the sound of the paving boards creaking, as Porfiry and Virginsky approached.

A sickly sweet waft of something spirituous hung about him.

Porfiry acknowledged his presence with a respectful bow. 'Are you here to witness the medical examination? I am the investigating magistrate in charge of the case.'

'I will not set foot in there again, sir.'

Porfiry raised one eyebrow for Virginsky's benefit. 'But you are here as one of the official witnesses? The law requires that we have two citizens present.'

'You cannot make me go back in there and look at that thing. It is too much to ask of a respectable citizen.'

'The other witness is inside, I take it?'

'The other witness took himself off entirely.'

'That is indeed unfortunate. We do need two witnesses.'

'I can hardly say I blame him.'

'Is it really so bad?'

The elderly gentleman's expression became sheepish. 'I'm afraid there was an unfortunate accident.'

'An accident?'

'At the sight of that thing ... the smell of it ... I was not able to hold on to my breakfast. I blame that doctor of yours.' The elderly gentleman shook his head disapprovingly. He produced a silver flask from his breast pocket and took a quick swig, releasing vodka fumes to the morning. 'I will be here if you need me. But I will not set foot in there again.'

Perversely, the witness's words only quickened Porfiry's eagerness to be inside.

As soon as he and Virginsky stepped through the entrance, they were met by the same swampy smell he had noticed by the Winter Canal. The light and air that flooded in with them seemed cowed by it, and hung back.

They found Dr Pervoyedov chatting blithely to his assistant – or *diener*, to use the accepted German term – next to a trestle table bearing the body to be examined. The cadaver's strange, waxwork-like face was uncovered.

Both Dr Pervoyedov and his assistant were dressed in long leather aprons, darkly stained. The *diener* was one of the orderlies from the Obukhovsky Men's Hospital, whom Pervoyedov had picked out on account of his aptitude for the peculiar work of the pathology laboratory. He had proven himself to have a strong stomach, in other words; one that held on to its own contents even when he was required to empty out the contents of others. That he was also a humourless and taciturn individual, as adept at retaining his thoughts as his recent meals, was perhaps understandable: Dr Pervoyedov accepted that here were two sides of the same coin. But he would have found almost any other temperament more amenable and certainly regretted the man's habit of assuming a doglike snarl whenever he set to work dismembering a cadaver.

'Ah, there you are, Porfiry Petrovich, there you are. And good day to you too, Pavel Pavlovich. At last, you are here. We may begin now, I presume?'

'One moment, doctor. There has been some difficulty with the official witnesses?'

Dr Pervoyedov winked slyly towards his unresponsive *diener*. 'Difficulty, you say? I can't imagine what you mean by that.'

'One has absented himself and the other refuses to fulfil his civic duty.'

'No matter, *no* matter. We don't need them. I always rather feel that the official witnesses are somewhat superfluous on these occasions, don't you? They haven't a clue when it comes to forensic medicine. If you ask them to perform the simplest task, they either keel over or vomit.'

'What did you ask them to do?' Porfiry's voice was heavy with suspicion. He had worked with Dr Pervoyedov for many years now. He knew the doctor well and liked him, although he did not always trust him. He was confident that such feelings were thoroughly reciprocated.

'Oh nothing really. I merely thought they might be interested.

Just trying to educate them, you know. One is never too old for a little *education*, now, is one? And besides, how can they be expected to bear witness if they haven't the least idea what's going on? It will be meaningless to them. Meaningless!'

'What did you do?' demanded Porfiry.

'I simply asked them if they wanted to smell some of the adipocere.'

Porfiry blinked in astonishment. 'And now we have lost our official witnesses! You are aware that we cannot proceed without them. You may resent the presence of unqualified laymen to supervise you, but the law requires it.'

'*Supervise?* I hardly think that is the right word.' A flash of indignation came into the doctor's tone. 'As I understand it, Porfiry Petrovich, the law merely requires that they sign the papers affirming that they have presented themselves here today in the capacity of official witnesses. I took the precaution of having them complete that minor administrative detail before uncovering the body.'

'And then you promptly scared them off.'

'Scared them off? Do you really think so?'

'Don't play the innocent with me.'

'I was only trying to demonstrate to them that the adipocere was the source of the rank smell that they had themselves commented on. I told them it was adipocere, but they looked at me blankly. So I had Valentin Bogdanovich scoop some out on a spatula and offer it to them.'

As if to confirm the doctor's account, the *diener* thrust out a wooden spatula towards Porfiry. On the end of it was a small mound of something soft and white.

'Adipocere is the most interesting substance,' continued Dr Pervoyedov, as Porfiry leant forward gingerly and inhaled. 'Many writers, the Englishman Taylor for instance, describe its odour as highly offensive. And yet, I wonder, if you did not know that it had been taken from a corpse, would you necessarily be repelled by the smell? It's an interesting question, is it not, Porfiry Petrovich?'

'There is no question about it,' said Porfiry, screwing up his face. 'It is a disgusting smell. Unequivocally.'

'*Un*-equivocally, you say? But what do you make of Casper, a German, and one of the foremost authorities of forensic medicine, who, I believe, rather likes the smell. *By no means disagreeable*, are his words – if memory serves me right. A little cheesy, but by no means disagreeable, is how he describes it.'

'I would say that Dr Casper has become too habituated to the smells of the charnel house.'

'Perhaps! That is certainly possible.' Dr Pervoyedov chuckled, as if at a private joke. 'I myself incline to Casper's view,' he admitted shyly.

'Then the same may be said of you,' commented Porfiry.

'But is it really *soap*?' asked Virginsky abruptly, having also sniffed at the sample on the *diener*'s spatula.

'Yes. Soap. Ammoniacal or, sometimes, calcareous soap. In the case of the latter, it is thought that the body first forms ammoniacal soap and that this is subsequently further converted by the presence of lime. But, yes, soap, of one form or another. The process by which the body is converted to adipocere is known as saponification.'

'Could you *wash* yourself with it?' wondered Virginsky. He looked down at the face of the unknown man on the trestle table.

Two glistening white patches showed where his cheeks once were. 'He is turning into a bar of soap.'

'He *was*. Since he has been taken out of the water and dried out somewhat, the process has stopped.' Dr Pervoyedov took a spatula of his own and prodded gently at one of the white cheeks. 'You will notice too that the adipocere on his face has hardened, due to its exposure to air.'

'How long does it take for a body to be completely converted to adipocere?' asked Porfiry.

'In the case of an adult body totally immersed in water, about a year.'

'And so, from the degree of saponification, you will be able to calculate how long he has been in the canal – giving us an approximate date of death?'

'Approximate, very approximate. One may not set one's watch by adipocere. It is an erratic and inconsistent material. It has no organic structure, you know. How it behaves in one case, on one body, may not necessarily be repeated in another.'

'And as for cause of death?' asked Porfiry, a little impatiently. 'Do you have any opinions pertaining to that?'

'All in good time, Porfiry Petrovich. We have not even commenced the examination. I have been waiting for you, you know.'

'You did not wait for me before you started dishing out mortuary wax.'

'I assure you that there is more than enough to go round.' It seemed that Dr Pervoyedov had misunderstood Porfiry's objection. He bowed to his *diener*, who began cutting away the dead man's clothes.

'But you must have already noticed the wound on the side of

the head?' Porfiry's voice was imploring. 'That's all I meant to suggest.'

'As you know, Porfiry Petrovich, I follow the Virchow method.' Dr Pervoyedov angled his head almost tenderly as he watched the *diener* work. 'In the Virchow method, the organs are removed and examined separately. In due order. However, adipocere has a rather interesting attribute that does somewhat compromise any forensic examination, whether by the Virchow method or any other.'

'And what is that?'

'All tissue, including organs, skin, musculature and fat – even blood and blood vessels – all is equally capable of conversion to adipocere. Indeed, in a body that has undergone complete saponification, it is impossible to distinguish the internal organs at all. One is simply confronted by a mass of soapy material. Similarly, it becomes impossible to distinguish flesh that has been subject to trauma from flesh that has not. Damaged tissue simply melts away and becomes one with the undamaged tissue. All is . . .'

'Soap,' completed Virginsky, wonderingly.

'Yes. And the more of his body that has turned to adipocere, the harder it will be to make any firm conclusions about the cause of death.'

The body now lay unclothed, the considerable bulk of the belly sprawling out on either side. Further patches of white were visible in certain places, noticeably at the chest, thighs and upper arms. Porfiry noticed that the man was circumcised.

Dr Pervoyedov looked down at the body wistfully. 'Even so, one must adhere to the method. If we abandoned the method, where would we be? And the first thing that the method calls for is that the physician conduct a thorough visual examination of the exterior of the body.' Dr Pervoyedov proceeded to put his words into practice, in a series of exaggerated swoops. He was like a hen pecking at grain, ducking his head sharply down towards the body on the table and back up again. All the time, he continued his explanation: '*Thorough*, Porfiry Petrovich. That's the watchword. I should be a poor pathologist if I confined my observations to the head and offered an opinion based only on what I saw there. What if a further trauma were subsequently revealed, upon removal of the clothing?'

Porfiry waited impatiently for Dr Pervoyedov to cease his examination. 'Well then, can you see any other wound, liable to have resulted in the victim's death?'

'There are a number of abrasions, particularly around the wrists and ankles.' Dr Pervoyedov pointed out the marks.

'He was tethered to some stones,' remarked Porfiry. 'I take it these abrasions could not in themselves have proved fatal.'

'They may even have been inflicted post-mortem. However, I have yet to examine the victim's back.' The doctor signalled to his *diener*, who hefted the body over with a savage grunt. Further white patches showed on the back, at the buttocks and kidneys.

'And yet . . .' There was a note of exasperation in Porfiry's voice. 'And yet, we do have evidence of a major trauma to the head, do we not? The only significant wound visible, as far as I can see. To your expert eye, does that wound appear sufficient to have caused this man's death?'

Dr Pervoyedov broke off from his swooping examination of the body and turned to Porfiry. His look was one of wounded disappointment, like a child who had been deprived of a favourite toy. 'Well, yes, it is difficult to imagine how anyone could survive such a trauma.'

'Thank you. And the blackening around the wound? Consistent with gunshot? A larger exit wound on the other side of the head, also consistent?'

'Porfiry Petrovich, would you prefer to conduct the examination yourself?'

'Not at all. I am not qualified. Although I have encountered similar wounds in the execution of my duties over the years.'

At a further signal from Dr Pervoyedov, the *diener* turned the body onto its back again.

'He was a Jew?' said Porfiry.

'Apparently so, although I have read studies by physicians who call for the removal of the foreskin on hygienic grounds.'

Porfiry watched as Dr Pervoyedov began the Y-shaped incision that would allow him to open the body up, across from shoulder to shoulder, and down from sternum to groin. No blood raced to his scalpel blade, of course. Instead, Porfiry felt the thump of his own quick pulse. He was intensely aware of the churning turmoil of his heart. It was almost as if he were willing himself to bleed on the dead man's behalf. He experienced a core of weightlessness in his being, a kind of empty intoxication where his soul should have been. It was an unbearable sensation, in which the instability and fragility of his organism overrode any other consideration. The sense of dread he felt was undeniably personal. It was a moment in which he was horrifically aware of his mortality. And yet he forced himself to continue watching, as Dr Pervoyedov teased his scalpel blade beneath the epidermis.

The skin came away in tatters, large looping holes where the formation of adipocere disrupted it.

'All flesh is as grass,' said Dr Pervoyedov, as the sheet of skin fell apart in his hands. 'Except when it is soap.' The doctor handed the remnants to his *diener* and turned back to the body.

'Look at this, Porfiry Petrovich.'

More than anything in the world, Porfiry did not want to accept that invitation.

He took a step closer. Dr Pervoyedov was probing the white mounds that had formed on the chest with a long metal implement. 'Here the adipocere goes deep. The heart has all but gone, it seems. I will be able to tell more when I cut the ribs away.'

'His heart has gone?'

'Yes. Turned to soap.'

Porfiry felt unspeakably sorry for the man on the table.

*

The air had never tasted fresher. Porfiry drew in great, bursting draughts as if he had just been rescued from drowning. He cocked his head to one side and listened to the riotous sounds of the nearby fair. And then lit a cigarette.

'We must not resist it, Pavel Pavlovich.'

'But should we not get back to the department?'

'Yes, of course. But first we must greet Yarilo.'

'I would rather not.'

'Are you afraid?'

'What do you mean? Of what could I possibly be afraid?'

'It takes courage to acknowledge every aspect of one's personality.'

'One may acknowledge the aspects to which you are referring without being enslaved to them.'

'Yarilo, god of regeneration. Of resurrection. Of life, reborn out

60

of death. Striking how these ideas recur, is it not? As if there is some deep, eternal truth behind them.'

'Or rather, it is because they answer some deep, eternal need in man. Man creates his gods to meet his needs.'

'Perhaps. But I have always loved the *balagany*.'

'I find them rather tiresome. If it is all the same to you, I shall see you back at your chambers.' Virginsky gave a curt nod.

Porfiry answered with a flurry of angry blinks. His smile hardened. 'As your superior, I command you. You will come to the fair with me.' Porfiry's hand tightened around Virginsky's wrist. 'Furthermore, you will enjoy yourself.'

*

Porfiry treated Virginsky to hot boiled potatoes from an old woman selling them out of her apron. He led the way through the crowd, holding his napkin of potatoes reverently out in front of him, as if it were a holy relic in procession.

He was happy to go where the crowd let him, carried along by the press of jostling shoulders. Every now and then, the throng eased around him and he would take the opportunity to guzzle a mouthful of potato. Following listlessly in Porfiry's wake, Virginsky left his fare untouched for as long as possible. But eventually even he could not hold out against the wholesome smell.

As they moved about the fairground, the clash of sounds around them constantly mutated. An ever-shifting power struggle was being waged. One moment, a trombone band dominated, blaring out a snatch of 'The Petersburg Theatre Goer'. The next, it was an organ grinder singing along to 'Katenka Goes Throughout the Village'; he turned the brass handle of his street organ to grind out the melody, as if it were a form of auditory sausage meat. The shimmer of a balalaika swayed in time with the swinging cradle in which a young man serenaded his sweetheart. The shrieks of children running in and out of their legs were chased away by the yelps of a hungry dog. A moment later, screams of unfettered delight from the slopes of the artificial ice mountains sent their gaze soaring.

And all the time, the barkers' cries rang out from competing booths.

Porfiry took in the sideshows with the air of a wine connoisseur given free run of a well-equipped cellar – with an unhurried excitement, in other words, and in the full expectation that he would not be disappointed. His promiscuous eye ranged over the dizzying choices. The flash and dazzle of the fire-eater's torches held him entranced until all the flames were swallowed out. He gasped at the speed of a juggler's batons spinning in the air. He felt his mouth kink into an anticipatory grin at the sight of an actor in harlequin costume, who was balancing on one of the balconies of an enormous booth, as if about to leap off into the crowd below. The fellow raised himself on his tiptoes and stretched his arms out to either side like wings. The assembled spectators drew in their breath as one, as the performer flexed his body with a few lithe dance steps on the balcony rail. At the next *balagan* window, puppet masters with magnificent priestly beards perched on the sill, dangling their brightly coloured marionettes or turning the wooden heads of their child-sized dummies. The most imbecilic displays were strangely compelling: a dog in a tutu dancing on its hind legs; a monkey in a hussar's costume riding a tricycle. Porfiry smiled at them both and turned to see if Virginsky shared his delight. He did not seem to notice the younger man's sullen glare.

Staggering like a drunk, Porfiry walked straight into a boy pushing a handcart of pastries for sale. He had finished his potatoes and was hungry for something else to consume, but the child got away from him, perhaps frightened off by his uncontrolled bulk. At the same time, his nostrils caught the scents from a nearby gingerbread and oranges stall. He was tempted by the cries of the ice seller: 'Ice! Ice! Chocolate, vanilla, coffee and rose! Who will taste my delicious ice?!' But in the end he settled on a gingerbread man each for himself and Virginsky. The younger man took the biscuit with a quizzical frown.

The next stall along sold puppets and dolls. Virginsky shook his head warningly at Porfiry, who seemed unduly interested in the goods on display.

'Are you quite well, Porfiry Petrovich?'

'What do you mean?'

'First you buy gingerbread men, now you are casting longing glances at these childish trifles. I fear you have reverted to some infantile stage of your existence.'

Porfiry gave a heavy sigh. 'Perhaps I am trying to recapture my lost youth. Can you blame me for that? Or it may be that I'm simply trying to get the smell of death out of my nostrils.' He craned his head towards some cherubs carved from wax, hanging from a willow branch. 'It amounts to the same thing, does it not?' He held out a hand towards one of the cherubs, and set it spinning. 'Even here I am reminded of what I seek to escape. It could be made from Dr Pervoyedov's adipocere, could it not?' Turning from the stall with a wistful smile, he surveyed the *balagan* booths, ready to make his choice at last. 'Pulchinella!' he announced, happily, and set off with renewed energy.

'Must we?' complained Virginsky, hurrying to keep up. 'I confess I can never make any sense of these shows.'

'That is because you are watching with the wrong part of your mind. You approach it too rationally. It is not your fault. It is the fault of your generation, and it applies to everything you do.'

'I am surprised to hear you, of all people, decry the use of too much rationality.'

'You're right, Pavel Pavlovich. I place great store by rationality. But it is like a muscle. One must exercise it, for sure. But one must also rest it from time to time.'

It was a pantomime show, presented on the platform of a makeshift wooden theatre. The actor playing Pulchinella was dressed in the traditional white costume, his face half-covered by a black mask. The performance had reached the part where Pulchinella – in his peculiar high, rasping voice – has announced his intention to marry. It seemed that a bride had been selected for him, a ninety-nine-year-old woman, living for some reason in the Semyenovsky Regiment.

'It makes no sense,' complained Virginsky. But Porfiry, like the other spectators, was delighted when the promised bride did not materialise and instead Pulchinella was attacked by a dog.

A seemingly random succession of characters came onto the stage in succession, to be attacked and fought off by Pulchinella. The action was chaotic. It culminated in the appearance of a devil, who it seemed had come to claim the incorrigible Pulchinella. A fight ensued, of course, ending with Pulchinella riding the devil like a horse. It was at this point, just as the drama was coming to its bewildering end, that Petrushka entered the stage.

'Why?' cried Virginsky, in exasperation. 'I ask you in all seriousness, Porfiry Petrovich, what purpose is served by his entrance? Why do we need Petrushka when we have Pulchinella? And why now, when the thing is nearly over?'

Porfiry waved away the objection.

'He is entirely superfluous to the drama!' But Virginsky appeared to be the only member of the audience who objected to Petrushka's appearance, for it was met with frenzied cheering by all around.

A canvas screen dropped down behind the actors, on which was depicted an enormous devil's head, with an open mouth. One by one, the cast climbed through the hole, apart from Pulchinella, who was pulled through by the hands of the others, resisting to the last.

A rendezvous with no one

Porfiry found the following letter waiting for him back at his chambers:

Dear Sir,

I have chosen to write to you because of your involvement several years ago in the case of the student who murdered the old woman and her sister. Covering the case as a journalist, I was obliged to attend the trial, where I was favourably impressed by the humane way you conducted the prosecution, as I believe I made clear in the account I wrote for a certain publication at the time. Indeed, it might have surprised you to have read such an account in such a journal.

I have an interesting story to tell you. Some sailors went swimming in the Winter Canal. Five men jumped in, but six men came out. How could that be?

If you would like to know the answer to this riddle, meet me at the Summer Garden, near the northern entrance, at three o'clock, today. It is my favourite time to visit the Summer Garden, when the statues emerge from their winter coffins. I would prefer not to visit you at your chambers because there are spies in every government department. If I am seen there it will mean certain death for me.

Of course, if this letter falls into the wrong hands, I will be dead by the time you come to meet me. Therefore I have greater cause than usual to hope that we shall meet this afternoon.

How will you know me? Do not fear. I will know you. Please come alone. I'm afraid this must be one of those tiresome anonymous letters, of which I am sure you receive far too many.

'Is it genuine?' asked Virginsky.

Porfiry handed the letter over to the younger magistrate. 'It appears to be. The letter bears yesterday's date. It was written and sent before the newspapers appeared. I think we may have found our mysterious onlooker.'

'He is a journalist, or so he claims. Perhaps he learnt about the incident professionally?'

'He mentions the number of sailors, which I do not believe was given in the information we released to the newspapers.'

'That's true,' conceded Virginsky. 'So you will go to meet him?'

'Of course.'

'Alone?'

'Is that not what he requests?'

Virginsky frowned. 'Do you have any idea who he is? He claims to know you.'

'I hope I shall find out soon enough,' said Porfiry.

*

He saw the padlocked chains from a distance. Both of the high, elaborate gates in the northern fence were secured. It should not have surprised him but it did. The Summer Garden was, of course, closed. It was that time in late April when visitors were kept from the park in order to allow the ground to recover from the thaw. Had his anonymous correspondent forgotten this? Possibly, though the letter had not explicitly said that they should meet inside the park, merely 'near the northern entrance'.

Porfiry approached the railing with a sinking heart. He had been looking forward to a stroll along the tree-lined avenues and had purposely arrived with a few moments to spare. The pink granite of the columns in which the gates were set seemed flushed by the glow of spring. The sun also sparkled in the golden embellishments to the wrought iron, almost compensating him for his exclusion. He peered through two vertical bars. The paths were indeed sodden, justifying the temporary closure. The grey wooden boards that protected the statues from the winter frost had already been removed, though the statues were still swathed in white sheets. There was something unmistakably eerie about the rows of enshrouded figures on podiums. They seemed to hold the potential for movement, as if they were simply waiting for the wrappings to be taken off, before springing to life. Porfiry must have been in a morbid frame of mind, for he added the thought: *And wreaking havoc.* It was not clear to him why the latent beings beneath the sheets should choose havoc-wreaking above any more harmless activity.

Checking his fob-watch, he saw that he was early for his appointment. He did not wish to draw attention to himself by loitering, so he decided to walk a circuit of the perimeter, striking off in the direction of the Summer Palace. The proximity of that modest palace, little more than a large house in fact, reminded him that he was very close to the spot where, almost exactly six years ago, Dmitry Karakozov had made his attempt on the Tsar's life.

He wondered whether this momentous event had played a part in his correspondent's choice of meeting place, consciously or otherwise.

Porfiry thought back to the trial of Raskolnikov, without doubt the murderous student referred to in the anonymous letter. The courtroom had been crowded with the gentlemen of the press, scrutinising his every word and even gesture. That was to be expected: Raskolnikov's crime, sensational enough in itself, had been interpreted as having a wider significance. It had been seen as a symptom of the nihilistic disease that was corrupting the younger generation at the time, and that had, if anything, become more virulent in the years since. Karakozov's assassination attempt had been made the following year. How the state dealt with Raskolnikov was to be seen as a litmus test for how it would deal with all its malcontent young men. Too much leniency would provoke the reactionaries; excessive severity would incite the radicals.

As always in Russia, a matter of justice had become a political battleground: Porfiry had found himself caught in the middle.

He tried to picture the journalists' faces. Had there been one among them whom he could identify as the writer of that letter? One man in whose eyes he had noticed a particular sympathy, the beginnings of a bond perhaps?

It seemed so long ago now. And at the time, he remembered, he had made a conscious effort to block out their faces, not to mention their pencils, sharpened for blood, hovering over their notebooks. If he had thought too much about what the press were going to write about him, he could not have done his job. He concentrated instead on the humanity of the young man whose terrible error had brought him to that courtroom. Yes, his error was grievous, his crimes appalling. But he was still a man. A human heart beat within his breast. He possessed a soul, one that had become infected with ideological disease admittedly, but a soul nevertheless. A soul capable of being saved. Indeed, it was the duty of all those older, wiser heads charged with the administration of justice – judges, prosecutors, defence attorneys, all – it was their duty to work together urgently to bring about this salvation. Porfiry had come to believe that Raskolnikov's soul was nothing other than the soul of Russia's youth. If they turned their back on him, they turned their back on a whole generation – on the future, in fact.

And so, with this thought in mind, he had called for clemency. He had joined with those who urged that the accused be treated with compassion, as one suffering from a mental derangement.

In short, he had not called for the maximum sentence. Further, he had himself brought to light many of the strange psychological contradictions in the case that had helped to convince the jury of Raskolnikov's insanity and had so led to mitigation in sentencing.

Which of those journalists, he now wondered, would have viewed this conduct with approval? Porfiry paused in his circuit. He closed his eyes and tried once again to bring their faces to mind. Nothing. However, he felt sure that he would immediately recognise the individual should he come towards him now. He opened his eyes and looked about him hopefully. There were not many people about (why would anyone come to the Summer Garden when it was closed?), but none of the faces he saw struck a chord.

Porfiry took the letter from his pocket. The line he wished to consult was, 'It might have surprised you to read such an account in such a journal.' *What could the writer have meant by that?* he wondered.

He folded the letter along its creases and returned it to his pocket. He had not yet completed his circuit and was still early for the meeting; nevertheless, he turned and headed back to the northern gate.

He looked expectantly into the faces of everyone who approached, including the women, and even, rather foolishly, the children. Not once did he feel any glimmer of recognition. More to the point, it was clear that no one recognised him.

Sudden activity within the park drew his attention: the squeak of a handcart being pulled around by couple of workmen in long artisan's waistcoats. Porfiry was unduly excited to see that they were about to take the covers off the statues. He watched as they picked away at the first of the sheets, pulling it away to reveal a female figure, in the classical style, semi-naked but nondescript. An allegory. Porfiry had to admit he was disappointed. She did not leap from the podium and run along the main avenue, her laughter tinkling stonily like dropped pebbles. Porfiry smiled at the fanciful image, which his imagination further embellished with the fantasy of the two workmen giving chase. In reality, the men simply busied themselves with folding up the redundant sheet, which they placed in the handcart, before moving on to the neighbouring sculpture.

Porfiry studied the statue that had been uncovered, wondering what the allegorical figure represented. She was depicted holding some kind of weapon, a rod or a sword of some kind. Of course, Porfiry realised, that was the *fasces*, the bundle of rods that symbolised the state's authority, a symbol also – as he well knew, being a magistrate – of its summary judicial power. Ah yes, he had contemplated this figure before, somewhere, if not here; drawn to it, perhaps, because of its particular relevance to him. She was Nemesis.

Porfiry consulted his watch again. It was now a quarter past the hour. He looked about him, his expectancy turned to unease, re-membering another sentence in the letter. 'If this letter falls into the wrong hands, I will be dead by the time you come to meet me.'

He would give it till four o'clock, he decided.

6

Chits

When Porfiry returned to his chambers later that afternoon, he found a small crowd of his colleagues already gathered there. As he entered the room, the mood of excitability that was clearly prevalent changed instantly. Everyone fell conspiratorially silent, regarding him with a mixture of glances, some guilty, others amused, but most pitying. He noticed, however, that they were unanimous in avoiding his eye.

He hung his coat on the stand without saying a word. Facing the room again, he acknowledged Nikodim Fomich's presence with an unsmiling nod. The chief of the Haymarket District Police Bureau received the greeting with a wince. His was the most pitying expression of all.

Also there was Virginsky, together with the clerk Zamyotov, as well as a number of other magistrates and clerks. There were about eight or nine men in all; perhaps not enough to truly constitute a crowd, but when he had first entered, their frenzied activity and agitated shouts had given the impression of a much larger gathering. Besides which, his chambers were not large.

One or two of the men thought it best to make their escape at this moment, almost tiptoeing out of the room. The remnant assembled suspiciously around his desk. They seemed to be united in their determination to prevent him from seeing whatever was on it.

Porfiry looked enquiringly to Virginsky for an explanation.

'There has been a slight mishap. An administrative error, one might say.'

'It was his fault,' put in Zamyotov, quickly.

'That's not entirely true, Alexander Grigorevich, and you know it!' countered Virginsky.

'An easy enough mistake to make,' smoothed Nikodim Fomich, ever the genial uncle.

'What has happened?' enquired Porfiry.

'It is to do with the poster,' began Virginsky. 'Technically, Imperial State has done an excellent job, considering the time in which they managed to produce the posters. The reproduction of the photograph is excellent.'

Porfiry took a step forward. The men shielding his desk bristled and closed ranks.

'Please, stand aside.'

No one moved, although one man felt compelled to cough.

'If I may first explain,' offered Virginsky. 'There has been a mis-understanding. The system, if you like, caught us out.'

'*Us?*'

'Very well, it caught me out, if you prefer. It appears I may have filled in the wrong chit. However, I must say in my defence that I filled in the chit with which Alexander Grigorevich supplied me.'

'It was up to you to check it,' insisted Zamyotov.

'Yes, I was remiss in not looking more closely at the wording.'

'The colour. The colour should have told you.' Zamyotov shook his head mercilessly.

'And so, which chit did you fill in?' wondered Porfiry.

'I . . . well . . .' Virginsky reached behind him and held up a copy of the poster.

74

It was printed on flimsy newsprint, tangy with the smell of fresh ink. Porfiry recognised the strange doll-like face staring out as that of the victim. The pockmarks were somewhat less defined in the photograph, but noticeably there, especially on the forehead. The most conclusive distinguishing feature, for Porfiry at least, was the blank-eyed presence of death. And it was that that rendered the poster's solitary word, printed in large block type, so absurd.

'Wanted?' read Porfiry.

'Yes, I apparently filled out the chit for a Wanted poster . . .'

'Pink,' interjected Zamyotov, with condemnatory terseness.

'Instead of for an Information Concerning poster.'

'Lilac.'

'Did you not specify any other wording?' asked Porfiry.

'Well, yes, actually, I did. I detailed the circumstances surrounding the finding of the body, the possible time of his disappearance – we believe, do we not, that he must have been deposited in the canal last year, just before or at the onset of winter? It must have been already cold, although not quite freezing, judging by the preservation of the body. I explained too about the changes to his appearance that had been wrought by the process of adipoceration. I drew particular attention to the pockmarks, and the unusually small size of the eyes. And I asked for anyone who might have any information regarding such an individual to make their presence known at their nearest police bureau.'

'Why did this wording not find its way onto the poster?'

'It seems that Imperial State ignored it, as it was not relevant to a Wanted poster, it being a Wanted poster chit that I had filled in.'

'You must take more care in future, Pavel Pavlovich. You know how important it is to pay attention to details when dealing with the bureaucracy.' Porfiry took the poster from Virginsky. 'Nevertheless, this will do. At least it will serve to publicise his face.'

'Are you not concerned that it will make us look rather . . . foolish?'

'I am more concerned that we find this man's killer, as soon as possible. Reprinting the poster will only occasion delay.'

Virginsky gave a quick consultative glance to some of the other magistrates, who nodded back encouragingly. 'But is there not the possibility that it may deter some individuals from coming forward? Friends of this man may not be willing to offer information if they think it is in connection with his arrest, whereas they might be very happy to help in tracking down his murderer.'

'But surely everyone will realise that he is dead? And that we cannot want to arrest a dead man?'

'We were talking about this before you came in, Porfiry Petrovich,' said Nikodim Fomich. 'I am afraid the prevailing view was that the poster will only confuse the public.'

A chorus of assenting murmurs reinforced the Chief Superintendent's words.

Porfiry gave the poster back to Virginsky with a defeated air. 'Hold on to this copy, but return the rest to Imperial State. Perhaps they can print up a patch to be pasted over the offending word. And this time, Pavel Pavlovich, please take care to fill out the correct chit.'

'I am not sure what the correct chit is for a patch,' admitted Virginsky forlornly.

'Alexander Grigorevich will be able to advise you.'

'There is no chit for a patch,' said Zamyotov, with a sharp shake of negation. 'Therefore it cannot be done.'

'Can you not go to the Imperial State Printing Works yourself and talk to the manager?'

The clerks who were present were evidently scandalised by this suggestion.

Porfiry waved them away. 'Take these out of my sight.' He handed the ream of posters, still wrapped in brown paper, to Virginsky.

The room emptied of all except Porfiry and Nikodim Fomich. Porfiry sat down at his desk and lit a cigarette without looking at the police chief.

'You alright, dear friend?' ventured Nikodim Fomich.

'It's damned frustrating.'

'Of course. But perhaps we won't need the posters, after all. Pavel Pavlovich tells me you went to meet a possible witness.'

'He did not keep the appointment.'

'Ah.' Nikodim Fomich sank into the sofa with a groan. 'How aggravating for you.'

'It's more than aggravating, Nikodim Fomich.' Porfiry took the anonymous letter from his pocket. He waved it vaguely at Nikodim Fomich, who was forced to heave himself out of the loosely upholstered sofa to receive it.

'I wouldn't place too much store by these ominous hints,' pronounced Nikodim Fomich. 'This letter may well be a fraud, written by some self-dramatising egoist.'

'He knew the number of sailors.'

'Very well, let us grant that it is what it seems to be. Even so, anything may have prevented him from meeting you. He may have been detained by a woman, or fallen into a ditch, or been waylaid in a tavern. He may simply have thought better of his original intention. If he is mixed up in this affair in some way, we may imagine that his state of mind is far from stable. You're the psychologist, Porfiry Petrovich.' Nikodim Fomich handed the letter back to Porfiry conclusively. 'It may simply be someone playing a trick on you. A great prankster like you ought to be constantly on the alert for hoaxes.'

Porfiry gave an offended flutter of eyelids. 'I don't think it is a prank. For some reason I have an ominous feeling.'

'Have you any idea who the writer might be? He obviously knows of you.'

'I've been trying to recollect. I did not read any of the newspaper accounts of the Raskolnikov trial at the time.'

'They will be archived.'

'Yes, that's true. I will look into it.'

'And so, what do you make of these fires?' asked Nikodim Fomich, settling again on the sofa.

'I know only what I have read in the papers. I have not been called to investigate in an official capacity.'

'A nasty business,' pronounced Nikodim Fomich. 'The Tsar must crack down heavily on the intellectuals. Suspend the universities. Tighten up censorship. It is the circulation of dangerous ideas that is responsible for these outbreaks, do you not agree, Porfiry Petrovich? The young people are too much in the thrall of these nihilists.'

'Certainly I agree with your last statement, though I cannot concur with the measures you propose. All that has been tried, without success. In fact, it is counterproductive, as it only results in greater resistance. It invests the dangerous ideas you speak of with a glamorous appeal they would not otherwise possess. It is that which draws the youth, like moths to a candle flame. Far better to expose these ideas to the fresh, cleansing air of careful scrutiny and rational dispute. Then the young people would see them for what they are and reject them. We must learn to trust our own children.'

'Good grief, Porfiry Petrovich. I never thought I would hear such views from you.'

'That is because you do not really know me, Nikodim Fomich.'

'But you are one of my oldest friends!'

Porfiry declined to comment; in fact, he scrupulously avoided looking at Nikodim Fomich. At last he muttered, 'Because we have known one another for a long time, it does not mean . . .' But he trailed off without completing the sentiment.

Nikodim Fomich watched his old friend closely, uneasily. 'What do they hope to achieve, Porfiry Petrovich? Can you tell me that?'

'They wish to build a new world, a fairer, better world. But first, they have decided that they must destroy the old one.'

'Even if that means killing women and children?'

'The end justifies the means.' After a moment, Porfiry added, 'They would say.' Porfiry considered the smouldering tip of his cigarette. 'However, it is not our concern, Nikodim Fomich. Another department investigates such crimes, as you know.'

Nikodim Fomich nodded morosely. 'The Third Section. Of course. I know you disapprove of their means, but I wonder, at times like this, perhaps their way is the only way?'

'You cannot fight criminality with criminality.'

'That's rather strong, isn't it?'

'I speak only from experience.' Porfiry Petrovich took a long draw on his cigarette.

Nikodim Fomich slapped his hands down on his thighs conclusively. 'No one can deny that you have your fair share of that!'

Porfiry fixed Nikodim Fomich with a critical glare. 'What do you mean to suggest by that?'

'Merely that you are one of our most experienced investigators.'

'In other words, that I am over the hill.'

'Now now, Porfiry Petrovich! It's not like you to take offence so easily! Experience is an exceedingly valuable quality in an investigator, as you know. When coupled with the energy of youth, which for you is provided by Pavel Pavlovich, the result is a formidable combination.'

'Now you are saying that I have no energy of my own!'

'Really, you are determined to twist my words. I wonder why you are so out of sorts.'

'Perhaps I have simply had enough for the day.' Porfiry stubbed out his cigarette. The vitality that he had absorbed at the fair seemed now to have deserted him. He closed his eyes for a moment, and saw once again Dr Pervoyedov's long metal probe sink into the waxy mass where the unknown man's heart had been.

When he opened his eyes, he could not say how much later, the room was in darkness and Nikodim Fomich had gone.

*

The following day, a Wednesday, and the third day since the body had come to light, Porfiry Petrovich left Virginsky to sort out the confusion over the posters and set out for a stroll along Sadovaya Street. He chose to walk as much to prove Nikodim Fomich wrong – *He did not need anyone else's energy!* – as to take advantage of the continuing fine weather.

At Nevsky Prospect, Sadovaya Street kinked north and became Malaya – or little – Sadovaya Street. This took him to Bolshaya –

or great – Italyanskaya Street, which ran parallel to Nevsky Prospect for a third of the latter's length, one block to the north. Until the previous year, it had simply been Italyanskaya Street, without the aggrandising adjective. The Ministry of Justice, at number 25, was on the corner with Malaya Sadovaya Street, at the congruence of the great and the small, or so the respective street names suggested.

A former residence of the Shuvalov family, the ministry building was a pale-blue baroque palace, three storeys high, extending itself over an entire block of Bolshaya Italyanskaya Street. It was ironic to think that a scion of the Shuvalov family, Count Pyotr Andreevich, was the current head of the Tsar's secret police, the notorious Third Section of His Imperial Majesty's Own Chancellery. It was a department that, to Porfiry's mind, had little to do with justice. Some dark exchange seemed to lie behind the coincidence. It was almost as if the Shuvalovs had vacated their home to justice, only to settle themselves into the seat of true power. It seemed to indicate a clarity of vision that was both blithe and ruthless, and therefore typically aristocratic.

The entrance was set in an imposing porch, banded with bone-white columns. It put Porfiry in mind of a general puffing out his chest to draw himself up to his full height: the usual baroque embellishments – festooned aprons, rusticated columns, three varieties of window styles – were the general's decorations.

The great lobby, a full two storeys high and therefore with a double set of windows to illuminate it, was flooded with a hovering silvery light. Something about it made him want to hold his breath. It seemed to have the same effect on others too: the atmosphere was hushed, despite the confluence of lawyers and civil servants. A representation of the double-headed eagle of the Romanov family crest, carved out of black marble, was set into a niche, high in the facing wall, looking down on all who entered with its strange bidirectional gaze. The floor was given over to a monochrome mosaic of that same allegorical figure that Porfiry had seen unveiled in the Summer Garden: Nemesis. The axe head projecting from the bundle of rods of the fasces was more clearly discernible here. In her other hand, she held the flame of truth.

His gaze must have fallen on that image countless times in his life. Small wonder that when he had seen the statue in the park he had the sense that he had contemplated the figure before. And yet he was not aware of ever consciously considering it. It was simply the ground he walked on whenever he came to the Ministry.

He took the stairs to the second floor. His step was slow and plodding today, and fell with a heavy reverberation. The exertions of the previous day had taken it out of him. Naturally, it had not been the first time in his career that he had attended the forensic examination of a corpse, but for some reason this one seemed harder than usual to get beyond. The trip to the fair had not wholly succeeded in dispelling his gloom – or in taking the whiff of death from his nostrils, as he had put it to Virginsky. The disappointments of the afternoon, the non-appearance of his mysterious correspondent and the mistake over the poster, had set him back disproportionately. He was aware of a winter tightness lingering in his chest. He acknowledged that it was getting harder each year to shake it off. And yet the exercise, surely, must do him some good? Why then did he feel like a swimmer who has been carried too far out to sea and is in fear of not being able to regain the shore?

Porfiry looked down, as if he could no longer sustain the weight of his head. The black and white tiles of the corridor brought to mind Pulchinella, dressed in white, with his black half-mask. Porfiry smiled to himself at the memory of Virginsky's bewilderment. It was simple really. Just the old antithesis: Death in life. Life from death. And why Petrushka as well as Pulchinella? Because life is abundant and excessive, and uncontrollably anarchic.

Porfiry lifted his head and quickened his step. He was picturing himself in Pulchinella's costume.

It was not long before he reached the Ministry of Justice library. It took a moment for him to catch his breath, then he made his request of the librarian.

The silver-whiskered clerk observed him with a critical and unpromising eye. 'You must fill in a chit.'

'Of course, yes. The inevitable chit.'

The librarian handed him a small printed form and a pencil stub. 'First, take a seat. Fill in your place number here. The date and title of the journal you require here.'

'But I may require more than one issue, of more than one title.'

'Then you will need more chits. Please help yourself to as many as you need.'

'I would really like you to bring all of the newspapers that you have from that time.'

'I will be happy to do so if you fill in the necessary chits.'

Porfiry placed a finger to the bridge of his nose and pressed, hard. 'Sometimes I cannot help thinking that there must be . . .'

'What?'

'Nothing. Never mind. I will fill in the chits. And if I do not find what I am looking for at first, I will fill in more chits.'

'That's the way,' nodded the librarian.

Porfiry took a seat at the end of a long table, subdivided by low screens into separate places. Next to him, a young magistrate was snoring over an open law book. Porfiry coughed sharply. His neighbour woke with a start and applied himself with renewed vigour to the case he had been studying.

Although he would not have admitted it, Porfiry found the necessity of filling in the chits useful. It forced him to focus his mind. The letter writer had expressed the view that Porfiry would be 'surprised' to read a favourable account of himself in the journal in question. That suggested a radical publication, by instinct unlikely to acknowledge anything praiseworthy in the behaviour of a state prosecutor. Then again, what had impressed the writer was the humanity of Porfiry's conduct, by which Porfiry took him to mean his compassion for the murderer. One would naturally be very surprised to find sentiments of that nature meeting with approval in any conservative paper. He had only to think of the fulminating leaders of *The Russian Soil*. On balance, he was inclined to start with the radical journals.

The leading radical titles at the time of the trial were *The Contemporary* and *The Russian Word*. The latter, with the emergence of the brilliant publicist Pisarev, was the more extreme of the two. Its stance was anti-state by default, leading to its enforced closure in the following year, in the aftermath of Karakozov's attempt on the Tsar's life. It would truly be surprising to find an article expressing approval of a government-employed magistrate in its pages.

The trial had lasted barely five days. Most of that time had been taken up in establishing the mental state of the perpetrator, and in arguments concerning sentence. His guilt had never been in question. Indeed, he had confessed to his crime. A disproportionate number of days had been consumed by the ultimately fruitless task of trying to understand why he had committed it. That was not to say that it was not a question worth asking. On the contrary, it was an essential question. It was just that Porfiry's colleagues had not had the remotest idea of how to go about answering it. The defendant himself was little help. And so the debate had raged, an emotional whirlpool of ever-increasing exasperation and incomprehension. The more they discussed it, the less they understood it.

The Russian Word had been a monthly journal, and so Porfiry filled in three chits, one for the month before the trial, one covering the trial itself, and one to cover its conclusion and aftermath. As a precaution, he completed chits for the corresponding issues of *The Contemporary*.

The elderly librarian's substantial eyebrows shot up when he saw the titles Porfiry had requested. 'You did not tell me that you wished to consult these particular papers.' The habitual dourness of his expression sharpened into horror.

'You did not ask me. Is there some problem?'

'Wait there.'

The librarian moved with a sprightliness that belied his evident age, and which Porfiry could only envy, to disappear through a door at the rear of the library.

A moment later he re-emerged, followed by what could only be described as a younger version of himself. The side whiskers had not yet turned silver but the eyebrows were well on their way to achieving a beetling prominence. More importantly, the gaze was equally discouraging.

It must have been a disconcerting experience for both parties to work together: one man confronted daily by the image of his future, the other by that of his past.

'You are aware,' began the younger librarian, who was evidently more senior in rank, 'that one of the titles you have requested is a restricted publication.'

'I was not aware of that. I was not even aware that there is a list of restricted publications.'

'That is hardly surprising. The list itself is restricted.'

'Ah, I see. I take it you are talking about *The Russian Word*?'

'Yes. There will be no difficulty with your seeing *The Contemporary*.'

'However, it was *The Russian Word* that I was particularly desirous of seeing.'

'That will not be possible.'

'But you don't understand, I am an investigating magistrate pursuing a murder enquiry. I believe there may be vital information in the issues of *The Russian Word* from that period.'

'Timofei Ivanovich will be happy to retrieve the copies of *The Contemporary* that you have requested from the stacks, if you will return to your place.'

'Yes, of course. That is indeed considerate of him, as I do not believe the journals in question will be able to walk to my place on their own.' The barb failed to dent either librarian's stony mask, and Porfiry immediately regretted it. Sarcasm was not the way to win these people over. 'It is true that I do want to look at *The Contemporary*, but I also want to look at *The Russian Word*. In fact, I particularly want to. You do understand, don't you? I want to consult both titles. There must be some way for me to see *The Russian Word*?'

'There is only one way,' said the younger librarian, but not in a way that encouraged hope.

'Yes?'

It is not our intention to diminish the true hor-
rimes. Merely to identify the true perpetrator. I
s not Raskolnikov. It is the system that created
It has been scientifically proven that in a system
socialist ideals, that is to say one in which the be-
uction are distributed equally throughout society,
ossible for crime to exist. One will simply do away
t a stroke by changing the socio-economic bases of
e sickness and poverty that caused Raskolnikov's
e eradicated, and with them Raskolnikov's crime.
would Raskolnikov have to kill a bloodsucking
r when there are no bloodsucking moneylenders
when, in addition, all his material needs are met?
is irrefutable and must lead, if pursued to its con-
he acquittal of Raskolnikov and to the presence bench of other individuals. (I need not name them,
names are known to all.)

se, encouraging as some of the recent verdicts of our
been, we must admit that the law courts do not al-
ate in accordance with the dictates of logic. Even if
el for the defence were to avail himself of the argu-
t we have put forward, there is no guarantee that they
with a sympathetic hearing. The chief difficulty in
cular case is that the defendant has already confessed
(would that he had read this article first!). There is,
nothing for the jury to decide, no verdict to deliver.
st only await the sentence. It is too much to hope that
uting judge will be swayed by an essay in *The Russian*
We know for a fact that many prosecuting judges read
sian Word; we will not speculate as to their reasons.)
r, in the person of one investigating magistrate at least,
justified in placing faith. It may surprise the reader to

'But that would mean filling in a different chit.' This was given
as an insurmountable obstacle.

'Of course! Whatever is necessary!'

'Which you must then have signed by the head of the Third
Section, Count Shuvalov himself.'

Porfiry was momentarily speechless. When he found his voice,
all he could say was, 'Count Shuvalov? Are you sure?'

The two heads of elder and younger librarian nodded in unison.

'Must we trouble Count Shuvalov with a trivial request for a
couple of old journals?'

'The request is not trivial. It is a restricted publication. If it falls
into the wrong hands, who knows what incendiarism it might
provoke.'

'I am a government employee! In fact, an employee of the Ministry of Justice. I require the copies in connection with work I am
conducting on behalf of the Ministry.' Porfiry held up his hands.
'Surely these are not the wrong hands?'

'We must believe that it has been restricted for good reason.'

'Ah, but you see, at the time, back in 1866, it was not restricted.
Anyone could read it! Indeed there must be many copies of this
very issue in open circulation, thousands even, gathering dust on
the shelves of respectable professional gentlemen.'

'Shall I tell Timofei Ivanovich to fetch the copies of *The Contemporary*?' There was something new to the younger librarian's
tone as he asked this. Porfiry was alert to the nuance and so he
nodded assent.

They both watched the older man on his way. When the door
had closed behind him, Porfiry looked over his own shoulder before taking out his wallet. 'How much?'

'I shall have to give Timofei Ivanovich something.'

Porfiry peeled off a red ten-rouble bank note.

The librarian's twitching fingers induced a second. Then he snatched the notes away with the alacrity of a hungry peasant.

The

ovna's deaths.
ror of these c
say again, it
Raskolnikov.
based on true
nefits of prod
it will be imp
with crime *a*
the state. Th
crime will b
What need
moneylende
to kill, and

The logi
clusion, to
fore the be
when their

Of cour
juries have
ways oper
the couns
ments tha
will meet
this parti
his guilt
therefore
One mu
a prosec
Word. (
The Ru
Howev
we feel

This young man is himse
that he is at a loss to ex
and sickness. He deserves
pity. Who is really respons
pawnbroker Alyona Ivanov
half-sister Lizaveta? It is not
though he wielded the impl
His sickness was to blame.
choose to be sick. Even his
claim. His sickness without d
gencies of the life he was forc
pelled from the university, bar
starvation, it is little wonder th
manner over which he had no
question, 'Who is responsible f
ovna and Lizaveta Ivanovna?', we
for Rodion Romanovich's povert
conscience will know in their he
tion. For who is responsible for the
Russians? Again, it does not need
swer.

As we are addressing men and w
without saying that every one of th
horrific circumstances of Alyona Iv

know that we are talking of the very man who hounded Rodion Romanovich into confessing.

We have been struck throughout the preliminaries of the trial by the humanity and tact of this individual's demeanour. We expected a wolf baying for blood. We found a human being sensitive to the plight of a less fortunate brother. The magistrate in question may not appreciate our approval, for we imagine that in official circles, to be praised by *The Russian Word* signals the end of a promising career. But the truth will out. The truth is that it was this magistrate's official duty to construct the case against Rodion Romanovich. The truth is also that he went so far in the opposite direction as to make certain evidence favouring the defendant available to the defence. Even as we write, he is engaged in advising the defence on the construction of an argument likely to lead to mitigation in sentencing. Granted, all this falls some way short of the ideal. Let us repeat: we are entitled to demand from the judicial process nothing less than the unconditional acquittal of Raskolnikov; nevertheless, it is a significant step in the right direction, for which P.P. (let us discreetly call our investigating magistrate P.P.) deserves credit.

Porfiry Petrovich allowed himself an inner chuckle. What would Pavel Pavlovich say! To see his old ideological adversary lauded in no less an organ than *The Russian Word*! For it was true that every time Virginsky had put forward similar views concerning the organisation of society, Porfiry had gently but thoroughly quashed them, counselling a more moderate, practical approach. He had even cautioned his young friend against initiating such debates in the bureau. Without doubt, Virginsky looked upon Porfiry with indulgent contempt, as a weak-livered, intellectually compromised, outmoded liberal. A man whose time had passed.

If only he had Virginsky there with him now, to show him the page!

Porfiry tried once more to visualise the journalists who had been present in the courtroom. He must have addressed them after the trial too. It was customary for them to identify themselves and their papers as they called out their questions. But he had no recollection of the occasion. A face floated into his mind, but he did not trust it. He felt that it was his imagination rather than his memory that supplied it.

But at least he had a name now. The article was credited to one D. A. Kozodavlev. Porfiry felt sure that this was one and the same as his anonymous letter writer, if only for a stylistic tic that both letter and article shared. Indeed, in such matters, it was closer to the truth to describe it as a psychological tic.

*

'Yes, but what makes you so certain?' There was a petulant tone to Virginsky's question, possibly occasioned by the concluding remarks of the article that Porfiry had just shown him.

It had taken a further three red banknotes, as well as completion of a yellow chit, to secure the removal of the relevant edition of *The Russian Word* from the library. Strictly speaking, a restricted publication could not be removed from the library under any circumstances. However, the fact that Porfiry had been allowed to view the journal created an anomaly, which was most simply resolved by temporarily removing it from the restricted list. (This was achieved by referring to an earlier version of the restricted list, which did not contain *The Russian Word*, and which by a bureaucratic oversight had remained in force.) If *The Russian Word* was not restricted, it followed that he was free to take it out, on completion of a standard yellow chit. The younger librarian had shown remarkable ingenuity in devising these strategies, which together with his willingness to accept bribes, boded well for his future in the service. There was every possibility that he would escape the fate that his aged doppelgänger seemed to represent. He would go far, in other words.

Porfiry did not answer Virginsky's question. 'You will notice this, from Kozodavlev's article: "It may surprise the reader to know that we are talking of the very man who hounded Rodion Romanovich into confessing." He is referring to me, of course. But note the phrase, "It may surprise the reader." Now, if we go back to the anonymous letter I received, we will find the following: "It might have surprised you to have read such an account in such a journal." What are we to make of this?' Porfiry did not wait for an answer: 'Here is a man who likes to surprise his readers! I feel sure it is the same writer. Now, all we have to do is track down Mr Kozodavlev. That shouldn't be so hard to do. *The Russian Word* was suppressed by the government in 1866. If my knowledge of radical journals is correct, the editor Blagosvetlov founded a new journal, *Affair*, which I believe is still in circulation, is it not, Pavel Pavlovich?'

'I believe so.'

'We need only to make enquiries at the Censorship Office to locate its address. Perhaps you would oblige me by drafting the necessary request, on the correct official chit, please.' Porfiry smiled and batted his eyelids in an attempt to be winning. It was an attempt laden with irony. 'I suggest we begin our enquiries there. Indeed, if we are fortunate, we may even find our Mr Kozodavlev in attendance. I imagine that all the contributors to *The Russian Word* transferred their allegiance to *Affair*.'

For some reason he could not explain, Porfiry felt his spirits revive. He felt the renewal of energy that he had hoped for at the onset of spring, and that the fairground had temporarily provided. Perhaps it had something to do with the fact that he had found himself favourably referred to in a defunct radical journal, though why he should take delight from this baffled him. Porfiry preferred to believe that it was simply the invigorating effect of a genuine lead in the case they were investigating. He was, he realised with pleasure, a hound with a fresh scent in his snout. His energy was the bound of exultation against the leash.

8

'Stenka Razin'

The following day, Thursday, 20 April, they received a reply to their enquiries made to the Censorship Office. The editorial offices of *Affair* were registered at an apartment in 16, Dmitrovsky Lane, under the name of the editor, G. E. Blagosvetlov.

The fine spring weather was strengthening its brief hold on the city and Porfiry was minded to make the most of it while it lasted. He invited Virginsky to accompany him. 'I expect you would like to pay your respects to these radical gentlemen. And besides, with you in tow, they may disclose more than they might otherwise.'

'What do you mean by that?'

'Simply that they will recognise you as one of their own. They will trust you.'

'I shall come with you, of course. It's my duty to do whatever you say.'

'And your pleasure also, no doubt?'

Virginsky hesitated. 'I do not like the duplicitous role in which you seek to cast me.'

'There's nothing duplicitous about it, Pavel Pavlovich. It's simply . . . good psychology.'

'And entirely unnecessary, in my opinion. If Kozodavlev is indeed the writer of the anonymous letter, as seems likely, then naturally he will tell you everything he knows. He approached you in the first place.'

'Ah, but you are forgetting. He is a gentleman who likes to surprise!'

They picked up a *drozhki* on Sadovaya Street. Along the way, Porfiry sang 'Stenka Razin' into the onrushing air. The sheepskinned driver was delighted with his fare's performance and joined in enthusiastically. Porfiry slapped Virginsky's thighs to encourage him to sing out too, particularly during the stanza in which Stenka Razin addresses the Volga river. Virginsky maintained a stubborn silence throughout.

'I would have thought that song would be to your taste, Pavel Pavlovich,' said Porfiry, as soon as the *drozhki* had deposited them. 'The stirring tale of a rebel leader who murders his new bride to prove his devotion to the cause.'

'I do not object to the song. It is the small matter of singing it in an open *drozhki* that I think indecorous. Particularly as we are magistrates engaged in a murder enquiry.'

'Indecorous? Good Heavens! I didn't realise that you radicals placed such store by decorum.'

'Porfiry Petrovich, kindly refrain from referring to me in that way.'

'In what way?'

'You make light of my political convictions. You use the word "radical" as if it were some great joke. The joke is at my expense. That's why you chose to sing that song, I suppose. You think that this is all very funny. Yet I will remind you, a man is dead. And we have come here in order to discover his identity. Furthermore, the political future of our great country is no laughing matter. If I have sincere convictions, it ill behoves you to mock them.'

Porfiry blinked out a face of bewildered innocence. 'You are right, Pavel Pavlovich,' he conceded, after a moment. 'Please for-

'But that would mean filling in a different chit.' This was given as an insurmountable obstacle.

'Of course! Whatever is necessary!'

'Which you must then have signed by the head of the Third Section, Count Shuvalov himself.'

Porfiry was momentarily speechless. When he found his voice, all he could say was, 'Count Shuvalov? Are you sure?'

The two heads of elder and younger librarian nodded in unison.

'Must we trouble Count Shuvalov with a trivial request for a couple of old journals?'

'The request is not trivial. It is a restricted publication. If it falls into the wrong hands, who knows what incendiarism it might provoke.'

'I am a government employee! In fact, an employee of the Ministry of Justice. I require the copies in connection with work I am conducting on behalf of the Ministry.' Porfiry held up his hands. 'Surely these are not the wrong hands?'

'We must believe that it has been restricted for good reason.'

'Ah, but you see, at the time, back in 1866, it was not restricted. Anyone could read it! Indeed there must be many copies of this very issue in open circulation, thousands even, gathering dust on the shelves of respectable professional gentlemen.'

'Shall I tell Timofei Ivanovich to fetch the copies of *The Contemporary*?' There was something new to the younger librarian's tone as he asked this. Porfiry was alert to the nuance and so he nodded assent.

They both watched the older man on his way. When the door had closed behind him, Porfiry looked over his own shoulder before taking out his wallet. 'How much?'

'I shall have to give Timofei Ivanovich something.'

Porfiry peeled off a red ten-rouble bank note.

The librarian's twitching fingers induced a second. Then he snatched the notes away with the alacrity of a hungry peasant.

7

The Russian Word

This young man is himself the victim here, driven to a crime that he is at a loss to explain, by the twin evils of poverty and sickness. He deserves not our opprobrium, but rather our pity. Who is really responsible for the deaths of the rapacious pawnbroker Alyona Ivanovna Kamenya and her unfortunate half-sister Lizaveta? It is not Rodion Romanovich Raskolnikov, though he wielded the implement that took away their lives. His sickness was to blame. We must allow that he did not choose to be sick. Even his prosecutors will not make that claim. His sickness without doubt derived from the dire exigencies of the life he was forced to lead through poverty. Expelled from the university, bankrupt of funds, delirious from starvation, it is little wonder that he found himself acting in a manner over which he had no control. And so, to answer the question, 'Who is responsible for the deaths of Alyona Ivanovna and Lizaveta Ivanovna?', we must ask, 'Who is responsible for Rodion Romanovich's poverty?' Every man and woman of conscience will know in their hearts the answer to that question. For who is responsible for the poverty of many millions of Russians? Again, it does not need this writer to supply an answer.

As we are addressing men and women of conscience, it goes without saying that every one of them will be appalled by the horrific circumstances of Alyona Ivanovna and Lizaveta Ivanovna's deaths. It is not our intention to diminish the true horror of these crimes. Merely to identify the true perpetrator. I say again, it is not Raskolnikov. It is the system that created Raskolnikov. It has been scientifically proven that in a system based on true socialist ideals, that is to say one in which the benefits of production are distributed equally throughout society, it will be impossible for crime to exist. One will simply do away with crime *at a stroke* by changing the socio-economic bases of the state. The sickness and poverty that caused Raskolnikov's crime will be eradicated, and with them Raskolnikov's crime. What need would Raskolnikov have to kill a bloodsucking moneylender when there are no bloodsucking moneylenders to kill, and when, in addition, all his material needs are met?

The logic is irrefutable and must lead, if pursued to its conclusion, to the acquittal of Raskolnikov and to the presence before the bench of other individuals. (I need not name them, when their names are known to all.)

Of course, encouraging as some of the recent verdicts of our juries have been, we must admit that the law courts do not always operate in accordance with the dictates of logic. Even if the counsel for the defence were to avail himself of the arguments that we have put forward, there is no guarantee that they will meet with a sympathetic hearing. The chief difficulty in this particular case is that the defendant has already confessed his guilt (would that he had read this article first!). There is, therefore, nothing for the jury to decide, no verdict to deliver. One must only await the sentence. It is too much to hope that a prosecuting judge will be swayed by an essay in *The Russian Word*. (We know for a fact that many prosecuting judges read *The Russian Word*; we will not speculate as to their reasons.) However, in the person of one investigating magistrate at least, we feel justified in placing faith. It may surprise the reader to know that we are talking of the very man who hounded Rodion Romanovich into confessing.

We have been struck throughout the preliminaries of the trial by the humanity and tact of this individual's demeanour. We expected a wolf baying for blood. We found a human being sensitive to the plight of a less fortunate brother. The magistrate in question may not appreciate our approval, for we imagine that in official circles, to be praised by *The Russian Word* signals the end of a promising career. But the truth will out. The truth is that it was this magistrate's official duty to construct the case against Rodion Romanovich. The truth is also that he went so far in the opposite direction as to make certain evidence favouring the defendant available to the defence. Even as we write, he is engaged in advising the defence on the construction of an argument likely to lead to mitigation in sentencing. Granted, all this falls some way short of the ideal. Let us repeat: we are entitled to demand from the judicial process nothing less than the unconditional acquittal of Raskolnikov; nevertheless, it is a significant step in the right direction, for which P.P. (let us discreetly call our investigating magistrate P.P.) deserves credit.

Porfiry Petrovich allowed himself an inner chuckle. What would Pavel Pavlovich say! To see his old ideological adversary lauded in no less an organ than *The Russian Word*! For it was true that every time Virginsky had put forward similar views concerning the organisation of society, Porfiry had gently but thoroughly quashed them, counselling a more moderate, practical approach. He had even cautioned his young friend against initiating such debates in the bureau. Without doubt, Virginsky looked upon Porfiry with indulgent contempt, as a weak-livered, intellectually compromised, outmoded liberal. A man whose time had passed.

If only he had Virginsky there with him now, to show him the page!

Porfiry tried once more to visualise the journalists who had been present in the courtroom. He must have addressed them after the trial too. It was customary for them to identify themselves and their papers as they called out their questions. But he had no recollection of the occasion. A face floated into his mind, but he did not trust it. He felt that it was his imagination rather than his memory that supplied it.

But at least he had a name now. The article was credited to one D. A. Kozodavlev. Porfiry felt sure that this was one and the same as his anonymous letter writer, if only for a stylistic tic that both letter and article shared. Indeed, in such matters, it was closer to the truth to describe it as a psychological tic.

*

'Yes, but what makes you so certain?' There was a petulant tone to Virginsky's question, possibly occasioned by the concluding remarks of the article that Porfiry had just shown him.

It had taken a further three red banknotes, as well as completion of a yellow chit, to secure the removal of the relevant edition of *The Russian Word* from the library. Strictly speaking, a restricted publication could not be removed from the library under any circumstances. However, the fact that Porfiry had been allowed to view the journal created an anomaly, which was most simply resolved by temporarily removing it from the restricted list. (This was achieved by referring to an earlier version of the restricted list, which did not contain *The Russian Word*, and which by a bureaucratic oversight had remained in force.) If *The Russian Word* was not restricted, it followed that he was free to take it out, on completion of a standard yellow chit. The younger librarian had shown remarkable ingenuity in devising these strategies, which together with his willingness to accept bribes, boded well for his future in the service. There was every possibility that he would escape the fate that his aged doppelgänger seemed to represent. He would go far, in other words.

Porfiry did not answer Virginsky's question. 'You will notice this, from Kozodavlev's article: "It may surprise the reader to know that we are talking of the very man who hounded Rodion Romanovich into confessing." He is referring to me, of course. But note the phrase, "It may surprise the reader." Now, if we go back to the anonymous letter I received, we will find the following: "It might have surprised you to have read such an account in such a journal." What are we to make of this?' Porfiry did not wait for an answer: 'Here is a man who likes to surprise his readers! I feel sure it is the same writer. Now, all we have to do is track down Mr Kozodavlev. That shouldn't be so hard to do. *The Russian Word* was suppressed by the government in 1866. If my knowledge of radical journals is correct, the editor Blagosvetlov founded a new journal, *Affair*, which I believe is still in circulation, is it not, Pavel Pavlovich?'

'I believe so.'

'We need only to make enquiries at the Censorship Office to locate its address. Perhaps you would oblige me by drafting the necessary request, on the correct official chit, please.' Porfiry smiled and batted his eyelids in an attempt to be winning. It was an attempt laden with irony. 'I suggest we begin our enquiries there. Indeed, if we are fortunate, we may even find our Mr Kozodavlev in attendance. I imagine that all the contributors to *The Russian Word* transferred their allegiance to *Affair*.'

For some reason he could not explain, Porfiry felt his spirits revive. He felt the renewal of energy that he had hoped for at the onset of spring, and that the fairground had temporarily provided. Perhaps it had something to do with the fact that he had found himself favourably referred to in a defunct radical journal, though why he should take delight from this baffled him. Porfiry preferred to believe that it was simply the invigorating effect of a genuine lead in the case they were investigating. He was, he realised with pleasure, a hound with a fresh scent in his snout. His energy was the bound of exultation against the leash.

8

'Stenka Razin'

The following day, Thursday, 20 April, they received a reply to their enquiries made to the Censorship Office. The editorial offices of *Affair* were registered at an apartment in 16, Dmitrovsky Lane, under the name of the editor, G. E. Blagosvetlov.

The fine spring weather was strengthening its brief hold on the city and Porfiry was minded to make the most of it while it lasted. He invited Virginsky to accompany him. 'I expect you would like to pay your respects to these radical gentlemen. And besides, with you in tow, they may disclose more than they might otherwise.'

'What do you mean by that?'

'Simply that they will recognise you as one of their own. They will trust you.'

'I shall come with you, of course. It's my duty to do whatever you say.'

'And your pleasure also, no doubt?'

Virginsky hesitated. 'I do not like the duplicitous role in which you seek to cast me.'

'There's nothing duplicitous about it, Pavel Pavlovich. It's simply . . . good psychology.'

'And entirely unnecessary, in my opinion. If Kozodavlev is indeed the writer of the anonymous letter, as seems likely, then naturally he will tell you everything he knows. He approached you in the first place.'

'Ah, but you are forgetting. He is a gentleman who likes to sur-prise!'

They picked up a *drozhki* on Sadovaya Street. Along the way, Porfiry sang 'Stenka Razin' into the onrushing air. The sheep-skinned driver was delighted with his fare's performance and joined in enthusiastically. Porfiry slapped Virginsky's thighs to encourage him to sing out too, particularly during the stanza in which Stenka Razin addresses the Volga river. Virginsky main-tained a stubborn silence throughout.

'I would have thought that song would be to your taste, Pavel Pavlovich,' said Porfiry, as soon as the *drozhki* had deposited them. 'The stirring tale of a rebel leader who murders his new bride to prove his devotion to the cause.'

'I do not object to the song. It is the small matter of singing it in an open *drozhki* that I think indecorous. Particularly as we are magistrates engaged in a murder enquiry.'

'Indecorous? Good Heavens! I didn't realise that you radicals placed such store by decorum.'

'Porfiry Petrovich, kindly refrain from referring to me in that way.'

'In what way?'

'You make light of my political convictions. You use the word "radical" as if it were some great joke. The joke is at my expense. That's why you chose to sing that song, I suppose. You think that this is all very funny. Yet I will remind you, a man is dead. And we have come here in order to discover his identity. Furthermore, the political future of our great country is no laughing matter. If I have sincere convictions, it ill behoves you to mock them.'

Porfiry blinked out a face of bewildered innocence. 'You are right, Pavel Pavlovich,' he conceded, after a moment. 'Please for-

Another was reading a manuscript. Two young women were together checking a set of galley proofs. Others were busy writing.

Porfiry was impressed by the relative youth of the journal's staff, but also by their universal attractiveness. *But by God, these radicals are a good-looking lot!* he thought facetiously. They were also, he noted, without exception intensely serious. No one spoke to another, each absorbed in his or her occupation. The women were dressed demurely, without ostentation, though their hair was carelessly tended, as if this was a fashion that they especially chose to follow. The men allowed their hair to grow long too, though it had not reached the waywardness of their female colleagues'. In general, the men's suits were in a more parlous state than the women's dresses. He had the sense that with them, threadbare elbows and frayed cuffs were badges of honour.

Porfiry smiled back at a roomful of myopically hostile faces. 'Ladies and gentlemen, I am looking for Mr Kozodavlev. I trust I have come to the right place?'

Someone gasped. Perhaps more than one person. It was certainly very loud.

A strange look passed about the room. And settled on a young man at the head of the T's stem. He rose to his feet, as if goaded by the glances of his fellows. 'One moment, please. I will fetch Grigory Elampievich.'

It was now Porfiry and Virginsky's turn to exchange a curious look.

The young man squeezed his way round the desks to slip through a door at the back of the office.

The first thing that struck Porfiry about Grigory Elampievich, when he appeared, was the unusual sensitivity of his eyes. It lent his expression a certain hesitancy, which was accentuated by a slightly weak chin. And yet there was also a burning energy kindling in those eyes. Here was a man, the face suggested, quick to take offence and also, perhaps, quick to act: as the chin receded, the rest of the face was projected forward. With its intensely dark moustache and brows, the face retained a youthfulness that was belied by a sweeping mane of silver hair. It was a handsome face, striking even, certainly holding its own in the roomful of radicals. Indeed, placing the man's age at around fifty, Porfiry decided that he was looking at an archetypal elder of the radical movement, smartly dressed in an immaculate suit and neatly tied bow.

The conflicting hesitancy and energy that Porfiry discerned in Grigory Elampievich's face was also evident in his gait. He came into the room as though he expected to be beaten back, and yet was ready to resist the onslaught.

'You were asking after Kozodavlev?'

'Yes.'

'You do not know?'

'Evidently not.'

'He is dead. That is to say, we believe he is dead. There was a fire at his building the night before last. He was due in the office for a meeting yesterday but did not appear. We became concerned. Kozodavlev is normally extremely reliable. He would always send word if he was unable to make an appointment. We were especially concerned when we heard about the fire. It appears that it was centred on his floor. His apartment was thoroughly destroyed. You may have read about it. A number of people died. Six, in fact. Five of the unfortunates were children. We believe he was the one adult. We have yet to receive any official confirmation, however.'

Porfiry found himself unable to speak.

'We are hoping that our fears may prove groundless,' continued the elder radical. 'But each day that goes by increases the likelihood of his death. We did not see him again today. I have been round to his apartment building. His floor is completely closed off. If he is still alive, he would have approached one of us, his comrades, for somewhere to stay. Naturally, we have made enquiries with the authorities, as journalists as well as friends. It seems that a body was recovered from Kozodavlev's apartment.'

'I did read about the fire,' said Porfiry at last. 'I did not know that it was Mr Kozodavlev's building.'

'You are friends of his? I do not believe we have ever met. I am Grigory Elampievich Blagosvetlov.' The editor of *Affair* held out his hand.

'I have never met him,' admitted Porfiry. 'He once wrote about me – I think in favourable terms. The day before yesterday I believe he wrote to me anonymously, requesting a meeting. If it was him, he did not keep our appointment – with good reason, it would seem.'

'Forgive me,' said Blagosvetlov. 'I do not quite understand. How do you know the letter was from him if it was anonymous? And why should Demyan Antonovich have written anything anonymously? Demyan Antonovich Kozodavlev is not a man to write anonymously. He would put his name to whatever he wrote, even if it resulted in him spending the rest of his days in the Peter and Paul Fortress.'

'I am a magistrate,' said Porfiry. 'An investigating magistrate. Demyan Antonovich claimed to have information pertaining to a case I am investigating.'

'Demyan Antonovich? An informant? Impossible. You are mistaken. This letter was not from him.'

'You are familiar with Demyan Antonovich's handwriting?'

Blagosvetlov reluctantly conceded that he was.

Porfiry took out the letter and handed it to him.

As he read, the fiery energy of his eyes prevailed, flooding out in a rush of colour over his cheeks. He thrust the note back at Porfiry in disgust.

'Do you recognise the handwriting? Is it Mr Kozodavlev's?'

It was a question that Blagosvetlov declined to answer.

'Do you know anything about the body recovered from the Winter Canal two days ago?' wondered Porfiry.

'Only what I have read in the newspapers.'

Porfiry turned to Virginsky. 'Pavel Pavlovich, will you kindly show Grigory Elamievich the copy of the poster?'

Virginsky took out and unfolded the erroneous Wanted poster.

'Please ignore the wording. There was a misunderstanding over the text. However, that is the body in question.'

'My God,' murmured Blagosvetlov. 'It's . . . grotesque!'

'Yes, well, the water has reacted with the tissue in certain places. But you will note the heavy pockmarking of the face, and the distinctively small eyes. Oh yes, and he appears to have been a Jew. Does that description, coupled with the photograph, bring to mind anyone – any associates of Mr Kozodavlev's, for example?'

'He does not look human.'

'Be assured, he was . . . human.'

Blagosvetlov shook his head. 'I don't know all Kozodavlev's friends.'

Porfiry smiled. 'Of course not. You are not his keeper, after all. Neither his brother nor his keeper.' Porfiry signalled to Virginsky to retrieve the poster then turned back to Blagosvetlov. 'Tell me, do you have any theories about these fires? My colleague here, Pavel Pavlovich – I am Porfiry Petrovich, by the way – Pavel Pavlovich is of the view that the fires may not have been started by disaffected students and radical elements, as many commentators are suggesting, but they may rather be due to the general combustibility of our city. Do I have that right, Pavel Pavlovich?'

Virginsky merely frowned.

'He is of the opinion, I believe, that the blame must be laid at the door of the regime. In short, it is all the Tsar's fault. That's Pavel Pavlovich's theory, anyway. Do you have one?'

Blagosvetlov regarded Virginsky with interest. 'You are an investigating magistrate also?'

'Yes,' confirmed Virginsky with a slight nod, possibly constrained by embarrassment.

'Oh, we have radicals in the department too, you know,' continued Porfiry brightly. 'So, what do you think, sir? About the fires, if I may press you.'

'You may discover my opinions easily enough,' said Blagosvetlov. 'By subscribing to our journal.'

'Ah! Very good! I like that! Never miss the opportunity to recruit a new subscriber, and why not. I dare say Pavel Pavlovich subscribes already. Perhaps he will bring some of his back copies into the department. Will you, Pavel Pavlovich?'

'If you wish.'

'Well then, I look forward to reading your views,' said Porfiry with a smile that suggested he was happy to let the matter drop. 'I wonder, does Mr Kozodavlev have a desk here in the office?'

'We all share desks.'

'Of course. That's precisely what I would expect!' cried Porfiry delightedly. 'You share desks. But each person must have somewhere to keep their own papers, the material they are working on from day to day? Did Mr Kozodavlev keep any papers here?'

Blagosvetlov bristled. The fire came back to his eyes.

'I understand your reluctance to co-operate with the authorities,' began Porfiry, speaking apparently to Blagosvetlov but in reality addressing them all. 'But I would ask you to bear in mind that I have come here today openly, in good faith, asking honest questions. I have not engaged in subterfuge or any of the filthy tricks to which other departments resort. I come in my service uniform, not in disguise. I have not sent spies or agents provocateurs. It is not my wish, or my intention, to close down your journal. On the contrary, I personally believe that the open airing of all shades of opinion is vital if Russia is to progress – as she must. I may not share your opinions, but I wish to hear them, and I wish others to hear them too. In short, I am not here to suppress you. I am here solely in my capacity as an investigating magistrate looking into the death of an unidentified man. I believe that your friend Kozodavlev knew something about that man. I believe also that he wished to share that knowledge with me. You may now condemn him as a police informant, and consider him a discredited comrade. However, before you do so, I ask you to remember the Kozodavlev you knew, to remember his principles and integrity, and ask yourself, would he have written this note unless he had good reason? I can only assume that what was a good reason for Kozodavlev will be a good reason for you too.'

The plea was met with silence, their faces sealed off in resentful misery.

'We were talking about the fires,' resumed Porfiry. 'Well, here is a theory for you. The fire in Kozodavlev's building was started deliberately with the sole purpose of killing Kozodavlev – or perhaps of incinerating his already-dead body. The other five victims were merely incidental. Collateral damage, we might say. The murderer's sole intention was to prevent Kozodavlev from going to the authorities with what he knew about the dead man in the Winter Canal. In which case, if that theory is true, then I am here investigating not only the death of the unknown man retrieved from the Winter Canal but also that of Demyan Antonovich Kozodavlev, your friend, your colleague. Your comrade. Please, I beg you, look deep into your heart before you wilfully obstruct me.'

'The heart is merely a physical organ pumping blood around the body,' put in a young man seated along one of the arms of the T of desks. Someone else sniggered.

Porfiry regarded the speaker with interest, taking note of his intensely dark, almost black eyes. There was an arrogance to his hostility that was lacking in most of the others, a self-conscious sneer that disfigured his good looks.

'And you must be Mr *Bazarov*,' said Porfiry, with a sarcastic smile.

The young man snorted derisively at the reference to Turgenev's archetypal nihilist. 'Bazarov is a fictional construct. A distorted character from a failed novel written ten years ago by a superfluous writer.'

'An interesting judgement, my friend. But am I correct in thinking that you believe all writers to be superfluous? That is the position of the radical youth, is it not? If it's a choice of Pushkin or a boot, you would take the boot.'

'Naturally. If a man has any talent for writing, he should devote himself to propaganda and publicity. For the cause, I mean. Utilitarian writing is the only kind that can be countenanced.'

'You are talking about manifestos?'

'Are you trying to entrap me?'

'I wouldn't dare. To have such a dangerous beast as you in my trap would surely earn me a savaging. I am simply interested in learning the opinions of young people today. If the human conscience does not reside in the heart – as natural science insists it cannot – where then would you place it? Or would you deny the very existence of human conscience?'

'What we experience as conscience, our moral outlook if you like, arises from the conditions of our upbringing, and from the norms of the society in which we are born. It is a mental construct, and therefore it resides in the brain.'

Porfiry considered for a moment. 'So conscience is relative, is that what you are saying? Different societies, different upbringings, will create different moral outlooks. There is no absolute right and wrong?'

'Amongst cannibals, it is perfectly acceptable to eat people.'

'And God? There is no room for God in this?'

The young man merely gave another derisive snort, by which he meant to repay Porfiry for the insult to his intelligence.

'And if a society with *norms* – is that the word you used?' Porfiry waited for the young man's dismissive nod before continuing. 'And if a society with norms that prohibit a certain act is changed to one that allows that same act, what happens to the conscience of those living in that society? Are they able to transform their consciences as easily as the society was transformed?'

'Those living at the time of the transformation will have to be retrained so that their consciences are brought in line with the new norms. All future generations who are brought up, once the transformed society has been established, will naturally have consciences that correspond to its norms.'

'I see. Thank you. I understand now. And if we go back to a time before the transformation has been effected, when it is in the process of being brought about, before its norms are established . . . this I would imagine would be a time of great turmoil and confusion for the human conscience?'

'It need not be.'

'It need not be? Please, elucidate, if you would be so kind.'

'A man, or woman, must simply choose whether his or her moral outlook is to be governed by the future or the past. Once that choice is made, everything becomes clear.'

'And if he –'

'Or she.'

Porfiry acknowledged the correction with a bow. 'If he or she chooses the future, then everything that pertains towards bringing about that future becomes permissible, and need not trouble his, or her, conscience?'

'That is correct.'

Porfiry turned back to Blagosvetlov. 'These are your views too?'

'Broadly speaking, yes.'

'And Kozodavlev's?'

'I believe so.'

'And was Kozodavlev – I am sorry to speak of him in the past, but assuming that he has perished in the fire – was he such a man as to choose his conscience from the past or the future?'

Blagosvetlov's eyes shone with certainty. 'The future.'

'He was a rational man too, I presume?'

'Eminently.'

'And so, everything that he did would be done in accordance with that choice? He would not be inconsistent?'

Blagosvetlov looked momentarily abashed, the hesitant aspect of his expression gaining precedence. 'It is impossible to say for certain . . .'

'But from what you know of Kozodavlev?' encouraged Porfiry.

'From what I know of him, then yes, I would agree with that statement.'

'So in writing to me, his conscience was governed by his commitment to the future? Whatever he hoped to initiate by this letter – which none of us can guess at – it would be consistent with his overriding desire to bring about this particular future? A future that you, and all of these here, are also working towards. That is where logic takes us, is it not?'

Blagosvetlov conceded Porfiry's point with a series of small but decisive nods.

'May I see Mr Kozodavlev's drawer?'

The opposing aspects of Blagosvetlov's expression shimmered momentarily in his eyes. A soft groan of conflicted anguish broke from his lips. His head fell in a gesture that might have been one of defeat or shame. Porfiry took it for assent.

9

In Kozodavlev's drawer

The opening of another person's private drawer is always an act freighted with a sense of transgression, even when it is committed by a magistrate going about his official duties. It may be done in the name of justice and in the interests of the law – still, when it comes down to it, one is simply prying. When the person in question is dead – or thought to be – this sense is even more acute. No permission can be either sought or granted. There is the mitigating feeling that it does not matter now, that they cannot be hurt by whatever is found; but for a man such as Porfiry, a man who could not shake off such outmoded ideas as the eternity of the soul, this was hardly persuasive. If he consoled himself with any thought, it was that Kozodavlev seemed to have led him to this drawer. He had a sense of the missing journalist standing at his shoulder, urging him to go on. This was a delusion, no doubt. Had Kozodavlev actually been there encouraging Porfiry's investigations, he would have been going against the grain of sentiment in the room. All that Porfiry could sense behind him was the sullen hostility of the younger radicals. Blagosvetlov had retired from the office, as if he could not bear to witness what he had set in motion.

Porfiry allowed himself a moment after opening the drawer to take in the sense of the space that had been revealed. He imagined himself as Kozodavlev, looking down on the drawer's interior. To the journalist, it would have appeared so familiar as to be hardly considered. And yet to Porfiry, it had all the strangeness and mystery of another man's soul laid bare.

If so, Kozodavlev's soul comprised: pencil parings and curls of tobacco, gathered in the corners with the darkness and dust; a copy of Chernyshevsky's *What Is to Be Done?*; a number of issues of the conservative journal, *Russian Soil*; a collection of writing materials, a couple of pens, a bottle of ink, some pencils of varying lengths; an empty cigarette packet; a loose pile of papers, in truth, not as many as Porfiry had hoped for; and a photograph in a dog-eared cardboard frame.

Porfiry seized most greedily on this last item. He called over the young man who had first gone to fetch Blagosvetlov. 'Which one is Kozodavlev?' There were about twenty people in the photograph, arranged loosely around a central group of five seated on a sofa. Even as he asked the question, Porfiry knew which of the figures the young man would point out. He recognised a number of the people shown as the young radicals of the magazine's staff. Blagosvetlov was there too, in the very centre of the composition. Of those he did not recognise, one man stood out. He was seated on the sofa, next to Blagosvetlov. This individual was not at all attractive, unlike almost everyone around him. But it was not for that reason alone that he drew Porfiry's eye. His face had a haunted expression. He looked towards the camera as if he believed it capable of capturing the secret that he undoubtedly nurtured.

The young man confirmed Porfiry's suspicion.

Porfiry handed the photograph to Virginsky. 'We will take that with us, Pavel Pavlovich.'

The young man let out a small cry of protest, then hurried through the door at the back of the office.

Leafing through the papers, Porfiry discovered what appeared to be two drafts of the same article, a review of a novel recently serialised in *Russian Soil*, which was presumably why Kozodavlev had copies of that journal in his drawer. Porfiry remembered that the novel in question, entitled *Swine*, had caused something of a sensation because of the interesting circumstances surrounding its author. Known only as D., he had supposedly once belonged to a secret revolutionary cell but had now renounced his former beliefs. The book was presented as a novel, but it was evidently to be taken as a memoir. Porfiry also found a letter from the editor of *Russian Soil*, in which this basic information was provided and the novel was heartily commended to Kozodavlev.

The first draft of the review was extremely critical. In it, Kozodavlev condemned the writer's portrayal of radical types as crude caricature. He denied, in fact, that the novel had any basis in reality and was rather the fantasy of a disordered and irredeemably reactionary mind. The novelist's supposed radical credentials were called into question; and even if true, they merely served to render his turn to conservatism all the more lamentable. The final verdict on the book was that it was a cynical fraud, designed to cash in on public fears about phantom revolutionary groupings. At the head of this article, Kozodavlev had written '*Affair* piece', which was underlined three times.

The second draft – under the heading 'R. E. piece', also triple underlined – took almost entirely the opposite stance. The novel under discussion was a warning to society, a work of visionary genius. The truth of the portrayal could not be doubted, given the novelist's own former radical credentials. The anonymous novelist was to be praised not only for turning his back on the errors of his youth but also for harnessing his undoubtedly painful experiences in order to create a work of art of such high moral conscience and integrity. Both versions were drafted in the same hand, which bore a striking resemblance to the hand the anonymous letter had been written in.

The only other item in the drawer was a scrawled note, on a sheet torn from a notebook. 'I don't give a damn what you do. Do you think I have ever cared?' This was the full extent of the missive, apart from the single initial serving as signature: 'D.'

Was it possible that this was the same D. as the anonymous author? It was too tempting a question to be answered in the affirmative. Porfiry recognised it as one of those traps of coincidence that are often met with in the course of an investigation.

Blagosvetlov came back into the room with the same mixture of combativeness and shyness that Porfiry had noticed earlier. He was beginning to find it endearing, and felt himself wanting to ease the man's suffering if he could.

'What have you found?' Blagosvetlov's tone was aggressive. He seemed to blame Porfiry for his own acquiescence in the search.

'I found this.' Porfiry handed him the brief note. 'Do you have any idea who this D. might be?'

Blagosvetlov shrugged. 'It might be anyone.'

'Might it be the author of the novel *Swine*? I believe Kozodavlev was working on a review for your magazine.'

'It might, I suppose.' Blagosvetlov drew himself up assertively. 'Ivan Ilyich tells me you intend to confiscate a photograph.'

'It's not a question of confiscating. That implies that I do not have your consent. Whereas, I am sure that you would consent to our taking anything that might shed light on the disappearance of your friend.' Porfiry did not wait for Blagosvetlov to respond. 'Is it possible that Kozodavlev knew the author of *Swine*? Perhaps he was about to reveal his identity?'

'You would do better to talk to Trudolyubov about that.'

'Trudolyubov?'

'The editor of *Russian Soil*, which serialised that trash.'

'Of course. That is a very good suggestion.' Porfiry studied Blagosvetlov in silence for a moment. 'Thank you.'

'Have you finished?'

'Yes, for the time being. If there is anything else that we need to know, I trust we may call upon you again.'

Blagosvetlov made no answer.

'In addition to the photograph, I am taking several other articles back to my chambers for further examination.' Turning to Virginsky, Porfiry added, 'Pavel Pavlovich, you will ensure that an official receipt of evidence is sent to Mr Blagosvetlov.'

Virginsky gave an automatic nod, assenting, and then shook his head like a horse that had just been stung.

Porfiry led the way out of the office and had in fact taken two steps onto the landing before he turned back, walking straight into Virginsky. The collision was observed with suppressed hilarity by the staff of *Affair*. Their laughter was made up of equal parts contempt and relief. This investigating magistrate was evidently something of a buffoon.

Begging Virginsky's pardon, Porfiry bowed past him to present himself once again in the office. He grinned sheepishly. 'I just remembered something as we were leaving. Pavel Pavlovich was right behind me. We had a little accident. But then, you all saw that, I imagine. It was my fault, my fault entirely.'

'Was there something else?' prompted Blagosvetlov impatiently.

'Oh, yes, thank you for reminding me. I nearly forgot again! What a dunderhead I am this morning. Were you aware that Kozodavlev wrote for other journals?'

'Other journals?'

'Yes.'

'He may have placed the occasional piece in *The Contemporary*. Its politics did not exactly coincide with his, but he could see the virtue of extending his readership. A liberal might be stung into radicalism.'

'But is there a journal, do you know, whose name begins with the letters R and E?'

'R. E.?'

'Yes. A name comprising two words, such as *Russian Word*. But in this case the letters are R and E. I imagine the first word must be "Russian." It seems to be a very popular epithet in journalistic circles.'

'There is only *Russian Era*,' said Blagosvetlov dismissively.

'Ah yes, *Russian Era*. Of course. Thank you. That must be it. Were you aware that Kozodavlev contributed also to *Russian Era*?'

'Never!'

'Never? Why not? Surely a journalist must place his pieces where he can?'

'But it's impossible to conceive of anything written by Kozodavlev appearing in that Slavophile rag. Not only would he refuse to submit to them, but they would not consider publishing anything by a radical journalist. They are unremittingly hostile to our goals.'

'But if he submitted under a false name?'

'Impossible!'

Porfiry fumbled for the two articles he had tucked away in an inner pocket. 'Let me see. Now where is it? This is the article he was writing for you. And . . . don't tell me I've lost it.' More fumbling in another pocket finally produced what he was looking for. 'This, here it is. Yes. "R. E. piece". That is what he wrote. At the top. Underlined three times.' Porfiry handed the sheets to Blagosvetlov. 'You helped me out by reminding me that the only title those two letters could possibly refer to is *Russian Era*.'

After a moment, the editor thrust the papers back at Porfiry. 'If Kozodavlev was not dead already, he is dead to me now.'

10

Men of the shadows

Back in Stolyarny Lane, Porfiry Petrovich called in on Nikodim Fomich. The chief superintendent seemed surprised to see him.

'I will not keep you long,' said Porfiry.

'Please, stay as long as you like.'

Porfiry seated himself on the government-issue sofa, identical to the one in his chambers. 'The other day we were talking about the fires, do you remember?'

'Yes, of course.'

'It seems that the individual I was to have met at the Summer Garden may have perished in the fire at the apartment building on Monday night. The fire which claimed six dead in all.'

'I see.'

'Do you know who is conducting the investigation into that? Is it a police matter, or has it been handed over to other authorities?'

'The Third Section, you mean?'

'That is what I am wondering.'

'I can find out for you.'

'Thank you. Either way, I wish to see the file.'

'If it is still under the jurisdiction of the police and an invest-igating magistrate, that won't be a problem. If it has gone to the Third Section, then I am not sure I will be able to help you.'

Porfiry nodded tersely in acknowledgement.

'Do you not have your own contacts there?' wondered Nikodim

Fomich. 'I seem to remember you were on amicable terms with one of the officers?'

Porfiry gave a startled look. 'You are referring to Major Verkhotsev?'

'That's the fellow.'

'He is hardly to be trusted.'

'My dear Porfiry, none of them is to be trusted.'

Porfiry's smile as he took his leave was guarded.

*

Porfiry sorted through an array of magazines and newspapers on his desk.

'It is hard to distinguish all these various publications, is it not, Pavel Pavlovich? We've had *The Russian Voice*, *The Russian Word* – there is a *Russian World* too, I believe. Not to mention a *Russian Messenger*, *Russian Soil*, *Russian Era* . . . They all lay claim to speak for Russia, and yet they have such contrary things to say on her behalf! Pity the poor readers, who must find it awfully confusing.'

'I don't find it confusing.' Virginsky had pulled up a chair to the opposite side of Porfiry's desk, so that he could more easily browse the newspapers spread out there.

'No? I suppose the trick is to ignore the *Russian* part of the title, which we may take for granted. So then it becomes a question of distinguishing between a *Voice*, a *Word*, a *Messenger*, the *Soil* and an *Era*.'

'*Russian Soil* and *Russian Era* are essentially the same paper – they are published from one address and edited by the same Trudolyubov that Blagosvetlov mentioned. *Era* is a daily and *Soil* a monthly. *Soil* is little more than an omnibus, or digest, of *Era*. It often repeats editorials.'

'And so Kozodavlev was reviewing *Swine* for the novel's publisher? No wonder that version of his review was so favourable!' Porfiry smiled and shook his head. 'My, my, that's the lowest kind of hackwork, is it not?'

'One moment, Porfiry Petrovich. We cannot be certain that R. E. does in fact refer to *Russian Era*. And even if it does, we do not know that Kozodavlev truly intended to submit the article. He may have written it as an intellectual exercise. To amuse himself, or perhaps even as a piece of satire aimed against *Russian Era*.'

'A curious waste of his time.'

'But not impossible.'

'The easiest way to resolve this would be to talk to this Mr Trudolyubov. He should know whether he was expecting a review of *Swine* from Kozodavlev. He may even be able to shed some light on the identity of the book's mysterious author. I see that *Russian Soil* is not at all reticent about its whereabouts. It prints its address for everyone to see. Liteiny Prospect.'

'Of course. It often serves as a mouthpiece for the Tsarevich. It is recognised as the means by which he airs his criticisms of his father's regime.'

'Ah.' Porfiry placed a hand wearily over his eyes. 'Please don't drag me back into those troubled waters.'

'I shall not drag you anywhere. But I cannot control where the case may take us.'

Porfiry nodded a distracted acknowledgement. He turned the pages of a copy of *Russian Soil* until he came to the first episode of the novel *Swine*. 'Have you read it, Pavel Pavlovich?'

It was a moment before Virginsky replied. 'Yes.'

'There is no need to be reticent. I will not think any the less of you for reading it. Indeed, I intended to read it myself. I cannot remember now why I did not. Certainly it is a work that must be of interest to an investigating magistrate. So . . . what did you think? That is to say, with which of Kozodavlev's judgements did you concur?'

'I judged it a poor piece of work.'

'You think it fails, as a warning to society?'

'I think it fails as a novel.'

'And the author? Do you have any opinions regarding his identity?'

'I do not see that it is at all material to the case we are investigating.'

'The novel concerns the activities of a group of would-be revolutionaries, is that not so?'

'Yes.'

'It seems likely that Kozodavlev was involved in revolutionary politics. I mean actively, rather than just observing from the sidelines and occasionally cheering on in editorials. His letter to me hints at that. He was worried about spies in the department. It is not inconceivable that there may be individuals employed by the state whose true loyalties lie elsewhere, is it, Pavel Pavlovich?'

'You are accusing me?'

'Not at all. I know you are far too sensible to get involved with any of that.' There was an undoubted hint of irony in Porfiry's voice, that could only be infuriating to Virginsky. 'To return to Kozodavlev. He went to the bridge over the Winter Canal on Monday, the day the thaw began, because he had a terrible presentiment that the body was going to come to light. He knew this because he had been present when it had been cast in the canal. We can speculate that our man from the canal was a member of a closed cell murdered by his fellows, one of whom may well have been Kozodavlev. The resurfacing of this old crime stings Kozodavlev's conscience, which had never been easy about the murder, and he writes to me. A spy in the department sees his letter, notifies the Central Revolutionary Committee, and an assassin is sent round to torch his apartment building. In the process, killing five other innocent residents.'

'Kozodavlev was not innocent. Not if he was an informer.'

'You think he deserved to be killed?'

Virginsky dipped his gaze, abashed. 'I had not meant to say that.'

'And what of the body in the canal? If he too was an informer, he too deserved to die?'

'We don't know what he was, or who.'

'These men . . . these men of the shadows.' Porfiry's sudden rage rendered him inarticulate. He was forced to light a cigarette to calm himself. 'Who gave them the right to take another's life?'

'No one . . . *gave* it to them.'

The faltering emphasis of Virginsky's answer implied a world of meaning that Porfiry was reluctant to explore. He looked at his junior colleague for a moment warily before inhaling deeply on his cigarette. 'There are two things that I would like to know for certain. The first being whether Kozodavlev was the man on the bridge who watched the sailors bring up the body.'

'The *Peter the Great* has sailed, has she not?'

'Regrettably.'

'And so we have missed our chance to present the photograph of Kozodavlev to Apprentice Seaman Ordynov?'

'We shall have a photographic copy made and sent on to

Helsingfors. The authorities there will question Ordynov when the ship docks, in a few days' time.'

'And the second thing?'

Porfiry's expression clouded suddenly, and he looked away from Virginsky. He snatched up the copy of *Russian Soil*. 'Whether this . . . novel . . . has any merit at all.'

Virginsky's frown made it clear he had detected the lie in Porfiry's voice.

*

Swine
By D.

PREFACE

Be in no doubt. The events set out in this narrative occurred. The personalities with which it is peopled exist. The crimes they commit are real and depicted without exaggeration or sensationalism. I say this with absolute authority. I was there. I am one of those personalities.

I share in the guilt of the crimes, even of the very worst.

Perhaps I did not pull the trigger, but I held down the man.

Why then have I chosen to write this account?

The simplest answer is to say that I have realised the error of my ways. I was in thrall of certain ideas, but am no longer. My intellectual captivation went hand in hand with personal fascination. There are men, and women, whom it is difficult to resist. Even when they utter the most flagrant and outrageous lies – for example, when they assert that black is white – one feels that they are telling the truth. Indeed, one is certain that they are capable only of truth-telling. It goes without saying that the truths they reveal are felt to be the most profound and devastating imaginable.

Their truths are the truths upon which one must act, and with a fierce urgency. When they call, whatever they may ask, one does not refuse.

You may find it hard to believe that any individual could exercise such power over another, that such scoundrels – such *swine* – are capable of commanding the loyalty of intelligent people. To which I can only say, believe.

They begin with seduction. The seduction of ideas, ideals, hope and goodness. They end with entrapment. The entrapment of fear and mutual suspicion. It is a web from which one cannot extricate one's self.

Every noble sentiment, every soaring aspiration, every burning desire to improve the lot of one's fellow man, is reduced to a simple formula of hate: kill or be killed.

One can accept this formula only for so long – that is to say, only for so long as one has not been called upon to act on it. As an abstract formula it may seem as logical, and reasonable, as any other. But the moment one acts upon it is the moment one grasps its true horror. One's soul is thrown into upheaval. One's sanity is fractured.

Of the personalities who appear in this narrative, all have suffered for the part they played. All are isolated from their fellow creatures – from God's creation, in fact – by the sins that hang over them. One man has already committed suicide. I would not be greatly surprised if others follow his example. It is a course of action to which I give due consideration daily.

Perhaps I wrote this narrative to defer that terrible, final crime. Perhaps I hope that the writing will atone for the crimes written about, and render my suicide unnecessary, that by offering this as a warning, I will redeem myself in some small measure.

Or perhaps it is simply the note I will leave behind.

D.

*

By the middle of the following afternoon, that of Friday, 21 April, Porfiry had finished reading all four instalments of *Swine*. He put the last copy of *Russian Soil* to one side with a dissatisfied expression. He could not say with any certainty what he had just read. Despite the assertions of that preface, much of the main narrative read as a novel, and a bad novel at that. It was full of cheap novelistic tricks. Indeed, the preface itself could be taken as the first of them. What more transparent novelistic trick could there be than to assert the truth of what is to follow?

And yet, the force of the preface gave him pause. The apparent authenticity of the sentiments expressed seemed to sit at odds with the lurid and contrived narrative that followed. The plot displayed a laughable reliance on coincidence and a lamentable taste for melodrama. The 'personalities' portrayed were flat and unconvincing.

That said, it did occur to Porfiry that perhaps individuals in such situations find themselves speaking and acting like characters in a bad novel; if a true account of their acts were written down, the result would be indistinguishable.

He had read the serial half in the hope that it might shed some light on the case he was investigating. On that front, he was not entirely disappointed, although he remained suspicious of the parallels he found. He was looking for a man shot through the head and cast into a canal, and he found him, or something similar. In point of fact, in *Swine*, the body was thrown into a lake, rather than a canal, and one located on a remote country estate and not in the centre of St Petersburg. Striking as any similarities were, Porfiry was not unduly excited by them. The crime in the novel was clearly modelled on a notorious case of a few years earlier, which had been widely reported when it came to trial. The body in that case, also shot through the head, had been disposed of in a lake.

Besides, when it came to disposing of their victims' bodies, there was a limited number of choices open to murderers. Immersion in water was not so unique that its occurrence in the novel and in the current case could be seen as significant. More significant, as far as Porfiry was concerned, was the location chosen for disposal: in the case he was investigating, this was the Winter Canal, right under the Tsar's nose. Nothing in *Swine* resembled this in any way.

More generally, he had hoped to gain some insight into the 'men of the shadows' who organised and controlled the types of grouping described in the novel. In *Swine*, such figures were given names that left one in no doubt as to their role in the narrative. The cruel and ruthless taskmaster who drove the revolutionaries to murder was 'Tatarin'; the shadowy mastermind whose fiendish plans set their crimes in motion was simply 'Dyavol', or *Devil*.

To Porfiry, these characters had no humanity beyond the traits encompassed by their names, which made it difficult for him to believe that they were based on real personalities. In fact, they reminded him of identifiable characters from other books; they were a little too much the stock villains of low literature.

This thought prompted him to turn his attention to the other novel found in Kozodavlev's drawer, Chernyshevsky's *What Is to Be Done?* The Peculiar Man of that novel, Rakhmetov, seemed to have provided the model for one of the characters of *Swine*, an ascetic called Monakh. Porfiry had read the book before, soon after its publication in 1863; almost ten years ago, he realised. The character of Rakhmetov, sleeping on a bed of nails to prepare for the struggle ahead, had struck him at the time as a rather preposterous construction. But then again, he was no less realistic than any of the other characters in the book. If the danger of such creations was that they might lead the youth of Russia to emulate them, then really there was no danger. One had to give the youth of Russia more credit. When it came down to it, they were just too sensible to fall for all that idealised nonsense, or so Porfiry believed. The self-negating sacrifice of Chernyshevsky's improbable hero Lopukhov (which, under the tortuous rationalising of the novel, was an act of supreme self-interest), faking his own suicide in order to leave his wife free to marry her lover – who in their right mind would wish to emulate *him*?

At the very moment Porfiry formulated that question, Virginsky came into his chambers. He was holding a large sheet of paper, the blank side of which was directed towards Porfiry.

'Ah, it has come in already, has it? The revised poster. And I see that everything is in order, this time.'

'But I haven't shown it to you yet,' said Virginsky, somewhat crestfallen.

'You don't need to. I can tell by the eagerness of your step, and by your smile, which though slight manages to transmit both relief and satisfaction. In addition, the fact that you are withholding the printed side of the poster, making ready to reveal it to me with a grand flourish, as if you were unveiling a masterpiece – all this leads me to suspect that the Imperial State Printing Works has not let us down this time.'

'Yes, well, here it is.' Virginsky turned the poster over. 'Do you approve it for release?'

Porfiry barely glanced at it. 'Is the wording correct?'

'It is.'

'Very well. Release it. Have it posted in all the city's police bureaux, and in the usual public places.'

'Do you not wish to check it?'

'I trust you, Pavel Pavlovich.'

The casually issued statement seemed to take Virginsky aback.

'Before you go,' continued Porfiry. 'This book.' He held up the copy of *What Is to Be Done?* 'You have read it, of course.'

'Of course. We have talked of it before, I believe. You have mocked me for admiring it too much.'

'You do admire it, don't you?' Porfiry's surprise at this fact was renewed in his voice. 'And bound up in your admiration of the novel is your admiration of the characters? These new men and women.'

'Yes.'

'You see it as a ... how can I put it? As a programme ... a manual ... or even a manifesto? It is not a novel, it is a guide to how one may live one's life?'

'Certainly, I believe that it may point the way to a better basis for relationships between the sexes.'

'But this character, Lopukhov, the one who fakes his own suicide . . .' Porfiry flicked through the pages. 'Let me find it. The note he left. Ah, yes. Here it is. "I was disturbing your peace and quiet. I am quitting the scene. Don't pity me; I love you both so much that I am very pleased with this decisive act. Farewell." I ask you, Pavel Pavlovich! How would you describe the man who wrote that? A doormat, perhaps? I mean to say . . . the way he just takes himself off like that! Can we really believe it? Would you do that?'

'If I believed that my disappearance was the only way to bring about the happiness of the woman I loved, and if I truly loved her, then, yes . . . I would like to think that I would be capable of such an act. It is not so strange. It is logical. He loves Vera Pavlovna. She loves another. He makes way for the man she loves.'

'But a real man would not act like that. You would not act like that. Not in that situation. Love is not logical, Pavel Pavlovich.'

'There are men – and women – who are living their lives in accordance with the precepts of that book. Marriage is the only way for many women to escape the control of their families. But traditional marriage only replaces one form of control with another. It is not true freedom for the woman. Therefore, many young people are entering into a new kind of marriage, a marriage of friendship and equality, in which the woman is not expected to bow down before the man. Such a marriage truly does bring about the liberation of the woman, because she is free to live her life as she wishes, not as her husband wishes. And if she wishes to take a lover, she is free to do so.'

'Yes, yes, that's all very well. But is it really possible to imagine a husband so devoid of jealousy that he negates his own life, faking his suicide and assuming a new identity, solely to allow his wife's future happiness?'

There was a pause before Virginsky answered: 'Yes.'

'Well, he is a fool.'

'I shall see to the distribution of the poster.'

'And really, does the author take us for fools? The police and the judicial authorities, I mean? That we would not see through the manifest fraud of that supposed suicide! A bullet in a cap! The cap was fished out of the water near Liteiny Bridge! The cap belonged to Lopukhov! Therefore, Lopukhov must have killed himself on Liteiny Bridge and fallen in the river!'

'Unfortunately, Chernyshevsky did not think to make you a character in his novel, Porfiry Petrovich.'

'Well, I would have seen right through it if he had.'

'I have no doubt.'

'I see that I must read this tiresome book again,' grumbled Porfiry. 'We cannot overlook the possibility that it may have some bearing on the case. But, good God, I do not find the company of these new men and women at all congenial!' He flashed a sour glance to Virginsky, as if he counted him one of their number.

*

Porfiry finished reading *What Is to Be Done?* on Sunday morning. He put the book down and left his apartment.

He headed straight for Haymarket Square, where he joined the traffic of worshippers flowing to and from the Church of the Assumption of the Virgin Mary. The cathedral stood like a bastion over the square, its minaret-like towers asserting the essential orientalism of the Orthodox religion. It both drew and repelled: it drew the faithful, the true believers, the true Russians, eastern- and inward-looking; and it repelled all those who would look to the west, outside Russia, for their ideas and influences.

Porfiry was drawn. He felt the simple need to be in an Orthodox church. Perhaps it was a reaction against the book he had just finished reading. He had never considered himself as a Slavophile; on the contrary, he had prided himself on being receptive to new ideas, from wherever they came. He knew that if Russia was to progress, as she must, she could not afford to isolate herself from the rest of Europe. It was simply that, increasingly as he grew older, he found himself comforted by the overwhelming scent of incense and the warm dazzle of the candle-lit icons. And the only God he could believe in was the Russian God.

Porfiry crossed himself as he entered.

The throng inside the church was lively, almost excitable. As always, there was a loose informality to the congregation. People came and went all the time, while the priests and monks continued to chant and drone. There was a soft murmur of chatter which echoed and overlapped, giving the impression that the multitude of saints and celestial beings depicted on the tiers of icons all around were joining in the conversations. The priests took a dim view of all this talking in church, but there was little they could do to stop it. The Church invited its flock to be as children in their Father's house. It could hardly be surprised if some of them behaved like naughty children.

The three doors of the iconostasis stood open, as they had done since Midnight Mass on Good Friday. This towering screen, a full six tiers of icons in height, shielded the altar sanctuary from the congregation in the nave. Encrusted with a grid of thick gilt frames, populated with holy personages, it symbolised the division between Heaven and Earth. For most of the year the doors were kept closed, with only the clergy being allowed to pass through them. The doors would close again later that day, at the None, or Ninth Hour of prayer, that is to say, at about three o'clock that afternoon. Porfiry felt a surge of emotion as he considered the symbolism of the doors' opening. He felt a corresponding opening of his heart. It seemed to be a gesture of transcendent generosity on the part of the Church. Heaven stood open to him, and to all the miscreant congregation. He was possessed by hope. And yet, at the same time, he was aware of the imminent closure. And so, he seemed to feel, and regret, the loss of that hope at the same time as he experienced the hope itself.

A priest intoned the day's reading, John, Chapter 20, Verses 19 to 31. It was the story of Thomas, of course, for this was Thomas Sunday. Thomas, who needed not only to see the risen Christ but also to thrust his fingers into His wounds before he would declare: 'My Lord and my God.'

The point was, of course, not that Thomas had doubted. But that he had come to believe. Porfiry thought of Virginsky. He moved his lips in prayer for his junior colleague.

11

A sheepskin coat tied with string

The following day, Lieutenant Ilya Petrovich Salytov stood before the poster that had just been pinned up in the receiving hall of the Haymarket District Police Bureau in Stolyarny Lane. Salytov had once been known as 'Gunpowder,' on account of his fiery temper. But ever since he had been disfigured in a bomb atrocity, about six years earlier, his colleagues had tactfully dropped the soubriquet.

The face in the poster fascinated him, possibly because it was even more grotesque than his own. But, also, it seemed somehow familiar to him. It stirred the muddy depths of his memory.

Salytov read the accompanying text, and, as directed, tried to discount the waxen patches on the cheeks. But he found that it was no simple matter to overlook something so startling, especially once it had been pointed out to him.

He concentrated on the eyes. He could not shake off the feeling that he had once before stared into two eyes as tiny and loathsome as these. He felt an eddy of anger rise up from those murky depths where that particular half-memory was buried, the resurgence of an old rage. But that was all that he could summon, for the moment at least.

Whether it was the strange transformation that had occurred in the face on the poster, or because the thought of his injury was never far from his mind, Salytov found himself thinking back to his hospitalisation after the bomb blast. He imagined the raw, shredded agony of his face once again wrapped in moist bandages. He pictured the nurse slowly easing and teasing the bandages away from his melded flesh. He saw again the involuntary look of horror that she could not suppress, and then the sad dip of her head as she avoided his eyes. At his insistence, she had held a mirror up to him.

He relived that moment now. Curiously, when, in his imagination, he turned his gaze to the glass, it was the face on the poster that he saw, not his own.

*

'Do you know what day it is tomorrow, Pavel Pavlovich?' said Porfiry. He too was studying the face of the unknown man recovered from the Winter Canal. He had pinned up a copy of the original poster, which bore the wording 'Wanted'. Perhaps there was something perverse about his preference for this version, now that the corrected posters had been delivered; the possibility could not be discounted that he kept it as a rebuke to Virginsky. Next to it he had fixed a photographic enlargement of Kozodavlev's face, taken from the *Affair* staff photograph.

'I should hope so. Today is Monday, therefore tomorrow will be Tuesday,' answered Virginsky.

'Yes, but what is special about this particular Tuesday?' It was almost as if Porfiry was addressing the face on the poster.

'If you are referring to some obscure religious festival, or saint's day, then I am afraid I cannot help you. I long ago gave up trying to retain the arcane intricacies of the Christian calendar in my mind.'

'But this is a very important one, for us at least.'

'For us?'

'Yes. As magistrates engaged in a murder investigation. Tomorrow is the Tuesday of Thomas Week. The festival of Radonitsa, when we are duty bound to remember the dead.'

'I see.'

'You knew really, didn't you? Your parents must have taken you to the cemetery on Radonitsa, to place painted eggs on the graves of your ancestors.'

'Perhaps so.'

'You feasted on funeral *kutia*, and all the other delicacies of the day.'

'If you say so.'

'I do. Tomorrow . . .'

'Yes?'

'Are you intending to visit a cemetery at all?'

'I had not thought to do so.'

'I would just like you to know that you have my permission.'

'I thank you, but that will not be necessary.'

'You should not cut yourself off from the rituals of your nation, Pavel Pavlovich. You might be surprised to discover a new sense of wholeness and well-being. The old rituals are there for a reason, you know.'

'But I do not believe,' said Virginsky flatly.

'It is not always necessary to believe. Sometimes it is enough to embrace. There is a rhythm and a pattern to the old ways that is deeply consonant with the rhythms and patterns of life. Tomorrow we feast in memory and celebration of the dead. If you are not going to the cemetery, then I will bring in some funeral *kutia* to eat here in chambers.'

'Please, there is no need.'

'It is no trouble.' Porfiry turned from the poster and crossed to his desk. 'During Bright Week, we celebrate the resurrection of our Lord and God. And then in Thomas Week, we look forward to the resurrection of all the dead, at least of all those who have died believing.' Porfiry gave Virginsky a warning look. 'In the meantime, we witness all around us the resurrection of nature, the rebirth and resurgence of life as spring bursts out from beneath the thawing snow. It is no coincidence that the marriage season begins in Thomas Week. After we have given due remembrance to the dead, we turn our hearts to the living and the continuance of life. It makes perfect sense, Pavel Pavlovich. You must see that. You must feel it.'

There was a knock at the door. Porfiry looked up to see Nikodim Fomich enter.

'Good day, Porfiry Petrovich.' The chief superintendent held out a brown envelope.

'What have you there?'

'The police report on the fire in Bolshaya Morskaya Street.'

Porfiry sprang to his feet and hurried over to Nikodim Fomich. He took the envelope eagerly. 'Ah . . . and so it is not as we feared? It did not go to the Third Section!'

'In point of fact, it did. The official file has disappeared into that department, in all likelihood never to be seen again. However, a diligent clerk – to whom we have cause to be grateful – made a copy of the police report and retained it in a separate file at the Admiralty District Police Department. I was able, through my contacts there, to arrange for the loan of that duplicate file.'

'You have read it?'

'Yes.'

'Does it shed any light on the disappearance of Kozodavlev?' Porfiry took out the report, a single sheet, filled with a clerk's neat copperplate, and scanned it.

'It seems most likely that your Kozodavlev fellow did indeed perish in that fire. We may reasonably conjecture that the fire had its beginnings in his apartment. The reasons for that conclusion you will no doubt read for yourself. I should warn you, Porfiry Petrovich, that if you do go raking over these particular coals you will stir up an unholy cloud of smoke. You will undoubtedly attract the attention of certain interested parties.'

Porfiry took Nikodim Fomich's hint. 'And what if I willingly make my chambers available to the officers of the Third Section, and offer my services to aid them in their investigations?'

'Perhaps they will accept your invitation. And perhaps you will wish that they had not.'

'Thank you for this,' said Porfiry. He held Nikodim Fomich for a moment with his gaze. There was a beseeching quality to Nikodim Fomich's expression. He seemed to be asking if he had been forgiven. Porfiry's nod seemed to answer that he had.

*

Some time before midnight of Monday, 17 April, fire engines of the St Petersburg Fire Co. attended a fire at the Koshmarov Apartment Building, Bolshaya Morskaya Street, 12. Police Officers of the Admiralty District were also in attendance. This report is entered on behalf of the attending officers, and is countersigned by them. The fire was concentrated on the fifth storey, although the storeys immediately below and above also sustained damage. All fatalities occurred on the fifth storey. The alarm being raised, a number of residents were safely evacuated, including many of those on the fifth floor, who had already come out of their apartments at the first whiff of fire. However, the ferocity of the flames on the fifth floor, coupled with the thick black smoke resulting, hampered attempts to save a small number of occupants living closest to the centre of the blaze. When the flames were finally dampened, approximately one hour after the first engine arrived on the scene, the bodies of six dead were discovered, including those of five juveniles. These latter were the children of the Prokharchin family, who had been left alone by their parents while they entertained themselves in a nearby tavern. The children are thought to have been sleeping, and to have died from smoke suffocation. The fire is believed to have originated in the apartment of the Prokharchins' neighbour, one Demyan Antonovich Kozodavlev, as the devastation and scorching is greatest there, particularly in the bedroom. It was here where the one adult body, that of a male, was found. This body is assumed to be that of Demyan Antonovich Kozodavlev himself, although a positive identification is impossible due to the severe disfigurement of the deceased's face through burns. Interviews with neighbours on his floor who survived the conflagration indicate that Kozodavlev was visited shortly before the fire by a disreputable-looking individual in a grubby sheepskin coat belted with string and a worker's cap. His appearance was variously described thus: 'He looked like a convict'; 'He had the eyes of a murderer'; 'A nihilist if I ever saw one.' Furthermore, it was noticed that this individual was carrying a large ceramic vessel, assumed to be a flagon of vodka. A violent altercation, in which voices were raised and oaths uttered, was heard to occur between the two men. The smell of burning was subsequently noted and various neighbours came out onto the stairwell, at which point the individual in the sheepskin coat and worker's hat was seen fleeing precipitously from Kozodavlev's apartment. Shortly afterwards, the fire took hold in earnest and the alarm was raised. Fortunately, the fire engines of the St Petersburg Fire Company were in the close vicinity, returning from a false alarm nearby. That the fire was not more widespread, giving rise to even greater devastation and casualties, is in large part due to the prompt arrival and brave action of the fire crews, who entered the building without thought of their own safety. A human chain was formed up the stairs, with fire buckets passing both ways along it. The parents of the deceased children arrived at approximately ten minutes past midnight on Tuesday, 18 April. The mother being in a highly inebriated state, and in addition distraught over the fate of her children, who were at that time unaccounted for, had to be forcibly restrained from entering the burning building. The father's inebriation was such that he failed to comprehend the gravity of the situation. He apologised for his wife's 'intemperance,' as he called it, and seemed to find the presence of the firemen and police amusing. When it was explained to him that his children were in danger, he answered with a smile, 'The little ones? No, they are tucked up safely in bed.' He then expressed the opinion that it was time they were home too. It was pointed out to him by a neighbour that this was his home, in answer to which he replied, 'I'm sure it can't be.' At first he laughed at the suggestion, but becoming gradually serious, he fell at last silent. Soon after it was confirmed that all five children had perished. A large ceramic vessel, of the kind described by witnesses as belonging to the man in the sheepskin, was found empty in the hallway just outside Kozodavlev's apartment.

12

Paying respects

That afternoon, Porfiry took a *drozhki* to the Koshmarov Apartment Building in Bolshaya Morskaya Street. He was accompanied by Virginsky, who could not help but notice the unusually sombre and taciturn mood of his superior.

'What do you hope to find, Porfiry Petrovich?'

Porfiry stirred from his morose self-absorption only to shrug his shoulders. In the tight confines of the rocking *drozhki*, Virginsky felt himself squeezed upwards by the gesture.

'Do you not think that the gendarmes of the Third Section will have removed any evidence from the scene?' pressed Virginsky. 'That is if there *was* any meaningful evidence left after the fire.'

Porfiry's eyelids descended in synchrony with a slow, grave nod of agreement.

'Then why go?'

Porfiry opened his eyes and turned the ice-grey irises to Virginsky. 'I wish to pay my respects to the dead.'

'I thought tomorrow was the day for that?'

'Tomorrow, today. It makes little difference.'

Virginsky raised an eyebrow. 'To the dead, it makes *no* difference.'

'Perhaps we do not do it for them. We do it for ourselves.'

'You betray yourself, Porfiry Petrovich. That suggests that you do not believe in the survival of the soul after death. It is the kind of thing an atheist would say. Or at the very least, a rationalist.'

'This week is Thomas Week. St Thomas doubted, before he came to believe.'

'And you doubt?'

'Sometimes. When five innocents perish in a fire that may have been started deliberately ... One struggles to see God's purpose in that.'

'And Kozodavlev? Was he not innocent?'

'Very well, six innocents.'

Virginsky paused a moment before resuming: 'Do we have ... how may I put this? Do we have jurisdiction to enter the scene? We are not, after all, assigned to the case of Kozodavlev.'

'Kozodavlev was a witness in the case we are investigating.'

'With all respect, Porfiry Petrovich, we do not know that for certain yet, and will not do so until we have confirmation back from Helsingfors that Kozodavlev was the man watching the sailors. And even then ...' Virginsky broke off. It seemed that Porfiry felt every word he uttered as a personal wound.

'There will be no jurisdictional aspect to our visit. As I said, we are simply paying our respects.'

Virginsky's mouth twisted up on one side, into a bemused smile. 'And if the Third Section find out? I cannot believe they will not have someone watching.'

'We have nothing to hide from the Third Section,' said Porfiry. After a moment, he added, 'Yet.' For the first time on the *drozhki* ride, something like his old liveliness came back into Porfiry Petrovich's eye. His eyelids oscillated frantically in celebration.

*

They had to step over the remnants of the door, which had been smashed through and lay scattered on the floor.

The pungent smell of charred wood and plasterwork mingled with a cloying dampness. The result was a peculiarly chill and despondent atmosphere. Black streaks marked where the flames had touched the walls and ceiling. The bedroom was so fire-blacked that it looked as though it had been painted that funereal colour, along with every strange, distorted object in it. The walls were gutted, deep black scars where the combusted laths had burnt through the plaster. Only the metal frame of the bed remained intact, though the mattress on it had almost completely disappeared; clumps of black matter hung together around the edges of the bed. The skeleton of a burnt-out armchair lay exposed beside a heat-contorted metal bookcase, its contents vanished. They were puzzling stumps of furniture, barely holding their form, weakened beyond all possibility of function.

Porfiry paced the empty apartment breathing the fumes of the extinguished flames. He quickly realised that he had to tread with caution. In places, where the fire had really taken hold, the boards had been burnt away, and elsewhere, those that remained were too fragile to support his weight.

A middle-aged man, all grizzled beard and velveteen coat, poked his head suspiciously through the empty door frame as they were making their survey. 'And who might you be?' he asked unceremoniously, pointing the stem of his smoking pipe at Porfiry, as if it were a rifle he was intending to discharge.

'Friends of the deceased,' said Porfiry. 'Come to pay our respects.'

'Strange I never saw your face when he was alive.'

'Do you see every visitor who comes to every one of the residents in this building?'

'I like to keep my eyes open.' His eyes, in fact, narrowed warily.

'You are the yardkeeper?'

'That's right.' The yardkeeper shifted impatiently. 'You'll have to go. This place is unsafe.'

'I should inform you that we are magistrates. We are here also in an official capacity.'

'Make your mind up. Magistrates or friends. Which is it to be?'

'Cannot we be both?'

'Demyan Antonovich was not the sort to make friends with magistrates.'

'Are you suggesting he engaged in illegal activities?'

'Just that he did not much care for the authorities.'

'Did you see the man who visited him shortly before the outbreak of the fire?'

'Yes.'

'Who was he?'

'He did not show me his passport.'

'Was he the sort of person you are wont to admit to the building? A respectable gentleman?'

'If I admitted only respectable folk, the place'd be empty.'

'Had you seen him around here before?'

'Mebbe. Mebbe not. Hard to say.'

'Did you hear their argument?'

'I did not eavesdrop if that's what you're suggesting.'

'Of course not. It's just that I assume you keep your ears as well as your eyes open.'

The yardkeeper thought for a moment. 'I couldn't tell you what it was about.' His expression became closed off. 'You'll have to go now.'

'Who is your contact at the Third Section?' asked Porfiry, abruptly.

'What's this?'

'Ours is Major Verkhotsev. You will have heard of Major Verkhotsev, of course?'

'No one told me any magistrates were coming.'

'Forgive me for saying so, but it is not felt necessary to inform you of everything.'

'I should have been told.'

'I hope I shall not be obliged to report to Major Verkhotsev that you obstructed us in our enquiries?'

'Your Excellencies will understand that I have to be careful. I cannot let just anybody wander in and out. That would not do.'

'Of course.'

'You will report that I was diligent?'

'We will tell him you were an exemplary spy.'

The yardkeeper nodded uneasily and backed out of the room, his pipe now clamped securely between his teeth.

'We will have to be quick,' said Porfiry. 'I suspect he will be back.'

'Quick?' wondered Virginsky, casting a disparaging gaze about. 'I see nothing to detain us further.'

'The gendarmes have undoubtedly picked the room clean. Even so, they may have missed something.'

Virginsky gave Porfiry a sceptical look.

Porfiry began in the bedroom, peering into the glistening black remains of the mattress, his nostrils twitching all the time. 'The worst of the fire damage is concentrated in this room.' He glanced up at the ceiling. 'In fact, the intensity of charring here is such that it would not be unreasonable to suspect the employment of an accelerant.'

'The earthenware flagon,' remarked Virginsky.

Porfiry nodded. 'By the time the accelerant had burnt out, the fire would have taken hold enough to spread to the adjoining room, but with less intensity.'

'It would be interesting to see the medical examiner's report on the body found in the bed,' said Virginsky.

'Indeed it would, Pavel Pavlovich.' Porfiry acknowledged Virginsky's train of thought with a smile. 'And what question would you most like the medical examination to answer?'

'Whether he died from the effects of the fire, or whether . . .' Virginsky looked down at the remains of the mattress.

'Go on.'

'Or whether he was dead before the fire started.'

'An interesting question. Though I must say it is an exceedingly difficult issue for a pathologist to settle. So perhaps we should not be too disappointed that we will never see the report.' Porfiry cast his gaze upwards again, and kept it focused on the ceiling.

'Heat rises, does it not, Pavel Pavlovich?'

'Of course.'

'And with it, specks of soot and other by-products of combustion?'

Virginsky gave his mouth a non-committal tightening.

'Please, help me move the bed into this corner. The damage here is less . . .' Porfiry broke off, squinting into an area of the ceiling that seemed to have been furthest from the heart of the fire. Virginsky tried to see what had caught the other man's eye.

Porfiry began to push the bed, but it snagged on the damaged boards. 'If you please, Pavel Pavlovich.'

The two men together manoeuvred the bed to Porfiry's satisfaction. He kept looking up to compare its position to some point on the ceiling.

'Your hand please.' Porfiry held out an arm, and with Virginsky's assistance climbed onto the metal frame. His quivering legs set off a deafening rattle. The bed seemed to be trying to jump out from beneath him. His torso swayed from side to side wildly. Virginsky pushed manfully against the latent force of Porfiry's inevitable descent. Porfiry's free hand flashed up towards the very corner of the room, his fingers snatching desperately. The rash movement hastened the end. Gravity prevailed. The short, plump magistrate toppled onto the taller, thinner one. The two men somehow found themselves sprawled uncomfortably across exposed beams, opposite one another.

'Got it!' cried Porfiry triumphantly.

'What?'

Porfiry opened his palm to reveal a tiny fragment of blackness, smaller than the nail of his little finger, a ragged semicircle, although with one precisely straight side. 'I don't know.' He smiled foolishly at Virginsky. 'I saw something standing slightly proud on the ceiling. That straight edge seemed peculiar and worthy of investigation.' Porfiry turned his find over. 'It appears to be a scrap of paper. Completely charred on one side. But it appears that something is printed on this side. Can you make it out, Pavel Pavlovich? My eyes are not up to it.'

Virginsky hauled himself over and peered into his superior's hand. 'It's just letters.'

'Yes, but what letters?' demanded Porfiry roughly.

Virginsky reached out and turned the fragment.

'Be careful! It's very fragile,' warned Porfiry.

The paper was indeed flimsy to the touch. 'It is this way up, I think,' said Virginsky. 'Four rows of letters. G-o. O-f, space m. S-t-i-t. N-o. *Go*, *Of m*, *Stit*, *No*. It's obviously a remnant from a larger sheet.'

'The rest of which was no doubt destroyed in the conflagration.' Porfiry looked up to the ceiling again. 'Or recovered by the gendarmes. Which amounts to the same thing, as far as we are concerned.' With a strenuous grunt, Porfiry heaved himself to his feet. He squinted into his palm, as if he were intent on reading his own fortune. 'This tiny scrap alone drifted up to adhere to the ceiling.'

'Surely there's not enough there to constitute a meaningful clue?' objected Virginsky. And yet even as he dismissed it, he felt that the wisp of paper might contain the significance Porfiry wished to impart to it. Perhaps it was something to do with the miraculous way Porfiry had plucked it out of the ravages of the fire. Or perhaps it was because the letters that he could make out were so tantalisingly close to meaning something that he could not accept their essential randomness. There had to be a message contained there. It was simply a question of decoding it. And if there was a message, it had to have a bearing on the case. He knew of course that this final piece of reasoning was flawed. Even so, it was hard to resist. Something about those few letters resonated deep within him.

'But it may be all we have, Pavel Pavlovich. And besides, I am sure that you will be able to make some sense of it.'

'I?'

Porfiry's smile made it clear that no thanks were necessary for the generous gift he considered himself to have bestowed.

*

'Now we must pay our respects next door,' said Porfiry quietly, as they stepped back out onto the landing.

Virginsky froze. The door to the apartment next to Kozodavlev's suddenly acquired a monumental presence. Glistening with fresh paint, it appeared to have been recently fitted. But there was something inhuman about its pristine edges. Given all that had happened inside that apartment, it seemed monstrous that someone had thought to repair the door, as if paint and joinery could set those horrors to rights. To Virginsky, the bright new door was a slab of desolation bearing down on him, the emptiness at the centre of the human heart. He did not want to go anywhere near it. 'Would it not be an intrusion? At this time . . . their grief . . .'

Porfiry gave him a curious distracted glance, as if he could not understand what Virginsky was saying, or even the language in which he was saying it. 'We must pay our respects, Pavel Pavlovich,' Porfiry insisted.

Virginsky did not care to probe his reluctance. Instead, he gave in to a surge of panic-tinged antagonism. 'All this talk of *paying respects* . . . that is not it at all, Porfiry Petrovich. It is unseemly. An unseemly prurience. All you want to do is goggle at their suffering.'

Porfiry met the accusation with a mild flurry of blinking, the softest of reproaches.

'Does it not seem odd to you that they have repaired the door?' said Virginsky abruptly. Now that he had voiced it, his thought of a moment ago struck him as absurd and unfeeling. He felt the need to defend himself: 'If I had lost five children, I would not have the presence of mind to summon a carpenter to mend a damaged door.'

'What would you have them do? Besides, the door was most probably paid for by their neighbours. That is the Russian way.' Porfiry considered Virginsky sternly. 'It does not mean they loved their children any less just because they have thought to replace the door to their apartment.'

With that, still fixing Virginsky with a recriminatory gaze, Porfiry tapped his knuckles against the controversial door.

It seemed that the old woman who opened up for them was expecting someone else entirely. An expression of joyous relief quickly collapsed into one of disappointment, which in turn sharpened into suspicion. She was wiry and angular, seemingly possessed of a stubborn strength. A black bonnet sat on loose grey curls. Her mourning dress was respectable and respectful.

'Madame Prokharchina?' The extremely sceptical emphasis in Porfiry's voice suggested that he did not for one moment believe she was the lady in question.

'No, I am Yekaterina Ivanovna Dvigailova. The landlady.'

'Of course.' Porfiry gave Virginsky a shaming glance. 'We are magistrates. We have come to pay our respects to the family.'

Yekaterina Ivanovna regarded him mistrustfully.

'Out of common human feeling. We read about the tragedy in the newspapers. We felt compelled to pay our respects. This being Thomas Week, you understand. Tomorrow is Radonitsa. We intend to say a prayer for the little ones.'

Virginsky stifled the cry of protest that was rising in his throat. The resultant sound resembled a sob of emotion. This seemed to decide the landlady. She pulled the door open to admit them.

Five white coffins of varying sizes were arranged on trestles.

The grimy, smoke-blackened room was crowded with the dead, who seemed to be falling over one another in their prostrate immobility. The coffins were open. Virginsky could not avoid looking into them, could not avoid engaging with the faces of the dead children. The youngest of them must have been about eighteen months old, an infant. A girl, she was dressed like a doll, in her christening gown. Her face was unbearably perfect, with no evidence of burning or scars. Unblemished, adorable, dead. A red-painted egg lay on her chest, in her cupped hands.

It was too much for Virginsky, but everywhere he looked he saw the face of a dead child: two boys, one about five, the other seven or eight, in sailor suits; and two more girls, one about three, and the other whose age was hard to gauge: from her face, you would have said she was the eldest, but she was smaller in stature than the elder of the boys. All of them nestled their Easter eggs in limp, lifeless hands.

A thin, washed-out woman with a black shawl pulled up over her head sat in one corner. Her lips were constantly moving, though no words could be made out, just a hoarse, soft gurgling. Her eyes were wide and raw. She turned them on Virginsky with a look that had gone beyond emotion. It asked nothing of him, but was simply a reflex turning of the head. Her face, he saw, was swollen and streaked with moisture. It was not that her expression was dazed, rather that it was emptied – spent. She had felt all that it was humanly possible to feel. Now all she could do was turn her blank, uncomprehending gaze onto whatever came within her purview. She existed as a kind of warning, and nothing more.

'You won't get much sense out of her,' said Yekaterina Ivanovna. 'And *he*'s out. At some tavern or other, I shouldn't wonder.'

Porfiry nodded his understanding. All the same, he took a step towards the woman in the corner. At his approach, a kind of startled horror flitted over her face. It was as if she were horrified not at Porfiry, but at the idea that someone, anyone, would want to approach her. She recoiled, withdrawing herself, buffeted by a violent repulsive force that seemed to surround her. Her chair scraped back along the floor.

'Madame Prokharchina,' said Porfiry gently. 'We have come to offer our condolences.' He reached a hand out towards her. The woman jerked away from it.

'This is not good,' hissed Virginsky.

Her movements were sudden and stilted, like a captured bird. It seemed imperative to her to avoid human touch at any cost.

Porfiry continued his efforts to reassure her. 'We are one with you in your grief.'

Virginsky felt a wave of anguish surge through him at Porfiry's words, so perhaps what he had just said was true. *But how could it be?* How could anyone's emotions at this moment compare with this woman's? It was just a platitude, hypocritical and therefore abhorrent. Perhaps the anguish Virginsky felt was simply the hypersensitivity caused by an intolerable excess of embarrassment. After they – or rather Porfiry – had uttered their condolences, they would walk out of that apartment, away from the roomful of white coffins, closing the newly hung door behind them. The woman's utterly worn-out face would fade from memory. In time, even the death-perfected faces of the children would be forgotten, or at least become harder and harder to recall.

Virginsky imagined the woman sitting in the corner of that room, the five coffins of her children in front of her, forever.

Suddenly he felt Porfiry's gaze on him, as though he expected him to add a consoling sentiment. The woman too looked up at him expectantly. He looked back at them both in turn, aghast. But suddenly he felt compelled to say something. 'I . . . I cannot imagine . . . cannot imagine . . . how . . . you bear this.'

The woman sighed. It seemed that she had somehow found relief, if not comfort, in Virginsky's words; that to have a stranger speak the truth to her was all that she wanted.

Porfiry bowed and turned away from her. Virginsky continued to search her emptied eyes, as though now he was the one needing consolation from her.

'It is a terrible tragedy,' said Porfiry to the landlady.

The landlady seemed to crumple under his fluttering gaze. 'I am to blame!' she suddenly cried. 'I promised I would sit with them. I promised I would look after them.'

'Now, now. Don't torment yourself, Yekaterina Ivanovna. You were not to know.'

'I only stepped out for five minutes, to answer the call of nature. And on the way back, I paid a visit on the Widow Sudbina. She lives on the third floor. Her husband died not long ago and she has been melancholy ever since. They were sleeping soundly when I left, the little ones. What harm could come to them, I thought?'

'It's not your fault. You did not set the fire.'

'You don't understand.' The landlady's eyes stood out as if they were trying to distance themselves from what she was about to confess. '*I locked them in!* For their own safety, you understand. You don't know who is prowling around these buildings. That yardkeeper is worse than useless. He never asks to see anyone's passport. He admits the most unsavoury characters. *I locked them in!* And then they wouldn't let me go back upstairs because of the fire.'

It took a moment for Porfiry to absorb what the woman had told him. 'No. You are not to blame. I repeat, you did not light the fire. You could not have known. My colleague and I are magistrates. Please rest assured that we will find the man responsible for this, and we will bring him to justice. Is that not so, Pavel Pavlovich?'

There was undeniably a challenge in Porfiry's question. Virginsky said nothing. He bowed his head and in so doing once again found himself looking into the face of the youngest of the Prokharchin children. He thought of the embalmer's hands on her tiny body, and wondered at the mysterious alchemy that had been worked to bring about her lifeless preservation. In truth, it was a brutal process, a cutting open, a ripping out, a filling in, a trussing up. A violation. The eyes could not turn to him in appeal, could not implore, held no rebuke, however gentle. He willed her grip to curl and tighten around the painted egg.

He felt certain that whoever had lit the fire, for whatever motives, had not wanted her dead. And yet the fire had been lit, and her death, however unintended, was the consequence.

Virginsky lifted his gaze from the child. But he found nowhere else in that room for it comfortably to settle.

13

Radonitsa

The solution came to Virginsky in the night while he was sleeping. He had not even started working on the problem, so it was indeed surprising that he had solved it so quickly. He woke from his dream with a start and sat bolt upright.

Lighting the tallow candle by his bedside, he pulled out the tin trunk that contained his collection.

Virginsky felt a strange sense of power, which was superseded almost immediately by one of revulsion. *This was mysticism!* He would not give in to it. He would not open the trunk. It was absurd to think he had dreamed the solution. He would leave the shamanism to Porfiry Petrovich.

He felt at once relieved to have made the decision. Opening that trunk would take him into a realm he had no wish to enter.

As soon as that realisation struck him, his relief evaporated. He stared in horror at the trunk. He imagined it containing some grisly secret: a severed body part, or the corpse of a child. The youngest of the Prokharchin children would just about fit inside it. No, it was inconceivable that he would open it. Not now, possibly not ever.

At the same time, he could not bring himself to push it back under his bed.

He was a rationalist. To unlock the trunk in the expectation of finding the solution he had seen in his dream was not the behaviour of a rationalist. And what if the solution turned out to be there, just as his dream predicted? The ramifications of that were devastating. He was beset by a fleeting premonition, a sense of imminent disintegration.

If his dream were proven to be true, he would be brought to a critical moment in his political as well as his inner live, a genuine crisis. It was far better that the lid remained closed, particularly as his rationalism told him that there could be nothing in it anyhow. One did not dream the solutions to the crimes one was investigating.

He pushed the trunk back under his bed.

He extinguished the candle and lay back down. He closed his eyes but sleep felt a long way off now. He tried to analyse what had just happened. There must be a psychological explanation for his dream, the rationalist in him decided.

The devastation at Kozodavlev's apartment had naturally made him think of Easter Sunday night when he had gone to witness the fires at the vodka warehouse. Furthermore, Porfiry Petrovich's theories about Kozodavlev's radicalism – together with his fixation on the novel *Swine* – had naturally influenced Virginsky. The dream, in which Kozodavlev had made an appearance, was therefore perfectly explicable. The details were already fading but he thought that it had been to do with a revolutionary cell. For some reason, the Prokharchin children were involved too. Had they been the members of the cell? A ridiculous idea, but that was the way with dreams. And therefore, all the more reason *not* to act on them.

Certainly, the urgent sense of discovery that had stung him from his sleep had faded. He could not even remember what it was that had almost convinced him to look in the trunk. He began to relax, welcoming the slow dissolution of his being that presaged sleep.

*

As he had intimated he would, Porfiry visited a cemetery on the Feast of Radonitsa. He had learnt from the landlady that the children were to be buried that day, at the Smolenksoe Cemetery on Vasilevsky Island. A procession would set out from the Koshmarov Apartment Building at ten.

There had been a subscription to help with funeral costs, to which both Porfiry and Virginsky had contributed. An edge of hostility had crept into Virginsky's voice when he answered Porfiry's question of whether he intended to give something, or not. It seemed that he had detected some kind of slight in the pause Porfiry allowed between the alternatives.

It was the finest day of the spring so far. There had been an explosion of buds in the city's gardens and parks. The bird-cherry trees were in blossom everywhere. In sending forth its shoots and stems, the earth seemed to be straining up towards the sky, drawn by its inhuman weightlessness. And yet it took a great effort of will on Porfiry's part to lift his face towards the exuberant light.

The Prokharchins' friends and neighbours had done them proud. Yekaterina Ivanovna alone had given one hundred assignat roubles. No expense was spared. To bear the five small coffins were two white funerary carriages, their elaborate canopies draped in lace and decked in spring flowers. Each carriage was drawn by a pair of white horses. Ahead of the hearses walked a line of attendants, their white flowing coats and white top hats flashing brilliantly in the sunlight. Behind came the mourners in black. The way was strewn with flowers, scattered from another carriage that led the procession.

The children's parents clung together. It seemed more that they were pulling each other down than giving mutual support. But somehow they managed to keep walking. They were impelled by the inevitability of the procession. *This is what a funeral procession is for*, thought Porfiry, *why it is necessary. So that those most struck by grief may know where to direct their feet.*

It was the first sight Porfiry had caught of Prokharchin. The man seemed to be in one of the stages of delirium tremens, so violently was he shaking. His feet came down with an exaggerated, slightly wayward tread, as if they were constantly trying to free themselves from the restraint of his ankles.

It was a long slow way to the cemetery, which was at the north of the island. They crossed the river over the Nikolaevsky Bridge. Now in full flow, the heedless Neva rushed away from the shuffling line of humanity, leaving it to its woes.

*

Virginsky wrote out the rows of letters:

    Go
    Of m
    Stit
    No

He felt immediately the hopelessness of the task he had been set. It was not a code. It was simply the first few letters of four lines of text. The letters in themselves meant nothing, or any meaning they suggested was illusory. They had been severed from their true meaning by a random accident. If the piece of paper had any significance at all, it was to be found in the larger, missing text. That is to say, it was beyond his reach. Therefore, no matter how much he applied himself, he would never be able to make sense of the letters in front of him.

The fragment seemed to start with an exhortation and end with discouragement. Between was nonsense. *All too appropriate*, decided Virginsky.

And yet, as Virginsky repeated the truncated chant that the letters spelled out – *Go, Of m, Stit, No, Go, Of m, Stit, No* – the significant detail struck him. Each of the four lines began with a capital letter. He could assume that the text these letters came from was a poem of some kind.

With this first realisation came another: he had seen these letters before. However, he was far less certain of this than he was of the letters' poetic provenance. He remembered waking from his dream the night before, but by now all the details of the dream were irretrievably lost to him. Had he also dreamt of pulling the tin trunk out from under his bed? His memory of that seemed to be of a different quality to the sense he had of the vanished dream.

The mood of the previous night came back to him, in particular his sense of appalled rationality. Now, in the cold light of day, he was not so sure that his refusal to open the trunk was in fact the right decision, even from a supremely rationalist standpoint. A rationalist would be able to accept that the mind – even his own mind – was at times irrational. He would reason that this aspect of the mind must not be ignored. Ignored, it would only grow and fester in secret. Far better to confront it with its own absurdities, to wage open war constantly against its calamitous influence.

Far better, in other words, to have opened the trunk and to have proven to himself the folly of his delusions.

Virginsky pulled a wincing face. He was reasoning himself into acting like a superstitious peasant, trusting to dreams and omens. No. The trunk must remain under the bed, its lid firmly closed. Until he had another manifesto to add to his collection, that is.

To do otherwise would be to give in to irrationalism, not to fight it.

* * *

It was after lunch when Porfiry returned to his chambers. To Virginsky, it seemed that his face was greyer than it had been when he had last seen him. There was a wan emptiness to his expression. He seemed hunched in on himself, reduced somehow. But when he spoke there was a rasp of determination, a fierce impatient quality to his voice. Judging by his voice alone, one would have said that Porfiry had been energised by the Feast of Radonitsa.

'How are you getting on with those letters? Have you deciphered them yet?'

'It is not a question of deciphering them,' complained Virginsky. He took Porfiry through his reasoning, though he omitted to tell him about his dream, and his consequent indecision.

'A poem? Good, yes. That is very plausible. Given Kozodavlev's politics, it is not likely to be some verses of Pushkin. You remember what our young nihilist said. Boots over Pushkin. No, this was probably some radical manifesto, severely utilitarian in purpose. Many of them are written in verse, you know. I suppose the writers believe it will make their message more memorable. If

158

the printed handbills are destroyed, the message will linger in the minds of those who have read it. Furthermore, it makes it easier to pass it on orally, if distribution becomes dangerous.' Porfiry pulled open a drawer in his desk. 'I have a small collection of such manifestos here . . .'

'*You?*'

'Yes. I. Why does that surprise you?'

'What possible reason could you have to collect such material?'

'Oh, all the wrong reasons, you would undoubtedly say. But I am interested to know what people are saying. And thinking. Many of these are in wide circulation. I have had a number posted to me anonymously, or thrust in my hand by passing strangers. It is not so hard to acquire them, and not so easy to destroy them. One feels that they are too interesting to destroy, although one cannot always agree with the sentiments expressed. I am a magistrate, after all. I must acquaint myself with the doctrinal edicts of the state's enemies, if they can be regarded as such.' Porfiry gave Virginsky a quick warning look. 'However, I must say that it would be quite another matter for anyone to harbour such a collection in the privacy of their own home. Magistrate or not. It is the fact that I keep my collection here, in my chambers, that makes it allowable. It is logged as official evidence, you see. There can be no unpleasant repercussions.' Porfiry took out a couple of handfuls of printed sheets. 'A rather tedious task for you, I'm afraid, Pavel Pavlovich. Sort through these and see if you can find a section that corresponds to our fragment. And well done, by the way. It was a breakthrough to perceive that it came from a poem.'

Virginsky frowned in bemusement as he took the manifestos from Porfiry.

*

It was a simple but laborious chore to look through the twenty or so pamphlets, isolating the beginnings of lines to find a sequence that matched the letters on the fragment. Almost all of the handbills were familiar to him from his own collection.

So when he found the poem he was looking for, it should not have been a surprise.

But it was worse than that. He felt a sickening vertigo. As soon as he saw it, he remembered his dream of the night before. For in the dream, he had held this very pamphlet in his hands as it caught fire, burning away the words as he read them.

He handed it to Porfiry without a word.

'This is the one?'

'Yes. There. The second verse.' Virginsky recited from memory. 'God is man-made, but no less real; / Of man's fears, does he consist. / Stitched from such stern material, / No wonder God's a Nihilist.'

'I see. Yes. Well done. A strange work. God the Nihilist.' Porfiry shook his head wonderingly. 'Perhaps he is. On days like this, one cannot help wondering.'

Virginsky's voice faltered as he asked: 'D-do you . . . do you remember where you got this?' After a beat, he added, redundantly: 'Who gave it to you?' He held in his own mind an image of the hatchet-headed man.

Porfiry leaned back in his seat and sighed. 'My memory is not what it used to be. That is in itself a cause for concern, Pavel Pavlovich. The investigator's memory is one of the chief weapons in his armoury. One must not only be able to hold on to the details of the current case one is investigating, but one must also be alert

160

to ripples of connection from past cases. Criminals do not burst forth spontaneously. They are like the spring buds. They give the appearance of spontaneous generation, but the plants that bear them may have taken root long ago.'

'Yes,' said Virginsky, shortly. 'I know that. You do not need to talk to me in this way. I am not a pupil in need of instruction.'

Porfiry looked aghast. 'Forgive me, I meant no offence. I am a foolish, forgetful old man. One falls into habits. And habits are by definition bad. I have acquired the habit of talking down to you. Whenever I succumb to it, you must reprove me, in the harshest possible terms.'

Virginsky shook his head impatiently. 'So you cannot remember who gave it to you?'

'In essence, no.'

Virginsky constricted his mouth and turned his back on Porfiry, as if in disappointment.

*

That night, Virginsky lit the tallow candle and pulled the tin trunk out from under his bed. He took the key from a drawer in his bedside table. He did not need to open the trunk to know that it was in there. He did not need to look at it, nor hold it in his hands.

Yet he did.

His dreaming mind had been right. He had known all along.

He stared at the lines of doggerel without reading them. Virginsky had to accept that his mind, in its totality, was a monstrously larger entity than his consciousness. It did most of its work without his knowing anything about it. This need not alarm him, he decided, although he was uneasy about the surrender of control that it implied. His emotions were racing to keep pace with his thoughts. A surge of panic was overtaken by anger: he would not relinquish his claims to be a rational being. On the contrary, his rationalism now had to encompass this newly recognised and undeniable fact. Calmer now, he realised that he must seek to grasp with conscious thought what his unconscious mind had been up to.

In the first place, there was the question of his resistance to opening the trunk the previous night. It would have been a simple matter to have looked inside, thereby confirming one way or another the solution which his dreaming mind had apparently furnished. A simple matter, and not at all irrational, for that was the only logical way to settle the question and restore his mental equilibrium. To confront his unconscious.

The irrational act had been to push the trunk back under his bed without looking inside.

It could only be that his unconscious mind had sensed the connection between Kozodavlev and the hatchet-headed man who had given him the manifesto. But why should that have provoked this strange reluctance? Of course, the answer to that was that opening the trunk and taking out the manifesto would have inevitably drawn Virginsky into the case they were investigating, and not simply as an investigator. His conversation with the hatchet-headed man would have come under scrutiny, as well as his motives and intentions at the time. He would have been forced to reveal far more of himself than he wished to, or was sensible.

The crux of the matter was this: the man had told him that he should look for him in the taverns around Haymarket Square. To pass this on to Porfiry Petrovich was tantamount to informing on him. Virginsky may have been a magistrate, but he was not yet ready to become an informant.

Furthermore, he himself, inevitably, would have been embroiled in whatever plan Porfiry came up with to catch the fellow.

To have opened the trunk and looked inside would have hastened the moment that Pavel Pavlovich Virginsky was finally made to choose between his principles and his conscience; the moment, in short, when he would have to decide who he was.

His principles and his conscience. It was unnerving to think that they were not one and the same. But when he tried to give shape to his principles, he had a vision of marvellous beings – very different from the grubby, venal populace of the day – living in vast communal phalansteries, which his imagination modelled on the Crystal Palace of the Great Exhibition in London. All would be equal. Every need would be met. Hunger, poverty and therefore crime would be at an end. The old institutions of church, marriage and the family would be dismantled. Women and men would be free to think – and love – as they wished. According to the principles to which he ascribed, whatever had to be done to bring about such a future was justified.

The image that his conscience imposed on him was very different. A little girl in a christening gown, her hands loosely folded around a painted egg, her eyes open but unseeing.

14

The Slavophiles

Two days later, Porfiry received a telegram from the authorities in Helsingfors. Apprentice Seaman Ordynov confirmed that the mysterious stranger who had watched him and his mates bring the body to the surface of the Winter Canal was the man identified as Kozodavlev in the *Affair* staff photograph.

'So, Pavel Pavlovich, what do you say now? Kozodavlev was on the bridge. He was there watching, as though he expected the body to come to light now that the ice was melting. Furthermore, we have found the trace of a nihilist manifesto in his apartment. You must at least admit the possibility that he was involved in a revolutionary grouping and was on the verge of informing on it when he was killed.'

'Of course. It is *possible*.' Virginsky's emphasis was intended to suggest that anything was possible.

'And so, we may look further into his background?'

'You do not need my permission. I believe we were waiting for the witness identification to come through. And now that we have that, it seems sensible to proceed.'

Porfiry's face lit up. 'Let us visit the Slavophiles then!'

*

If – thought Porfiry – one were to choose one's politics based on the physical attractiveness of the proponents of this or that cause, then the radicals would certainly win out over the Slavophiles. For one thing, the men (for they were without exception male) who comprised the editorial staff of *Russian Era* and *Russian Soil* were markedly older than their counterparts at *Affair*. They were all heavily bearded. Their expressions, stern to the point of forbidding, created the distinct impression that they held a grievance against anyone who dared to cross their threshold. They looked out from the territory of their office on Liteiny Prospect with the same suspicion and hatred with which they looked out from Russia. According to their siege mentality, which was clearly visible in their faces, everything that came in from outside was inevitably evil and had to be repelled.

In other respects, the office was very similar to the one he and Virginsky had visited exactly a week ago. It was basically a domestic apartment converted to a business. There was a central arrangement of desks with hardly any space to move around them.

A facetious thought occurred to Porfiry as he sought to appease the automatic hostility of the room with a deep bow. He knew of many famous men who had begun their careers as radicals, only to become conservatives in later years. Did they, as the more reactionary views took hold on their minds, undergo a physical transformation to match their ideological one? Of course, they would have worked on their beards. But he was thinking of something more fundamental than that: a gradual rearrangement of the structure of their faces, inevitably a contraction, a hardening.

The oldest and most thickly bearded man in the room rose shakily to his feet. He was a frail figure, of slight build. His beard was white and divided into two points. He wore a soft velvet hat on the back of his head, which gave him a strangely bohemian appearance. His eyes were little black points in a luminously pale face. He had a large domed forehead in comparison to which the rest of his face seemed shrunken away. Both eyebrows were steeply arched, one higher than the other, in an expression of permanent quizzicality. 'How may I help you gentlemen?' His voice was unexpectedly kindly and welcoming. Porfiry felt at once that he had been unfair to the Slavophiles. If their expressions appeared serious, it was only because they were engaged in a serious business: that of survival, both personal and national.

'I am looking for Mr Trudolyubov.'

'I am he. Who might you be?'

'I am Porfiry Petrovich, an investigating magistrate. And this is my colleague, Pavel Pavlovich Virginsky.'

Trudolyubov's pinpoint eyes widened slightly in alarm. 'What is this about?'

'We are investigating a body found in the Winter Canal. The victim of a murder, we believe.'

'Good Heavens! What has that to do with us?'

'Did you recently commission a review for your publication *Russian Soil* of the novel *Swine*?'

'I did.'

'The novel was serialised in your other publication, *Russian Era*, was it not?'

'It's a common practice.'

'Yes, of course. I understand,' said Porfiry smoothly. 'A practice known as advertisement, I believe.'

Trudolyubov recoiled at the suavely delivered barb.

'From whom did you commission the review?'

'From one of our regular contributors.'

'And the name of this regular contributor?'

166

'He prefers to remain anonymous.'

'But surely you know who he is?'

'Not at all.'

'Then how do you communicate with him?'

'Through an intermediary. An agent, if you like.'

'And who is this agent?'

'A gentleman by the name of Prince Dolgoruky.'

'Prince Dolgoruky? A distinguished name,' observed Porfiry.

'The Dolgorukys are an ancient and noble family,' said Trudoly-ubov complacently, as if this was somehow to his own credit.

'The Tsar, I believe, is a friend of Prince Mikhail Dolgoruky.' Porfiry paused to blink significantly before adding: 'And his daughter, Yekaterina.'

'This is a different branch of the family. I am talking about Prince Konstantin Arsenevich Dolgoruky. He is only distantly re-lated to the Tsar's . . . friend.'

'How interesting. Does Prince Dolgoruky act in this capacity – as an intermediary or agent – for any other writers whom you publish?'

The aged editor paused before answering, his face atremble. 'Yes.'

'And who would that be? Another anonymous writer?'

'Yes.'

'Allow me to hazard a guess. Are we talking about the anonym-ous author of *Swine*, the notorious D.?'

'That is so.'

Porfiry gave a delighted chuckle. 'Did it ever occur to you that the writer of the novel and the reviewer of the novel might be one and the same person?'

'The writer of the novel is D. The writer I commissioned the review from is K.'

'K. Of course. Yes. D. and K. Clearly two very distinct individuals.'

'Besides, Prince Dolgoruky assured me –'

'Prince *Dol*-goruky?' cut in Porfiry. 'Perhaps he is himself D.? Though if that were the case, he would certainly have signed the pages "Prince D.," wouldn't he?'

Trudolyobov wrinkled his nose at Porfiry's sarcasm.

'I believe I have the review you commissioned on me.' Porfiry fished out the article from inside his frockcoat. 'Does that look like the work of your fellow K.?'

'It is certainly more or less what I was expecting.'

'Would it surprise you to learn that your regular contributor K. also contributes to the radical journal *Affair* under his full name of Kozodavlev?'

'This is Kozodavlev? Impossible!' Trudolyubov snapped the paper with the fingernails of one hand.

'I assure you. I took it from Mr Kozodavlev's drawer at the offices of *Affair* last week. The handwriting was identified as his by the editor of that journal.'

'But Kozodavlev is against everything we stand for. He has attacked us in the most vicious terms on numerous occasions.'

'And yet you wrote to Kozodavlev, soliciting a review of *Swine*. I found your letter in his drawer.'

'I wrote to every journal I could think of. I knew *Affair* would hate it, of course. I *wanted* them to hate it. That would be the greatest endorsement of the work.'

'You sought controversy?'

'I suppose you could say that.' Trudolyubov's eyes seemed to twinkle. He looked down at the review again. 'But Kozodavlev cannot be K.! K. even attacked Kozodavlev, singling him out for the bitterest vituperation.'

'I believe it was a game he liked to play. Perhaps it was his way of working out the conflicts that buffeted his soul.'

'But it makes a mockery of all the principles any of us hold, on whatever side.'

'I don't think so,' said Porfiry. 'Have you always held the views you now propound with such force in your publications? Were you not once, in your younger days, in the sway of entirely opposite ideas?'

'I learnt the error of my ways.'

'Yes, but you will accept that it is possible for two contrary opinions to reside in the same man?'

'At different times of his life, perhaps.'

'But were not the seeds of your current views taking root in your mind at the very time that you were openly expressing sentiments of a decidedly radical tendency? Are not both viewpoints, though on the face of it polar opposites, more closely related than they first appear? Might we not say they are two sides of the same coin? The coin being a sincere and deeply held love of Russia. For it seems to me, if I may say so – I am not a political individual, so my comments may strike you as naive – nevertheless, it does seem to me that the radicals and the Slavophiles are both motivated by a genuine desire to do what is best for Russia. It is just that they disagree as to what that is.'

Trudolyubov thrust the article back at Porfiry. 'No. I won't accept that. This is just cynical sport.'

'He was a professional writer,' said Porfiry reasonably. 'He had to place his work where he could.'

'Was? You just said "was." Is Kozodavlev the one you fished out of the Winter Canal?'

'In the first place, I did not myself fish the body out. In the second, no – I do not believe so.' Porfiry turned to Virginsky. 'Pavel Pavlovich, do you have the poster?'

Virginsky nodded and took out the folded poster, which he handed to Trudolyubov.

'This is the body from the Winter Canal,' explained Porfiry. 'We have seen a photograph of Mr Kozodavlev – or K., if you prefer – and it is not the same person. However, Mr Kozodavlev *is* missing, and, I regret to say, presumed dead.'

Trudolyubov did not appear to have heard. His gaze was concentrated on the photograph in his hands. 'What has happened to this poor fellow?' He spoke in a barely vocalised whisper.

'He would not have looked like that in life. A chemical reaction has occurred in certain places. It has transformed his flesh into a soapy substance. Please try to ignore that and concentrate on the areas that are not affected. You will notice the pockmarks and the small eyes. They are distinctive features, I think.'

Trudolyubov looked aghast at Virginsky. 'They would take away God from us. But if you take away God, what are you left with, sir? This.' He handed the poster back to Virginsky.

'Do you recognise him?' asked Porfiry.

Trudolyubov shook his head. 'So, Kozodavlev is dead too, you say?'

'It seems he perished in a fire that took hold of his apartment building on Monday night.'

'How ironic.'

'Why do you say that?'

'You could say he has only himself to blame. His inflammatory articles without doubt contributed to the unrest and vandalism that has beset our city in recent days.'

'And yet the articles he wrote for you might have served to counteract it.'

The elderly editor seemed unconvinced.

'I would be interested in seeing cuttings of the work K. contributed to your publications,' said Porfiry.

'I can arrange that. If you provide me with an address, I will send them on for you.'

'Thank you. Here is my card. Also, I would very much like to meet Prince Dolgoruky.'

'The family home is not far from here. I seem to remember that it is also in Liteiny Prospect. If you don't mind waiting, I will have someone look up the address for you.'

'Most kind.'

Trudolyubov consulted with one of his colleagues, who lifted his head slowly, thrusting his beard in Porfiry and Virginsky's direction. A moment later the address was handed over.

15

A timid creature

'May I say something, Porfiry Petrovich?' began Virginsky, as they walked back along Liteiny Prospect towards the Nevsky Prospect end. 'And I hope you will not take it amiss.'

Porfiry blinked frantically as he gave consideration to Virginsky's words. 'If it is something that I may take amiss, then perhaps it is better not said.'

'Very well. I will keep my thoughts to myself.'

Porfiry regarded Virginsky out of the corner of his eye, with an indulgent spasm of the lips. 'Oh dear, Pavel Pavlovich, so easily discouraged? That's not like you. I worry that you too often keep your counsel these days. It suggests either that you do not trust me, or that you do not trust yourself. I'm afraid to think which horrifies me more. To be honest, I don't like either much.'

Virginsky frowned thoughtfully. This man – plump, ageing, short-winded, with his preposterously mannered tics, always blinking and smirking as if he were some silly lovesick girl and not a senior investigating magistrate – this man was constantly surprising him. It could only be because he, Virginsky, was constantly underestimating Porfiry Petrovich. He had fallen into the trap again, despite consciously being on his guard against it. And Porfiry, with just a few words and a sly, sidelong glance, had shown that he knew precisely what was going on in Virginsky's soul.

'How do you do it, Porfiry Petrovich?'

'Is that what you were going to say?'

'No. And you know that it was not.'

'Very well. "How do I do it?" you ask. "How do I do what?" I ask.'

'You have an unerring knack.'

Porfiry blinked expectantly.

'For voicing the very thing that is on my mind.'

'Oh? And what was that? I've forgotten what I said, you see. My memory is not unerring.'

'You spoke of . . . trust.'

'And you hesitated, just now as you said the word. That is all there is to my knack, such as it is. I pay attention to the little signals.'

'You feel that there is some loss of trust between us?'

'Do you?'

'Our differences . . .'

'Are as nothing. *Nothing!*' cried Porfiry, with an emphatic wave of his arm.

'. . . may not be as easy to overcome as you might hope,' insisted Virginsky.

'What are you trying to tell me, Pavel Pavlovich? I hope to God it is not what I fear.'

'I am a man of principles. I am no Kozodavlev.'

'You judge him too quickly and perhaps too harshly. We do not yet know what has prompted him to act in the way he has.'

'You defend him. That is because he flattered you in an article.'

'Please, give me more credit than that. Who knows what lies behind Kozodavlev's strange . . .' Porfiry pursed his lips as he waited for the right word to come to him.

Virginsky provided it: 'Hypocrisy.'

Porfiry gave a remonstrative look.

'What I was going to say,' began Virginsky again, 'is that I fear Kozodavlev may be a false trail.'

Porfiry smiled. 'I am glad you have overcome your reticence. Please continue.'

'We do not, in point of fact, have anything conclusive linking Kozodavlev to the man in the Winter Canal – the case we are supposed to be investigating, if I may remind you.'

'We have the word of Apprentice Seaman Ordynov.'

'Well, yes, we now know that Kozodavlev saw the sailors bring up the body. And that he failed to raise the alarm, as he had said he would. But that does not prove beyond doubt that he knew the man. He may simply have been frightened.'

'There is also the letter that I received. The letter taken together with Ordynov's testimony is conclusive.'

'An anonymous letter.'

'Handwriting comparisons strongly suggest it was written by him.'

'You know that handwriting similarities are not conclusive,' pointed out Virginsky. 'And are indeed highly circumstantial. The fact is, there may have been someone else there, unnoticed by the sailors. That someone else may be the writer of the anonymous letter and the person who is connected to the body in the canal. It would be a strange coincidence, but it is not beyond the bounds of possibility that this other person has a similar handwriting style to Kozodavlev. You cannot build a case on conjecture based on the similarities of a number of unsigned writing samples. Any half-decent defence lawyer will tear it to shreds. With all due respect, if I may say so, Porfiry Petrovich, it is your vanity that led you to the offices of *Affair*, where you promptly found what you were looking for.'

'Vanity? I –'

Virginsky pressed on. 'What if the letter was not written by Kozodavlev, after all? If there was someone else there, the writer of the letter, then we have been wasting our time. We are still wasting our time. If the man from the Winter Canal has nothing to do with Kozodavlev, then he has nothing to do with *Affair*, or *Russian Soil*, or the novel *Swine*. Or Prince Dolgoruky – whoever he may be.'

'He appears to be a distant cousin of the Tsar's current mistress,' observed Porfiry tartly.

'You wish to drag the Tsar into this?'

Porfiry's expression was panic-stricken. 'No! Please God, no! It is simply a curious coincidence. I am confident there is nothing more to it than that. The Dolgoruky family has multitudinous offshoots. Indeed, it is a name claimed by many, even those who have no right to it. Perhaps that is the case here with this Dolgoruky of Trudolyubov's.' They carried on walking in silence for some moments. 'So, Pavel Pavlovich. What would *you* have us do?'

Virginsky gave an ineffectual shrug.

'Nothing? Drop the case? Is that what you are suggesting?'

'I fear that we must wait until we have a positive identification of the victim. Until we know for certain who the man in the canal was, we are chasing phantoms.'

'But we may never have that.'

'Then the case may never be solved.'

'I confess I'm disappointed. I was hoping you were about to propose a wager.'

'You know I do not gamble, Porfiry Petrovich. Particularly when it is to do with the execution of our professional duties. That is to reduce a matter of deadly seriousness to mere sport, is it not?'

'Once again, I consider myself justifiably rebuked, Pavel Pavlovich.'

They continued several paces in silence.

'But Kozodavlev is dead,' ventured Porfiry at last. 'And if the fire in which he perished was started deliberately, then that too is murder.'

'But we have not been assigned to that case,' Virginsky pointed out.

'And what of the children? Whoever killed Kozodavlev killed them also.'

Virginsky did not reply. The speed with which the colour drained from his face indicated that Porfiry had touched a nerve.

'You did not go to the graveside. You did not witness the mother's collapse. She fell forward. Perhaps it was deliberate – she threw herself. At any rate, she had to be pulled out. The father ... the father's cries ...' Porfiry broke off. He lit a cigarette before continuing. 'Have you ever been to the Zoological Gardens, Pavel Pavlovich?'

Virginsky hesitated before replying, 'Y-yes.' He was thinking back to Easter Sunday night.

'His cries were like the bellow of a wounded beast. Such suffering cannot be borne. The landlady too was in a terrible state.'

'If she had stayed with the children ...'

'You will blame her? We must find out who lit that fire, Pavel Pavlovich, and bring them to justice. We promised. We promised Yekaterina Ivanovna – or have you forgotten?'

'*You* promised.'

'And you gave your promise too, I seem to remember.'

'But we are not assigned to it.' There was a despairing quality to Virginsky's words, as if he was pleading with Porfiry to leave him alone.

Porfiry considered his junior colleague carefully for a few moments. 'There is something about Kozodavlev that makes you uncomfortable,' he said. 'That you do not wish to look into. That is why you shy away from him.'

'You are wide of the mark this time, Porfiry Petrovich.' The despair in Virginsky's voice tipped over into panic.

Porfiry continued to watch him closely. 'Quite possibly . . . dear boy,' he said quietly, almost tenderly. They had reached the number of the apartment building where one branch of the Dolgoruky family resided. Porfiry looked up at it regretfully. 'So what is it to be? Do we just go back to the bureau and wait for someone to recognise our corpse?' He seemed to be waiting for Virginsky's permission to enter.

'Now that we are here . . .' began Virginsky sullenly.

It was like a trap springing open. Porfiry was away before Virginsky could finish speaking. He called something over his shoulder that could have been, 'That's the spirit!' But it was lost in the speed of his flight up the steps.

*

The Dolgoruky apartments were, naturally, at the front of the building, looking out on Liteiny Prospect. They were on a grand scale, and seemed to be inhabited, at first sight, exclusively by servants.

As far as Porfiry was able to discover, the extensive household existed to serve the needs of one tiny individual, to whom he and Virginsky were eventually presented. The dowager Princess Yevgenia Alexeevna Dolgorukaya was like the hard kernel of the woman she had once been. Her face was the shape of an almond, and as deeply lined. Her lips were held in a permanent pucker of disapproval – or perhaps it was pain, caused by the severity with which her hair had been parted and pinned. She did not blink. As soon as Porfiry noticed this, he was greatly disconcerted by it. He immediately thought her capable of anything.

Her extremely diminutive stature, which was in inverse proportion to her importance in the household, was exaggerated by the voluminous skirt of her purple satin dress. The widow's colour seemed to be a vortex of grief into which she was in danger of sinking. She was also dwarfed by a pair of enormous oriental vases balanced precariously on narrow stands and positioned at either side of the golden velvet sofa on which she was perched.

Seated next to her, though at the furthest possible distance on the same sofa, was a young woman working at an embroidery hoop. She was a pretty enough girl, thought Porfiry, though her expression was timid, almost cowed. It did not seem that she was the older woman's daughter – more that her relationship to her was one of subservience, or indebtedness. At any rate, there was no clear family resemblance, and the companionship with which she provided the Princess did not seem to be freely given. Neither party gave any impression of deriving enjoyment from it.

Porfiry bowed as he introduced himself and Virginsky. The Princess invited them to be seated on a sofa that was positioned at right angles to her own. Somewhat inhibited by the semicircle of attendant maids and footmen, as well as the giant vases, Porfiry cleared his throat to state his business. 'I regret the necessity of disturbing your peace, Madame. In point of fact, we wish to speak to Prince Konstantin Arsenevich Dolgoruky. Your son, perhaps? Is he by any chance at home?'

'I know of no one by that name.'

When Porfiry had thought her capable of anything, his imagination had not encompassed this. 'I beg your pardon? We were assured that this was the Dolgoruky family home, the same Dolgoruky family to which Prince Konstantin Arsenevich belongs. Is that not correct?'

She repeated her unblinking chant, as if it were the response in an often-repeated liturgy: 'I know of no one by that name.'

The young woman next to her threw herself from the sofa as if it had suddenly come to life and bitten her. Her embroidery hoop fell to the floor. As she rushed from the room, her skirt, which was almost as voluminous as the Princess's, brushed the stand of one of the oriental vases and set it rocking. The attendant servants watched mesmerised, as did Porfiry and Virginsky, as the vase tottered and at last toppled. The smash was devastating and magnificent.

No one moved, though all eyes turned on the dowager princess.

Surely now she must blink! thought Porfiry.

But as far as he could discern, she did not.

*

They were shown to the door by an elderly butler by the name of Alexey Yegorovich.

'You have been with the family for a long time?' ventured Porfiry.

'All my life. I was a house serf, freed in the Great Reforms.'

'And do *you* know of anyone by the name of Prince Konstantin Arsenevich Dolgoruky?'

'Of course.'

'Am I right in thinking he is Princess Dolgorukaya's son?'

'Yes.'

'But she no longer acknowledges him?'

'Clearly.'

'And the reason for this has something to do with the young lady who ran most precipitously from the room?'

The butler's face masked whatever feelings he may have had on the subject. 'Marfa Timofyevna? I cannot say.'

'You are very discreet. I commend you for that.'

'I cannot say because I do not know. I am not privy to the confidences of either Princess Dolgorukaya or Marfa Timofyevna.'

'But servants talk.'

'Is it your business to gather the tittle-tattle of parlour maids? I for one pay no heed to it. I advise you to do the same.'

Porfiry acknowledged the rebuke with a series of blinks. 'What about Prince Dolgoruky? Are you privy to his confidences?'

'I have known the Prince since he was a babe in arms. I dandled him on my knee. My wife, God rest her soul, was his wet nurse.'

'He confided in you?'

'The Prince does not confide in anyone, wholly. Is he in any trouble?'

'Would it surprise you if he were?'

The old servant did not reply, but his face fell eloquently.

Porfiry smiled. 'I merely wish to speak to him about a gentleman who is known to be one of his associates.'

'It is his associates who are to blame!' said Alexey Yegorovich, forcefully.

'Yes, of course. He has fallen in with a bad crowd. It often happens. It is this bad crowd that I am interested in. What we must do is separate Prince Dolgoruky from the bad crowd, so that his goodness can be allowed to flourish. Is that not so?'

'He was not a bad little boy. Very sweet-natured and loving. He doted on my wife. As she did on him.'

'Then there is certainly hope for Prince Dolgoruky now. What can you tell me about these associates?'

'He did not generally receive his friends here. They are not such that you would admit into a respectable home.'

'I see. And he never mentioned any names to you?'

Alexey Yegorovich shook his head doubtfully. 'He may have. But the names meant nothing to me.'

'Do you at least know where he is now?'

'He is not far from here. In fact, he has merely crossed two courtyards.' The butler looked up and down the hallway conspiratorially. 'I sometimes take him things. Food. Books. Whatever he asks for that will not be missed.'

Porfiry thought for a moment. 'I would like to show you some photographs.'

Alexey Yegorovich shook his head blankly at the image of the man taken from the Winter Canal, and in fact looked at Porfiry as if he were mad for showing it to him. The photograph of the staff of *Affair* provoked a more promising reaction, at least when Porfiry pointed out Kozodavlev.

'I have seen him once or twice with that man. He may have even brought him to the house. I rather think the Prince considered him to be one of his more respectable friends.'

'Do you know who he is?'

'I believe the Prince referred to him as Demyan Antonovich.'

'Thank you. The man is indeed Demyan Antonovich Kozodav-lev.'

The click of a door handle turning drew their attention. The door in question creaked open a few inches, then closed again quickly. Porfiry thought that he had seen two moist, timid eyes peer out.

'Marfa Timofyevna?' he whispered to Alexey Yegorovich.

The butler nodded.

'I would very much like to speak to her. It may help the Prince.'

The butler bowed and crossed to Marfa Timofyevna's door, knocking gently. The door opened a crack, through which a whispered exchange was passed. At a nod from Alexey Yegorovich, Porfiry and Virginsky were admitted.

The room was tiny, the walls crowded with reproductions of mostly sentimental genre paintings.

Marfa Timofyevna indicated the bed for them to sit upon, but Porfiry declared that the interview need not take long. At that, the young lady swayed uncertainly on her feet.

'But please,' relented Porfiry. 'By all means, you may sit down.' He watched her solicitously for a few moments. 'You are not well, Marfa Timofyevna? May we fetch you a glass of water?'

'Thank you, no. That won't be necessary. I am a little fatigued, that is all.' She dabbed her eyes with a minuscule, lace-trimmed handkerchief.

Porfiry and Virginsky both felt awkward standing over the girl. Nodding simultaneously, they settled down on either side of her.

'I could not help noticing,' began Porfiry gently, 'that when we were talking to Princess Dolgorukaya, you left the room in something of a hurry.'

'Yes.' Marfa Timofyevna gave a self-mocking smile that entirely won Porfiry over. He could not say which was more touching, its bravery or its fragility.

'The reason, if I am not mistaken, has something to do with her rejection of her son, Prince Dolgoruky.'

'I owe everything to Princess Dolgorukaya,' said Marfa Timofyevna, hotly.

'Yes, of course. I understand. That makes it very difficult for you to say anything against her.'

'Is Konstantin Arsenevich in trouble?'

'No. I merely wish to speak to him about a friend of his. Did he ever introduce you to any of his friends?'

Marfa Timofyevna shook her head quickly, almost violently. For the first time, she turned her eyes directly on Porfiry. 'It is not what you think.' She looked away sharply, as soon as she had confided this.

'Ah, it is interesting that you should say so, as I am not sure *what* I think.' Porfiry smiled.

Marfa Timofyevna's tone darkened. 'You think that Konstantin Arsenevich seduced me.'

'And that is not what happened?'

'I . . .' Marfa Timofyevna bit her lower lip and closed her eyes. She could not bring herself to say any more.

'Yes, I think I understand,' said Porfiry, softly. 'And so, perhaps, you hold yourself responsible for the Prince's exile from his family home?'

Marfa Timofyevna seemed shocked by the suggestion. 'No, I . . . ! Why do you say that?'

'Then, forgive me, I do not understand. Except that I understand how painful and delicate these affairs are. And that the truth of the matter is often very different to the way it is vulgarly represented. What is left out – quite often – are the feelings. How the heart is stirred. Noble, beautiful – and above all delicate – feelings. But if you take those away, what are you left with? For they are the truth, the whole truth, nothing but the truth. Without allowing for those feelings, then you are only dealing with a travesty of the truth. A lie, in other words.'

Marfa Timofyevna's mouth was open in a wondering O. She studied Porfiry's eyes carefully. 'I knew what was said about him,' she said at last. 'The rumours.'

'Which were?' Porfiry asked the question a little too eagerly.

Marfa Timofyevna shook her head impatiently. 'Oh, that he had seduced many women. That he kept three apartments, with a separate mistress in each. That he had committed crimes.'

'Crimes?'

'Yes. And blasphemies.'

'You knew all this,' stated Porfiry, his tone confirmatory.

'I had heard all the rumours. The very worst. I heard them all from him, you see.'

'From Konstantin Arsenevich?'

'Yes. He often said such things against himself, as if to frighten me. But I would not be deterred. And so, he arranged for the printing of a manifesto in which he accused himself – and condemned himself – of the vilest crimes. He brought it willingly to me.'

'How extraordinary.'

'He told me that every word in it was true. He told me to read it carefully, and if, at the end of reading it, I still loved him, then he would be mine, mine alone, for ever.'

'And so?'

Marfa Timofyevna gave a sudden startling sob that convulsed her whole body. 'I was not good enough!' she gasped.

'You could not love him,' said Porfiry flatly.

Marfa Timofyevna squeezed her eyelids tight.

'May I see this document?'

'I don't . . . have it . . . anymore.' Marfa Timofyevna's eyes were glistening. 'I realise now that he is gone, that I do, I can, I *must* love him. It is his only hope. And mine.'

'And what of Princess Dolgorukaya? Does she know of this document? Had she read it? Is that the true reason why she cast him out?'

'I . . .' Marfa Timofyevna's eyes widened in recollection of the single most appalling act of her young life. 'I took it to her.'

'What has become of it now, do you know?'

'She destroyed it, of course.'

Porfiry absorbed the news with a flutter of blinking. 'Can you remember any of the charges that the Prince laid against himself?'

'You will not hear them from me. You may torture me all you want, but I will not say a word of what was printed on that paper.'

'My dear young lady – please! – be assured that I have no intention of torturing you!'

'They were lies anyhow. I realise that now. Lies he had made up to test me. And I failed. Oh, how I failed!'

Porfiry laid a hand consolingly across one of hers. She looked up, startled by his touch. Her eyes implored him for some consoling word. Her face trembled with anguish and despair.

'If you have a message for him, I will happily convey it,' Porfiry offered.

Marfa Timofyevna breathed in deeply, drawing herself up fully, only to collapse in defeat on the exhalation. She hung her head and waited for them to go.

16

A Russian Byron

For a small consideration, Alexey Yegorovich escorted them across a series of courtyards, each muddier than the last. He pointed out a squalid entrance and left them to it. The door was rotten and looked as if it were about to fall off its hinges. A dark stairway led down to the basement. They were at the very rear of what was essentially the same sprawling building that housed the lavish apartments of the Dolgoruky family. It was here where one found the filthy garrets and cellars, and the dingy rooms sublet into 'corners,' into which multiple families and individuals were crammed.

Prince Dolgoruky had merely moved from the front of the building to the rear, and yet he might as well have crossed an entire continent. If the apartment building was a microcosm of Russia, he had been cast into its Siberia.

An old woman came through a door as they reached the bottom of the stairs. She regarded them suspiciously out of the gloom, holding herself stock-still. When Porfiry announced that they were looking for Prince Dolgoruky, her manner became highly animated and almost coquettish. She smiled an entirely toothless grin.

The old coquette led them into a large room hung with washing lines. The drying clothes served as informal partitions, dividing the space into its various living areas. Small windows set high in the walls, at ground level on the outside, let in a meagre light.

She pointed to a shabby curtain that was strung across one corner of the room. 'You had better knock first!' she recommended with a knowing leer.

As they approached the curtain, they could hear the sounds of laughter coming from behind it; more specifically, the laughter of two people, one as unmistakably male as the other was female. The sounds had an intimate tinge, as if the two people making them believed themselves to be utterly alone. The curtain sealed them off in the universe of their mutual abandon.

Porfiry cleared his throat loudly. 'Prince Dolgoruky? Prince Konstantin Arsenevich Dolgoruky?'

A strained silence descended on the couple on the other side of the curtain. However, after a moment or two, a fit of giggling burst from the female.

'Who wishes to speak to him?' The male voice was charged with aristocratic hauteur.

'My name is Porfiry Petrovich. I am an investigating magistrate. I wish to talk to Konstantin Arsenevich about the journalist Kozodavlev.'

'A magistrate, you say?'

'Yes.'

'So, you've caught up with me at last!' The quip provoked an appreciative giggle from Dolgoruky's companion. There was the sound of a palm striking flesh, followed by a squeal of mingled pain and delight. The scents that came from the corner left little doubt as to what had very recently occurred there.

Porfiry looked around the room. The interview was drawing the attention of a number of the other residents. In particular, an audience of small and ragged children had gathered. Some of them even sat on the floor at his feet, looking up expectantly for the entertainment to continue. One or two held crusts of black bread in their grimy fingers. 'Perhaps you would care to draw back the curtain, or come out from behind it, so that we may talk to you in a more convenient manner,' said Porfiry.

A man somewhere in his late thirties pulled back one side of the curtain and stepped through. He was dressed in a loose shirt and tight breeches. He kept his sand-coloured hair long, swept back in waves from a brow that was higher than it once had been. The angle of his head matched the hauteur that Porfiry had earlier detected in his voice. There was an amused, self-satisfied glimmer in his eye, and a one-sided twist to his mouth. Porfiry saw no trace of the sweet-natured boy the butler Alexey Yegorovich claimed to remember.

'Kozodavlev, you say? What's the old fool been up to now?'

'Are you aware that there was a fire in Mr Kozodavlev's apartment building on Monday night, in which several people perished? It is feared that Mr Kozodavlev may have been one of them.' Until he had asked the question, Porfiry did not know that he was going to frame it in that way. Indeed, he had not known he was going to start with the fire at all. He wondered if he had been motivated solely by a desire to wipe the smile from Prince Dolgoruky's face.

If so, he was not fully prepared for the effect his words had. All colour drained from Dolgoruky's complexion. The man seemed to age ten years before his eyes. 'Kozodavlev is dead?' His voice was a frightened whisper.

'It is feared so. Obviously, in the case of death by fire, one cannot always be certain of the identity of the victims. But a man did perish in Mr Kozodavlev's apartment, and he failed to attend a number of appointments on the following day, including one with me.'

Prince Dolgoruky considered this information thoughtfully but said nothing. The colour slowly returned to his cheeks and he seemed to regain his composure.

'You acted on his behalf as an agent for certain of his journalistic endeavours, did you not?'

'So, you know about that.'

'We know that he was K. We also know that you acted in a similar capacity on behalf of the author known as D. Who is D.?'

Prince Dolgoruky shrugged, his face contemptuous.

'You will not tell me?'

'Perhaps I do not know.'

Porfiry reached into his pocket and took out a bundle of papers. He found the sheet he was looking for and handed it to Prince Dolgoruky. 'We found this in Mr Kozodavlev's drawer at the office of *Affair*. Do you recognise it?'

'Yes. I wrote it.'

'You are the D. in this note?'

'I am.'

'What did you mean? "I don't give a damn what you do. Do you think I have ever cared?"'

'The words are clear enough, I think.'

'You had quarrelled with Mr Kozodavlev?'

'It's not a question of a quarrel. It is simply a statement of the – how shall I put it? – of the factual basis of our relationship. From time to time, Kozodavlev had to be reminded.'

'You were never on friendly terms with him?'

'I have never been on friendly terms with anyone. It is the first article in the code of conduct by which I live my life.'

'Are you the author of *Swine*?'

'Ah, you are very clever, I see, Mr Magistrate,' mocked Prince Dolgoruky. 'We shall have to be careful with you. Was it the letter D that alerted you? But are there not other names that begin with the letter D? Some of them, I believe, belong to more noted literary gentlemen than I.'

'The plot of *Swine* concerns a revolutionary grouping. A closed cell, I believe it is called.'

'I have heard the term.'

'I'm sure you have. In *Swine*, one member of the cell is suspected of being an informer, and is for that reason murdered by the other members.'

'I am sure the author will be gratified to know that you have read the novel.'

'To be honest, I have not finished reading it. However, I am familiar enough with the novel and the circumstances surrounding its publication. It is rumoured that the author once belonged to such a group and in fact participated in a similar crime.'

'It is not a rumour. It is the truth.'

'You do not deny it?'

'Why should I?'

'Because you must see that your action places you in a difficult position vis-à-vis the law. If you are the author –'

'*If!*'

'Even if you are not, by concealing the identity of the author, you are concealing the identity of a criminal.'

'And if you have in fact read the novel, you will know that the author distances himself from the act of his fellows – whom he sees as swine. Hence the title. It is out of moral disgust that he decided to write his account.'

'He would have done better to inform the authorities, supplying the real names and addresses of those involved.'

'But he is not an *informer*,' said Prince Dolgoruky with disgust. 'That would make him worse than those you would have him inform against.'

'To inform is a greater crime than murder?'

'Of course.'

'I believe that Mr Kozodavlev had made up his mind to inform the authorities of something. Given certain hints that he put in a letter he wrote to me, it would seem reasonable to speculate that it concerned political – one may say revolutionary – crimes. He expressed the fear that this would place him in mortal danger.'

'If that is so, then he was right to be afraid.'

'If Kozodavlev is the author of *Swine* –'

'What on earth makes you suggest that?' cried Dolgoruky.

'Let us for the moment imagine that he is. There would be those who would object to the fact that he had written the book in the first place. If they found out for certain that Kozodavlev was the author, they might have decided to punish him. For that betrayal, the only fit punishment would be death. Of course, it would have required someone to have pointed the finger.' Porfiry gave Prince Dolgoruky a meaningful look.

'But you are assuming that D. is Kozodavlev! I have by no means confirmed that he is.'

'You would save us a lot of trouble if you simply told us who the author is.'

'I do not exist to save you trouble.'

'I can have you arrested.'

'I would welcome it. I am not afraid of the Fortress. I hear one is well looked after there.'

'Is it true that you wrote and had printed a manifesto in which you accused yourself of a number of crimes?'

'Have you seen it?' asked Prince Dolgoruky brightly.

'No.'

'Would you like to?'

'Is there any truth in it?'

The contempt evaporated from Prince Dolgoruky's expression. He seemed surprised by Porfiry's question.

'Marfa Timofyevna claims to believe that it is all lies,' explained Porfiry.

'She is a dear sweet girl. I regret deeply what happened between us.'

'What did happen between you?'

'Nothing. That is what I regret.'

'You are quite the Russian Byron, aren't you? And yet, why is it I feel this is all a pose with you?'

'That is an insult. I have killed men for less.'

'Then certainly I should have you locked up.'

'Do you wish to see my manifesto?'

'Are you really so eager to show it to me?'

'Unfortunately, I have destroyed all copies of it.'

'Then I will have to imagine what it said. I think I can, easily enough.'

'I doubt your imagination will be up to the task.'

'You forget, my imagination is fuelled by a lifetime of investigating the crimes of men.'

'But you will not have encountered crimes as black as mine.'

Porfiry sighed wearily. 'You are a veritable genius of crime, I'm sure. And, as such, the true Hero of our Time.'

'Again you insult me?' Prince Dolgoruky's questioning tone betrayed his uncertainty. It seemed he did not know what to make of Porfiry. 'You are not interested in my crimes? Is it not your duty to be interested in my crimes?'

'I find that I am not very interested in *you*, Prince Dolgoruky. You bore me.'

Prince Dolgoruky was visibly shaken. 'I cannot bore you. Dolgoruky does not bore anyone.'

'You bore me, and I suspect you bore yourself. And that is your tragedy, to the extent that you may be said to have a tragedy. But I am not sure that you can be said to have a tragedy. If you are allowed to have a tragedy, there is the danger of your becoming slightly interesting.'

'You are not serious?'

'One last thing before I leave you to your . . .' Porfiry glanced at the curtain. His smile was strangely mocking. '*Crimes*. I would like you to look at a photograph. Please try to ignore the white patches on the man's face.' He nodded to Virginsky to show the poster of the body from the Winter Canal.

'My God, what has happened to him?'

'His face, in life, would not have been like that. It is likely to have been deeply pockmarked all over. I will draw your attention also to his eyes, which are quite small, I think.'

'Piggy eyes. The eyes of a swine!'

'Do you recognise him?'

'Recognise *that*? It is a monstrosity. If I had ever seen such a face, it would haunt my nightmares for ever!'

'Do you have nightmares, Konstantin Arsenevich?'

'Yes. Every night, the same one. I dream that the Devil has come to fetch me. I know he is the Devil, though I never see his face.' Prince Dolgoruky's voice trembled weakly, all hint of hauteur gone. His face appeared shockingly vulnerable, even afraid. He looked down at the photograph on the poster. 'Perhaps I have seen it now.'

'I am glad that we were able to be of service. We have provided a face for your nightmares.'

Prince Dolgoruky turned his attention to the semicircle of children watching, as if he had only just noticed them. He looked into their faces searchingly, addressing his words to them now: 'It is not just my nightmares. Sometimes I can hear his step during the day, when I am awake. And when something moves in the shadows, I am sure it is him.'

Porfiry studied Prince Dolgoruky with narrowed eyes. It seemed he had at last begun to interest the magistrate.

17

An old obsession

'What do you make of that?' asked Porfiry as they stepped into the yard. He breathed deeply for a few moments and then lit a cigarette.

Virginsky answered with a question of his own: 'Did he really not interest you at all?'

'Oh, perhaps a little. But I did not want to give him the satisfaction of knowing it. There is something rather infantile about his desire to scandalise. He is like a little boy who wishes to be thought very wicked.'

'So you do not consider him capable of any great crime?'

'I consider him capable of great idiocy, which may well amount to the same thing. You noticed that he knew our man in the canal?'

'Can you be sure?'

'Oh absolutely. He is a bad liar. A simple "no" would have been more persuasive. Instead he had to work himself up over nightmares of the Devil and such like. He as good as confessed.'

'*You think he killed our man?*' Virginsky was astonished.

'I think he may have had something to do with it, yes. As I think that Kozodavlev had something to do with it too.'

'And what of this manifesto of crimes?'

'It's hard to say, without having seen it. But I would not be surprised if it turned out to catalogue every crime he has dreamed of committing but to omit the one crime of which he is actually guilty.'

'I wonder that you can speak with such confidence on something that is necessarily a matter of conjecture.'

'There is something cowardly and weak about him, I sensed. And yet also, a vileness that he is fully conscious of himself – and disgusted by. He plays with the idea of confession, as he does with that of wickedness. I would say he is torn by two contradictory impulses. The first, the desire to plumb the depths of his own evil, to commit the worst crime of which he can conceive. The second, the need for redemption, to achieve which he must confess his crimes – his true crimes, I mean. But before he is able to reach that point, his cowardice intervenes and subverts his intention. He has the boldness for wickedness but lacks the courage for salvation. At heart, he is a Christian, I think. And we must not forget that he is a Russian too. Yes. That is all it comes down to in the end. In many ways, he reminded me of myself. All investigation is ultimately self-investigation.'

Virginsky's mouth gaped, but he was so far from formulating a response that all that came out was a strangulated gasp.

*

When they returned to Stolyarny Lane, Porfiry found Lieutenant Salytov waiting outside his chambers.

'You wish to see me, Ilya Petrovich?' Porfiry opened the door to admit them all.

'I have seen him before,' declared Salytov, intensely.

Porfiry and Virginsky exchanged a quizzical glance. 'Seen ... whom, exactly?'

'Him.' Salytov pointed at the waxen face on the poster pinned to the wall.

'Our drowned rat? Please, tell me more.'

'Four years ago, I was investigating a revolutionary cell based in a confectioner's on Nevsky Prospect. Ballet's, the shop was called.'

'But there was no revolutionary cell at Ballet's!' objected Virginsky, who was for some reason suddenly agitated.

Salytov directed the full force of his loathing towards the junior magistrate. 'Is it not strange that my investigations were cut short by the bomb blast which accounted for this?' Salytov swept a hand in front of his own face. It was the gesture of a stage magician, summoning up the disfigurement.

'But that atrocity had nothing to do with the confectionery shop, as you know,' insisted Virginsky. 'You were following a false trail.'

'This man.' Salytov's conjuring hand stabbed towards the poster emphatically. 'I once saw this man in Ballet's. He was mixed up in something, I am sure.'

'*Mixed up in something!*' mocked Virginsky.

Salytov's stare snapped onto him once again. 'My instincts have been proven correct, have they not? He would not have been killed and dumped in the canal if he were not mixed up in something.'

'If it is the same fellow,' muttered Virginsky sceptically.

'Do you know his name?' asked Porfiry, his tone smoothly appeasing.

Salytov hesitated. His gaze drooped, abashed. 'No.'

'But you are sure you saw him in Ballet's?'

'Yes. It was clear that he was an associate of the individual I was investigating, the lad Tolya. If you remember, Porfiry Petrovich, he was found with illegal manifestos in his possession.'

Porfiry wrinkled his face as he squeezed out his memory. 'I do vaguely remember something about it. But I fear that Pavel Pavlovich is right. There was nothing in it. The boy had nothing to do with any revolutionary cell.'

'That we could discover. At the time.' Salytov's doggedness was wearingly impressive.

Porfiry's expression became momentarily pained. 'Very well. Look into it. Talk to this Tolya. He may be able to supply a name, at least.'

Salytov clicked his heels and left the room in a series of quasi-military spins and steps.

'That man . . .' began Virginsky.

'. . . is, at the moment, the only chance we have of identifying our corpse,' completed Porfiry.

'But do you not see, Porfiry Petrovich? The confectioner's was an obsession with him. Is there not a danger that the same thing will happen again? Indeed, is it not simply the resurfacing of that old obsession that has prompted him to make this connection? I defy anyone to make a credible identification based on that photograph! Perhaps if it was someone you knew well, a husband, or a brother, or a close friend. But he is talking about a man he saw once in a confectionery shop four years ago. Are you not concerned that you are encouraging him in an unhealthy fixation?'

'I repeat. At the moment, he is the only chance we have.'

*

Once again, the tallow candle was lit and the tin trunk pulled out from under the bed. Virginsky sat with his copy of 'God the Nihilist' in his hands. Its celebration of human reason rang hollow, as did its faith in the ascendancy of the human conscience. It seemed to assume that the two were identical, that if a man acted in accordance with his conscience it went without saying that he would be acting reasonably, and vice versa. But Virginsky had come to realise that they were very much at odds. One could reason out a course of action against which one's conscience screamed rebellion.

Without knowing that he would do it, he tipped the tin trunk up, emptying the contents onto the floor. He stared sullenly at the unruly sprawl of ideas. Words and names jumped out at him, as if in retaliation for his childish petulance: 'Saint-Simon', 'utopia', 'communism', 'phalanstery', 'freedom', 'the woman question', 'atheism', 'Bakunin', 'organisation', 'revolutionary', 'freedom', 'destruction', 'nihilist', 'Nechaev'. He sensed an escalation of intent, a hardening of resolve, leading right up to the ultimate phrase, the ruthless encapsulation of all the other radical concepts: *the end justifies the means*. It was a supremely reasonable formula.

The stove in his room was a fat white pillar bulging out from the corner. Two black cast iron doors were set into it close to the floor, one for access to the firebox, the other for cleaning beneath the grate. Virginsky knelt down and opened the larger door.

It was almost as if the flames were waiting for him. They lapped out towards his face as he opened the stove, their eagerness spilling out with a hungry crackle.

Generally, he kept the fire low. The stove was efficient. As long as he maintained it, a small flame was enough to keep the chill from his room, even in winter. The days were warmer now, but a night frost could still surprise.

But the fire in his stove was more than the means by which he warmed his room. It was a small, intense fragment of the greater fire. Staring into it, he imagined himself back in the time of that first revolution, when fire had just been discovered, and those who knew how to create and control it had power over their fellows. One could share or withhold. In the same way, one could use it benignly or destructively. Human nature being what it was, the jealous, destructive choice would always prevail. There was something, too, in the nature of fire that demanded this.

Virginsky moved his copy of 'God the Nihilist' towards the aperture of the stove and fed the handbill quickly into the consuming flames.

He put the rest of the manifestos back into the trunk and pushed it under his bed. A moment later, he put on his overcoat and went out.

*

Instinct drew Virginsky to the filthiest, darkest drinking dens on and around Haymarket Square. That is not to say that he narrowed his search down to any meaningful degree. It would have been hard to find taverns in the district that did not fit that description.

He bought a five-kopek measure of vodka in each place he visited, which he drank quickly. After six taverns, he gave up all hope of finding the man. Frankly, it was a relief to do so, as he had no clear idea what he would say to him if he did find him. The more the evening wore on, the more likely it was that he would say something inept and revealing, thereby making a fool of himself, and also, possibly, placing himself in danger.

His plan, such as it was, had been flawed from the outset. After all, it was perfectly possible for the man to enter a tavern he had already visited, the moment after he had left it. Their paths need never cross. As an investigative technique – if that was what it was – it was hardly more sophisticated than stumbling around aimlessly.

And so Virginsky gave himself up to drinking and abandoned any pretence of looking for the hatchet-headed man who had given him the manifesto.

Then it came: the hand on the shoulder, the voice in the ear, the plunging vertiginous lurch of fate – or something worse, doom – and he realised that he had never wanted to find this man, who had now found him.

'My friend, we meet again.'

Virginsky hid his panic with feigned blankness.

The man's mouth spiked on one side sarcastically; the suddenly familiar expression took Virginsky back to the night of Easter Sunday. 'You mean to say, you were not looking for me?'

'I . . .' But Virginsky was at a loss for a convincing lie.

'Still and all, you found me.' The man increased the angle of his sarcasm.

'Very well,' said Virginsky. 'Let's say I was looking for you. Now I have found you. What next?'

'Come over and join me. I have a table in the corner. Away from prying ears.'

'Are you here alone?'

'Are you here as a magistrate?'

'You remembered.'

'It would be hard to forget. I was here with some friends, but . . .' The man looked around, scanning the scattered drunks, indistinguishable with their expressions of glassy-eyed stupor. 'They have gone. Come on. I will introduce you to their shadows.'

On the way to the corner, Virginsky almost fell over as his foot caught against some obstacle on the floor. He looked down and in the dim candlelight could just about make out a man sprawled face-down, unconscious.

As he took a seat on a rickety chair, he felt but could not see the layer of grime on the table. 'To answer your question . . . no. I am not here as a magistrate.'

'Then what?'

'I was very interested in the poem you gave me.'

'Yes. Go on.'

'And what you said, about hunger . . . the hunger you saw in my eyes. I think it's true. I do have that hunger.'

'And what would you do with it?'

'I wish to serve the cause.'

'The cause?' The man's mocking laughter scythed the air. He became abruptly serious: 'Do you even know what the cause is?'

'Revolution.'

'Just a word. Is it not?'

'At the moment, perhaps. But it is my earnest desire to turn that word into an act.'

'So? What do you want from me?'

'You . . . are close to those directing this great . . . endeavour . . . are you not? I am not wrong in thinking that?' There was a pleading note to Virginsky's question.

The man did not immediately reply. Behind the circular lenses of his spectacles, his eyes narrowed in assessment. At last he said, 'Have you changed your views?'

'My views?'

'The last time we met, you said that you could not condone the loss of life.'

'There are other means of achieving destabilisation, are there not?'

'What do you have in mind?'

'The circulation of manifestos, such as that you handed to me. Education, in other words.'

'That is just the beginning. Words can only convey so much. There is a point at which it is necessary to translate them into deeds.'

'But must they necessarily be violent deeds?'

'Not all will be violent. There is a range of action in the revolutionist's repertoire. Vandalism, sabotage, the desecration of churches. One method that we have used with some success is the introduction of counterfeit banknotes. It all falls under the rubric of propaganda. Even acts of violence. Everything carries a message – the message being that the Tsar is losing his grip on power. But we must use all means. You cannot pick and choose. If you are called upon to act for the cause, you are not at liberty to discriminate on the grounds of squeamishness.'

'But surely it makes sense to use each according to his abilities, and opportunities.'

The hatchet-headed man considered this, and finally nodded in agreement.

'I am a magistrate,' went on Virginsky. 'I work for the Ministry of Justice. I have access to official documents. Briefings, reports . . . orders.'

The man nodded thoughtfully. 'Bring us something. Something useful. Then we will see.'

'What?'

'I will leave it to your discretion.'

'How will I get in contact with you again?'

'You found me now, didn't you? You will find me again.'

'But it's . . . that's . . .' Virginsky wanted to give in to the vodka swoon that was making it hard for him to string his words together.

'What?'

A great effort of concentration led to sudden clarity: 'Surely we cannot afford to leave it to chance like that?'

'Don't worry your head, my magistrate friend. If you can't find me, I know where to find you.' Although the man was smiling, it was his usual one-sided leer of sarcasm, which only served to accentuate the hint of a threat in his words.

18

The Devil's Professor

The following day, a large envelope arrived for Porfiry Petrovich from the office of *Russian Soil* and *Russian Era*. A number of folded rectangles of newsprint slumped out limply like so many dead butterflies, landing in a heap on his desk. Porfiry spread them out, sorting them first by size, then resorting them in chronological order. There were about thirty to forty snippets of paper, with articles going back approximately three years. A covering letter from Trudolyubov explained that these were all the articles that had appeared in his publications written by the journalist he knew as 'K.'

The most recent piece was one that Porfiry remembered reading. It was the attack on Virginsky's former professor of jurisprudence, Tatiscev. It seemed that over the years K. had waged something of a campaign against this man, and was, as far as Porfiry could tell, the originator of the soubriquet 'The Devil's Professor.'

Porfiry now rearranged the clippings thematically. There were seven articles attacking Tatiscev, as well as five other articles which mercilessly lampooned another individual, one Vissarion Stepanovich Lebezyatnikov. This gentleman appeared to be a former professor of history, a liberal of a previous generation, whom K. deemed to be utterly without purpose or point. In short, he considered him to be a 'superfluous man' and called upon him to do the decent thing, which was – in K.'s opinion – simply to disappear.

Other individuals also served as targets for K.'s barbs, but none to the same extent as Tatiscev and Lebezyatnikov.

'He seems to have a singular antipathy towards academic gentlemen.' It was only after Porfiry had given voice to this musing that he realised there was no one there to hear it. Virginsky had not yet presented himself at the department. Porfiry consulted his fob watch. It was close to eleven.

Porfiry rose from his desk and peered outside his chambers to confer with his clerk. 'Alexander Grigorevich, have you seen Pavel Pavlovich this morning?'

Zamyotov gave a minimal shake of the head, putting far more effort into producing a disdainful snort.

'While I think of it, I need you to make an enquiry at the Address Office. The name is Vissarion Stepanovich Lebezyatnikov. A former professor of history. I require his address as soon as possible, if you please.'

Porfiry returned to his desk and read again the series of articles attacking Professor Tatiscev. The charges in each piece amounted to more or less the same complaint, continually restated: simply that the writer held the new law courts responsible for the decline in morality evident everywhere in society. Professor Tatiscev, as a noted supporter of the new courts, was held up as the human embodiment of all that was evil.

Of course, reasoned Porfiry, it would not do for the writer to attack the Tsar – at least not in these publications. The Tsar was above criticism. But the fact remained that it was the Tsar who had signed off the reform of the legal system. Tatiscev was outside the government, and, as far as Porfiry could tell, had never been in a position to influence the Tsar or his ministers. It was not even known if his opinion had been sought. The only charge that could be laid against him was that some of his former students had gone on to profit from the new system by becoming highly successful defence attorneys. What made him a natural target for these conservative papers was that he was a well-known radical, and also that he was an educator, with access to and influence over the younger generation. In other words, it was men like Tatiscev who were responsible for the gulf that had formed between fathers, who read publications like *Russian Soil* and *Russian Era*, and their sons, who preferred *Affair*.

Is that all there is to it? wondered Porfiry.

The political basis of the attacks was undoubtedly thin, perhaps deliberately so. If anything, Tatiscev came across as a straw man. Porfiry reminded himself that the writer of the articles was, under his real name, a radical journalist, who would undoubtedly have approved of Tatiscev's political stance. If Kozodavlev wrote these pieces purely for money, as hackwork, he would be careful not to inflict serious damage on the cause in which he truly believed. And yet he might be willing to vilify a man he personally disliked, especially as he was doing so under the cloak of anonymity.

A cannonade of innuendo was fired off. Was it any wonder that our country was in crisis when a whole generation of jurists had sat at the feet of a man who had learnt his ethics from the serpent? The Devil's Professor was not content to call for an end to the institution of marriage but had manfully taken it upon himself to bring it about, marriage by marriage. He was always ready with his own firm answer to the woman question. And just so that there should be no doubt what that answer was, it was asserted that Tatiscev had taken down the icon in his study and replaced it with a statue of Priapos.

To be frank, it was all rather juvenile, not to mention libellous. Beneath one of the articles, and seemingly linked to it, was a piece about the desecration of some icons in a church and the theft of relics and religious gems. In fact, there was no explicit connection made to Tatiscev, and indeed this piece appeared not to have been written by K.; nonetheless, the proximity of the articles associated the hapless professor with this crime too.

The four articles attacking Professor Lebezyatnikov were altogether different in tone, more light-hearted, entirely lacking in any scurrilous suggestions, but rather treating the former historian as a harmless buffoon. These lampoons could almost be said to be affectionate, celebrating rather than savaging their target. Porfiry was hard-pressed to see the point of the articles, as Professor Lebezyatnikov was now a retired gentleman, with practically no influence in society. If he might be described as 'superfluous,' what did that make the articles satirising him? Apparently, if K.'s satire was to be believed, he retained a high opinion of his importance, despite abundant evidence of his worthlessness. No doubt that made him ridiculous; it also made him somewhat pathetic. The attacks on him amounted to little more than a catalogue of the follies of a deluded old man.

It was past noon when Virginsky finally appeared. His face, drained of all colour, looked as though it had been slightly inflated, which had the effect of shrinking his eyes into narrow slits.

'My God, Pavel Pavlovich, what has happened to you?'

'I ran into someone.'

'With your face?'

Virginsky squinted. 'The sunlight is particularly bright today, do you not find?'

'I do not find it especially so. Perhaps you would like to move your chair, so that you are not looking directly into the window. Would you care for some tea?'

Virginsky shook his head. 'Are you not going to reprimand me?' He winced, as if he felt Porfiry's solicitude to be an intolerable cruelty.

'I prefer not to. I imagine that your own conscience, the inevitable pangs of . . . uh, remorse that you are suffering, will serve as both reprimand and warning. I will, however, express my concern, Pavel Pavlovich. Permit me to say that this is not like you. In all the years I have known you, I have observed you to be an admirably sober young man. To call you abstemious would not be overstating it. Therefore I consider this evident lapse to be out of character. I trust it does not presage the onset of a new habit and is rather the temporary influence of Yarilo, coupled with the accident of meeting an old friend.'

'He was not an old friend.'

'A new friend then?'

'Why are you so interested in him? Am I not permitted to have a life outside the department, of which you are not a part?'

'My dear, of course you are permitted! What an extraordinary thought! Let us put this behind us. In point of fact, I am secretly rather pleased that you have allowed yourself to relax to this extent. So long as it does not become a regular occurrence, I can only think that it will do you good to go on a binge once in a while.'

'It was not a binge. I do not go on binges, Porfiry Petrovich.

I . . .' But Virginsky broke off. A confessional flicker in his eyes was as close as he got to confiding in Porfiry.

'I understand completely. It is because you are not used to indulging in alcoholic consumption at all that a small amount had such a deleterious effect on you. There are some taverns in Haymarket Square where one only has to breathe in the atmosphere and the room begins to spin.'

'How did you know I was in Haymarket Square?'

'I did not. I only mentioned Haymarket Square because it is notorious for the density of its drinking dives. I rather imagined that you and your friend entertained yourselves in a far more respectable establishment. Somewhere like the Crystal Palace, no doubt?'

'Why Crystal Palace? What do you mean by that?'

'I mean nothing by it, Pavel Pavlovich! Good Heavens, what has got into you? You are so very sensitive this morning.'

'It is a satirical reference to my political aspirations, is it not?'

'In all honesty, no. I merely mentioned it because I know it to be a lively place where young people are wont to meet.' Porfiry blinked his face into an expression of severity. 'Enough, Pavel Pavlovich. I must ask you, are you here to work or to pick a fight with me? If it is the latter, then I have no use for you, not today, not any day.'

'I . . . I apologise, Porfiry Petrovich. I will endeavour to fulfil my duties as well as I am able. I trust that you will not be disappointed.'

'If you are up to it, I would have you look at these. Kozodavlev's cuttings from *Russian Soil* and *Russian Era*. When you have finished reading them, I suggest we pay a visit to the university, where I hope you will introduce me to your old professor.'

Virginsky surveyed the narrow infinity of parquet flooring ahead of him. He was standing at one end of the great, elongated hallway of the Twelve Collegiums building on Vasilevsky Island. The hallway ran the entire length of that determinedly linear structure, connecting all the faculties and disciplines – linking History and Philology to Philosophy and Law, Physics and Mathematics to Oriental Studies – in one long sequence of learning. The unifying principle of the architecture had been inherited from Peter the Great, who had originally commissioned the building to bring together the disparate departments, or colleges, of his bureaucracy.

It was two weeks since Good Friday. Lectures were over for the year. The place was almost deserted.

Virginsky felt again the same sickening mixture of apprehension and anger that he had known as a student walking the hallway. Perhaps that was where his habit of counting his steps had originated, for he knew that it was three hundred and sixty-four paces from one end to the other. He remembered the awe that the seemingly endless corridor had inspired in him the first time he had confronted it. It came to represent an uncertain and bewildering future. His hope had once been that, as he walked its length, he would acquire the knowledge and skills he needed to make his way in the world. Of course, it had not quite worked out like that. He had acquired something, been prepared for something, but in the process his ideas about what constituted 'making his way in the world' had been subject to constant revision. It was ironic to think that such a long, straight corridor could lead in so many directions.

Along one side of the hallway were the arched windows that

looked out onto University Line, with benches projecting from the wall beneath them; along the other, glass-fronted bookcases and the doors to lecture rooms and faculty offices. The vast length of the corridor was punctuated by statues and portraits of benefactors and men of learning, put there, perhaps, as much to inspire the students as to honour the dead. To the student Virginsky, they had been distant and intimidating presences. Indeed, he could now look upon his whole time at the university as an attempt to overcome the sense of inadequacy that those figures provoked, to reach a point where he could consider himself, if not their equal, at least entitled to be their critic.

One man had encouraged him in this aspiration, the man they were now coming to see, Professor Alexander Glebovich Tatiscev.

As he passed the figures now, Virginsky barely gave them a second thought.

'Significant, is it not, that the university rolls together the disciplines of law and philosophy into one faculty?' mused Porfiry. 'It inevitably makes philosophers of our lawyers. I wonder if this singular circumstance is not responsible for all the recent developments in our society, those which publications like *Russian Soil* inevitably perceive as ills.'

'There is nothing surprising about it,' answered Virginsky. 'How a state administers justice – or fails to – makes that state what it is. It is necessarily a philosophical, as well as a political, consideration. Similarly, when one begins to think deeply about the concept of justice, one is inevitably led to question the administrative arrangements within which justice is expected to function. If those arrangements are flawed, one naturally calls for change. The teaching of jurisprudence is inherently inimical to the status quo.'

'Inherently? Only if the status quo is itself unjust, surely?'

'Well, yes. That goes without saying. As it goes without saying that the status quo here in Russia *is* unjust.'

'Good gracious, Pavel Pavlovich! How emboldened you are by this return to your alma mater!'

'The very fact that you consider what I have said to be bold, when it is simply a statement of fact, proves my point, Porfiry Petrovich.' And yet there was some truth in what Porfiry had said, although Virginsky would not acknowledge it. A nervous excitement had been mounting with each step he took along the hallway. It was overlaid by a complicated nostalgia, not wholly, or even predominantly good. He had been so often hungry and unhappy as a student that it could hardly be a simple pleasure to feel himself walking back into that past.

His feelings about meeting his former professor were equally complex. He ought not to feel such trepidation. But he could not shake off the anxiety that he would be a disappointment to his erstwhile mentor. Had he not, after all, chosen a career path that appeared to put him on the side of the enemy? He was barely able to admit to an even worse fear: that Tatiscev would be a disappointment to him.

Virginsky slowed and stopped. Had he subconsciously been counting his steps all the time? Somehow, without looking, he knew that they had reached Professor Tatiscev's door, two hundred and three paces from the southern end of the hallway. A glance at the brass nameplate confirmed his instinct.

Porfiry smiled and made a gesture of encouragement. He was allowing Virginsky the privilege of knocking.

'Enter!' As the invitation rang out, Virginsky was taken deeper into his emotional memory. He was once again the student who had not quite put enough work into his essay; whose hand as he reached for the door trembled with dread at the prospect of the imminent tutorial; who was nagged by a perpetual sense that he was squandering the valuable opportunities cast his way. And then something that had not occurred to him until now suddenly deflated his confidence even more: *He will not remember me!*

But as this new thought sunk in, Virginsky found it strangely liberating. He turned the handle and stepped into the professor's study.

Everything was as he remembered it: the vaulted ceiling that gave the room something of the feel of a grotto; the two arched windows hung with layers of elaborate drapes; the assortment of bookcases of varying sizes, fitted in willy-nilly, making the accumulation of knowledge seem like a haphazard venture, as perhaps it was; the same paintings and photographs hung on the wall; around them, the same dreary brown pattern of festoons, unchanged apart from being somewhat more faded; and at the centre of it all, the monumental desk, a great slab of mahogany on four square-set pedestals.

Tatiscev was seated at the desk, half-concealed by a console of low bookcases that rose from the front of it. His head was bowed over a large notebook in which he was writing. At last he looked up with a quizzical, distracted frown, half-impatient as if he were expecting a student. Virginsky felt an intense frisson of shock, caused not by how different Professor Tatiscev looked to the last time he had seen him, but how similar. He had always had something of the look of a Russian monk about him, yet he combined long flowing hair, and flat triangular blades of beard, with impeccable European tailoring, invariably from Kincherf's. Now, that beard was streaked with grey, and the hairline began a little higher up a forehead that had gained in prominence. His figure was still trim and sprightly. His eyes burned with a quick, perceptive energy. He seemed to take in Virginsky's presence without missing a beat. He did not even need to search his memory before exclaiming, with a jaunty stab of the finger: 'Virginsky!'

'That's correct, sir. I was sure that you would not remember me.'

'How could I forget you? You were my most . . . challenging student.'

'I hope in a good sense?'

'Well, I like to be challenged, so any sense is a good sense. But yes, I meant it in the best possible sense. Your questions kept me on my toes.'

Virginsky had the slight suspicion that his old professor had him muddled with someone else. 'I . . . am flattered, sir.'

'I see you have entered the service.' Was there a note of disappointment in the question?

'Yes, sir. I hope to reform it from within.'

This provoked a burst of deep, unrestrained laughter from Tatiscev. Virginsky felt himself blush. 'Forgive me. I see you are in earnest.' Tatiscev smiled indulgently. 'Still and all, it is good to see that your radical spirit remains undimmed.' He turned his crimped eyes on Porfiry Petrovich. 'You have brought a friend with you, I see.'

'This is my superior, Porfiry Petrovich.'

'I am honoured to meet you, Professor Tatiscev.' Porfiry blinked pleasurably and bowed his head.

'So, this is the great investigating magistrate, Porfiry Petrovich.' Tatiscev rose from his seat and extended a hand.

'You have heard of me?'

216

Virginsky tightened his lips in displeasure. To him, Porfiry's astonishment seemed affected.

'I am a professor of law,' said Tatiscev, gesturing for his guests to sit down. 'I make it my business to follow all the important cases passing through our courts. I think it's fair to say that you have been associated with many of the most notable, not to say sensational.'

'I have not deliberately courted sensation.'

'I was particularly interested in a case of several years ago. That of the former student Raskolnikov. It interested me, amongst other reasons, because I had taught the fellow.'

Porfiry took in the news with two sharp blinks. 'How interesting. I did not know.'

Tatiscev seemed to detect something recriminatory in Porfiry's response. 'In my defence, I would say that I have taught many students who did not go on to become murderers. In fact, by far the majority of those graduating from my classes show no signs of murderous inclinations whatsoever.'

'So you do not consider yourself responsible for Raskolnikov's misguided acts?'

'In all conscience, I can say that I do not.'

'There are some who would blame you for every crime committed in Russia.' Porfiry's tone was bantering. 'Or perhaps you are not familiar with certain editorials appearing in a number of conservative publications.'

'The number being two, both of which are edited by the same man. You are talking about *Russian Era* and *Russian Soil*, I take it?'

'I am.' Porfiry smiled.

Tatiscev dismissed the articles with a sweep of the hand. 'Have you really come here to talk about libellous innuendo printed in those disreputable Slavophile gutter rags? And, I might add, written by a pseudonymous hack.'

'Curiously, we have.'

'We do not take them seriously, of course,' put in Virginsky.

'I hope I have made that clear,' added Porfiry. 'As far as I can see, there is no substance to the vitriolic attacks, which seem rather to have been prompted by a personal vendetta than any credible political opposition. What interests us is the identity of the author.'

'I cannot help you there. I have no idea who wrote them.'

'Oh, but we do.'

Professor Tatiscev gave Porfiry a startled glare. He quickly recovered his composure. 'How interesting. Are you intending to prosecute him?'

'I fear it may be too late to do so,' said Porfiry.

'What do you mean?'

'We fear he may be dead. A body was found in the burnt-out wreck of his apartment. A definite identification is impossible. But it seems very likely that it is the man who wrote the attacks on you.'

'I don't understand.'

'Have you ever heard of a journalist called Demyan Antonovich Kozodavlev?'

'Kozodavlev? But Kozodavlev would not write for Trudolyubov. He despises everything that man stands for!'

'So you do know Mr Kozodavlev?'

'Not personally,' said Tatiscev quickly. 'I know *of* him, of course. I am a great admirer of his work. I subscribe to a number of journals he contributes to. He would never write for Trudolyubov. It is inconceivable.'

'And yet he did. Under the pseudonym of K.'

'I don't believe it!'

'It can be proven,' said Porfiry wearily, as if he would rather Tatiscev did not call upon him to do so. He compromised with an appeal to Virginsky: 'Is that not so, Pavel Pavlovich?'

'It seems to be the case,' confirmed Virginsky, heavily.

'What interests us, and, frankly, why we are here, is the question of why Mr Kozodavlev took it into his head to pen these terrible and baseless attacks on you. Especially if, as you say, you did not know him personally, but only through his work – that is to say, the work he produced under his own name.'

'I really have no idea.'

'You described the attacks as libellous. Did you never think to seek redress in the courts? You are a lawyer, after all.'

'Like you, I did not take them seriously. They were an irritant, but one that it was easy enough for me to ignore. In all honesty, I did not consider that they damaged my reputation, so much as that of the scoundrel who published them. The best action, I decided, was to take no action.'

'At any rate, it appears that you need not concern yourself any more about the continuation of these articles.'

'Are you suggesting that I had a motive for killing this man? But I had no idea he was behind it all. How could I? And I rather suspect that Trudolyubov will find some other hack to take up the cudgels against me.'

'They call you the Devil's Professor, you know.'

'Do they really? I have no idea *what* they mean by that.'

'It is an allusion to your atheism, I believe.'

219

'But that really is absurd. Yes, I am an atheist. Which is to say, I do not believe in God. By the same token, neither do I believe in the Devil. An atheist cannot also be a Satanist. They have proven themselves to be imbeciles, as we always suspected.'

'Perhaps that was why Kozodavlev wrote the articles,' said Virginsky suddenly. His former professor and his superior looked at him with interest. 'Not to attack Professor Tatiscev, but to subvert Trudolyubov. By tricking Trudolyubov into publishing these ridiculous articles, he succeeded in bringing his newspapers into disrepute. Perhaps he was hoping to provoke Professor Tatiscev into pursuing a defamation charge.' Virginsky addressed Tatiscev directly: 'Which he was confident you would win, sir. What he could not bank on was your admirable restraint.'

'If so, it was rather a subtle plan of his, and one which I rather wish he had not undertaken – at least not without consulting me first.'

'But perhaps he did,' said Porfiry, mischievously.

'But I have already told you that I did not know this Kozodavlev.'

'Oh, yes, you did, didn't you!' Porfiry grinned foolishly. 'Sometimes it is difficult to retain all the essential elements of a case in one's mind. Particularly as one gets on in years. Generally, I rely on Pavel Pavlovich to be my memory.' Porfiry reached across and clasped Virginsky's arm firmly. 'He is a pillar of strength to me.'

Virginsky very much wanted to shake Porfiry off, but contented himself with glaring resentfully down at the hand on his arm.

Porfiry at last released his grip and leant back complacently in his chair. 'If you don't mind me saying so, Professor, you look to me very much like a man who ought to believe in God.'

'What on earth do you mean by that?'

'You have the look of a mystic.'

Tatiscev gave a derisive snort. 'If Kozodavlev had written that, then I would have sued for defamation, truly.'

'Have you ever heard of Vissarion Stepanovich Lebezyatnikov, a former professor of history, I believe?'

'Lebezyatnikov? I have heard the name.'

'He too was a victim of K.'s attacks.'

Professor Tatiscev shrugged. 'Again, I do not know him personally. But of course, in this case, there is no reason why I should.'

'In this case?'

'I merely meant that with Kozodavlev, you might have expected our paths to cross, given our shared interest in radical politics.'

'But you have never met Professor Lebezyatnikov?'

'I cannot say that. There is a chance we may have encountered one another. Was he a professor here at the university?'

'For a time. Perhaps one of your colleagues in the History and Philology Faculty will remember him?'

'Perhaps.'

Porfiry brought both hands down on the arms of his seat. 'We will take up no more of your time. Thank you very much for your help, Professor Tatiscev.'

'But I fear I have been no help at all!' There was a glimmer of desperation in the professor's eyes.

'It is always helpful to talk a case through, especially with a distinguished professor of law such as yourself.'

Virginsky was horrified to see his superior flutter his eyelids in a manner so insincerely sycophantic as to be insulting. He noted that Professor Tatiscev was by no means taken in. He regarded Porfiry Petrovich mistrustfully. It seemed he did not quite know what to make of him, and for that reason alone perhaps, reserved a small portion of fear amongst his evident contempt.

19

The pastry vendor

It took a moment for the genteel chatter of the confectioner's to fall silent. But Salytov knew that the silence would come, to be broken only by gasps and the perilous clatter of silverware on china, as heavy-handled forks fell from involuntarily relaxed grips. It was the moment it took for everyone to notice him, for the full horror of his melded face to be absorbed.

He was used to this. Every time he walked into a roomful of strangers, he experienced a similar reception. And yet it did not lessen his willingness to go abroad. He had no intention of turning himself into a recluse. On the contrary, it was with a certain pride that he held himself upright, thrusting his posture upwards against his cane, facing down the looks of shock and pity with angry contempt. He wanted to scream back at them, *That's right, look at me! I got this face for you, you ungrateful pigs!*

Eventually, as happened now, the conversation would resume. Those who had stopped to stare at him would gradually tear themselves away from the freak show of his face, and turn their attention once again to their pastries and their companions. For Salytov, it was almost worse when they did. For in that moment he was left alone with his disfigurement.

The fat German woman avoided looking at him as he approached. No doubt, she would not recognise him from the last time he had visited the shop, before the bomb blast. Perhaps that was just as well, thought Salytov, without exploring his reasons for thinking that.

'I am looking for Tolya.'

Recognition skittered wildly in her eyes at the sound of his voice. She looked up and stared searchingly into his eyes. 'You?'

Salytov lifted the angle of his head disdainfully.

'You have nerve, coming here.'

'Tolya,' insisted Salytov.

'Master will not be happy to see you.'

'Do you think I care? But I have not come to see your master. I have come for Tolya.'

'Always Tolya. Still you persecute that boy. He is a good boy. You leave him alone.'

'I merely wish to speak to him. He is not in any trouble. That is to say, he will not be in any trouble so long as he co-operates with me.' After a moment, he added, 'And is not found to have done anything criminal. If that is the case, then, naturally, he will feel the full force of the law come down upon him.' Salytov rammed the tip of his cane against the floor to reinforce his point.

'He is not here. Master let him go. After all the trouble.' From the woman's scowl, it was clear that she held Salytov responsible.

'Where is Tolya now?'

The German woman's nose wrinkled distastefully.

Salytov lifted his cane and slapped it threateningly into his spare hand. 'I'm sure you don't want any trouble, like last time. Then your master had Tolya to blame. Now . . .' Salytov pointed the tip of his cane at the woman.

'I heard he sell pastries in Gostinny Dvor.'

As the door closed behind him, he sensed the explosion of relief, as the customers burst into conversation, far more garrulous and excitable than that which his entrance had quelled.

*

Everywhere Salytov looked, he saw a reflection of himself. He was standing on Sadovaya Street, facing the longest of Gostinny Dvor's frontages. This stretch of the great bazaar, where the mirror sellers clustered, was known as 'Glass Line'. Here, the windows of the vaulted arcade were given over to displays of looking glasses of every size and shape, fragmented walls of reflection that threw the observer's image back in his face. It was not a comfortable place for Lieutenant Salytov to stand. And yet he did not, for the moment at least, turn away or move on.

There was no doubt a streak of masochism in his nature that kept him rooted there, confronting the multiple glimpses of his damaged flesh. It was as if he needed to remind himself what he had suffered, in order to understand who he had become. But however many mirrors he stood before, and however long he looked into them, he would never be able to relate the grotesque stranger he saw to his own sense of himself.

He thought of his wife. That woman never tired of looking into a glass. In her younger days, it was no doubt because she had been gratified by what she saw. She had once possessed a fresh, heedless prettiness that could trip his heart. The years, in which she had borne him seven children, had taken their toll on her looks. Now when she scoured the surface of a silver-backed glass, it was as if she was desperately seeking an image of herself that she knew must be in there somewhere, but which had somehow slipped out of sight. Or perhaps she was simply watchful, not trying to recapture her youthful looks but determined to track and capture every sign of their disintegration. There was something obsessive about her fascination with her own face. It had acquired an added piquancy since Salytov's accident. He had the feeling that his wife looked more intently into her own face now that she could no longer bear to look into his.

Salytov entered the market and pushed through the cluster of mirror sellers' stalls. A tradesman in blue kaftan and cloth cap approached him from the side and accosted him with the usual spiel: 'Step this way, sir . . . only the finest examples of the mirror-maker's art . . . such a flawless reflection as you have never –'

Salytov waited until the man had got this far before turning his full face towards him. It was enough to silence him. He began to back off, one hand gyrating in confusion and apology, his face drawn in horror. 'Halt,' commanded Salytov. 'Do you know a pastry seller by the name of Tolya?'

The stallholder continued to back away as he answered Salytov: 'There's a fellow I sometimes see wandering the lines. Could be a Tolya.'

'Have you seen him yet today?'

'He has not been this way yet, sir. He treads a well-worn route. There is a pastry cook who has a concession upstairs in the gallery, over on Linen Line side. By the name of Dasha. She should be able to tell you where to find this Tolya at any given time of the day. It could even be that Tolya works for Dasha, sir, if you see what I mean – taking her pastries abroad for her.'

Salytov gave a curt nod, which was as close as he came to expressing gratitude.

He left the arcade and stepped into the central court of the bazaar. The cries of stallholders vying for business echoed around him, at times drowned out by the squawks of the caged birds they kept hung around the entrances to their shops. From those who were busy came also the sharp clack of flying abacus beads; from those who sat idle, the clatter of dice in the cup and the click of backgammon pieces on the board.

The looking-glass traders gave way to art dealers, first those selling secular paintings, and then the icon dealers. Jewellers, watchmakers, cabinetmakers, dealers in tables, chairs, beds ... the place was like a living encyclopedia of household commerce, arranged in categories and sub-categories, a criss-cross of themed lines. Sometimes the transition from one group to another was gradual and subtle, as if one trade was slowly mutating into another.

Now and then, a trader – not simply to amuse himself it seemed, but more to strengthen links with his neighbouring stall-holders – would hoof a ball along the line, over the heads of the hapless shoppers, landing it skilfully at the feet of his mate a hundred or so *arshins* away.

It was with some relief that Salytov ducked out of the central courtyard, to take the stairs to the upper gallery.

He found the pastry stall near the corner of the Nevsky Prospect and Surovskaya Line arcades, a simple matter of following his nose. The greasy odour provoked a rush of salivation and a twisting sensation in his belly, as if his guts were being wrung out.

He waited for the woman stallholder to finish serving a savoury pie to a young man in a battered top hat. His complexion was as flaky and pale as the pastry. The pie flew to his mouth as if subject to some strange magnetism. He did not see Salytov; his whole being was absorbed in the consumption of that pie. Salytov communicated his distaste with a conscious sneer.

The woman met Salytov's gaze with the shopkeeper's look of habitual, almost disengaged, expectancy. She had the napkin ready and the tongs poised over her array of pastries. She gave the impression of having been on her feet at her stall since the first days of Gostinny Dvor, over a hundred years before, with every expectation of remaining there for a hundred more years.

'Where will I find Tolya?' Salytov demanded abruptly. He allowed his police uniform to explain his interest.

A flicker of commercial disappointment showed in her face, but she quickly recovered from it. 'You could try the Linen Line. He treads the same path every day, and at this time of the morning he is usually there or thereabouts.' It was clear that she wanted to be rid of Salytov as quickly as possible. Salytov sensed this and hated her for it. To punish her, he lingered pointlessly, keeping his eyes fixed on her warningly. 'Will there be anything else?' she asked at last.

'What?' he snapped, as if outraged by her effrontery.

'A pie perhaps?' Was there a trace of mockery in her smile?

Salytov glowered. 'Madam, a man of my position cannot be seen to buy pies from the likes of you.'

'If you don't want a pie, then you'd best be gone. You're scaring away the paying customers.'

'I could close you down . . .' Salytov clicked his fingers. 'Like that.'

'I have a business to run. I've told you what you want to know. Why do you pick a fight with me?'

The question seemed to take Salytov by surprise. At last he began to back away from the stall, although he kept his eyes fixed on her warningly.

Returning to the inner courtyard, the clamour of the caged

228

songbirds seemed louder and more insistent than before. Salytov allowed his instincts to lead him, through avenues hung with lace and shawls, to the Linen Line. He made enquiries as he went, and eventually closed in on the itinerant pastry vendor, clamping a hand on his shoulder as he pushed his cart away from him.

As Tolya turned to see who was detaining him, his look of mild enquiry changed to horror.

'Do you recognise me, lad?'

'You?'

Salytov nodded. He worked at the muscles around his mouth to produce something that he hoped would approximate a smile.

'What do you want from me?'

'This face – do you know how I got it?'

Tolya shook his head.

'It was not hawking pies, I can tell you that.'

'How . . . did you?'

'A *bomb*,' cried Salytov, his voice exultant. 'I was one of the lucky ones. I survived. Some of my friends, my fellow officers, did not. They tell me you had nothing to do with it. But I am not so sure I can believe that. All I know is that I was investigating you and your associates at the time. And then . . .' Salytov pointed at his face. 'This.'

'I had nothing to do with it.'

'Do you remember that day I broke your stilts?'

'Yes.'

'I can do much worse than that, let me tell you.' Salytov looked down at Tolya's cart with a threatening leer.

'What do you want from me?'

'Answers. The last time we met, you were working at Ballet's. There were two men in there. Friends of yours. Disreputable-

looking individuals. One of them has turned up dead. This one.'
Salytov handed Tolya a photograph of the man from the canal.
'He had a badly pockmarked face. Give me a name.'

Tolya looked as if he was going to be sick. 'Pseldonimov.'

'Who was he? What was he? How did you know him?'

'He was a customer at the confectioner's.'

'Don't play games with me, lad. He was more than that.'

'He was a printer, I think, or something like that.'

'Something like that?' Salytov barked back sarcastically. 'What
does that mean? Either he was a printer or he was not.'

Tolya drew himself up. The years since his last encounter with
Salytov seemed to have emboldened him. 'You are a difficult man
to help, Lieutenant Salytov. I was going to say, there were rumours.'

Salytov glared at him, as if outraged at his impertinence. 'What
rumours?' His tone was suddenly less abrasive.

'Rumours that he engaged in illegal activities.'

'Pamphlets? I remember we found pamphlets at your lodgings.'

'Pamphlets, yes. But also . . . counterfeiting.'

'I see. And when was the last time you saw him?'

'I haven't seen him for years, I swear. Not since I left Ballet's.'

'You expect me to believe that?'

'I need not have told you about the counterfeiting,' cried Tolya
in outrage.

'Oh, but you know that it would have been worse for you if you
had not.'

'I swear, I have seen neither him nor Rakitin since that time.'

'Rakitin?'

'The one who was always by his side.'

'I remember him. Grubby individual. Where is he now, this Rakitin?'

'He used to live in the Petersburg Quarter. I don't know if he lives there still.'

'Give me a pie,' demanded Salytov.

Tolya angled his head warily. 'What sort of pie would you like?'

'I don't care.'

Tolya selected a pastry and wrapped it in a napkin. His movements were constrained by suspicion. Reluctantly, he held it out to Salytov. 'That will be five kopeks.'

Salytov stared blankly at Tolya, as if he had not heard. He did not take the pie.

Tolya started to withdraw the pie.

'What do you think you're doing?' Salytov touched Tolya's wrist with his cane, halting the withdrawal.

'Do you want it or not?' demanded Tolya.

'That's very kind of you.' Salytov snatched the pie. He held it for a moment and then tipped his hand so that it fell onto the floor. A moment later, he raised his foot and stamped it down on the pie, squashing it into the ground. 'Give me another one.'

'Are you going to pay me for that one?'

'You gave it to me. A gift. Remember.'

'This is my livelihood. I cannot afford to have you–'

'My livelihood,' cut in Salytov, 'is tracking down criminals. When you withhold information, it is just the same as me treading on your pies.'

'I'm not withholding information. You didn't give me a chance. You don't have to do all this. I would have told you everything I know anyhow. I have told you everything I know. I haven't seen Rakitin for years. All I can say is he used to live in a house in the

Petersburg Quarter. I did go there once. If you wish, I can tell you where to find it. But I cannot promise that he still lives there. He may do, but if not, someone there may know where to find him.'

'Are you telling me how to do my job, lad?'

'No.' Tolya closed his eyes, his face trembling in exasperation.

'Because I would not presume to tell you how to sell pies.'

Tolya clamped his lips together.

'Right. Let's get going.'

'Where?'

'To this house in the Petersburg Quarter, of course. You're going to take me there.'

Tolya looked down in despair at his cart.

'You won't be needing that.' Salytov made a sharp gesture with his cane to hurry the pastry vendor along.

20

A friend of the family

'How extraordinary,' murmured Porfiry Petrovich, as he closed the door to his chambers.

'What is it?' asked Virginsky.

Porfiry handed over the slip of paper that he had received from his clerk Zamyotov only a moment before.

Virginsky read: *The Dolgoruky Residence, Liteiny Prospect, 10.* 'What is so extraordinary? That is the correct address, I believe.'

'I asked Alexander Grigorevich to make enquiries about Lebezyatnikov's address. This is what he discovered.'

'Lebezyatnikov lives with the Dolgorukys?'

'That would seem to be the case,' said Porfiry. 'I wonder what his connection with the family is. Princess Dolgorukaya does not seem to be the sort to take in paying lodgers. Still, appearances can be deceptive. When necessity speaks, and all that.'

'Perhaps his relationship with the ageing princess is not that of a landlady and tenant. Perhaps he lives there on entirely different terms.'

'What are you suggesting, Pavel Pavlovich?'

Virginsky shrugged. 'He may be a friend of the family.' He handed the address back to Porfiry with an ironic ripple of his brows.

*

Porfiry detected no hint of surprise on the elderly butler's face as he opened the door. Years of serving an aristocratic Russian family had no doubt habituated him to the suppression of that emotion, to the extent that he now seemed incapable of feeling it. His tone was impatient and weary: 'I shall tell the Princess that you are here.'

'There is no need to disturb your mistress, Alexey Yegorovich. We have come to speak to Vissarion Stepanovich.' Porfiry enjoyed a moment of satisfaction as a tremor of elusive surprise did at last cause a small convulsion in the butler's face.

Alexey Yegorovich recovered himself quickly. 'Vissarion Stepanovich is out of sorts today.'

'I am sorry to hear that. However, I am afraid that we must insist on talking to that gentleman.'

The butler bowed and showed them into a drawing room, furnished and decorated in impeccable European style.

Some moments later, Princess Dolgorukaya herself burst into the room, a tiny purple tornado of agitation. 'It is out of the question. You cannot talk to Vissarion Stepanovich. I will not allow it.'

'With all respect, dear lady, you cannot prevent it.'

'He is an old man. An old fool. It will do you no good to talk to him.'

'Allow me to be the judge of that.'

Princess Dolgorukaya scowled severely at Porfiry. 'I insist on being present while you interview him.'

'That will not be necessary.'

'Do you suspect him of some misdeed? Vissarion Stepanovich is a confused and silly old man, but he is not a criminal. You have my word on that.'

'Really, Madame, this is a matter between ourselves and Vissarion Stepanovich. We are not at liberty to discuss it with a third party.'

'How dare you! I am not a *third party*. I am that man's sole benefactor and friend. You will have me to answer to if Vissarion Stepanovich is upset.'

'Please, be assured, it is not our intention to upset him. We merely wish to ask him some questions.'

'Oh, but you don't understand. That's the very thing that will upset him. He finds it very, *very* difficult to answer questions. It is simply the cruellest thing you can do to him.'

'Nevertheless, we must speak to him.' Porfiry watched the elderly princess closely. Remembering the cool demeanour she had shown yesterday, with her chilling denial of maternity, it was hard to believe that this was the same individual in front of him now. What was consistent – he saw now – was her wilful obstruction. In neither case had he interpreted her behaviour as obstruction. She was simply the disappointed mother and the anxiously solicitous friend. But for the first time he began to suspect that there might be an element of pretence to her conduct. She was presenting personas.

The Princess seemed to detect something she did not like in Porfiry's attention. 'Very well, speak to him if you wish. He is not a child. I am not his mother. He must answer for himself, and pay the consequences. I have done all I can to protect him.' She was withdrawing from the fray, certainly, but only because she saw that it was necessary to do so. She had sensed Porfiry's suspicion, and chose to nip it in the bud. However, she had missed the right psychological moment to do so.

At any rate, she left the room abruptly, possibly to take herself out of the range of Porfiry's consideration.

The door opened one more time and a gentleman entered the room with such force that it seemed he had been propelled into it. This could only be Vissarion Stepanovich Lebezyatnikov.

He was past the prime of his life, though by no means as advanced in years as Princess Dolgorukaya had led them to believe. In fact, the man was little older than Porfiry himself, or so he judged. He was dressed carelessly, a silk dressing gown thrown over crumpled trousers and a grubby waistcoat. His shirt lacked a collar and he wore no necktie. Strands of white hair stood up from a naked skull. A stubble of several days' growth silvered his face.

Lebezyatnikov clutched a large, far-from-clean handkerchief in one hand, which he dabbed to his rheumy eyes. 'Forgive my appearance. I was not expecting guests. They told me I didn't have time to dress. *Quelle dommage!* I appear before you *en déshabillé*. And you are magistrates, they tell me.'

'That is perfectly alright. You are Vissarion Stepanovich Lebezyatnikov?'

The Princess's anxiety about the effect of questions on her protégé's nerves was borne out. 'What? What is this? Good Heavens. I never. Am I Vissarion Stepanovich Lebezyatnikov? My good sir! What kind of a question is that? If I am not, then I do not know who I am. And even if I am, then perhaps the same may be said. Am I Vissarion Stepanovich Lebezyatnikov indeed! How is one to begin to answer such a question?'

'A simple yes will suffice.'

'Oh, but will it? Will it, indeed? Let us say, for the sake of argument, that I possess the name you mentioned. Where does that get us? Does it get us any closer to understanding the essential man behind the name? I am more than just a name, I hope, even if that name be Vissarion Stepanovich Lebezyatnikov.'

'But that *is* your name?'

Lebezyatnikov held his finger down the length of his nose and inhaled noisily. 'I prefer that question.'

'Will you deign to answer it?'

'That is my name. That is to say, it is the name by which I am known. To go further, the name by which I have always been known. It is not too much to speculate that it will be the name by which I will continue to be known in the future, for the rest of my life we might say, and perhaps beyond, if I am remembered at all after I have gone. Perhaps I will be remembered fondly by some of those I have touched, in one way or another, on this journey through life. By some of my former students perhaps. Of course, it is my fervent hope that my name will, from time to time, form itself upon the lips of my lifelong friend and benefactor, Yevgenia Alexeevna. However, she is an old woman, not in the best of health. One must face the possibility that I may outlive her, though how I will survive when she is gone, I tremble to think. I can only trust to her generosity and consideration. Oh, she scolds me horribly – every day! But she has a heart of gold. She will not abandon me, even in death.'

Porfiry and Virginsky watched spellbound as Lebezyatnikov dabbed non-existent tears from his eyes and then took a moment to recover his composure.

'As for any wider remembrance of my name by the general public,' he resumed at last, 'that is too much to hope for. Except that there were some verses of mine published in my youth. I flatter myself to think that they may have left the imprint of my soul on the receptive ears of unknown readers. Oh dear – can a soul leave an imprint on an ear? I'm not sure. It seemed that it could, but now, I think perhaps it can't. I shall have to think about that one. To return to the name of Vissarion Stepanovich Lebezyatnikov, yes, it is mine, but it was given to me by my parents. Not so much given to me as thrust upon me. I had no choice in the matter. And I will say this to you, there are times, even now, when I wake in the middle of the night in a cold sweat with the question "Who am I?" ringing in my ears. The answer comes, "You are Vissarion Stepanovich Lebezyatnikov!" In response to which, the further question, "Yes, but who is he?" '

'For our purposes, it is enough that you are willing to acknowledge the name as yours.'

'If you gentlemen are satisfied with that, then so am I.'

'I can see that we are going to have to proceed carefully,' said Porfiry. 'I do not wish to unsettle you with unnecessary . . . questions. However, there are certain matters we wish to talk to you about. Indeed, we are utterly compelled to talk to you about them.'

Lebezyatnikov gasped.

'There is nothing to be alarmed about. I wish to talk to you about the articles that appeared in certain newspapers concerning you.'

'What is this? I have been defamed in the press?'

'Some lampoons appeared. The author was given as "K." '

'I have always had my enemies.' Horror dawned on Lebezyatnikov's face. 'And so you have come to arrest me! On the basis of these slanderous lies.' Lebezyatnikov clumped the handkerchief into a ball, which he as good as stuffed into his mouth. He took two tottering steps backwards and fell onto a sofa. He tried to speak, but his voice was muffled by the handkerchief. Removing it, he cried, 'I recant! I recant! Whatever I stand accused of, I recant! Let me write a letter to the Tsar. I will throw myself at his mercy! I will confess to everything. I will go back to the Church. I have never stopped believing, in my secret heart.'

'My dear sir,' soothed Porfiry. 'Please do not distress yourself. You do not stand accused of anything. The articles were clearly malicious – and really there is no substance in them. It is simply that we believe that the man who wrote them is now dead. We are talking to a number of people whom we can connect to him. In a general way, you understand.'

'And you have connected me with this man?'

'There must have been some reason why he chose to attack you in print.'

'The poems, I told you about the poems. That is where I can trace all this enmity back to. They may be interpreted metaphorically, you see. And there are those who do not like such an interpretation. Powerful individuals. I should never have allowed their publication. If I could take one thing back in my life, it would be that. But I was vain. I allowed myself to be flattered. The vanity of youth! It should have been enough for me that they were circulated in private, that certain influential figures read and approved of them. But I was prevailed upon. They said I had a duty to publish.'

'When ... was this?' asked Porfiry nervously. It seemed a simple question, but so too had asking the man's name.

'When? But what is the passage of time, when we are concerned with eternal absolutes? There exists, beyond the time-sullied world we know, a pure, perfect, *ideal* realm. I may be a creature of the former world, enslaved by appetite, shackled to the runaway locomotive engine of time, but my ideas belong to the latter realm, that of eternal absolutes. I trust my images are not too subtle for you?'

'Please, rest assured, they are not. But I believe you said the poems were published in your youth.' Porfiry consciously removed any interrogative intonation from the statement. 'The articles attacking you appeared quite recently. We must consider the possibility that something other than your metaphors provoked them.'

'I can think of no other reason why anyone would attack me.'

'The writer, we believe, was a journalist called Demyan Antonovich Kozodavlev.'

'Kozodavlev? Kozodavlev attacked me?'

'It would seem so.'

'But Kozodavlev is my friend.'

'So you do know Kozodavlev . . .'

'He is my friend, I tell you. He came on my name day. We drank champagne together.'

'He was a friend of Prince Dolgoruky too,' suggested Porfiry.

'Will you show me these articles?'

'I don't have them with me. I assumed you would have already seen them.'

'I never read the papers. Sometimes, I look back at old almanacs. It seems to me that that is the only way to understand events, with hindsight. I find what is happening now to be altogether too tumultuous. It overwhelms me. What is a man to do in the face of all these happenings?'

'I sympathise. I spend my life contending with the tumult of happenings. Tell me about Prince Dolgoruky. He has become estranged from his mother.'

'Yevgenia Alexeevna has a heart of gold, as I think I have told you. *Un véritable coeur d'or*. Mais, en effet, it is a peculiarly brittle kind of gold. Like gold that has been left out in the ice and snow. The frost has permeated it and it has become ... brittle. For Heaven's sake, do not tell her that I said this! She does not understand the subtlety of my images. She would not understand a heart of gold permeated with frost. Assuming such a thing is possible, of course. My subject is history, not the natural sciences. I do not know if gold becomes more brittle when subjected to the action of frost. I suppose it may be possible to conduct an experiment.'

'You mentioned history. You taught at the university, I believe.'

'The happiest days of my life ... until my enemies caught up with me.'

'I am surprised to hear you say that you have enemies.'

'Do you think I am too ridiculous to have enemies?'

'Forgive me, no. That is not what I meant to suggest. Too benign, too innocent.'

'It amounts to the same thing. It was Yevgenia Alexeevna who told me that I am too ridiculous to have enemies. Who would waste their time in becoming my enemy? That is her question to me. But I do have enemies. Perhaps it is my innocence that they hate.'

'You were talking about Prince Dolgoruky.'

'Ah, dear, sweet Konstantinka. Little Koka.'

'He didn't seem so little to me.'

'Not now, but when I taught him.'

'Ah, I see. You ...'

'I was his tutor for many years. In his boyhood ... You may say I stood *in loco parentis*, or more accurately *in loco patris*. His father died when he was an infant. Yevgenia Alexeevna . . . she . . . has a heart of gold, that woman.'

'Yes, of course, it goes without saying.'

'Her heart was in the right place, but it has to be said that she did not understand how to bring up a boy.'

'I see.'

'She was his mother, but she left much of his upbringing to me. It may be said that I was his solitary guiding influence during his formative years.'

'Oh . . . that is a great responsibility.'

'A burden! But I saw it as my duty, and I fulfilled my duty to the utmost of my abilities. In all conscience, I did the best I could for that boy.'

'I'm sure you did.' Porfiry smiled uneasily. 'Prince Dolgoruky –'

'My dear Kostyasha!'

'Your dear Kostyasha . . . acted as an intermediary – as a kind of agent, we might say – between Kozodavlev and the publisher of the articles against you. Without doubt, he profited from the transaction. He facilitated their publication.'

Lebezyatnikov let out a bleating cry and fell back in an affected swoon. 'You drive a dagger into my heart! A dagger, sir! And my heart is not metallic. Oh no, *my* heart is all too weak and fleshly.' Lebezyatnikov's gaze veered wildly, and then he seemed to fix on a distant point. Some kind of realisation came over him. 'I am to blame. I am to blame for everything.' He spoke quietly, though his voice was strangely firm. For all his absurdity and self-deception, he did not baulk at confronting this single devastating truth.

'Professor Tatiscev.' Porfiry simply said the name, and left it hanging there.

Lebezyatnikov turned a bewildered expression on Porfiry. 'What about him?'

'According to Kozodavlev, *he* is to blame for everything.'

'But that makes no sense.' Lebezyatnikov frowned at Porfiry. Then his expression became wary and sealed.

'Kozodavlev called him the Devil's Professor.'

'But Kozodavlev was an atheist.'

'And Prince Dolgoruky is hounded by the Devil.'

'He is an atheist too. I made sure of that. I taught him to turn his back on all such superstitious nonsense.'

'Even so, he sees the Devil. Perhaps that is proof of the Devil's existence, if he can be seen by a man who does not believe in him.'

'The Devil is a pervasive delusion.'

'There is something else I wish to tell you about Prince Dolgoruky.'

'Something worse? You have saved the worst till last?'

'He had printed a certain document, accusing himself of a number of crimes.'

Lebezyatnikov frowned darkly as he considered this information. Then his face suddenly lit up. 'It is his conscience! The boy has printed up his conscience! He acknowledges his crimes against me, and seeks forgiveness. There is hope!'

But Lebezyatnikov's face, in the aftermath of this assertion, was the most pathetic that Porfiry had ever seen. Behind the mask of optimism, the eyes showed utter desolation. The vaunted hope was nowhere to be seen.

21

The house of the retired Arab

The further they got from Bolshaya Street, the muddier the streets became, and the more disreputable the dwellings. Most of these were tumbledown wooden hovels.

The Petersburg Quarter had once been the heart of the city, its streets lined with the homes of the wealthy and well-to-do. Peter the Great had built his first palace here, albeit a modest one, as an example to his nobles. But the rich had followed the power south, across the river, closer to the heart, rather than the edge, of Russia. They had left the bleak northern quarter, the unpropitious territory reclaimed from Finnish swamps, to be colonised by the poor.

The streets were mostly unpaved, many not even boarded. Compared to the broad, brightly lit avenues of more southern districts, these were mean, dark, dangerous alleys. In places, the area could feel like nothing more than a maze of filthy dead ends.

Tolya directed the *drozhki* driver down a boarded thoroughfare, which, in the absence of an official name, had been dubbed Raznochinnyi Street – *the street of the classless ones*. The wheels clanked over the loose planks. They bounced in its wake like the bars of one of Gusikov's xylophones. At the far end of the street was Dunkin Lane, more a swamp of conjoined puddles, down which the driver quite sensibly declined to venture.

At Tolya's lead, they walked a short distance down Dunkin Lane, pulling their feet high with each step to free them from the clinging mud. Tolya stopped in front of a house that had once, fifty or so years ago, been a pleasant enough timber cabin. He studied the yellow nameplate on the gate. 'Yes, this is the place. The residence of the retired Arab.'

Salytov glowered at the nameplate. 'What does that mean? The residence of the retired Arab?'

'The gentleman who owns the house, Ivan Ivanovich – he is a retired Arab. That's how I can be sure we have come to the right place.'

'What in God's name is a retired Arab?'

'I don't know. It was once explained to me but . . .' Tolya trailed off despondently.

'Right. We will get to the bottom of this.' Salytov hammered on the gate with his cane. There was no bell.

Tolya took a couple of tentative steps backwards, away from the house, keeping his eyes on Salytov all the time.

'Where do you think you're going, lad?'

'I've brought you here. You don't need me anymore.'

'Oh no you don't. Only when I have Rakitin in my hands will I think of letting you go.'

'But he may not be here.'

'You had better hope that he is.'

An old gentleman, as pale as a candle from head to toe, dressed as he was in a white dressing gown and white *tarboosh*, came out from the house to open the gate for them. 'How may I help you?'

'Are you the owner of the house?' demanded Salytov sceptically.

'I am.'

'The retired Arab?'

'That is correct.'

'You do not look like an Arab. Your skin is whiter than mine.'

'I am not an Arab by race. But I am one officially, you see.'

'No, I do not see. Some kind of fraud has been perpetrated here, I'll warrant.'

'No fraud. My transformation to Arabhood was sanctioned by the authorities. I went through all the proper channels. It was my wife's idea. She heard that Arabs are retired from the service with twice the pension of ordinary Russians. "Ask them if you can retire as an Arab," she said. And so I did. I put forward a petition, stating my reasons –'

'Reasons? What reasons could you possibly have?'

'Well, my main reason was that I could do with the extra money.'

'That is a reason any of us could put forward!'

'There is nothing to stop you.'

'And your petition was granted?' Salytov was incredulous.

'My boss took pity on me. To be honest, I think the idea amused him. At any rate, he put me down on the rolls as an Arab and I retired on an Arab's pension. I recommend it, sir, when the time comes for you to retire.'

'I will not pass myself off as an Arab, not for any money.'

'It's twice the pension.'

'Enough!' barked Salytov. 'We have come for Rakitin. Does he still reside with you?'

'He does.'

'And is he at home today?'

'I have not seen him go out, your Honour.'

Salytov gave a nod of satisfaction. But the look he turned on Tolya was entirely devoid of mercy.

*

A knot of misery and fear tightened in his chest. The lieutenant was leaning with his back against the wall, next to the door jamb, looking out at him. If the door was opened, Salytov would be out of sight of anyone inside the room. Tolya could not look him in the face. It was not the ugliness of his disfigurement that repelled him but the unrelenting, unreasoning hatred in his eyes.

Tolya felt the cords of his emotions twisting and tightening even more, as if he were being bound and gagged from within.

He closed his eyes, so that he would not have to watch his own act of betrayal, and rapped his knuckles lightly against the door. There was an answering flurry of movement inside the room.

Salytov prompted Tolya further with an urgent nod.

'Rakitin? Are you there? It is I, Tolya. From Ballet's. Do you remember?'

The door opened a crack. An almost handsome face, marred by dark rings around the eyes, peered out. 'Oh. You. I thought it might be . . .' Rakitin broke off; his eyes shifted nervously.

'Who?'

'Never mind. Come in then.'

Salytov shook his head slowly at Tolya.

'No. I . . . I don't want to take up too much of your time.'

'You must come in,' Rakitin pleaded. 'You never know who is listening.'

Tolya sensed Salytov's smile. He was clearly enjoying the irony. A thread of anger now twisted itself in amongst the tangled mass of Tolya's emotions. 'Pseldonimov is dead,' he blurted.

'How do you know?'

'The police came to me. I didn't know what to think.'

'The police? What did you tell them?'

'The truth. That I haven't seen Pseldonimov, or you, for years.'

'Me? Why did you have to bring me into it?'

'You were his friend. You were always together whenever you came to Ballet's.'

'And so? You were not obliged to tell the police this.'

'You don't understand.'

'And now it won't be long before they come snooping round here. Thanks to you.'

'No, you don't understand. They knew all about you.'

'What are you saying? Was this the Petersburg police . . . or the Third Section?'

'The police. A policeman.'

'What did he know?'

'He knew that you were a friend of Pseldonimov's.'

'What of it? That is not a crime, even in this country.'

'But Pseldonimov is dead. He wants to speak to you about Pseldonimov.'

'Impossible. I cannot be drawn into this. It is too dangerous. Far too dangerous.'

'Why do you say that? Was he murdered? Do you know who killed him?'

'I cannot talk about it anymore. If you will not step inside, then I must –'

Salytov spun out of his hiding place and rammed his cane into the crack of the open door, leaning into it to prise it open further.

'You led them here!' cried Rakitin. He ran back into his room, clambering over furniture to get away from Salytov. After a moment of indecision, he threw himself towards the window, struggling to open the latch.

Salytov grabbed the belt of his trousers and hauled him back. 'Don't think of it. Don't . . . you . . . dare . . . think . . . of it.' The words were punctuated with blows from his cane, landed viciously on either side of Rakitin's torso. Rakitin fell to the floor and pulled himself up into a whimpering ball, his arms wrapped protectively around his head.

Tolya did not stay to witness the sequel to these events.

*

'Good,' said Porfiry quietly, as he turned away from the cell door. His voice lacked any enthusiasm for the sentiment expressed.

Virginsky flashed a questioning glare towards his superior. Porfiry answered with a minute shake of the head. But Virginsky would not be silenced. 'You commend *this*? The man can hardly walk.'

'He tried to escape,' said Salytov.

'Did you even have a warrant for his arrest?'

'I was acting on my own initiative. There are times when a policeman, out in the field, must do what he feels is necessary. He does not always have time to consult the rulebook.'

'You do not need the rulebook to know that you should not beat a witness!'

'One used to be able to. Before the reforms.'

'Well, it is no longer allowed.'

Salytov ignored Virginsky's objection. 'I brought him in, didn't I? It's up to you now. You can draw up the damned warrant now, if you're so determined to have one.'

'After the event?'

'That's how we used to do it.'

Virginsky shook his head in despair. 'Will we be able to get anything out of him though?' He directed his protest to Porfiry. 'The man is scared out of his wits. I am not sure he is even capable of speech any more. We should have a doctor examine him, Porfiry Petrovich. You know that.'

'Yes, of course. You will see to it, Pavel Pavlovich. If the doctor says he is well enough to be interviewed, we will proceed. In the meantime, we will allow him to rest.'

'May I also remind you, he is not a suspect. He is possibly a witness. Is this the best way to ensure the co-operation of a witness?'

'Very well, Pavel Pavlovich. You have made your points quite eloquently,' said Porfiry. 'However, we cannot undo what has been done. A policeman is granted licence to use all necessary force in the conduct of his duties. I am confident that Ilya Petrovich will not have exceeded the limits of *necessary* force.'

Virginsky's mouth fell open. 'What has happened to you, Porfiry Petrovich? What have you become? You say "necessary force", as if this is a perfectly civilised concept. But when the abuser is the one who determines what is necessary, what hope is there for the abused? Furthermore, why is he being kept in a cell? We do not normally throw witnesses in cells.'

'But he tried to escape,' insisted Salytov.

'No no,' intervened Porfiry. 'It is rather that we are short of space. We do not have any other rooms for him to recover in.'

'Why lock the door then?'

'Now that we have him, it would be a shame if we lost him, would it not? I believe that happened once before, Ilya Petrovich, and it caused us an inordinate amount of inconvenience.'

The red of Salytov's complexion intensified.

'But his rights! The man has rights, you know. The Tsar himself set them down in law.'

'His rights will be respected.' There was a hint of impatience in Porfiry's voice, anger almost. 'Now, back to my chambers. Ilya Petrovich, you will accompany us? I wish you to tell us all you can about this witness.'

'If you will excuse me,' said Virginsky, 'I will see to the doctor, as you requested.'

*

When Virginsky entered Porfiry's chambers later, he found the magistrate alone. A mist of tobacco smoke filled the room, and the air tasted pungently of Porfiry's familiar brand of cigarettes.

Porfiry blinked, as if the fug was bringing tears to his eyes. That did not prevent him from lighting a fresh cigarette. 'What did the doctor say?'

'Three broken ribs. Do you approve of that?'

Porfiry sighed out smoke. 'I do not like his methods any more than you do.'

'And yet you allow them. More than that, you encourage them. You complimented him.'

'I do not think I complimented him.'

'You said "good"!'

'I was not referring to Salytov's treatment of the witness. Merely to his success in tracking the man down.'

'Do you think Salytov is capable of making that distinction?'

'Men like Salytov . . .' began Porfiry.

'Yes?'

'His generation of policemen – those who entered the force before the reforms – will not endure. You are young. You must simply bide your time. The new recruits are being trained to honour the rights of our citizens.'

'But they still have the example of men like Salytov, whom they see encouraged by a respected magistrate.'

'I hardly think that one word, uttered in careless distraction, counts as encouragement. Besides which, if I remember rightly, you hardly gave me an opportunity to admonish him. For all you know, I may have been going on to say, "Good . . . Good *God*, Ilya Petrovich, have you any idea how damaging your behaviour is?"'

'Were you?'

Porfiry looked away sheepishly. 'That's beside the point. The point is that this witness may prove to be crucial in the case. I cannot regret that we have him in custody, even if I regret the means by which this was achieved. The fact that he did attempt to flee from a policeman is enough to confer suspicion on him. There is flexibility within the law – within the new law – for Salytov's conduct. A warrant has been drawn up.'

'In retrospect?'

'His known association with the dead man necessarily makes him someone we are desirous to interview. If he will not co-operate with our desire, I'm afraid we must resort to a warrant.'

Virginsky shook his head dismissively. 'This ability to compartmentalise the deeds of men like Salytov, accepting those that are expedient but turning a blind eye to the inconvenient abuses they commit, is the reason why such abuses persist. I would go further: it is the foundation upon which all the injustices of the regime are constructed. So long as men like you, Porfiry Petrovich, say nothing, then the state may do as it pleases. You urge me to bide my time, to simply wait for the extinction of Salytov's generation. I am afraid I must also be impatient for the passing of men like you, Porfiry Petrovich. If you will not stand up to the Salytovs of this world, then one must seriously wonder if you have any role in society left to you.'

'We are investigating a murder. My role in society is to keep on asking questions until we have discovered the person or persons responsible. It is as simple as that. I urge you to adopt a similarly narrow focus of concentration.' Porfiry ground out his half-smoked cigarette with premature finality, as if he had suddenly sickened of it. 'In my conversation with Lieutenant Salytov on our return from the cells I was able to glean a number of significant facts. Our man from the canal, the man with the pock-marked face, now has a name: Pseldonimov. I have asked Alexander Grigorevich to submit an enquiry at the Address Office. We should have Pseldonimov's last known address later today. We also have an occupation for him. He was a printer. There is more to it than that. He is rumoured to have turned his hand to certain illicit activities, such as the printing of manifestos, and counterfeiting.'

'Counterfeiting?'

'Yes. I am afraid so. Perhaps – after all – his death has more to do with common criminality than revolutionary politics.'

Virginsky hesitated a moment before asking, 'W-why do you say that?'

The slight falter in Virginsky's question provoked Porfiry's attention. Under his superior's calm and interested scrutiny, Virginsky felt himself blush.

'What is going on, Pavel Pavlovich? Do you know something about all this?'

'What do you mean? Why do you ask that?'

'You're blushing. And there was a decidedly guilty tone to your voice just now. And now you have adopted a bullishly aggressive one.'

'What nonsense!'

'What have you got yourself mixed up in, Pavel Pavlovich? Whatever it is, I urge you to confide in me.'

'I have been . . . pursuing a line of enquiry of my own.'

'And when did you intend to share this with me?'

'When I had something more concrete to go on.'

'What if, in the meantime, this line of enquiry of yours leads you into the company of dangerous men? And they find out who you really are – Pavel Pavlovich Virginsky, magistrate. The next thing we know, we are fishing you out of a canal.'

'They already know I'm a magistrate. So . . .' Virginsky shrugged. And then grinned, rather sheepishly.

'You fool! These men do not play games, Pavel Pavlovich.' Porfiry's hands were shaking as he reached for his cigarettes. 'Now, you will tell me everything. For God's sake, sit down. I cannot have you standing over me like this. My nerves will not tolerate it.' He threw his enamelled cigarette case back onto his desk without taking a cigarette out.

'I-I-I met a man.' Virginsky lowered himself hesitantly onto the artificial-leather sofa. 'On Easter Sunday. The night of the first fires, you will remember. I suspected him of being a *pétroleur*. It was something he said. Something along the lines of, I would always find him at such events. Anyhow, he gave me a copy of a manifesto. "God the Nihilist". You know the one. You had it in your collection. It was the one we linked to Kozodavlev. Through the scrap of paper we found in his apartment.'

'*We* found?'

'Very well, you found it. At any rate, I had been thinking about it, and last night I decided to seek him out again. I found him in a tavern in Haymarket Square, as he had said that I would. I offered my services to the cause. We talked about methods. He mentioned counterfeiting.'

'I see.'

'It is a method of destabilising the government. He said that they had employed it with some success. So, you see, it is not simply an activity of common criminals. Revolutionists engage in it too.'

'Do you have any idea of the risk you were exposing yourself to in talking to this man? There is not simply the danger from him and his associates to consider. Suppose he is being watched. That would bring you under suspicion – if you are not already.'

'I know what I am doing.'

'What? Does this mean you intend to continue in this course of action?'

'I can hardly back out now.'

'I cannot allow it.'

'Come now, Porfiry Petrovich. You and I both know that if there ever comes a time when you consider it necessary to the progress of the case, you will certainly allow it.'

Porfiry gave Virginsky a reproachful look, quickly averted.

The two men sat in silence for some time. Eventually, Porfiry picked up his cigarette case again and opened it, but only to count the cigarettes remaining. 'Seven,' he murmured, as if he were communing with his cigarettes.

'Porfiry Petrovich.' Virginsky's tone was sharp, almost hostile.

Porfiry looked up, startled, it seemed, to discover Virginsky still there.

'The man I met . . . he said I was to take him something, information, to prove my commitment to the cause. Do you have any suggestions? Something we can feed to them?'

Porfiry's expression was somewhere between bewilderment and anger. That is to say, he turned a flurry of blinking on Virginsky. 'But I forbid it. It is too dangerous. It will not happen.' He gave a decisive nod to underline the force of his intent. 'Now, I suggest that we interview our witness as soon as possible, so that he may be released without inconveniencing him any more than we have done already. It would be regrettable if he were forced to spend the night in the cell.' With that he began to heave himself up from his chair.

22

A visit from an old friend

'Are you quite comfortable?'

Rakitin looked up from the plank bench affixed to the damp wall of his cell. The grubby patches of exhaustion around his eyes seemed to intensify, shrinking in extent, but growing darker, as if the skin there was a touchpaper to his emotional state. The dark patches expanded now, closing in over his eyes. He looked around the cell and gasped in disbelief.

Porfiry blinked in astonishment at the mute bitterness of the response to his question. 'You do not want for anything?'

'Are you . . . mad?' Rakitin looked from Porfiry to Virginsky, his mouth lolling open in disbelief.

Porfiry held out his enamelled cigarette case. 'Would you like a cigarette, for example?'

Rakitin winced. 'It hurts . . . when I breathe.'

'We regret that it was necessary to use force to apprehend you. However, if you had co-operated with Lieutenant Salytov . . .'

'I've done nothing wrong!' The violence of his protestation caused Rakitin to double over in pain.

'I am glad to hear it. In which case, you will soon be out of here. I would also like to assure you that there will not be any charges brought against you for resisting arrest or obstructing the course of justice, provided you co-operate from now on. As soon as you have answered our questions, you will be released. It need not take long.'

'I have nothing to say to you.'

'Oh, I think you have. When you were told that Pseldonimov was dead, your reaction – according to Lieutenant Salytov – was not one of surprise, or shock. It seemed that you already knew about his death. "How do you know?" was what you said to Tolya. Is that not the case?'

'I didn't say that. Or if I did, I didn't know what I was saying. I was in shock. I must have been. Don't you see? Pseldonimov was my friend. So, yes. It was a terrible shock to me. I hadn't seen his ugly mug all winter. I had begun to fear the worst. I knew that he was mixed up in – well, things he shouldn't have been mixed up in. And so, when Tolya came to me with this news, it seemed that my worst fears were being confirmed. I wanted to be sure. I wanted to know from whom he had heard it. I didn't want to believe it.'

'Do you know who killed Pseldonimov?'

Rakitin hesitated a moment. He did not look at Porfiry when at last he gave his reply. 'No.'

'What *was* he mixed up in?'

'I don't know.'

'You just said he was mixed up in things he shouldn't have been. To what were you referring?'

'I don't know. It was just something to say. I meant nothing by it.'

'What are you frightened of? That the men who killed him will come for you?'

'I have told you all I know. You must let me go now. You have no reason to keep me.' Rakitin turned to Virginsky. 'Is that not so?'

Porfiry blinked quizzically at his assistant, while continuing to address Rakitin. 'I don't think you've told us all you know yet. Pseldonimov was a printer, was he not?'

Rakitin shrugged. 'It was no secret. He was a printer. What of it?'

'Where was his workshop?'

The smudges around Rakitin's eyes seemed to pulsate, as a tremor of panic vibrated under the skin. 'His *work*shop?' The intonation was designed to convey the evident absurdity of Porfiry's question, as if to say, *Why on earth would you want to know where his workshop is?*

'Yes, his workshop,' insisted Porfiry calmly. He at last turned to Rakitin with a beaming smile, above which his eyelids fluttered. It was so excessively and deliberately coquettish that, in the circumstances, it could only be interpreted as a threat.

'I don't know.'

'Did you never visit his workshop?'

'No.'

'And he never divulged its location to you?'

'No.'

'Not even in the most general terms? May we, for example, assume it is somewhere in St Petersburg?'

Rakitin shrugged. 'You can assume what you like.'

'My friend, this is not good. This does not help us. And if you do not help us, we cannot help you. Did they tell you where Pseldonimov was found?'

'What's that got to do with anything?'

'That's right, in the Winter Canal,' said Porfiry, ignoring

Rakitin's actual answer. 'Here, this is a photograph of what remained of him. Not a pretty sight, is it?'

'That is Pseldonimov?'

'The white patches are caused by the action of water on the flesh. You must disregard them. It is difficult at first – such is the transformation that has been effected. However, Lieutenant Salytov recognised him from the pockmarks on his face. The identification was confirmed by the pastry vendor. Can you not see it?'

'It could be him. It could be anyone.'

'I understand. You do not wish it to be your friend. How much more you must wish that it will not be you.'

'What do you mean?'

'We can protect you against the men who did this.'

Rakitin gave a derisive snort. 'If you don't mind, I would rather do without your protection.' He put a hand tenderly to the side of his chest and grimaced.

'Very well, you may go,' said Porfiry abruptly. 'You are right. We have no reason to hold you. It seems you do not know the dead man as well as we believed you did. Certainly, you cannot be counted among his friends. A true friend would not wish his murder to go unavenged. It is just as well you were not Pseldonimov's friend. Otherwise, his soul might consider your reluctance to help a betrayal.'

'You don't understand. It's not that simple.' Rakitin's eyes seemed to recede into the twin shadows of despair in which they were sunk. 'I begged him. I pleaded with him. I told him . . . not to get involved.'

'With what, exactly?'

'He was not . . . political. Not really. So it was no business of his. He was a grumbler, yes, and always short of funds. That didn't make him a revolutionist!'

'So he was involved in a revolutionary cell?'

'No!' The first force of the denial quickly decayed. Rakitin hung his head. 'I don't know,' he murmured. 'He went to meetings.'

'Did you go with him?'

'You expect me to inform on myself?'

'You are an intelligent man, I can see that. However, we are not the Third Section. We are magistrates, investigating a murder. The murder of your friend. That is all we are concerned with. We will not pass on any information you reveal to any other department.'

'I may have talked to people. Attended name days, or birthdays – perfectly legal gatherings – where discussions were conducted.'

'Discussions?'

'Yes.'

'Which touched upon . . . ?'

'Which touched upon matters that you may deem . . .'

'Revolutionary?'

'*Free* . . .' After a beat, Rakitin added, '*ranging*.'

Porfiry nodded thoughtfully. 'May I ask, what is your occupation?' The courtesy with which Porfiry framed the question was strange, given that he had asked far more probing questions far more bluntly.

Rakitin drew himself up with a self-conscious shiver. Somehow the gesture combined diffidence and assertiveness. 'I . . . am a writer.' The answer was a challenge, but one issued almost apologetically.

'My goodness, Pavel Pavlovich, what a troublesome breed these writers are! And who do you write for, *Russian This* or *Russian That*?'

'I don't understand.'

'It is his little joke,' explained Virginsky.

'You are a journalist?' asked Porfiry. 'I don't think I have come across your name in the thick journals, or the dailies for that matter.'

'I write for the *lubki*. Novels, mostly. I am sure you do not condescend to read such material.'

'Ah! I see! Literature for the masses! In my youth, I used to enjoy reading *lubki*. I do not have time now for such entertainments, I am afraid. My reading matter is largely professional. And woefully lacking in pictures, unlike *lubok* stories. But I would be interested in reading one of your . . .' Porfiry's inability to produce the appropriate word could perhaps be seen as insulting. He overcompensated with '*oeuvres*.'

'You can buy them at the usual places.'

'And do you write under your own name?

'I do. I'm not ashamed of my writings. On the contrary, I am proud of them. I know what my readers want. And I know how to give it to them.'

'And so, you are a literary gentleman. Do you mix in literary circles then? Do you, for example, know a journalist by the name of Kozodavlev?'

'They look down on us.'

'Us?'

'*Lubok* hacks like me.'

'Ah, I see. There is a table of ranks within the literary world.' Rakitin shrugged.

'So you have never encountered Kozodavlev? Perhaps at one of the name days or birthday parties you mentioned? Such events bring together individuals from every level of society. They are very democratic in that way.'

'*I* don't know any Kozodavlev.' The stress on the first-person pronoun was barely perceptible. But it was all that Porfiry needed.

'Did Pseldonimov ever mention a man called Kozodavlev to you?'

Rakitin avoided Porfiry's eyes, as if by so doing he could make the question go away.

'Think very carefully. Your friend, your dead friend, urges you to answer honestly, for his sake.'

'You speak for the dead now, do you?'

'Of course. That is my job. You have described my job very succinctly. I can see you have a gift for the well-polished phrase. I speak for the dead. I ask my questions on their behalf – on his behalf, Pseldonimov's. And I do not stop until I have the answers that will satisfy them. They have no one else to speak for them.'

'Kozodavlev, yes. I heard him mention a fellow called Kozodavlev once or twice.'

'Kozodavlev is dead too, you know.'

'No!'

'We believe so. His apartment was burnt out. A body was found. There is another name I wish to ask you about. Prince Dolgoruky. Do you know him? He operates on the fringes of the literary world, as some kind of go-between. He certainly worked in that capacity for Kozodavlev. Perhaps you have had dealings with him? Perhaps he even attended one of the gatherings you went to?'

'You are determined to turn me into an informer!'

'Not at all. We know that Prince Dolgoruky arranged to have

something of a personal nature printed up. There is a chance he gave the commission to Pseldonimov.'

'He wasn't the only printer in Petersburg.'

Porfiry smiled. 'Ah, so the workshop *is* in St Petersburg. And did Prince Dolgoruky ever visit it, I wonder?'

'Why don't you ask this Prince Dolgoruky of yours?'

'I am sure we will, when we next have an opportunity to speak to him. However, in the meantime, I am asking you. Did Pseldonimov ever mention Prince Dolgoruky?'

Rakitin opened his mouth as if to answer. But instead of words, the action seemed to produce a volley of urgent hammering. Porfiry bowed in apology to Rakitin, although it was clear he was relieved at the intrusion.

The cell door opened. The clerk Zamyotov peered in. His demeanour was unusually diffident. 'Porfiry Petrovich. There is someone who insists on seeing you, right now. I am to say that he is your old friend, Major Verkhotsev.'

'Verkhotsev? Here? Now?'

'Yes.'

Porfiry looked down pityingly at Rakitin. 'Please forgive me. I must talk to this person. I will be back to continue our conversation. Pavel Pavlovich, a word please.' He drew Virginsky over to one corner of the cell. 'Stay with him,' he hissed into Virginsky's ear. 'Get him to tell you about the workshop.' Porfiry gave a confirmatory nod and then looked once more, almost regretfully, at Rakitin, before stepping out.

Major Verkhotsev was waiting for him outside the cell, dressed in his sky-blue gendarme's uniform and accompanied by two of his junior officers, similarly attired.

So, this was an official visit.

'My dear, dear friend!' Verkhotsev held open both arms. Porfiry allowed himself to be embraced, and kissed several times on each cheek.

When he was at last released, he wagged a finger at Verkhotsev. 'This is not a friendly visit. One does not visit old friends with one's henchmen in tow.'

'Henchmen? What an awful word! But you're right. This is not entirely a social call.' Verkhotsev produced a sealed warrant and handed it to Porfiry. 'I have come for the witness.'

'The witness?'

'My witness, whom you have kidnapped.'

'I have kidnapped no one.'

'Now now, Porfiry Petrovich, don't play games with me. I think we know one another too well for games. And that reminds me, I hear you have been broadcasting my name, putting it about that I am some kind of contact of yours at the Third Section. That was very naughty of you.'

'We needed to look at the apartment.'

'No need at all. I'm sure you have enough cases of your own without poking your nose into other people's.'

'But I was working on my own case. That was what led me there.'

'You were investigating the death of Pseldonimov.' It was a statement, not a question.

'You know the identity of the body we found? But that has only just come to light.'

'We have known its identity for some time.'

'And you did not think to share your information with us?'

'We do not operate like that, my friend. It is not the way of the Third Section to share information. Although we do insist that others share their information with us.' Verkhotsev broke off to twirl one of his long waxed moustaches as he smiled at Porfiry. 'I sometimes think it must be very tiresome for the departments who are forced to co-operate with us.'

'You cannot force someone to co-operate, my friend. Co-operation is by definition given willingly. When force is involved, it is coercion.'

'Let us not split hairs. We will take Rakitin off your hands now. We had been watching him for some time and were about to bring him in when your Lieutenant Salytov pre-empted us. Ah, good old Lieutenant Salytov! I remember him well. Of course, how could one forget Lieutenant Salytov? Is he still trading in dead bodies?'

Porfiry ignored the question. 'I have not yet finished interviewing Rakitin.'

'No matter.'

'No matter?'

'It doesn't matter,' expanded Verkhotsev with a wink. 'To me.'

'Please don't start winking at me.'

'*You* cannot criticise *me* for *winking*!'

'What are you suggesting?'

'Come now, Porfiry Petrovich, let us not argue about such nonsense. The time has come to hand over Rakitin. You will see that the necessary documentation is all in order, signed and countersigned by the appropriate authorities.'

'Of course the paperwork will be in order. The Third Section is always scrupulous about its paperwork.'

Verkhotsev beamed delightedly. 'Ah! A savage attack disguised as a compliment! We are scrupulous in paperwork, but not in other matters. The barb was not lost on me, Porfiry Petrovich.'

'Tell me, how is your daughter, Maria Petrovna?'

'She is very well. Busy with her school, as always. And shows no sign of marrying. I shall tell her that you asked after her.'

'Do more than that. Convey to her my deepest affection. Please let her know that I wish her every happiness. And I hope to hear news of a betrothal before too long.'

'With pleasure. Now, is there anything else you wish to say to me before we take away the witness?'

'What do you mean?'

'I know what you're doing. You're seeking to delay me while your man – what's his name? Virginsky, isn't it? – continues to question the witness in there. You know, I could have just burst in and snatched him away.'

'That is effectively what you are doing.'

'Enough, Porfiry Petrovich. Deliver up Rakitin.'

'And what is to become of my case? Pseldonimov.'

'Consider yourself relieved of it. I have already supplied your clerk with instructions concerning the files, which will be delivered to Fontanka, 16 forthwith.'

'Very well. I wasn't getting anywhere with it anyhow. I will be glad to be rid of it.'

'That's a blatant lie, Porfiry Petrovich. If I know you, you were very close to solving it. It is not as difficult a case as some you have successfully concluded.'

'Ah, but as I have had occasion to say to you before, Pyotr Afanasevich, the moment the Third Section becomes interested in a case is the moment it ceases to interest me.'

'Then you will not object to me taking your witness?'

'Finally, you admit that he is my witness! But only when you sense that there is no danger of my contesting your appropriation of him. No matter, you may have him.' Porfiry gestured to the open cell door.

Verkhotsev gave one last contemplative twirl of his waxed moustache as he bowed to Porfiry. 'Might I suggest that you go in first and explain to him what is happening? We don't want to alarm him, do we?'

Porfiry blinked in ironic astonishment at Verkhotsev's apparent solicitude.

The rings around Rakitin's eyes were darker than ever: it looked as though he had rubbed them with inky knuckles.

Porfiry sighed despondently. 'I'm afraid matters have been taken out of my hands. You are to be handed over to another department.'

'What other department?'

'You have heard of the Third Section of His Imperial Majesty's Chancellery?'

Rakitin shifted back on the bench. He reminded Porfiry of a nervous animal scuttling for safety. 'No! Please! Don't let them take me!'

'There is nothing I can do to prevent it.'

'You said I could go, once I'd told you what I know. I'll tell you everything.'

'You mean there is something you have held back?'

'Call off the Third Section and I will tell you everything.'

'I'm afraid that's impossible. Besides which, I don't have any use for your information. I myself am no longer investigating Pseldonimov's murder.'

'But what about the dead? You speak for the dead, that's what you said. You ask questions on their behalf. And don't stop until you have the answers that will satisfy them. That's what you said,' insisted Rakitin.

'Yes, but I have been removed from the case. There are some men outside. They have come to take you with them.'

'Don't let them take me. I'll stay here with you. I'll tell you everything!'

'I'm sorry. There's nothing I can do.'

'Do you know what they will do to me?'

Porfiry held a clenched fist over his mouth, as if to prevent an answer inadvertently escaping.

The cell door creaked. The two officers Verkhotsev had brought with him came in.

'You must go with them,' said Porfiry quietly.

'No! No-o! I would rather die! Kill me! Kill me now!' Rakitin leapt to his feet but did not try to escape. Instead, he began fumbling with the belt of his trousers.

It took Porfiry a moment to realise what he was doing. In that moment, Rakitin had drawn his belt through the air, looped its tongue through the buckle and thrown this improvised halter around his own neck. He now pulled the belt tight. The two gendarmes rushed forwards and wrestled his hands away from the belt. Rakitin sagged forwards. The gendarmes caught him under the armpits and dragged him towards the door. For the most part, Rakitin was passive in their hands, defeated.

Just as they got him to the door, his torso shook violently and he managed to turn himself enough to face Porfiry. His eyes seemed, briefly, brilliantly white.

23

The secret agent

Zamyotov intercepted Porfiry just outside his chambers. The clerk's expression was unusually contrite. 'I really didn't know what to do for the best, Porfiry Petrovich.'

'That's quite alright, Alexander Grigorevich. You did what you had to do. You have sent off the file, I trust?'

'Yes.'

'Good.'

'You're not angry?'

Porfiry shrugged and shook his head. He laid a hand reassuringly on Zamyotov's arm.

'Porfiry Petrovich, they threatened me, those men.'

'What's this?'

'They took me into your chambers and threatened me. They said they knew all about me. About my . . . inclinations.'

'Alexander Grigorevich, I –!'

'I have tried to fight them, Porfiry Petrovich, but sometimes it is too much. I have to give in. I know I am vile and worthless. But the Third Section – they must have been spying on me. Or they have spoken to . . . my friends. They said they would expose me and prosecute me unless I co-operated.'

'This is an outrage!'

'So I had to tell them, Porfiry Petrovich.'

'My dear Alexander Grigorevich, what did you have to tell them?'

'The name of the victim. Pseldonimov. That's right, isn't it? I overheard Lieutenant Salytov tell you. I was not eavesdropping but you were standing right in front of me at the time.'

'You mean, they didn't know?'

'They didn't seem to know. Indeed they were most eager to find out.'

'I see.' Porfiry stood for a moment, giving himself over entirely to the act of blinking. 'The sly old fox.' He suddenly roused himself and bowed to Zamyotov. 'Thank you, Alexander Grigorevich. There is no need to worry. I shall see to it that nothing comes of this.'

'Thank you, Porfiry Petrovich.' Zamyotov gave a broad smile of relief. Then suddenly remembering something, he rushed back to his desk. 'Oh, and there is one more thing. This just came in. I didn't know what to do with it now that the file is closed. Should I send it on to Major Verkhotsev?'

Porfiry glanced down at the official slip. 'No need,' he said cheerfully.

*

'A long and eventful day,' sighed Porfiry, staring down at his empty desk. 'I suggest we hasten its end. There is nothing more for us to do, after all.'

'You are content to surrender the case to those . . . vipers?'

'I have no choice, Pavel Pavlovich.'

'I am surprised to find you so . . . passive. You are no Oblomov, after all.'

'You once, not so long ago, took great delight in comparing me to that exemplar of lethargy.'

'You remember that?'

'It wounded me.' Porfiry gave a pout.

'Well, I was wrong.' Virginsky's brows drew together in thought. 'He told me the address, you know. Rakitin. Of the workshop.'

'Oh, Pavel Pavlovich. What are we to do?'

'Should we not at least go there?'

'But what would be the point? No. What we *should* do is forward this information to Major Verkhotsev immediately, so that he can decide what action to take.'

'You cannot be serious?'

Porfiry considered briefly. 'You're right. If it turned out to be a false lead, then we would have merely wasted Major Verkhotsev's valuable time. It would be better, I think, to look into the matter ourselves, on our own time, and if we find anything we consider pertinent, only then need we trouble the Major. I'm sure he will appreciate our discretion. It can do no harm if you tell me where the print shop is, I suppose. If it is not out of our way, we will pay a visit. If it is too inconvenient, we will not trouble ourselves.'

'What if Major Verkhotsev finds out you are continuing in the case?'

'I'm *not*,' said Porfiry, ironically insistent. 'Do you not remember the hash the Imperial State Print Works made of the latest commission with which we entrusted them? It is possibly time for us to investigate other suppliers. Many government departments employ private print shops, I believe.'

Virginsky smiled and shook his head admiringly. 'Do you really think he will be taken in by that?'

'It is the truth! That is to say, it is one truth. We do need to look into sourcing new printers. Tomorrow is Saturday. We shall visit Pseldonimov's print shop, as prospective clients, in the morning.'

'Provided it is not too inconvenient to do so,' reminded Virginsky, mischievously.

'I trust it is not.'

'It is on Voznesensky Prospect. Close to where it crosses the Fontanka.'

'It is practically on our doorstep.'

Virginsky's smile broadened. But a shadow of doubt – or perhaps even fear – chased it away. 'And in the meantime, tonight, there is no time to waste . . .' He was aware of a heavy, fateful timbre in his own voice. The kick of his heart was suddenly stern, an inner alarm rousing him to a state of nervous expectancy.

'What are you talking about?'

'I must meet with my contact, the *pétroleur*. It must be tonight. I will tell him that Rakitin is in the hands of the Third Section.'

Porfiry said nothing.

'It is a piece of information of immense significance, and must be urgently communicated to him. He will know that Rakitin will talk. A man like Rakitin will not be able to hold out for long against the Third Section. You saw that in the terror of his reaction. His pathetic attempt to strangle himself. Of what do you think he was so afraid? Simply that he would betray his associates. That he would not be able to help himself. He *will* name names. And then, it will not be long before the Third Section closes in on those he betrays. Therefore, my contact will appreciate this information, because it enables the central committee to steal a march, to disperse . . .'

'And then what good would be served? We will lose them.'

'No. By then, I will have gained his trust. I will be on the inside.'

'But what if Rakitin is what he says he is? That is to say, a man without any real connections to any revolutionary grouping – the information will be of no interest or significance at all. You will be exposing yourself to unnecessary risk.'

'Yes, there is a risk. But there is always a risk. Even if I do nothing. Better to take the bull by the horns. Besides, I do not see another way for us to move forward in this case.'

'But there is no case anymore. Or have you forgotten?'

'We cannot simply allow these hoodlums to sidestep the judicial process,' cried Virginsky. 'Who knows what they will do to Rakitin, or if he will ever be seen again alive? One day they will be held to account.'

'I wonder, Pavel Pavlovich, whom you are intent on investigating: Pseldonimov's murderers or the Third Section of His Imperial Majesty's Chancellery?'

'It is not beyond the bounds of possibility that they are one and the same.'

'We have no evidence to suggest that.'

'And nor will we ever, unless I meet with my contact again. Tonight.'

Porfiry's expression grew pained. 'If anything happened to you, I would never forgive myself.'

'I take responsibility for my own actions, Porfiry Petrovich.'

'That suggests that even if I do not give my consent, you will go through with this. That – of course – would make you a revolutionary spy, you know, feeding secret information to the state's enemies.'

'Then you had better give your consent.'

Porfiry shook his head in forlorn protest. 'I thought you didn't gamble, Pavel Pavlovich. And yet this . . . this is far worse than any monetary wager. Here the stake you are playing for is your life.'

Virginsky clicked his tongue dismissively. He looked down at the floor, away from Porfiry's warning, to await his eventual acquiescence. He heard the cigarette case click open again. This time it was followed by the scrape and sulphurous whiff of a match igniting. When Virginsky at last looked at his superior, he saw him exhale a long cone of smoke. At the same time, he gave an upward tilt of his head, fixing Virginsky with a gaze that was for once utterly unblinking.

*

Virginsky stepped out onto Stolyarny Lane and thought of food. It was night. The lamps were lit. For its size, Stolyarny Lane was well illuminated: the presence of a police bureau counted for something. He felt a strange reluctance to take himself outside the protective glow. No harm could come to him, he felt, for so long as he could be seen. He sensed a voracious darkness lurking beyond the lamps' soft auras.

His stomach grumbled angrily. The claw of pain in his head dug in its nails. It had been clutching his brain all day, but now that he was released from duty, it tightened its grip for one last stab of torture. He knew that he was in no fit state to undertake the mission that he had so rashly, and perhaps feverishly, proposed. Equally, he also knew that it had to be done tonight, if it was to be done at all.

It was hard to believe it was only the night before that he had met the hatchet-headed man in the tavern on Haymarket Square. It seemed a lifetime ago. He realised, with a dawning sense of his

275

own stupidity, that he had been in such a state of intoxication at the time that he had no clear memory of which tavern the encounter had taken place in. However, he distinctly remembered the man's last words to him: 'If you can't find me, I know where to find you.'

He wondered if the man was watching him now, hiding in the vast darkness that surrounded the small pockets of illumination. He had the sense that the true city was constructed out of darkness, with shadows for inhabitants. By keeping to the light, he was drawing attention to himself as an outsider.

He had to remind himself that he wanted the man to find him. The plan relied on their meeting again. But Virginsky was so distracted by headache and hunger that he could not be sure what the plan was anymore. It was no longer clear to him whom, or what, he was serving, or even where his loyalties lay.

To distract himself, he fell into his old habit of counting his steps: *One, two, three . . .*

The first thing to do was to eat something. But that would not ease the pain in his head. For that, there was only one cure that he knew.

He counted his way to Haymarket Square. *Seventy-six, seventy-seven, seventy-eight . . .*

A boisterous crowd of *muzhiks* were passing the bottle around. Virginsky shied away from them and headed for the nearest tavern. His mouth was salivating as he stumbled down the stairs to the basement.

When it came to it, he ordered vodka first. He saw that his hands were trembling as he waited for his drink. The idea of the drink was more soothing than the drink itself, which did not provide the instantaneous easing of his discomfort that he had hoped for. However, for the time being at least, it seemed to steady his hands. Certainly, the bottle did not shake as he poured the second glass.

A display of collapsed pies drew his attention. In all honesty, he had never seen anything more unappetising. Nevertheless, he picked one out and watched with a mixture of impatience and horror as the landlady plated it for him.

It was the punch of petroleum in his nostrils that alerted him to the presence at his side. He turned and saw a familiar face, with a familiar lop-sided grin fixed in place. 'Hungry?'

'Yes, I am, in fact.'

The hatchet-headed man looked Virginsky up and down. 'Well, well, look at you, magistrate. Come to see me in your service uniform.'

'I have come straight from the bureau. I have something to tell you that cannot wait.'

'My goodness, you are an eager little magistrate. At least eat your pie first. The sound of your stomach churning is deafening. Come, there is a booth in the corner. We will be able to talk more freely there.'

They transferred to the booth, Virginsky making sure to take the vodka as well as the food with him. The table was covered in crumbs. A candle flickered, almost burnt out, the feeble flame surrounded by frozen rivulets of wax.

Virginsky took a bite of the pie, as he had been bid. He discovered it contained some kind of fish mixed with rice. It was devilishly dry. Despite his hunger, he had great difficulty swallowing the first mouthful. A swig of vodka helped to wash it down. 'There is something you must know. I trust you will pass it on to the appropriate people.'

'I am the appropriate people. As far as you are concerned.'

A chilling thought struck Virginsky. Suppose this man was not who he purported to be. Suppose he was simply a solitary crank, a fantasist without any connections to the revolutionary movement. The only link with Kozodavlev and Pseldonimov was the manifesto. But it was a common enough piece of trash. Even Porfiry had had a copy in his possession. Virginsky took a second bite of the pie, followed by more vodka. 'An urgent situation has developed. The Third Section have Rakitin.'

'Who is Rakitin?'

'Please. Don't insult me.'

'Why do you think I should be interested in this information?'

'If you do not understand the significance of it, you should pass it on to those who will.'

'You are sweating, magistrate. What's the matter? Is it hot in here?'

'I suffer from a medical condition. This comes upon me without warning. And for entirely no reason.'

'A medical condition, or a guilty conscience?'

'No. It is . . .' Virginsky drained his glass.

'Doesn't the vodka exacerbate the condition? Most of the drunks I know suffer terribly from the sweats.'

'It's not the sweats. It is something more . . .' Virginsky poured another drink. The bottle rattled in the glass. His hand was shaking again.

'Dear dear, the shakes as well. That does not bode well. We need men we can rely on, you know. Not alcoholics.'

'You must understand,' began Virginsky. 'This is very difficult for me. I am putting myself at great risk. I have given you valuable secret information. And what if you are an informer? You say you need men you can rely on. But how do I know I can trust you?'

'It is not necessary that you trust me. Simply that, when the time comes, you obey me.'

'But how can I give obedience without trust?'

The guttering candle finally went out. The man's features grew less distinct, his sarcastic smile lost in the shadows. 'Blindly. That is what we require of you. Blind obedience.' The man shook his head discouragingly. 'Now then, my dear magistrate, this information you have given me. It is nothing. It does not help us. We will need more than this before we trust you.'

'What do you mean?'

'Perhaps you could see to it that this . . . what was his name?'

'Rakitin. You know who he is.'

'Perhaps you could see to it that this Rakitin does not betray his friends, whoever they may be. Perhaps you could personally see to it that he is silenced.'

'Impossible. He has been taken away by the Third Section, I tell you.'

'Do you not have contacts in the Third Section?'

Virginsky thought for a moment before replying. 'No.'

'Then you know what you must do. Apply for a transfer into the Third Section.'

'But I despise them. I am against everything they stand for!'

'That remark reveals you to be a very naive individual.'

Although he could not see it, Virginsky sensed the man's sarcastic grin was back in place. He felt himself flush. 'If I may say so, your proposal is quite absurd. Even if I were able to secure a transfer, which is by no means certain, it would take time. That effectively rules out your plan as a means of silencing Rakitin. He would have informed before I had a chance to get anywhere near him.'

'Then you are no use to us. Superfluous. But it is no matter. We already have our people inside the Third Section. If the central committee decide that this is a matter that requires acting on, there is someone in place to silence this fellow. Indeed that is how you may know that you can trust me. Wait for news of Rakitin's . . . silencing.'

'You would have him killed?'

'If what you have said is true, then that would be the logical course of action.'

'Would it not be safer for the central committee to disperse?'

'The central committee is not interested in what is safer, but in what is necessary. If they disperse, the work will be abandoned. And all that we have struggled to achieve so far will be in vain. Yours is the suggestion of a coward.'

'I am not a coward.'

'I require you to prove it.'

'I have brought you this information.'

The man made a dismissive gesture with his hand. 'We knew it already.'

'Lie.'

'No matter. Whether it is a lie or not is irrelevant. It is not enough. We require more of you.'

'What?'

'Names. The names of police agents who have infiltrated re-volutionary cells.'

'Can't your spies in the Third Section discover this for you?'

'There is a list. But it is not widely circulated, even inside Fontanka, 16.'

'And do you think I would have access to it?'

'Oh, but it is essential that you should. As I am sure your superiors will agree. Tell them that you have the opportunity to infiltrate a terrorist cell yourself. Tell them as much of our history as you think is necessary to make the story persuasive. They will naturally give their consent. However, at this point, you will raise an objection. What if there is already a police agent in place? That would seriously complicate matters, and might put both of you in an awkward position. You would be working against one another, rather than together. If you are to undertake such a dangerous task, it is only reasonable that you should be forewarned with this information. They will see that. You will be given the list.'

'I'm not convinced your plan will work.'

'So far I have asked you to perform two tasks for the cause. You have raised objections to both.'

'I can only do what is possible. If you ask me to reach down the moon . . .'

'I would expect you to do it.'

'Is there not a danger that if I broach the subject of infiltrating a cell, it will arouse my superiors' suspicions? Furthermore, I will be expected to supply them with information about the cell to make the story credible.'

'Of course. We will select what you tell them. There is something that is very like information, but is in fact its opposite. Disinformation, you might call it.'

'There's no need to talk in such a roundabout sort of way. It serves no purpose. I understand perfectly well what you are talking about. Disinformation. Just say it.'

'So you will do it?'

Virginsky poured another vodka.

'Go easy on that, my friend. Remember, you are no use to us if we cannot rely on you. The cause requires sobriety and dedication. An almost ascetic devotion to the furtherance of our great task. Study the lives of the martyrs. You must become a contemporary martyr. No more fish pies and vodka. You must learn to live simply. To endure privation. And pain. Are you capable of that?'

'Yes. Of course.'

'My friend. We are not ungrateful. We realise that you have put yourself at some risk. That you brought us the information about Rakitin in good faith.' Virginsky detected a softening in the man's tone. 'We recognise in you considerable potential. We wish to encourage you, but you must be made aware of what lies in store for you if you continue down the path you have set out upon. In a word, danger. There will be rewards too, of course. When the time comes, you will be in a position to reap them.'

A waiter brought over a fresh candle. In its glow, Virginsky saw that the hatchet-headed man was smiling. His smile was almost kindly, and for once without any sarcasm. But as soon as the candle was placed on the table, the man stood up, as if the presence of light repelled him.

'Where are you going?' Virginsky's question had an edge of desperation to it.

'A friend of mine is having a party. It is his name day.'

Virginsky drained his glass and slammed it, more heavily than he had intended, on the table. A wave of vertigo rocked through his head as he sprang to his feet. 'Take me with you.'

'My dear magistrate . . .'

'My name is Pavel Pavlovich.' After a moment, he added, 'Virginsky.'

'I know that.'

'And what may I call you? It is absurd, if I am to accompany you to a party, for me not to know your name.'

'I have not yet said that I will take you.'

'Do I not deserve some reward for what I have brought you?' Virginsky's tone was becoming strident.

The other man looked around the tavern warily. The clientele was universally absorbed in its own dramas and drunkenness. No one was paying any attention to them. Even so, when next he spoke, his voice was hushed: 'We do not operate like that. Either an individual is committed to the cause, or he is not. The motivation must come from within and must be capable of withstanding every discouragement.'

Virginsky's crumpled expression suggested that he was far from being up to that challenge.

Perhaps the man took pity on him; certainly, his expression was contemptuous. 'My name is Alyosha Afanasevich.'

Virginsky tracked his implacable back as he left the tavern.

24

The name-day celebration

Alyosha Afanasevich set a brisk pace, zig-zagging east from Haymarket Square in the direction of the Moskovskaya District. It was all Virginsky could do to keep up, but he was determined not to let the man out of his sight. Alyosha Afanasevich had not, in fact, explicitly consented to take Virginsky to the party, but neither had he flatly refused. Since leaving the tavern, he had not addressed a single word to Virginsky, ignoring the questions that Virginsky fired at his back. All this, together with the speed of his march across the city, could be taken as an indication that he was trying to shake Virginsky off. Certainly, Virginsky had the impression that the man would not have turned a hair if he had simply stopped following him. But he himself could not bear the thought of losing Alyosha Afanasevich.

They walked along the northern embankment of the Fontanka, passing the riverside façade of the Ministry of Internal Affairs. The sight of the building reminded Virginsky of an earlier case, the first that he had worked on with Porfiry Petrovich. There would come a time, he imagined, when every building in St Petersburg would bring to mind one case or another.

It was a clear, mild night: under different circumstances, one for ambling unhurriedly alongside the river, anticipating the pleasures of the white nights that lay only a couple of months ahead. But this was no romantic stroll.

The force of the pace, coupled with the vodka he had drunk, was causing Virginsky to overheat. Despite his indulgence over the last two nights, Virginsky was not a habitual drinker. He welcomed the exercise as an opportunity to clear his head.

As Alyosha Afanasevich turned right onto the Chernyshov Bridge, Virginsky put on a spurt to draw level with him. Their footsteps reverberated over the arching stonework. 'Isn't it a bit strange, you fellows celebrating name days? I thought you urged the desecration and destruction of everything connected with the Church. Name days, after all, are Orthodox festivals.'

As their feet came down on the other side of the bridge, Virginsky at last succeeded in provoking a response from his companion. It was perhaps not the one he would have hoped for: 'Once again you reveal your naivety through your remarks. I hope you do not say anything so foolish when we are at my friends' apartment. Indeed, it would be best if you did not say anything at all.'

'Will your friends not think me rude?'

'I will tell them you are a mute.'

'Would it not be better to educate me as to why my question was so foolish? Then I will guard against making similar mistakes in the future. To me, it seemed a perfectly reasonable question, bearing in mind the manifesto that you once gave me. To mark the saint's day corresponding to one's name – one's *Christian* name – does seem a little at odds with the notion of God the Nihilist, do you not think?'

Alyosha Afanasevich gave a heavy sigh. 'Naturally we do not celebrate name days as devout Orthodox Christians celebrate them. Indeed, amongst ourselves we do not use the names our parents gave us at all. We have given one another new names, names more in keeping with our roles and our destinies. And you may take it from me that we do not give a damn for the calendar of saints' days.'

'What is yours?'

'What?'

'The name that your friends have given you? I take it they do not call you Alyosha Afanasevich.'

'No. To my friends, I am Hunger.'

'Hunger?'

'It is not a reference to physical hunger, to the hunger of appetite, but rather to my hunger for the revolution.'

'I see.'

'Mine is the hunger of the flame.'

'Yes. Quite. But why then are we going to a name-day party?'

'Because it is not a name-day party.'

'What is it then?'

'A pretext.'

'Ah, I see.' Virginsky nodded his approval. His eyes widened as if in excitement, but he said nothing, and indeed kept silent for the rest of the way.

*

Alyosha Afanasevich led them to a four-storey stone apartment building at the corner of Kuznechny Lane and Yamskaya Street. The neighbourhood was noticeably run-down. Not surprisingly: the Moskovskaya District was a predominantly working-class area, with a high proportion of peasant workers, migrants from the villages. Somehow, the dreariness of the area reflected the fact that the majority of its inhabitants were men living without women.

286

The nearby shops were all shuttered up, reminding Virginsky that there was also a significant Jewish population in Moskovskaya District. It was Friday, the Sabbath. While many of the shops on Nevsky Prospect might keep late hours tonight, those in Moskovskaya would not.

A few steps led down to the entrance of the building, below the level of the street. The porter nodded Alyosha Afanasevich in, as if he were a regular visitor.

They took the stairs up to the second floor. In truth, the interior of the building was better kept than Virginsky had been led to expect from the air of general neglect outside. The doors of the apartments they passed were all closed, presenting blank, demure rectangles of respectability. Perhaps they were the apartments of Jewish families, devoutly observing the Sabbath within. But even the door to the apartment they were visiting was closed.

'This doesn't look like the apartment of someone who is celebrating a name day,' Virginsky observed, as they waited for Hunger's complicated series of knocks to be answered. He thought he could detect the murmur of voices within, tense rather than celebratory. 'If you wish to construct a pretext, you should do so more carefully.'

'We cannot afford to admit all and sundry.'

'Then it is clearly not a Russian party.'

'It is intended to be an intimate gathering of close friends.'

The door began to move, drawing Virginsky's attention. He felt the thump of apprehension in his chest, sensing that he was standing at the threshold, not simply to an apartment in the Moskovskaya District but to a formless and irresistible abyss – to the future, in other words.

The face that greeted him, if such a look of hostility and suspicion could be said to be any kind of greeting, was elusively familiar to him. After a moment's concentration, he recognised the young 'Bazarov' who had discussed the physiology of the heart with Porfiry Petrovich at the office of *Affair*. Without opening the door to its full extent, the young man turned sullenly to Virginsky's companion. 'This man is a magistrate. Why have you brought him here? Have you betrayed us, Botkin?'

'Don't be stupid.'

Virginsky was struck by the fact that 'Bazarov' had used neither Alyosha Afanasevich nor Hunger in addressing the man.

'In the first place,' continued Virginsky's companion, 'I of course know that he is a magistrate. That is the very reason why I have brought him here. In the second place, you know better than to address me by that name.'

'Are you not Botkin?'

'Don't compound your stupidity with insolence!'

'If you have brought this magistrate here, then presumably you think you can trust him. And if you trust him, you will not object to him knowing your real name, Alyosha Afanasevich Botkin.'

'And what if I tell him your name?'

'I dare say he already knows it. He was at the office the other day.'

'I don't know your name,' said Virginsky to the young man.

'He is rather naive,' explained Botkin. 'Touchingly so, at times.'

'And so you think you will be able to manipulate him?'

'It is not a question of that. He wishes to help the cause.'

The young man regarded Virginsky sceptically, his expression slightly pained. 'I shall have to ask Kirill Kirillovich. It is his name day, after all.'

'That has nothing to do with anything, as you well know,' said Botkin.

'There are important people here. It is said that we are to be visited by a member of the central committee. Though, of course, none of us will know who he is.'

'How do you know that I have not brought him?' Botkin now treated the young man to the sarcastic smile he had practised on Virginsky.

The young man's expression grew unpleasant as he considered Virginsky afresh. 'Make up your mind. Either he is a new recruit who wishes to help the cause, or he is an important personage on the central committee. Which is it to be?'

'Let us in,' said Botkin, pushing at the door.

When it came to it, the young man did not resist. He let the door go with a strangely girlish laugh. 'On your head be it,' he threw out as he turned his back on them.

They followed him into an entrance hall with a number of doors coming off it. One door stood open, revealing a carelessly furnished drawing room where the assembly was already gathered, about twenty guests in all. The conversation was sub-dued, and in fact ceased completely as they entered. Virginsky was surprised to see women as well as men there. He thought he re-cognised some other faces from the office of *Affair*. Certainly he had the sense that he was recognised, and that the faces that were turned on him were far from welcoming.

A lean, somehow slovenly looking woman of about forty was handing out tea, which she served from a samovar on an oval table draped with a threadbare cloth. She bustled about the room with a sarcastic joviality, suggesting that she resented the presence of these guests in her apartment. She was taking great delight in keeping up the pretence of a name-day celebration. A man of about the same age as her, balding and anxious, rose from a sofa and approached Botkin. His face was careworn, brows pulled down in a permanent frown.

'Who is this?'

'Kirill Kirillovich, may I introduce Pavel Pavlovich Virginsky. A magistrate who wishes to perform a great service for the movement.'

'Can you trust him?'

Botkin did not reply, except to crank up the angle of his lopsided leer, as if to say that it did not matter to him one way or the other if Virginsky could be trusted or not.

'What do you mean by that?' demanded Kirill Kirillovich indignantly.

'Can I trust you? Can you trust me? Can he trust us? I mean to say, my dear Kirill Kirillovich, that trust is not an absolute. It is always relative, always provisional, never stable. Trust, whatever it is, is a highly volatile substance. I am not even sure it exists at all. And so, there is no meaningful answer to the question you asked. One must act as if there is trust between us, otherwise we could get nothing done. Still and all, at the same time, one must never lower one's guard. In essence, trust no one. Do not even trust yourself, Kirill Kirillovich.'

'That is absurd. More of your mysticism, Alyosha Afanasevich. You know that there is to be an important personage here tonight? I trust that nothing untoward will occur.'

'How do you know that there will be someone here tonight?'

'Why, you yourself told me!'

'Exactly. Therefore, I hardly think you need to issue such warnings to me.' Botkin scanned the room. 'Our people are all here, I see.'

'We are still awaiting Dolgoruky.'

Virginsky cocked his head sharply at the name. 'Prince Dolgoruky is coming tonight?'

'We do not recognise such titles,' answered Kirill Kirillovich. 'But yes, Dolgoruky is expected. Do you know him?' His frown darkened as he considered Virginsky.

'I have . . . met him. His name came up in connection with a case I was investigating.'

'And are you here investigating a case?' asked Kirill Kirillovich.

Before Virginsky could answer, the woman handing out tea thrust a cup into his hand. 'Everyone must have tea! If this is to be a proper Russian name day. Any friend of my husband's is a friend of mine.'

Kirill Kirillovich's frown changed its tenor in the presence of his wife. It seemed to go from something fierce and disapproving to a look of helpless despair. 'Varvara Alexeevna, this is not necessary, as you know.'

'Oh but it is, Kirill Kirillovich,' insisted his wife. 'We must create the semblance of a true name day, in the event of a police raid. At any rate, it is your name day. And we have guests. Why should I not give them tea?'

'Let us get on with it,' said Botkin. 'Dolgoruky is late. We cannot wait for ever.'

Kirill Kirillovich gave a sharp nod of assent. 'I for one am anxious to begin.'

Just as this was decided, there was an exuberant rap on the door.

'Dolgoruky,' said Kirill Kirillovich sourly.

'He does not even use the entry code!' complained Botkin.

'That is how we may know it is Dolgoruky.'

'If he will not trouble to learn the code, then he must not be admitted,' declared Botkin. 'We must teach him the discipline that he is incapable of instilling in himself.'

'Not admit the Prince!' cried Varvara Alexeevna, bustling past them to the door. 'It will be a sorry party without the Prince.'

25

The girl with the broken laugh

An explosion of laughter accompanied Dolgoruky's entrance to the apartment. Virginsky waited tensely for his appearance in the drawing room. He was suddenly aware that he had sobered up completely. At that moment, it seemed unlikely to him that he would ever drink vodka again.

Prince Dolgoruky stepped into the room with a faintly mocking smile on his face, as if he was struggling to take the whole thing seriously. It was also apparently impossible for him to suppress entirely the aristocratic disdain with which he habitually greeted everything – and everyone – he encountered. There was no sign of the tormented side of his Byronic nature, the devil-haunted individual Virginsky had briefly glimpsed at their last encounter.

Dolgoruky was accompanied by a much younger woman. Whether they had arrived together by accident, or whether Dolgoruky had brought her with him, was not clear. An instinct for jealousy inclined Virginsky to prefer the former explanation. Virginsky felt that he had seen the woman's face before. Perhaps she simply conformed to a type that was becoming familiar to him. She was physically attractive, although not in an easy or approachable way. There was something guarded and even aloof about her gaze, which was accentuated by an unusually long neck. He was sure he had not seen her at the offices of *Affair*. It was some time before that, perhaps long ago. He had the sense that she had changed enormously since the last time he had seen her, and that she would not have appreciated being reminded of it. He sensed the wariness in her assessment of him, and the flicker of alarm when something like recognition showed on her face. She was someone he had encountered in his official duties, he felt sure of that.

In the event, he was denied the opportunity of giving it any further thought. Dolgoruky approached him with a jabbing finger. 'I know this man. He is a magistrate. Did you know that, Kirill Kirillovich?'

'Yes. Botkin brought him here.'

'Botkin? Is this wise?'

'He is sympathetic to the cause. He wishes to help us. A magistrate could be very useful to us.'

'He was snooping around asking questions about Kozodavlev. Leastways his superior was. A most eccentric individual. He claimed I did not interest him!'

Virginsky sensed Botkin and Kirill Kirillovich regard him with a new and dangerous interest. 'It's true,' he confessed. 'We *were* investigating the death of Kozodavlev, in connection with a body found in the Winter Canal. The body of Pseldonimov. The secret information I gave to you, Alyosha Afanasevich, relates to that case. The fact of the matter is that we are no longer working on it. It has been taken from us. As I told you, Rakitin is in the hands of the Third Section. I have never hidden from you my position as a magistrate. On the contrary, I have shared with you useful information acquired through that position.'

'The information he gave me was, in fact, of limited usefulness.'

There was a chilling finality to Botkin's utterance. It had the ring of a sentence being pronounced.

'You see what you have done!' cried Kirill Kirillovich, in sudden panic. 'What kind of a man you have brought here! You have put us all in danger.'

Virginsky felt as if the room was closing in on him. Many of the guests had risen from their seats. They were pressing forward in response to their host's shrill cries. He noticed a vindicated smile on the face of the young man who had admitted them.

'What do you propose we do with him?' asked Botkin darkly.

'That is a question for you to answer,' bleated Kirill Kirillovich. 'You brought him here.'

Virginsky felt that his fate was being decided, and that the decision would not go his way.

'Wait!' It was the voice of the woman who had entered with Dolgoruky, clear and naturally authoritative. She seemed to turn the mood of the gathering with just one word. 'Let me ask you outright: What are you proposing? That we kill this man and dispose of his body?'

Now that she had expressed the matter with such chilling and almost gleeful directness, it seemed that the others began to back away from the idea. They were suddenly desperate for her to talk them out of it.

'Let me tell you, if that is what you're thinking, you are no worse than a gang of common criminals. We did not instigate the revolution in order to give men like you the licence to commit violent acts. Yes, we will be ruthless when the time comes. We will strike, and we will strike hard. If a head needs cutting off, I will be first in line with an axe. But we must choose our targets carefully. An ill-considered attack, prompted by panic, and executed without due diligence, can only serve to bring us to the attention of the authorities.'

She broke off to consider Virginsky. A wrinkle of distaste upset the balance of her face. 'This man may be a police agent, but I doubt it. Really, would even our police be so stupid as to send a serving magistrate to infiltrate a revolutionary grouping? I have had some experience of spies and informers, you know. In Paris, during the Commune. Invariably, it turns out to be the one you would least suspect. If you want to find the agent amongst us – and yes, you may be sure that there is already an agent amongst us, and has been long before this young man's appearance – there is no great mystery to it. You simply look for the man who most exemplifies the common stereotype of a revolutionist. Botkin is more likely to be a police spy than him. Or Totsky,' she added, as if to lessen the implicit accusation she had made against Botkin. The afterthought caused the young 'Bazarov' to blush, indicating to Virginsky that he was the Totsky she had referred to. 'The police – or the Third Section, or whoever wishes to infiltrate us – would naturally want their agent to fit in, not to stand out, as this fellow so pitiably does. Why, he did not even bother to get out of his service uniform!'

Her observation, facetiously made, provoked mocking laughter from the other guests. With it, the tension was released.

The young woman had possibly saved Virginsky's life. He sought out her eyes gratefully. It seemed at first that she was avoiding him, but when their eyes did meet, her expression was not what he had expected, or hoped for. There was the cast of something unmistakably unpleasant there, something indistinguishable from contempt. She looked away from him quickly. Her gaze had now acquired a constantly drifting restlessness that took

Virginsky more concretely back into his memory. For now he was certain that they had met before, and he remembered under what circumstances too. Now that he was able to place her, he realised that his intuition had been correct: she was very much changed.

'I would also say,' she continued, addressing the room at large, 'that the way to ensure the loyalty of those we recruit to our cause is not through terror but through education. When people understand what we are fighting for, when they share not only our convictions but also the fervour with which we hold them, we need not fear that they will betray us.'

Virginsky could hardly believe this was the flippant, cynically knowing girl he had met once before, the spoilt daughter of a lecherous father, the girl with the broken laugh, whose dangerous appetite for experience had brought her close to ruin. There was no note of cynicism in her voice at all now, and in her eyes no hungry glimmer, no desperate seeking after men's attention. 'Let us say,' she went on, speaking with a calm, unforced confidence, knowing that she could hold the room through her words alone, 'that there is here amongst us one who has come with the intention of spying on us. If, after an evening in our company, he has not converted wholeheartedly to our cause and volunteered to spy on his former masters on our behalf – well, then, we are sorry revolutionists. You might even say we would deserve to be informed against! For every word we utter is a revolutionary act. Therefore, we must make our every word count and carry the fight with us wherever we go. Comrades, to kill one who has come amongst us is a sign of our failure, as much as his disloyalty. It must only ever be done as a last resort.'

'But you do not deny that force may be used when necessary?' It was Botkin who asked the question.

'There! You see!' cried the young woman exultantly. Only now did Virginsky detect a sign of the nervous excitement that had once dominated her behaviour. She laughed, and it was the same broken laugh he remembered. 'How he seeks to entrap me! How like a spy!'

'Not at all. I was merely seeking to . . .' Botkin shook his head angrily. 'Oh, never mind. You know that I have the greatest respect for you, Tatyana Ruslanovna. Your experience during the Commune counts for a lot. No one doubts that you are a tireless worker for social revolution. However . . . you do not know men like I do. Sometimes, a measure of healthy fear can accomplish a lot.'

'I understand that.'

'Tatyana Ruslanovna.' Virginsky murmured her name wonderingly.

The young woman, serious again, gave a minute, almost imperceptible shake of the head, as if she were denying any connection with the person he might have associated with that name. Or possibly the gesture was a warning. Either way, it seemed that she remembered him.

'Enough of this,' said Kirill Kirillovich. 'We have kept our people waiting long enough.'

The meeting began chaotically. Kirill Kirillovich attempted to take the floor, on the grounds that it was his name day. However, he was shouted down, on the grounds that that was simply a pretext and had nothing to do with anything. Reluctantly, he gave way, although the look of sour disappointment remained on his face for the rest of the evening.

A grey-faced professorial type, older than most others there, stood up with a thick ream of papers in one hand. The groan of dismay was palpable rather than audible, an evident respect for his learning and revolutionary credentials acting as a restraint. He began to read from the papers. After a rather incoherent introduction, his thesis developed into a critique of Fourierism, tremendously pedantic and hard to follow. What made it worse was that his reading voice was a dreary monotone, pitched in an extraordinarily high register, making it uncomfortable to listen to.

He had not got far into his argument when Dolgoruky, who was perched on the arm of a sofa, interrupted: 'How much more of this is there?' His face wore an expression of disgust, and his tone was deliberately insolent.

The professor angled his head so that he was addressing Dolgoruky without looking at him. 'It is a complex subject. I have looked into every aspect of it.'

'How many pages do you have there, man?'

'One hundred.' The professor thumbed his pages and added, 'And seventeen.'

'You cannot seriously be proposing to read out all one hundred and seventeen pages!'

'If there proves to be insufficient time to read it all this evening, I will present the remainder at our next meeting.'

'But we will be here for all eternity. Trapped in this room, listening to you drone on and on about God knows what. And meanwhile the revolution will have taken place without us! This is what is wrong with you people! Don't you see? What we need is action. Acts! Not words. Especially not these words.'

Dolgoruky's outburst was greeted with stunned silence. Eventually, the professor gathered his wits enough to say, 'But there must be some theoretical basis for action.'

'Of course! And everyone here understands the theoretical

basis well enough. The tsarist regime is corrupt, inefficient and unjust. It must be got rid of. So, let us get rid of it!'

'But there is the question of how that is to be achieved. Ways and means.'

'I am very happy to join in that discussion.'

'And then there is the question of with what you will replace it.'

'I thought that was settled. Don't all you people want democracy?'

'Ah, but it is not so simple as that,' objected the professor, allowing himself a small smile of intellectual superiority. 'How does one ensure social justice after the initial revolutionary goals have been achieved?'

Dolgoruky waved his hand airily. 'We will cross that bridge when we come to it.'

'I agree with Dolgoruky,' said Botkin. 'To the extent that I think we should concentrate our discussions on practical matters. However, I also agree that it is important that our people have a firm grasp of the theoretical and intellectual bases of our movement.' He turned to the professorial type. 'I propose that you write a précis of your paper, which may be circulated amongst our people, for them to read at a more convenient time.'

'But it is impossible to précis my arguments. They must be heard in full, otherwise the nuances will be missed.'

'We do not have time for nuances.'

'Botkin's proposal is a good one,' declared Tatyana Ruslanovna. Her tone was conciliatory as she addressed the professor. 'We are grateful to you for the work you have put into this. And anxious that the fruits of your labour should not be wasted. Do you not see that a précis is the best way to ensure the propagation of your important ideas among the widest number of people?'

'But so much will be lost,' he complained forlornly. 'A précis will be meaningless.'

'You must try,' insisted Tatyana Ruslanovna. 'And now, let me, if I may, summarise what I believe to be the theoretical basis upon which any revolutionary act is based. As many of you know, a few years ago I lived for a while in Zurich, where I was sent by my family following certain unfortunate incidents in my private life.' She could not resist flashing an almost desperate look in Virginsky's direction. Rightly or wrongly, he had the impression that she was addressing her remarks solely to him. 'The man I loved was murdered. My father was even suspected of murdering him – in defence of my *maidenly honour* of course.' The harsh irony that had once, at the time of the events she was referring to, characterised almost all her utterances broke through her otherwise measured discourse. 'But in time I realised that I did not love that man after all. What I was in love with was the idea of escape, escape from my family, and in particular my father. I had looked upon the man I thought I loved as the means to achieve this escape. Indeed, that was why I persuaded myself that I loved him. But I might just as easily have fallen in love with a locomotive engine, or a horse. I was surprised when my family consented to my journey to Switzerland, granting me the escape that I had longed for. In truth, I think they saw me as a problem to be got out of the way. I was to enrol at the university there, which as you will all know not only allows female students to attend lectures but even allows them to take their degrees.'

The room was by now thoroughly settled, and content to listen to Tatyana Ruslanovna's narrative. The personal nature of her speech made it all the more compelling, especially coming as it did after the professor's dry, abstract dissertation.

'In Zurich, I received two educations, the first in medicine at the university, the second in political science, from the other Russian émigrés I met there. I began to realise that the latter was far more important to me than the former. To qualify as a doctor would enable me to lead an independent life, free of my family and the necessity of shackling myself to a husband. It was the way to personal freedom. But to gain an understanding of political science, and to bring that understanding back to Russia – that would lead to a far greater freedom, the freedom of my country.'

Her eyes seemed to flare with a visionary intensity. It was reflected in the eyes of all her listeners. Virginsky felt his own spirit ignited by it.

'And so I cut short my medical studies – I had gained enough practical knowledge to serve the Russian people as a doctor, if ever I was called upon to do so – and travelled to Paris. I was anxious to meet certain individuals there who could complete my political education. My time in the French capital coincided with the establishment of the Commune. Yes, I fought on the barricades. My medical knowledge was put to the test, treating the wounded Communards. As was my revolutionary zeal. I learnt how to shoot. I took aim at the enemies of the Commune and fired. I was prepared to kill for the cause, and, in the heat of conflict, I did. There were traitors to deal with, and I was as merciless as the Devil.'

Virginsky pictured her on the barricades, her face transformed by blood.

'Why was I there? Why had I thrown myself into the struggles of another nation? I was there for the millions who toil in back-breaking labour under the yoke of oppression. For the millions held back by ignorance and poverty, enslaved by an iniquitous economic system. I was there because my conscience demanded it! I came from a privileged background. I was the spoilt and capricious daughter of wealthy parents. I was one of the exploiters! How it shamed me to realise that. The whole of my life up to that point had been based on the exploitation of others. It was pointed out to me by one of my émigré friends that my father and mother, being of the gentry class and therefore exempt from taxes, contributed nothing to the welfare of the state. Far from it – their lives of comfort and ease were paid for by the people! It shocked me to learn that the entire burden of taxation in this country is borne by the peasants. That simple fact alone is the entire intellectual basis of social revolution. I have gone beyond shame now. Indeed, I hope that by renouncing my privileges, I have put my shame behind me. It is a question of necessity now.'

There were fervent cries of agreement from the young people in the room, and even some cheers.

'You are an inspiration to us all, Tatyana Ruslanovna,' said Botkin, but still with his usual sarcastic smile. 'You speak of necessity. Do you mean that the time has now come to erect barricades in the streets of Petersburg?'

'We must bring the struggle here to Russia. It is a struggle for the hearts and minds of the Russian people. Yes, if called upon, we will build barricades. But we must ensure that we have fighters to man them. That is why we must take our message to the people. We must go amongst the people. We will patiently explain to them how they are oppressed and that the time has come for them to throw off their yoke. The revolution must come from the ground up. It cannot be imposed from above.'

'You do not know the Russian peasant like I do. They are ignorant and lazy, not to mention superstitious. It is unlikely that such an initiative will be successful. What is more, they are stupidly loyal to the Tsar, their little father.'

'You must have faith in the people, Alyosha Afanasevich.' Tatyana Ruslanovna's tone was imperious, as if she believed in the power of command to change men's hearts.

'If you will forgive me, Tatyana Ruslanovna, that remark reveals your privileged background as much as your educated voice and aloof demeanour.' He smiled and added quickly, 'I hope that as comrades we may be honest with one another, without causing offence where none is intended. However, it is a tendency of the privileged intellectual to idealise the peasant, without any thoroughgoing experience of the peasant's true character. I speak from a position of expertise because, unlike you, I have lived amongst this class. My father was a village priest. He carried his scythe into the field on his back, and ploughed the land, and spread the muck, and brought in the harvest alongside the peasants. I have seen their superstition and ignorance at first hand. I know the uselessness of even attempting to educate these people, apart from a few rare exceptions. No, the education you talk about must take place after the revolution. First must come education through deeds. Education through fire, if I may put it like that. Political action *is* political education.'

'I agree with Botkin,' said Prince Dolgoruky. His voice had a sinuous, seductive quality. 'First we must open their eyes through terror. Then, when we have their attention, we will educate them.'

'It is not a question of political education *versus* terrorism,' conceded Tatyana Ruslanovna. 'We must engage in both. We must continue to propagandise, while destabilising the government through acts of violence and sabotage.'

'Quite,' agreed Botkin. 'I am suggesting nothing else. We must strike at the heart of the regime. We must lay bare the Tsar's weakness. When the people see that he is not even able to protect his own, that he is more concerned with the imminent birth of a bastard child than he is with their well-being, that he loves his mistress more than he loves them . . .' Botkin broke off to leer sarcastically at Dolgoruky.

Dolgoruky returned the compliment with a burst of cynical laughter. 'Yes, it is ironic to think that my dear cousin Katya is doing more to undermine the Tsar's position by bearing him a bastard than we ever could by blowing him up!'

'At any rate,' concluded Botkin, 'they will lose faith in him as their protector.'

Tatyana Ruslanovna smiled approvingly. 'An exemplary assassination? Is that what you are proposing?'

Botkin nodded, his smile reflecting her own. 'A government minister perhaps. Or a magistrate. What is more, we now have in place the individual who can undertake such a commission.'

Every pair of eyes in the room followed Botkin's gaze and settled on Virginsky. The eyes he was most interested in were those of Tatyana Ruslanovna. He saw in their gleam a challenge and an appetite to which he could not fail to respond. 'It would be an act of singular daring,' she said.

26

The print shop in the Spasskaya District

To the clerk Zamyotov's critical eye, Pavel Pavlovich Virginsky appeared extremely pale and distracted when he presented himself at Porfiry's chambers the following morning. No doubt Virginsky had been carousing into the early hours, in all likelihood ending his night of debauchery with a visit to one of the city's brothels. (Zamyotov had read all about such places in the *lubok* literature.) Virginsky was not even wearing his civil service uniform, but was dressed instead in a pale grey suit. The clerk shook his head woefully.

He had not been expecting either magistrate to make an appearance today. It was Saturday, after all, and, as far as he knew, there were no urgent cases in progress. Indeed, the case they had been working on had been taken from them. He himself had handed over the files.

And so, Zamyotov was more than a little intrigued when the two magistrates shut themselves in, Virginsky's tense, almost luminously pale face the last thing he saw in the closing of the door. At a suitable moment, that is to say when no one was looking, he placed his ear to the door, but it was hard for him to distinguish anything that was said within.

*

'Are you quite well, Pavel Pavlovich? You seem a little pale. I trust you have not been indulging in excessive alcoholic consumption again. Though, of course, what you do in your own time is no business of mine – provided you do not break the law, or bring the department into disrepute.'

'I fear that I may be about to do precisely that, Porfiry Petrovich.'

A strange, trembling tone in Virginsky's voice startled Porfiry into affording him the closest scrutiny. 'Whatever is the matter?'

Virginsky looked at his superior for a long time as he considered his answer.

*

Zamyotov's frustration deepened. It was quiet in the bureau today, but not entirely without traffic. And so his vigil on the other side of the door was regularly interrupted.

To compound it, even when he was able to press his ear to the door, it was practically impossible to hear anything, except for the groan of the wood against his flesh. Their voices barely rose above a mumble; they could have been discussing anything from Virginsky's dissolute nightlife to the price of straw. He was aware that the risk he was taking far outweighed any reward he received. And yet he could not completely tear himself away from the door.

He didn't have much warning: a sudden increase in volubility; footsteps within, hurriedly approaching the door. They were coming out. He darted back towards his desk, turning round with a look of feigned surprise just as the door opened.

'Ah, Alexander Grigorevich, there you are. Pavel Pavlovich and I have decided to do something about our printing difficulties,' announced Porfiry Petrovich, pulling on his frock coat as he came through the door.

'I beg your pardon?' said Zamyotov, in some amazement.

'You remember the mix-up over the poster? We have found out about another possible supplier and will look into it this morning.' Porfiry quickly locked his chamber door. He was evidently in a hurry to visit this particular print shop.

There was something suspect about this, Zamyotov felt sure. He looked from Porfiry Petrovich to Virginsky. Certainly the younger magistrate looked as relaxed as he might when about to set out on such an innocuous mission. The colour had returned to his face, which showed no sign of its earlier ravaged tension.

'But Porfiry Petrovich,' objected Zamyotov, 'you need not concern yourself with such administrative matters. Give me the details of the supplier and I will look into it myself.' After a beat, he added, 'At the soonest opportunity.'

'Well, you see. There you have it. The soonest opportunity. Pavel Pavlovich and I find that we have just such an opportunity available to us now. Our most time-consuming case was taken from us, so why should we not occupy ourselves productively in this way? If we are satisfied with what we find, we will naturally pass the details on to you to arrange the purchasing contract.'

'This is highly irregular.'

'Not at all. Think nothing of it. Good day.' Porfiry gave a small bow on the hoof, treating Zamyotov to a brief and excluding smile.

*

The sky above Sadovaya Street was clouded over, the endless strip of grey a memory of the winter gone. There was moisture in the air, which began to form into a light drizzle. The pale grey of Virginsky's suit was soon spotted with small dark circles, the size of five-kopek pieces. It seemed as though the seeping sky had singled him out, prompted by a misguided spirit of affinity, its grey communing with his.

The two men said nothing as they walked. Indeed, it seemed that there was nothing left for them to say, at least not until they had discovered whatever else the morning had to reveal to them.

The fourth Spasskaya ward neighboured on the Moskovskaya District, which Virginsky had visited the night before. Both had a significant Jewish population. As they approached the junction with Voznesensky Prospect, Virginsky noted an increase in the number of Jewish shops and business premises. The characters of the Hebrew signs were to him tantalisingly alien. Each one seemed to hold the secret to its own great mystery, and the promise of revealing it, if only he would step inside. But this was impossible, today being Saturday.

Virginsky thought back to the closed doors that he had seen as he had climbed the stairs of the apartment building, following Botkin to that fateful meeting. He thought of the lives of the families that he imagined living behind them; Jewish families observing the Sabbath. He felt an overwhelming surge of envy for what he took to be the simplicity and certainty of their lives, their innocence. As they lit the ceremonial candles, and enjoyed their Sabbath Eve meal, they knew nothing of the plots being hatched in the apartment on the second floor. He realised that he envied them their religion, as he envied Porfiry Petrovich his Christian faith. Perhaps he was not cut out to be an atheist, after all.

But religion was a lie; atheism an unblinking confrontation

with the truth. The former offered deluded consolation; the latter left him bereft, an aching weight of loneliness pulling at his heart. Atheism required men to model their own certainties, which crumbled to dust as soon as they clutched them.

In a godless universe, every door of that apartment building would have been closed on an identical meeting to the one he attended, the same plans discussed, and the same momentous decisions made. Even he, as an atheist, found that a chilling thought.

He stole a quick glance at Porfiry Petrovich. His face was calm, a mask of imperturbability. *Was that the effect of his faith?* wondered Virginsky. Was he really incapable of being shaken to his core? Could nothing, ultimately, surprise this plump little gnome of a man? For Virginsky knew that all his displays of astonishment, the endless flurries of blinking and grimacing, were nothing more than play-acting. This blank impassive screen of flesh that his face had for the present become, his face in repose, was the true Porfiry. He was in control of every tic that passed across it. And behind the face, what was there of Porfiry Petrovich that could be known? What of his soul?

Virginsky could not speculate about that. All he could say for certain was that the old man looked a little tired. Other than that, he showed no sign of unease.

They were walking south along Voznesensky Prospect, past the great Novo-Alexandrovsky Market. Recently constructed, it was the largest market in St Petersburg. It amazed Virginsky how it had so quickly taken root as part of the city's commercial establishment. At the time of its construction, the vast market, thrown up almost overnight, struck many as a reckless venture. Did they not have enough markets already? Where would the people come from to shop in it? And yet now, barely five years later, it was hard to imagine how they had managed without it.

This morning, the place was bustling with life. Again, Virginsky experienced a pang of envy, this time for the shoppers who streamed through it, troubled by nothing other than the need to acquire the day's provisions, or the desire to squander their week's wages on a small luxury. It was another kind of faith, another kind of certainty that drove them. And Virginsky almost wished it was enough for him. What would they make of the plots that had been hatched in their name? A part of him longed to follow the shoppers into the market, to lose himself in its avenues of stalls, to wander there aimlessly until the catastrophe of his life had passed him by.

But his feet were locked onto another course, from which he was unable to extricate himself. All he could do was count his steps, and as soon as he started to do so he felt strangely comforted.

They reached the Fontanka. And Virginsky suddenly felt that something more immediate than faith or certainty was lost to him, something acutely personal. Not even the counting of his steps could reconcile him to it.

*

The address that Rakitin had confided to Virginsky was for a building on the opposite side of the road, just where Voznesensky Prospect met the Fontanka embankment. The print shop was in the basement, entered directly from the street by a small flight of steps.

They walked into a din of black iron and lead, a rhythmic,

rolling clatter as ink was hammered onto paper and literature coughed out with a mechanical retch. Oil and ink tingled in their nostrils. The workshop contained three presses, all in operation, driven by belts from a rotating axle fixed to the ceiling. Each machine was tended by its own inky-fingered man in a long apron, like a worker bee fussing around its queen. The man at the first press looked around vaguely at Virginsky and Porfiry's entrance, but did not break off from what he was doing. Off to one side, a row of stoop-shouldered compositors stood at high angled workbenches, placing the metal type into formes with the absorption of surgeons.

At length, another man, also wearing an apron over a merchant's kaftan, emerged from a side door. He cast a foreman's eye over the work of the others, cursory but critical, and then approached the magistrates. 'Can I help you?'

'We wish to enquire,' Porfiry began, but his words were entirely swallowed up by the noise of the machine. He drew breath to shout: 'You are the foreman here?'

'I am the owner.'

Porfiry gave a mechanical smile.

'And the foreman. I see to everything.'

There was a sudden reduction in the noise from the machines, as one of them appeared to have come to the end of its paper supply. It was enough to allow Porfiry to speak more comfortably: 'You are the very man we need to speak to. We wish to know whether you can supply printed material to the Department of Justice.'

'That depends,' answered the printer, dubiously. 'How quickly you need it. How complicated the job. What is it for?'

'There is no specific job at the moment. We are simply looking into your . . .' Porfiry waved a hand around the workshop. 'Facilities. Typically, however, we require items such as posters and leaflets, to be produced very quickly.'

'We are not equipped for a fast turnaround. Right now, our presses are booked up for months to come. I have to plan jobs carefully, you see. There is a schedule of work. Perhaps if you came to us just as we were finishing a print run, we could fit your job in before we set up the presses for the next big one. But that would be a matter of luck. I couldn't stop the presses to accommodate you.'

'That seems rather inflexible. Does it not curtail your commercial potential?'

'It is simply the kind of work we are set up for. We have stop cylinder platen machines which we use for book and periodical production. We used to have a treadle-powered letterpress, which was ideal for the sort of jobs you describe. But it was stolen.'

'A printing press was stolen? Good Heavens.'

'It's not unheard of. It was a small machine, not like these beasts.'

'Who would have stolen it?'

'Well, you know . . . There are those who find it rather useful to have an illegal printing press, if you know what I mean.'

'It is a pity that you cannot help us. We had been led to believe that you could.'

'Really? By whom, may I ask?'

'Mr Pseldonimov.'

The foreman gave a snort of incredulity. 'Pseldonimov? I sincerely doubt it. Pseldonimov is not the type to have friendly dealings with the Department of Justice!'

'What do you mean by that, if I may ask?'

313

'Why, he is the one I suspect of stealing my press!'

'I see. And why is that?'

'For one thing, he disappeared soon after the press was stolen. I was dropping hints about it and things got too hot for him, so he scarpered. Good riddance, I say.'

'When was this?'

'Oh, it must have been six months ago. More. Last autumn, I believe it was.'

'How interesting. Did you report the theft of your press to the authorities?'

'Oh yes.'

'And your suspicions regarding Pseldonimov?'

The foreman gave a shrug. 'I couldn't prove anything. What was the point?' But his head was angled down, his eyes averted away from his interlocutor, evasively, or so it seemed to Virginsky.

'Perhaps you knew that he would meet his comeuppance anyhow,' said Virginsky.

The foreman gave him a startled look, as if he were astonished to discover that he could speak.

'Pseldonimov is dead, you know,' continued Virginsky. 'It might be said that you had a motive to kill him – or to organise his death.'

'I don't know anything about that. Look here, what is all this about? I thought you wanted to purchase some print work.'

Porfiry gave Virginsky a disparaging look. 'We do. That is to say, we did. But now we know that you are not able to help us. Unless, of course, you are intending to replace the stolen printing press?'

'I would love to, of course, but at the moment I don't have the capital. Our profit margins are very tight.'

'But with the promise of ongoing work from the Department of Justice, perhaps you could persuade the bank to supply a loan.'

'That's possible, I suppose.'

'Perhaps then, you would allow us to have a look around? Just to reassure ourselves that your facilities are up to the task. There are certain minimum standards that every government department requires.'

'Be my guest, though there isn't much for you to see. I don't have the press that I would use to do your work, as that depends on me getting the contract.'

'Understood,' said Porfiry, blinking suavely.

Virginsky frowned, as much to himself as for Porfiry's benefit. He was not entirely sure what they were looking for. It was so long since Pseldonimov had been at the workshop that he doubted they would find any meaningful evidence relating to him. And as for assessing the print shop's suitability as a supplier for the Ministry of Justice, he was hardly qualified to make a judgement on that.

None of this seemed to concern Porfiry, who gave every impression of being in his element. He wandered over to the nearest printing press and looked down at the growing pile of printed sheets, each bearing four pages of type, ready for folding and cutting into quartos. He gave a startled blink as each sheet jumped out from the jaws of the press. He soon appeared to be mesmerised by the action of the machine.

He turned to the foreman with a look of wonder. 'What is this?'

'We are printing a *lubok*.'

'A *lubok*! How fascinating. Perhaps you know a gentleman called Rakitin. He is an author of *lubki*. Perhaps you have printed some of his work?'

'We do not generally have dealings with authors.'

'But he was a friend of Mr Pseldonimov's, I believe.'

The foreman shrugged, as if this information was not of the least interest to him.

Porfiry gave a small bow to indicate that he had seen enough.

*

'What now, Porfiry Petrovich?' A small, blindingly white rupture in the clouds above Voznesensky Prospect drew Virginsky's gaze. The rain had dried up. The air was clearing.

Porfiry took out a folded piece of paper and handed it over. 'Pseldonimov's last known address,' he explained. 'It came in after the file had gone off to the Third Section.'

'Obvodni Canal Embankment, 157. You think we should go there?'

'It's not far. Just across the Fontanka and down Izmailovsky Prospect.'

'Yes, but we are not supposed to be investigating this case any longer. What possible reason could we have for going to Pseldonimov's lodgings?'

'A citizen has only just now reported the theft of a valuable piece of equipment. Do you not think he would be grateful if we were able to recover it?'

Virginsky shook his head in begrudging admiration, his mouth cranked into an involuntary grin.

*

Number 157 was only one door away from a dosshouse, on the

northern embankment of the Obvodni Canal. Facing the building, on the other side of the canal, was the Varshavsky Railway Station, and next to that the Cattle Yards. This was at the southern threshold of the city. There was a bleak, fragmented feel to the area, as if it barely cohered as a neighbourhood. It seemed an appropriate location for a night shelter for transients; equally fitting that the former lodgings of a murder victim should be next door.

They discovered that Pseldonimov had shared an apartment with six other men. That was nothing unusual for the Narvskaya District, of course, one of the poorest in the city. The yardkeeper who admitted them was a wily individual with cheeks so ruddy they seemed to be painted on and eyes that were little more than chisel slits in the hardened fabric of his face. The impression was superficially cheery, but if you looked into those permanently narrowed eyes, you saw reflected back at you an empty, instinctual cunning and a dark-hearted contempt. Pseldonimov's vacated bunk had long ago been filled, of course, and the yardkeeper pretended to know nothing of any possessions that had been left.

A man with a liverish complexion lay on a plank bed, covered by a coarse blanket. He was either drunk or dying, and at that time of the day, the latter was more probable. He raised himself with difficulty onto one elbow and pointed a trembling finger at the yardkeeper. In a voice that was astonishingly clear and robust, he said, 'He stole it all.' He fell back on his plank and closed his eyes. He lay very still now, and it almost seemed as though this surge of effort had hastened his end.

'He's delirious,' said the yardkeeper.

'Of course,' agreed Porfiry. 'But still, it is a serious charge. For a yardkeeper, who holds a position of trust and responsibility, to be accused of such a crime . . . it must be investigated. You will have to come with us back to the police bureau. Unless, of course, it is all a misunderstanding? Perhaps you were simply looking after Mr Pseldonimov's possessions until his relatives came to claim them? If that were the case, there would be no need for any investigation. It would be enough for you simply to show us the items and we could arrange for them to be collected and passed on to the parties concerned. I am sure there might even be a reward, if everything is found to be intact.'

'Yes, that's it. That's what I was doing. Looking after them. I have them downstairs.'

They descended to the yardkeeper's cellar, which was like a peculiar reversal of Aladdin's cave, in which it seemed items of the least possible value had been hoarded: empty pomade jars, chipped cups, broken figurines, cracked lanterns, handleless pans, shattered mirrors, as well as piles of old newspapers. The only explanation was that the yardkeeper's instinct to purloin was greater than his ability to discriminate.

The yardkeeper led them to the back of his one-room apartment. An olive-green drape hid a shapeless mass of further objects. Virginsky naturally imagined that these must be the items of genuine value secreted amongst so much dross. He pictured the mountains of jewels and precious metals, heaped coins and polished lamps that would be revealed when the drab cloth was lifted. The reality was inevitably disappointing. It did seem to be the case that these objects were more valuable than those on open display, but in truth that was not saying much.

The yardkeeper bent down and pulled out a cardboard box from under a table. 'These belonged to Pseldonimov.'

It was a box of handbills, printed on cheap paper. Porfiry pulled one out and handed it to Virginsky.

'God the Nihilist,' read Virginsky.

'My dear friend,' said Porfiry to the yardkeeper, his voice heavy with foreboding. 'This puts a rather different complexion on the affair. Here you are in possession of illegal manifestos. How do we know you are not intending to distribute them?'

'No, no! It's not like that. It's as you said. I have been keeping them. Looking after them. The reward! Don't forget the reward!'

'I'm afraid it is no longer a question of a reward. This is a very serious matter. As a yardkeeper, you are in a position of great position and influence. Why, it is almost the same as if I, or my colleague here, as if we magistrates, had such material in our possession. The courts come down very heavily on yardkeepers and magistrates who stray. An example must be set. Besides, the new juries do not like us, you see. They take great pleasure in punishing us.'

'But it need not come to court, your Excellency. I am sure I can persuade you to overlook this. What would it take?'

'Be careful, my friend. Do not add attempted corruption to the already serious charges you face.'

'But in all honesty, I didn't know anything about it. I hadn't looked inside that infernal box until just now. These were Pseldonimov's handbills, not mine.'

'Was there anything else of Pseldonimov's that you have been taking care of?'

'Just this box. That was all. If he had any other possessions, I don't know where he kept them.' Fear made the yardkeeper's words convincing.

'Very well. We will let the matter go this time. I will send a police officer to collect this illegal material.'

'And what about the reward?'

'Don't push your luck, my friend.' Porfiry nodded tersely to Virginsky and the two magistrates left the yardkeeper to his grubby trove.

*

The following day, a Sunday, Porfiry attended mass at the Church of the Assumption of the Virgin Mary in Haymarket Square. Rumours passed through the congregation that Katya Mikhailovna Dolgorukaya had that day borne the Tsar a son, and that His Imperial Highness had given thanks to God. The news was indeed highly scandalous. Porfiry pretended to be affected by the general agitation, though in truth he was secretly pleased. After the ceremony, he was moved by the desire to visit old friends. In particular, he had long been troubled by a sense of estrangement that had entered his relations with Nikodim Fomich. He was greeted by the police chief and his wife like a prodigal son. That is to say, he was offered tea and honey-soaked *pirozhky*. The couple's unmarried daughters entertained him with songs at the piano, performed with great exuberance and accomplishment. Fortunately, Porfiry was too old to feel obliged to choose between them. The afternoon was rounded off delightfully by a visit from the eldest daughter, accompanied by her husband and two small children. Porfiry was pressed to stay for dinner, but made his excuses in a private conversation with Nikodim Fomich in the latter's study. There was one other call he wished to make that day, he explained.

Dr Pervoyedov was equally surprised, and delighted, to find the magistrate at the door of his Gorokhovaya Street apartment. He called excitedly to his wife, 'Anya! Anya! Come and see! It's Porfiry Petrovich!'

His wife came out from the kitchen to greet the magistrate with a shy smile, which was nonetheless illuminated by an ironic intelligence. She had never met Porfiry Petrovich before this day, a fact which seemed to have escaped her husband. But, in truth, he had talked so much about Porfiry over the years that she might have felt that she knew the magistrate as well as her husband seemed to assume she did. She smiled indulgently at Pervoyedov as he gabbled on; in her look, Porfiry detected a depth of love that for a moment exalted them all. The good doctor then insisted that Porfiry should be introduced to his son and demanded from his wife the boy's whereabouts. She confessed that she hadn't the least idea.

A search of the apartment was made and young Gorya was at last found, much to the adults' delight, under the table in the dining room, completely hidden by the long fringed cloth that trailed the floor. He was coaxed out with offers of bonbons, and introduced to the magistrate whose hand he shook with appropriate solemnity. The little boy seemed in awe of the strange plump man, even frightened of him.

Porfiry dropped down onto his haunches with a grunt. 'Close your eyes, Gorya.'

The little boy obeyed. Porfiry ducked under the table, disappearing behind the hanging tablecloth, with a wink to Dr Pervoyedov's wife.

His parents' laughter prompted Gorya to open his eyes. The stranger was nowhere to be seen. Of course, the first place he looked was under the table. Porfiry held a finger to his mouth, urging the boy to silence. Quick-witted Gorya played along, pretending that he had not seen the magistrate behind the tablecloth. The adults' look of patronising amusement changed to confusion. They were forced to look for themselves, and seeing Porfiry with his hands over his face were only more bemused, until Gorya's piping laughter told them that they had been taken in. Porfiry dropped his hands and leered triumphantly. After that, he and Gorya were firm friends.

This time he accepted the invitation to stay for dinner; indeed, an invitation was barely offered and it was simply assumed that he would eat with them. And it was hard to refuse as the *zakuski* were laid out on the table, dish after dish, all manner of pickled vegetables and salads topped with sour cream or served with vinaigrette, together with little dishes of smoked sturgeon, tender chicken roulade and rollmops of herring. The colours of the different *zakuski* delighted his eye. The table became a palette of dining, the rich reds of the tomatoes, beetroot, cranberries and red caviar giving way to the pinker hues of the boiled pork, and the gold of the carrots, smoked salmon and aspic, all contrasting with the white of the sour cream and potatoes. Porfiry could not help himself. But all this was just by way of an appetiser. The feast of *zakuski* merged into a second feast, of *pelmeni*, the little parcels of noodle dough stuffed with various fillings. Porfiry tasted meat *pelmeni*, fish and mushroom *pelmeni*, cabbage *pelmeni* and mashed potato *pelmeni*; all perfectly cooked, the soft mouthfuls melting away in explosions of salivation. But Porfiry discovered the most surprising filling of all when his teeth clamped down on something unexpectedly hard and resistant to biting. He pulled out a button and showed it to the company, to the amusement of everyone, especially little Gorya.

'Ah, you've found the button!' said Dr Pervoyedov, with an appreciative smile to his wife. He did not know how she had arranged it, but it was appropriate that the prize should have fallen to their guest. 'That means good luck.'

'I accept it. I am very much in need of some good luck,' said Porfiry, pocketing the button, with a wink to Gorya.

Porfiry took his leave of Dr Pervoyedov at midnight, at the same time as he took his leave of the month. He held onto the doctor's hand for an unusual length of time, as if he believed that in relinquishing it he would relinquish all hope of happiness. He pressed his friend, with a strange insistence, to call on him the following morning.

27

An act of singular daring

On the morning of Monday, 1 May, Pavel Pavlovich Virginsky entered his superior Porfiry Petrovich's chambers at nine thirty. He closed the door behind him. There was nothing unusual in this. Afterwards the head clerk, Alexander Grigorevich Zamyotov, would say that he had noticed Virginsky's expression to be unusually strained that morning, his complexion noticeably pale.

There were few people in main receiving room of the police bureau at the time, and so Zamyotov was able to steal a few moments to listen at the door. He had no great expectation of hearing anything of interest, and assumed the role of eavesdropper more out of habit than mischief. It was almost as if he believed it was expected of him.

Nothing prepared him for what he heard.

The explosive discharge of a gun threw him away from the door. A moment later, there was the clatter of something heavy and metallic falling to the floor and then Virginsky burst through, now flushed in the face. He stared into Zamyotov's eyes, as though he were an acquaintance he had not seen for many years whose name he was struggling to remember. Gathering his wits, the junior magistrate bowed politely and began walking away from Porfiry Petrovich's chambers. Looking back on the moment, it seemed strange to Zamyotov that Virginsky did not at any point break into a run, but merely walked calmly out of the bureau. But at the time, it was the junior magistrate's calmness that went a long way to persuading Zamyotov that nothing untoward had happened at all, and that he must have been mistaken in thinking he had heard a gunshot.

But as soon as Virginsky was out of sight, it was as if Zamyotov was released from a spell. He rushed into Porfiry Petrovich's chambers, where he found the magistrate clutching a hand to his chest, high up, to the left, just below the shoulder. The clerk was horrified to see blood seeping through the magistrate's fingers. He noticed that there was blood on the magistrate's cheek too. It seemed strange to him that the blood coming from the chest appeared darker than the blood on his face.

Porfiry Petrovich was breathing hard. 'Get Dr Pervoyedov,' he rasped into Zamyotov's anxious face. 'Only Dr Pervoyedov. No one else. Keep this. Quiet. No panic. Do you understand, Alexei? Go softly.'

'What about Nikodim Fomich?'

'Yes. Get him too. Quickly. But Pervoyedov is the only doctor I will allow to look at me.' Porfiry Petrovich closed his eyes and slumped back in his seat. His face relaxed into something that for a moment resembled contentment, as if he welcomed the wound and held onto it jealously. But that impression was not long-lasting. The shift in his position seemed to take its toll on Porfiry, tightening his face into a wince of manifest pain.

'Do not stir yourself, Porfiry Petrovich,' said Zamyotov. 'I shall return with a doctor forthwith.'

'Pervoyedov,' groaned Porfiry. 'Only Pervoyedov.'

Zamyotov shook his head as he ran out of the chambers. Clearly, the old man was delirious. God only knew why he had got it into his head to insist on that eccentric. Zamyotov hated to go against him but this was a matter of life or death. To send to the Obukhovsky Hospital for Dr Pervoyedov would waste valuable time. The crucial thing was to get a doctor to Porfiry Petrovich as quickly as possible. Any delay might prove fatal. And if there were an inquest, how could he justify sending for Pervoyedov when there were other doctors just as capable closer at hand?

And yet Porfiry Petrovich had been strangely insistent. *Perhaps*, thought Zamyotov, *I had better talk it over with Nikodim Fomich first.*

But, of course, there would be no time for that.

It had been many years since Zamyotov had prayed in earnest, not since his boyhood, in fact. He and religion had gone their separate ways long ago. But now he closed his eyes tightly, fervently, and mustered all the sincerity of which his soul was capable. He opened himself up to an idea of God that, without his knowing, still resided within him. To that God he made all manner of rash promises, which perhaps he would not be able to keep. But at the time he made them, he was sincere and that is all that counts in these matters. *Just save Porfiry Petrovich*, was the burden of his prayers. *Just save Porfiry Petrovich and I will live a different life.*

It is a frightening thing, to open your eyes from prayer and see the answer to your prayers before you. It is not something you can ever be prepared for. And when you have made the answering of those prayers conditional upon nothing less than a wholesale upheaval of your being, you do not necessarily welcome such a sight. Indeed, it may inspire in you as much dread as joy.

Zamyotov opened his eyes to see the miracle of Dr Pervoyedov himself, walking towards Porfiry Petrovich's chambers, as calmly as Virginsky had walked away from them.

'Doctor! Thank God you're here! Something terrible has happened.' Zamyotov's startling cry, equally laden with panic and relief, changed the tenor of the day for good: 'He has been shot! Porfiry Petrovich has been shot!'

*

Virginsky rapped urgently on the door. As soon as he had done so, he regretted not using the coded sequence of knocks that he had witnessed the last time he had visited the apartment.

Despite that oversight, the door was opened. The woman who had served tea to the guests, Varvara Alexeevna, appeared to be on her way out, with a shawl pulled up over her head and a large cloth bag in one hand. She clearly recognised Virginsky, but made no move to admit him. 'Kirill Kirillovich is not here.'

'I will wait for him.'

'He will not return until this evening. And I must go out. I have been called away. I am a midwife, you know.' Varvara Alexeevna volunteered this information with a self-important tilt of the head. 'I was just about to leave when you knocked.'

'You must let me in. I have nowhere else to go. And . . .'

Varvara Alexeevna cocked an eyebrow questioningly.

Virginsky scanned the landing nervously. 'I think I have just killed a man.'

'You think?'

'I did not stay to find out for certain.'

'And you believe this will incline me to let you in?'

'I did it for the cause. For them. I have put myself in a position of extreme . . .' Virginsky broke off, as if unable to define the position in which he had in fact put himself. 'I have nowhere else to go,' he said simply.

Varvara Alexeevna nodded and stepped to one side.

'Do you know how to contact Alyosha Afanasevich?' asked Virginsky. 'Or Tatyana Ruslanovna?'

'There will be time for that later. Stay in the apartment and do not answer the door to anyone. Kirill Kirillovich will know what to do.'

With that, she was gone. And if Virginsky had ever felt lonely in his life before, it was nothing compared to this.

*

When Kirill Kirillovich appeared at around four that afternoon, his face had already assumed the look of sour disappointment that seemed to come most naturally to it. 'Why did you come here?'

'Where else was I to go? The police will be watching my apartment.'

'You acted without authorisation.'

'It was what we talked about at the meeting. Alyosha Afanasevich called for action. You agreed. You all agreed.'

'We were talking about general principles. No order was given. How could it have been? We do not generate our own orders. We must wait for them to come from the central committee. It had not even been definitely decided that you were to be accepted into the group.'

'I trust there will be no doubt about that now?'

'I would not be so certain. You have revealed yourself to be a highly unreliable and dangerous individual. A volatile character. You place us all at risk.'

'As soon as you become involved in political activity, you place yourself at risk. You must have the courage of your convictions. You cannot call for the overthrow of the Tsar and then baulk at the assassination of a magistrate.'

'You took matters into your own hands. That is ill disciplined.'

'To me, it was clear what was called for at the meeting on Friday. I was called upon to use my position within a government department to carry out an act of singular daring. Those were the very words Tatyana Ruslanovna used.'

'Yes, yes, that was what was discussed. But it goes without saying that we would have to wait for confirmation from the central committee before any action was taken. That is the way things are done.'

'I believe there was one there who was authorised to speak for the central committee. And yet no voice was raised calling for delay.'

'Nonsense. No one speaks for the central committee.' Kirill Kirillovich's expression became even sourer as he assessed and somehow dismissed Virginsky. 'At any rate, you cannot stay here.'

Virginsky looked around. The apartment seemed large without the presence of the name-day guests. He also saw that it was more comfortably furnished than he remembered, even luxuriously so, as if some objects of value had been removed for that last occasion. This was either as a precaution against damage, or because Kirill Kirillovich and his wife had not wanted their guests to see that they possessed such items. One article in particular caught Virginsky's eye. 'I see that you have an icon in the corner.'

'Why not? It is for form's sake. Our neighbours expect us to be devout Russians. It does no harm.'

'It was not in place last Friday.'

'Naturally. There was no one present who needed to be deceived as to our true convictions.'

Virginsky frowned distractedly as he considered Kirill Kirillovich's explanation. 'You can't kick me out. Not until the central committee have decided what to do with me.'

There was a knock at the door, the coded knock that signalled one of 'our people.' It was Alyosha Afanasevich Botkin, his face illuminated by a wild excitement. He held a newspaper in front of him. 'You fiend! You are a veritable fiend! That's what we will have to call you from now on!'

'Just as they call you Hunger?' remarked Virginsky, raising one sardonic eyebrow. 'May I see that?'

It was a late edition of the *Police Gazette*. Virginsky read on the front page:

Magistrate in Critical Condition after Shooting

A senior investigating magistrate employed by the Department for the Investigation of Criminal Causes, a subdivision of the Ministry of Justice based at the Haymarket District Police Bureau in Stolyarny Lane, has been taken to the Obukhovsky Hospital following an apparent assassination attempt. He is said to be suffering from a gunshot wound to the chest. Dr Pervoyedov of the Obukhovsky, who attended the victim, described the wound as 'grave'. The victim's name has been given only as Porfiry Petrovich; he is thought to be the magistrate who achieved prominence through his prosecution of the former student R. R. Raskolnikov some years ago. The authorities are anxious to speak to one Pavel Pavlovich Virginsky, also a magistrate, in connection with the incident. Witnesses saw Mr Virginsky flee the victim's chambers shortly after a gun was fired there. No motive for the dreadful crime has been given.

Kirill Kirillovich snatched the paper and shook his head over the account. 'A wasted opportunity,' he declared.

'What do you mean?' asked Virginsky.

'*No motive for the dreadful crime has been given,*' read Kirill Kirillovich. 'What is the point of committing such an act if you do not make it clear that it is political? The least you could have done was to shout some slogans.'

'I . . .'

'And why did you run away? You should have waited there for them to arrest you.'

'That's insane!' objected Virginsky.

'No,' said Botkin. 'He's right. It is better for the cause when the assassin is arrested. For one thing, it shows that we are not ashamed of our acts. For another, it allows the possibility of a trial. A trial is essential; indeed, it is the main point of a political crime. It affords us, in defending our actions, to speak directly to the Russian people. By avoiding arrest, you have held back the cause of the revolution.'

'But am I not of more use to the cause free? Can I not be used to lead and inspire further unrest? Besides, the timing of my attack was everything. The timing proves its political aspect. I struck the very day after the Tsar's mistress gave birth! While he was busy fawning over his illegitimate son – abandoning not only his own family, but the whole of Russia. When people see that his decadence allows us to strike at the heart of the administration with impunity, they will cease to believe in the regime's ability to protect them. You must at least admit that my action will be successful in destabilising the government?'

'But we must let it be known beyond doubt that it is a political act. We must put out a manifesto to that effect, claiming responsibility. It is a pity that . . .' Botkin broke off.

'What?'

'Nothing. I have notified the central committee of these developments. We may expect a visit from one of their number, imminently.'

'A member of the central committee is to come here? Openly? A member of the central committee is to reveal himself to us?' Kirill Kirillovich was beside himself at the prospect.

'Such an extraordinary development calls for extraordinary measures,' said Botkin.

Virginsky gave a tense grimace.

They heard the apartment door. Varvara Alexeevna came into the room, stooped and worn out, her eyes ringed with exhaustion.

'In the meantime, let us have some tea.' Kirill Kirillovich gave his wife a commanding nod.

Varvara Alexeevna turned on her heel with a sudden burst of alacrity.

'Of course, tea! I shall bring in the samovar. What an excellent suggestion, Alyosha Afanasevich. It is no wonder you are held in such esteem by your friends.'

Botkin frowned at her back as he tried to unravel the nuances of her sarcasm.

*

They drank tea steadily for the next five hours, while they waited for the visit from the representative of the central committee. At one point, Varvara Alexeevna provided *buterbrody* of ham and cheese, with a selection of pickles.

Little was said. They morosely watched the stilted, ponderous progression of the filigree hands of an ormolu and enamel clock, decorated elaborately with dancing nymphs. Each time the hands approached the hour, and the antique clock wound itself up to chime, the watchers' air of tense expectancy increased. It seemed they believed, irrationally, that the visitation would occur precisely on the hour, although which hour did not seem to matter. At midnight, this feeling was greatest of all, but it was also mixed with a sense of dread that the longed-for visit would not after all occur, and the day would end without them knowing what to do.

As the prolonged midnight chimes came to a close, Botkin gave vent to his frustration by roundly abusing the clock that had announced the time. 'What are you doing in possession of that filthy object? You call yourself a revolutionist? You're worse than the most decadent aristocrat! I have a good mind to throw it from the window and watch it smash upon the courtyard.' He even stood up and took a step towards the mantelpiece.

'If you do, you will have me to answer to, Alyosha Afanasevich!' warned Varvara Alexeevna.

'My wife is fond of it,' explained Kirill Kirillovich, despondently.

'I am surprised at you, Varvara Alexeevna,' said Botkin, turning away from the offending clock. 'I know you share our convictions. Indeed, I always took you to be a more rigorous political theoretician than your husband.'

'And so I am. If you wish to discuss this sensibly, then I will ask

333

you this. Is the purpose of social revolution to bring all down to the level of the meanest pauper, or to raise all up to the level of the privileged few?'

'The latter is impossible, Varvara Alexeevna,' said Botkin dismissively. 'We cannot all live as wealthy aristocrats. That is the way to perpetuate the disparities of the current system, merely transferring the privileges of the few to a different elite. And so, inevitably, the production of equality necessitates a process of levelling off. We will all meet in the middle somewhere, I imagine.'

'And there will be no more fine things?'

'Everything that is necessary will be provided. There will be no more want. Still and all, *this* . . .' Botkin turned and pointed at the clock. 'This is not a question of necessity. It is luxury. For sure, there will be no more luxury.'

'And what will become of all the fine things that already exist?'

'They will be destroyed.'

'What purpose does that serve?'

'It clears the way. It educates. It punishes.'

'And I will be punished for owning this clock? You know I was given it as a fee by a countess who had fallen on hard times and got herself into trouble. You could say it was redistribution in action. At any rate, I worked long hours to earn that clock, and all the other nice things you see here.'

'You will fall into the category of education, rather than punishment. You are essentially suffering from a misguided aspiration. You aspire to the decadent practice of connoisseurship which you have appropriated from another class. It would be better that you did not.'

'But is it not a form of social revolution when people such as I can own such objects?'

'And in the meantime there are millions who cannot afford to feed their families. Are you aware, Varvara Alexeevna, that men died to produce luxuries like this?'

'You go too far, Alyosha Afanasevich!'

'Not at all. The process of laying on the ormolu involves the evaporation of mercury, which causes first the insanity and then the premature death of the artisans involved. In France, a more enlightened country than ours I think, the process was long ago declared illegal.'

'The clock is over a hundred years old. The man who made it is certainly dead, whether prematurely or not. His oppression will not be lightened one iota by smashing it.'

'Surely you are familiar with the Catechism? The revolutionist knows only one science: the science of destruction. Before we can establish a new order, we must destroy everything associated with the old. Your precious clock falls into that category. It must be swept away.' Botkin appeared carried along by his own words. Although he had so far restrained himself, he now reached out and lifted the clock from the mantelpiece.

Varvara Alexeevna shrieked.

Botkin's eyes were gleeful. 'I see now it is my duty to destroy it. As it is your duty to rejoice in its destruction.'

It was at that moment that the long-awaited knock at the door was finally heard. The clock between Botkin's hands indicated the time to be twenty-one minutes past twelve. For some reason, Botkin was distracted by the time, perhaps by its numerical symmetry. The moment for destroying it passed. He returned it to the mantelpiece.

Kirill Kirillovich went to see to the door. He returned a moment later with Tatyana Ruslanovna. The room became energised at her entrance.

'You!' cried Botkin. 'You are the representative of the central committee?'

'Does that surprise you?'

'No. It pleases me immensely. It delights me.'

'It is a good thing,' agreed Varvara Alexeevna. 'You are a woman,' she added, to explain her position more clearly.

Tatyana Ruslanovna turned her attention to Virginsky. 'And so, my friend, what have you done?' Her smile was kindly.

'I have struck at the heart of the administration.'

'Hardly the heart. But you have struck one of its prominent limbs.'

'Yes, but he should have made clear the political aspect of his act, should he not?' insisted Kirill Kirillovich. 'If he had been dragged off shouting "Long live the Revolution!," the crime would have had more of an impact. As it stands, it is possible for the authorities to represent it as the isolated action of a lone madman. He should have stayed to make clear his position as a revolutionist.'

'The central committee is of the view that Pavel Pavlovich acted correctly in saving himself. In allowing Porfiry Petrovich's attacker to remain at liberty, the authorities reveal their ineptitude. It increases public terror. The central committee is of the view that all our people must co-operate in keeping Virginsky out of the authorities' reach. This is now a priority. For the time being, he will remain here.'

'Here?' Kirill Kirillovich screwed up his face distastefully. 'Who is to pay for his food?'

'You are. Sacrifices are required. This will be yours. You will also supply him with clothes, preferably a workman's. You, Pavel Pavlovich, are advised to do whatever you can to change your appearance. Grow a beard. Adopt a different gait. You will be surprised what a difference a change in gait can effect. You will also be supplied with a false passport, of course. As soon as this is ready, we will move you out of Petersburg.'

'I don't want to move out of Petersburg.' Virginsky's voice was childishly petulant.

'It doesn't matter what you want.'

He tried to affect a more reasonable tone: 'But I can be more use here.'

'It is hard to see how you can be any use at all to us now, other than as an idea, a phantom. That is the only reason we are determined to keep you safe. There is also the consideration that we cannot be sure you will not betray us if you are arrested.'

'I would hope that I have proven myself on that score,' protested Virginsky.

Tatyana Ruslanovna did not reply. And the smile that flickered briefly over her lips was hard to interpret.

28

A new man

He slept on the sofa in the main room of the apartment. More accurately, he lay down on it and closed his eyes intermittently. After a while, it was hard to distinguish between the swirling grey fuzz of the room around him, and the non-dimensioned darkness, streaked with flaring lights, that he entered when he closed his eyes. Both were filled with the ticking of the ormolu clock, meting out the hours with inhuman patience. He found its measured insistence oppressive, and began to wish that Botkin had made good on his threat to destroy it. He self-consciously framed the intention that, before the end of his stay in the apartment, he would smash the infernal clock himself, if no one else did. He laughed wildly into the darkness, his eyes straining with defiance at the boundless obscurity of the night. It seemed that he was capable of anything now. Soon, however, he became irrationally afraid of the clock. He imagined that it had grown to gigantic size, and that its hands were swinging axes, as sharp as guillotine blades. He knew at that moment that he was asleep, and dreaming. And as soon as the realisation struck him, he woke up. The reality of his situation was immediately depressing. He felt trapped, as indeed he was. He imagined eternity as a nocturnal room like this, with an unseen clock tapping relentlessly at the darkness. He began to count the ticks of the clock, and for some reason that made him feel a little better.

He knew that he would not get to sleep again that night. But that decisive realisation was also somehow liberating. He settled down to address the turmoil of his thoughts, without being distracted by the anxieties of insomnia.

Surprisingly, perhaps, he found himself thinking about Prince Dolgoruky; or, more specifically, about his demon. He imagined it there in the room with him, squatting foully on its haunches, leering in the darkness. He could not quite believe in it. When he tried to put a face to it, his mind – peculiarly – supplied the face of Porfiry Petrovich. And so it was a demon with pale, almost translucent skin, with a face as feminine and cunning as a peasant woman's, with eyes the colour of ice and transparent lashes flickering restlessly over them. He sensed the bulbous prominence at the back of its head, and was repelled by it.

But this demon, it seemed, had the power of metamorphosis, for he saw that its face had changed into that of Alyosha Afanasevich Botkin. And so it was now a hatchet-headed demon, with a wild incendiary stare trapped behind circular spectacle lenses. No sooner had the demon settled into this incarnation than it began to change. Its neck stretched out impossibly. Virginsky's mind's eye craned upwards to see the face of Tatyana Ruslanovna Vakhrameva looking down at him with an expression of aloof indifference. This was the Tatyana Ruslanovna of old, the sexually knowing woman-child with the drifting, dangerous gaze. He felt an ache of longing and unhappiness. He knew from her glance that she was utterly unattainable, no matter what crimes he might commit to please her.

He didn't like to see the demon as Tatyana Ruslanovna. He willed it to assume another form. But the demon seemed to want to torment him, for it held onto Tatyana Ruslanovna's features with obstinate cruelty.

Of course, at no point did he actually believe that there was a demon there with him in the room. *Was that the difference between him and Prince Dolgoruky?* he wondered. Virginsky, ever the materialist, knew full well that the demon was simply a product of his own mental processes, that it was something he himself had created, possibly to represent that aspect of himself that was capable of evil. (He took it for granted that he was capable of evil.) Indeed, he had no real sense of the demon as existing outside his mind. Pursuing this impeccably rationalistic analysis, he saw that the projection of other people's faces onto the demon was an attempt by his unconscious mind to shift the blame for his negative acts onto others.

He shook his head without raising it from the cushion it rested on. Such moral cowardice would not do. He had to take responsibility for his own acts, for all of them. And so he attempted to will his own face onto the demon, for that would be the only honest representation. But even after a conscious, creative effort, he could not make the demon wear his face. It was as if the part of him that had conjured it into being simply refused to countenance such an outcome.

He was growing tired of the demon. He wanted it to be gone. He wanted to prove his mastery over it, over the negative aspects of his personality. And the last face it wore, before it dissolved into the soft grains of night, was that of his old professor, Tatiscev.

*

The walls of the apartment blazed with panels of luminosity, sharp geometric sections of sunlight. A wash of cold pallor spread across the parquet floor.

'You are to stay in the apartment. Don't go out. Don't answer the door. Stay away from the windows, too. You must not be seen by anyone, do you understand?' Kirill Kirillovich's habitual look of sour disappointment was momentarily transformed into one of sour disapproval.

Virginsky experienced a nostalgic pang as he contemplated the angled projections of spring. 'Tatyana Ruslanovna said you are to get me clothes.'

'There will be time for that later.'

'But if someone comes to the apartment and I am seen in my civil-service uniform, they are more likely to suspect something. If I am dressed as a workman . . .'

'If you are dressed as a workman, you will convince no one. I have never seen a more unlikely workman.'

'That was Tatyana Ruslanovna's wish. It was the wish of the central committee.'

'Sometimes, like a theologian interpreting the Bible, one must interpret the commands of the central committee. Having done so, I do not feel it is necessary to supply you with the clothes.'

'But that is not interpretation. It is contradiction. Furthermore, you chose a suspiciously reactionary analogy.'

Kirill Kirillovich regarded Virginsky without enthusiasm. 'This is all beside the point. I have already told you that you are not to open the door to anyone. What need is there for disguise?'

'Is there any news of . . . of the man I shot?' The question surprised Virginsky as much as it did Kirill Kirillovich.

'I don't know. I haven't been out yet. I haven't had a chance to see a newspaper.' He frowned impatiently and then added, 'Do you care?'

'No,' said Virginsky quickly.

'You don't care whether he lives or dies?'

Virginsky felt unsure how to answer, sensing the question was a trap. *It will be like this from now on*, he thought. 'No. I really don't,' he claimed.

Kirill Kirillovich did not seem to be impressed. 'I suppose it makes little difference to you now. They will not go any easier on you if he lives. However, as far as the cause of social revolution is concerned, it would be better if he died.'

His wife, Varvara Alexeevna, came into the room as he said this. Her face assumed an uneasy expression. She averted her gaze sadly to the floor and spoke with quiet determination: 'You know, Kirill Kirillovich, that I share your aspirations concerning the foundation of a more just society in the future. However, I cannot, in all conscience, condone such bloodthirsty sentiments. I spend my days bringing new life into this world. I see what a precarious and treasured thing it is. I will not sit at the breakfast table, fill myself with pancakes and then blithely call for another being's destruction. The deed is done. Perhaps it was a necessary deed. I don't know anything about that. But as far as it was a political act, it is complete. The political point has been made. So let us hope that this magistrate survives, as his death adds nothing, and pleases no one, or so I would hope.'

Virginsky felt obscurely shamed by her words.

Kirill Kirillovich sighed. 'We have talked about this before, Varvara Alexeevna. And as I have had occasion to remark in the past, you must put aside such sentimental prejudices. It is simply not consistent for you to say that you share my aspirations but reject my means – for you know in your heart that there is no other way. The future can only be born out of the destruction of the past. Just as some women inevitably give up their own lives during childbirth, for all your best endeavours.'

The colour rushed to Varvara Alexeevna's cheeks at this intrusion of the personal. 'But not all women die in childbirth!' she protested.

'No, but those who do . . . do. What I mean is that it is inevitable in certain cases. In the same way, it is equally inevitable that some, perhaps many, will have to die before a new order can be established. We cannot prevent it. Therefore we should not lament it.'

'Only a man could be so glib.'

'And only a woman could be so . . .' Kirill Kirillovich broke off to consult the ormolu clock. 'I must go.'

'What? Only a woman could be so *what*?' demanded his wife.

But Kirill Kirillovich only shook his head in sour distraction, as he rose to leave.

*

'Your husband refused to get me any clothes. The clothes that Tatyana Ruslanovna ordered you to provide for me.'

'What do you need clothes for? You're not going anywhere, are you?'

'Suppose the police come to the apartment.'

'What good would a change of clothes do you?'

'I might be able to effect my escape.'

'And how would you do that? By flying out the window?'

'If I were in disguise, I might be able to slip past them.'

343

'You do not think they will send someone who can recognise you, no matter what clothes you are wearing?'

'What if it is not the police, but someone who might inform on me?'

'You are not to open the door to anyone. Is that clear?'

'If I am to be a prisoner here, then I may as well hand myself in. At least then we will have the political advantage of a trial.'

'If that is what you wish, I shall not stand in your way.'

'But it is not what the central committee wishes.'

'Then do not do it.'

'So I *am* to be a prisoner!'

'My friend,' began Varvara Alexeevna more gently, 'we are all prisoners. It is simply that when you put yourself outside the law, outside society, your imprisonment becomes visible. You notice it for the first time, and you rail against it.'

'I thought I would become free.'

'Yes, and that is what makes it all the harder to endure.'

'I would feel better if I could wear some different clothes. Safer.' After a moment, Virginsky added, 'These are the clothes I was wearing when I shot him.'

Virginsky's voice had taken on a distant quality, half wistful, half appalled. He seemed chastened. This proved decisive to Varvara Alexeevna. 'You may help yourself to my husband's clothes.' She looked him up and down, her gaze softly scrutinising. 'You are about the same size, you and he.'

'But he is not a workman,' objected Virginsky. 'Tatyana Ruslanovna said I was to be given a workman's clothes.'

'No, he is not a workman. He is a skilled engineer.' Varvara Alexeevna's head tilted sharply with pride. 'Tatyana Ruslanovna also said you were to grow a beard. How are you getting on with that?' Varvara Alexeevna's tone was gently mocking.

'I intend to devote all my energies to it.' Virginsky smiled. 'I fear I will have little else to do.'

Varvara Alexeevna's expression suddenly darkened. 'You are a cold-blooded man,' she said. 'You frighten me more than the others. They have no experience of the things they dream about. But you . . . you raised a gun at one of your colleagues and fired. And here you are, a day later, calmly sitting down to breakfast and arguing about a suit of clothes. Are you really not afraid that he might die, and that the sin of his murder will be on your soul?'

Virginsky thought for a long time before replying: 'I do not believe in the soul.'

Varvara Alexeevna shuddered and quickly put on her shawl. 'Yes, of course. None of us believes in the soul, these days. Or at least that is what we *profess*. To be able to act on such a profession, however – that is a different matter.' Varvara Alexeevna stared at the floor for a moment before continuing. 'I must go out.'

'I hope I am not driving you from your own apartment?'

The look she gave him was not reassuring. 'There is tea in the samovar if you need it. I believe you will find some bread for lunch. I trust we shall see you later.'

She closed the door behind her with unseemly alacrity. It shocked Virginsky to realise that she was afraid to be in the apartment alone with him. He frowned as he listened to the sound of her locking him in.

29

New people

If her look had made him feel like a murderer, to be left alone in the apartment made him feel like a thief. Her invitation for him *to help himself* to her husband's clothes did not help.

The couple's bedroom adjoined the sitting room. It was a dark, sag-draped space, clogged with furniture and ornaments. Varvara Alexeevna's taste for frivolous possessions seemed to emanate from here, spilling out into the rest of the apartment in the centrifugal scatter of a storm.

There was a hook on the inside of the bedroom door which fitted into a metal loop on the frame, to form a rudimentary lock. For some reason he could not explain, knowing he was alone in the apartment, he pushed the hook into its eye.

Tatyana Ruslanovna had warned him to stay away from the windows. But the angular projections of light that were distributed about the apartment like so much celestial bunting were more compelling than her injunction. He stood to the side of the frame and looked down at the courtyard. A solitary figure, a man in artisan's clothes, could just be made out, lurking by the entrance. It could have been Virginsky's imagination, but he felt sure that the man was looking up at the apartment. This was precisely what he expected. In fact, it comforted him to see the man there. Everything was as it should be, as far as that was possible. He moved slowly back from the window.

He had not expected Kirill Kirillovich to be the owner of an extensive wardrobe. In addition to the work suit he was wearing that day, Virginsky had counted on finding an additional suit for best, although he was not sure that a committed revolutionist would succumb to such conventionalities. However, Virginsky had not reckoned on the fact that a resourceful revolutionist might find it expedient to accumulate a range of clothes, which might be termed outfits, or even disguises. He could think of no other reason why Kirill Kirillovich would possess a number of different coloured peasant smocks, as well as a merchant's kaftan, and a tailored European suit with a swallow-tailed jacket. He was not altogether surprised to find a priest's robe hanging in the wardrobe. He chose a pair of loose workman's trousers and a rough red smock. He then searched the bottom of the wardrobe and found a pair of felt boots, which he tucked the trousers into. Finally, he put on a leather belt to cinch the smock.

It was strange to stand before a mirror in another man's clothes. He was surprised how unlike himself he looked. He wondered whether that was the result of the change of clothes, or of a greater change that had taken place inside him. But in St Petersburg, a city of costumes and uniforms, the power of appearance could not be underestimated. It was never a question of *mere* appearance. A man could make himself whatever he wanted to be, simply by appearing to be it.

He was startled out of his self-absorption by a knock at the apartment door. His heart picked up the sharp rhythm and echoed it internally. He froze. The silence after the knocking ceased throbbed with catastrophe. The knocking was repeated. Virginsky thought he recognised the complicated pattern of the entry code. He relaxed minutely, though his heart still kept up its percussive chorus.

He let himself out of the bedroom and moved noiselessly to the apartment door. He sensed the presence of the other in the silence. He laid a hand flat on the door, as if to reach out to whoever was there. He withdrew the hand as the knocking was repeated, the same pattern, more urgently.

A voice, Dolgoruky's, hissed: 'Magistrate! Open up. It's me, Dolgoruky.'

'I can't. She's locked me in.'

There was laughter from the other side. 'She's not taking any chances, that one.'

'What do you want?'

To Virginsky's astonishment, he heard a key fit into the lock. A moment later the door was open. The Prince's gaze swept over him hungrily. 'My, my, magistrate, what have you done?'

Virginsky closed the door quickly. 'You have a key?'

'Of course. This is my apartment. That is to say, it was. I put it at the disposal of the central committee and they handed it over to Kirill Kirillovich and Varvara Alexeevna. I must have forgotten to surrender all the keys.'

'But you live in that squalid room? With all those others.'

'One must make sacrifices for the revolution.'

The look Virginsky bestowed on Dolgoruky was almost one of admiration. There were many questions he could have asked. He settled for, 'Why did you knock, if you had a key?'

'It's hardly polite, is it, to go barging in uninvited.' Dolgoruky's sheepish expression suggested another motive.

Only now did Virginsky think of the question he should have asked in the first place: 'How did you know I was here?'

'Everyone knows you are here. That is to say, all our people do, at least.'

'Which means that the authorities will by now. Tatyana Ruslan-ovna believes there is an agent in our midst.'

'Oh, it is never as simple as that, in my experience. Do you not agree?'

'I don't know what you mean.'

'And so you shot him!' cried Dolgoruky abruptly. 'You really shot him, that horrible little man. I must say, I couldn't be more pleased.'

'I didn't do it to please you.'

Dolgoruky seemed surprised by this. 'Why did you do it?'

The question seemed to throw Virginsky. 'I would have thought that was obvious. To strike at the heart of the administration . . . The central committee called for an act of singular daring . . .'

'Yes, but why did you take it upon yourself to be the one? And why did you shoot *him*?'

'Do you have any news . . . concerning his condition? Is he . . . ?' Virginsky was unable to complete the question.

'He's still alive, if that's what you mean. He is being cared for at the Obukhovsky Hospital. Perhaps we should go there and finish the job off?' Dolgoruky grinned maliciously.

'I . . . I imagine he is closely guarded.'

'Yes, but to a daredevil like you, what does that matter? I like your disguise, by the way. That will serve you well. You can turn up at the hospital pretending to be a workman – there is always some work or other to be done in those filthy, crumbling wrecks. In amongst your bag of tools, you hide a gun, or some dynamite – do you know what dynamite is?'

Virginsky nodded.

'There! What could be simpler?'

'I don't have . . . any tools,' objected Virginsky lamely. He added, 'I cannot conceive of acting without the authorisation of the central committee.'

'Why not? You did before.'

'No, you are mistaken. As I said, I was called upon –'

'I think not. I was there, remember. I don't think anyone explicitly called upon you to do what you have done. You acted on your own initiative. The central committee would be within their rights to hang you out to dry.'

'They would not dare!'

'Oh my goodness, listen to him! Now he threatens the central committee!'

'What do you want, Dolgoruky?'

'Do you have any tea?'

'No. There is no tea. And no one to provide it.'

'What did it feel like?'

'I beg your pardon?'

'When you squeezed the trigger and saw what you had done. When you saw him there bleeding . . . *What did you feel*?'

Virginsky hesitated before answering. 'I don't know. It's hard to say. I felt . . . different. I felt as if my life would never be the same again.'

Dolgoruky shook his head impatiently. 'Of course! That goes without saying. That is nothing. But . . . you felt free? For the first time in your life, you were free!'

'Yes, for a moment. In the instant I pulled the trigger. As the bullet was released. Yes, then, in that moment, I was free.' Virginsky shook his head violently, as if he were trying to cast out from it a weight of unhappiness. 'But look at me now. I am a prisoner in

350

this infernal apartment. Can you believe she locked me in?! And when I am moved from here, I will be a prisoner somewhere else.'

'Until the moment when your crime is multiplied across society. When an army of men like you each stands up and shoots . . . a magistrate here, a minister there, a governor in this province, the marshal of the nobility in that! When your lead is followed, and widespread destruction is unleashed, you will be once again free.'

Virginsky sighed, as if he found Dolgoruky's vision oppressive. He gave him a critical look. 'And what if no one rises up?'

'Don't be despondent, my friend. The day will come. And you have helped to hasten it. I was talking to someone who . . .' Dolgoruky broke off, and began to pick his words more carefully: 'Someone who . . . considers himself . . . to be a friend of yours . . . to have your best interests at heart. Who, it might be said, has followed your career with interest.'

'Who is this?'

'I am not at liberty to reveal his name. It is too dangerous for you, as well as for him. Still and all, this man – let us just call him "Dyavol," for that is a soubriquet it amuses him to answer to – this man –'

'Dyavol? The Devil? Is this your demon that you're talking about?' Virginsky gave a sarcastic laugh.

'No. This is a real man. A man of flesh and blood. He is known as Dyavol amongst our people, though in truth, I look upon him more as some kind of god. He has had a tremendous influence on me.'

'Not Lebezyatnikov?!' cried Virginsky incredulously.

'Don't try to get his name out of me. I will not even answer your questions. However, as I was saying, if you would only let me finish you would hear something that redounds to your considerable credit . . .'

'Go on.'

'This man, this great man, believes that your action may well prove crucial in heralding in the next, necessary phase of the struggle that will bring about the end of the regime. Widespread violence and destruction are on the brink of being unleashed. This is palpable. I for one feel it. When the time comes, you will take your place amongst the heroes of the revolution.'

'I would like to meet this man. Would this be possible?'

'Quite out of the question.'

'You know,' began Virginsky tentatively. 'Last night, I thought about your demon. I imagined I had a demon of my own. I will not say he was real to me. But certainly I considered the possibility of his reality.'

Dolgoruky's reaction was unsurprised, matter-of-fact. 'This is what happens when you take the step that you and I have taken. When one transgresses . . .'

'What did you do, Dolgoruky? What was your crime?'

'The more one transgresses, the more real one's demon becomes. All this is very perplexing and ironic. I don't believe in demons, and the only god I acknowledge is . . . myself. And perhaps, also, the great man I have just told you about. And to prove that I don't believe in it all, I set about . . .' There was something shocking about the innocently mischievous giggle that Dolgoruky let out. Virginsky had the sense that it was far from appropriate to the enormity of Dolgoruky's actual crimes. 'Sinning.' He put his hand in front of his mouth like a naughty child. 'Yes. I sinned to banish the demon, but it only made him more real.'

Virginksy looked over Dolgoruky's shoulder. 'Is he here now?'

'I left him outside the apartment.'

'Shall we not let him in?'

'It will do no good. You will not be able to see him. I took him to see Lebezyatnikov. I thought if anyone could see him it would be my old tutor.'

'Did you introduce him to Kozodavlev?'

'Why bring up Kozodavlev? You're not still interested in Kozodavlev, are you? That was before. When you were with *him.*' Dolgoruky screwed up his face distastefully. '*He claimed that I did not interest him!*'

'It's just that when you mentioned Lebezyatnikov, I naturally thought of Kozodavlev.'

'Why naturally?'

'Because Kozodavlev attacked Lebezyatnikov in print.'

'Ah yes.' Dolgoruky gave a distracted smile.

'I believe you acted as an agent in the transactions.'

Dolgoruky's air of distraction deepened. Virginsky had the sense that it was an evasive strategy.

'As you did in the articles Kozodavlev wrote attacking my former professor.'

Dolgoruky could not prevent himself from being interested in what Virginsky was saying. 'Your former professor? You mean . . . ?'

'Tatiscev.'

'I see. So you know Professor Tatiscev.'

'And knowing him to be a man of great integrity, a man whose radical credentials are beyond question, who is furthermore known to be sympathetic to the cause of social revolution, I must confess that I was surprised to find him the target of Kozodavlev's barbs. Equally, I am disappointed that you played a part in that transaction too, a sordid part, if I may say so.'

'But you don't understand. All that was . . . well, let's just say, it was Dyavol's idea.'

'Is Dyavol a member of the central committee?'

Dolgoruky shrugged. 'Dyavol is Dyavol. He needs no one's authority but his own.'

Virginsky's face lit up with sudden realisation. 'Dyavol is "D." The author of *Swine!*'

Dolgoruky's cracked grin left room for the possibility that he was right.

'And, if I remember rightly,' continued Virginsky, 'there is a character in the book called Dyavol. He wrote the book and put himself in it! But why? Is he an anti-revolutionist? It does not portray our people in a very good light.'

'He wrote it primarily as a warning. If you betray the cause, this is what will happen to you. But perhaps it amused him to write it too. He often does things because they amuse him.'

'Did it amuse him to have Kozodavlev attack Professor Tatiscev?'

Dolgoruky gave a delighted giggle. 'Oh, yes! That was the most amusing diversion he had ever concocted!'

'And why did Kozodavlev go along with it? That's what I don't understand. Kozodavlev's convictions, at least as evidenced by the articles he wrote under his own name, were every bit as radical as Professor Tatiscev's. Ideologically speaking, you could not put a cigarette paper between the two men.'

'Yes, yes, of course. That's true. But what you are forgetting is that, many years ago, Professor Tatiscev stole Kozodavlev's wife.'

'No!'

'It's true! It's wonderfully, fantastically true! Although perhaps it is not so correct to talk of his stealing her. In truth, Kozodavlev rather gave her up. He was very much the new man, you see. He loved his wife as an equal, or so he claimed. And when he saw that she was in love with . . . with your old professor, he would not stand in her way. So he allowed her to choose. And she chose Tatiscev. It's just like that book, you know, *What Is to Be Done?* Except he did not fake his own suicide. He just gave her up.'

'How could he do that? How could any man?'

'Well, the point is, and here this is my own theory you understand, but I think psychologically the facts bear me out . . . the thing is, he was a little bit in love with Professor Tatiscev himself! And he was driven, I think, as much by a desire to make the professor happy as to give his wife her freedom. I told you he was a new man.'

'But then to attack him in the press?'

'What could be more natural? Because, yes, of course, he proved himself capable of acting in the most selfless, noble way imaginable. But, you know, that's going to hurt. That's going to breed resentment. That's going to inflict a wound that festers. And so when, all these years later, out of a devilish desire for amusement, it is suggested to him, by none other than . . . than, well, by Dyavol himself . . . naturally, he agreed. And I was happy to act as intermediary.'

'But what political purpose was served by all this? How did it aid the cause of revolution?'

'It allowed us to control what was said about our people in the enemy's press. Yes, of course, we defamed ourselves, but in the most ludicrous ways imaginable.' Dolgoruky seemed to remember himself. 'And of course, we picked harmless targets, straw men. We made the reactionaries look in one direction, while the real work was being done elsewhere. That, I believe, was the theory. Lebezyatnikov, for example, was never anything to do with anything.'

'And Professor Tatiscev?'

'Professor Tatiscev is a respected member of the University of St Petersburg's teaching staff, as you know.'

'Why did Kozodavlev have to die?'

'Did he?'

'Did Dyavol kill him? Perhaps it amused him?'

'He may have put the idea in someone's head. The Devil works like that, you know.'

'But you don't believe in the Devil.'

'It's a useful figure of speech.'

'And Dyavol is a man.'

'Sometimes I forget.'

Virginsky smiled. 'What do our people call you, Dolgoruky? Alyosha Afanasevich is called Hunger . . .'

'He is?'

'So he tells me.'

'I have never heard anyone call him *that*.'

'He says that I shall be known as the Fiend.'

'I think we shall just call you Magistrate. Or Magistrate-Slayer.'

'He is not dead. Porfiry Petrovich is not dead.' Virginsky spoke urgently, pleadingly almost.

Dolgoruky frowned distractedly. 'Not yet. But we may hope.'

'Of course.' Virginsky nodded strenuous agreement. He affected a joviality that was not entirely convincing. 'But you didn't answer me. They must call you something.'

'I am the Prince, of course.' Dolgoruky cackled to himself, his eyes skittering wildly as if buffeted by the shockwaves of his laughter. Then he fell silent, as abruptly – and madly – as he had begun laughing. His expression snapped into seriousness. 'But, God, you must be bored, cooped up in here.'

'I have no choice, for the time being.'

'Of course you have a choice. One always has a choice.' Dolgoruky took hold of Virginsky's arm and began to pull. There was something boyish about his eagerness and insistence. 'Come on! A bit of fresh air will do you good.'

'I have been told to stay put. Not even to show myself at a window. It is for the best.'

'Nonsense.'

'What if I am picked up? The central committee –'

'Hang the central committee.'

'But Tatyana Ruslanovna . . .'

'Ah now! That's a different matter! Tatyana Ruslanovna! What an admirable woman! You do admire her, don't you, Magistrate?'

'Yes.'

'Naturally. We all admire her. And she admires you. Your recent escapade has impressed her tremendously. That I have heard.'

'You have?'

'Indubitably.'

'From Tatyana Ruslanovna in person?'

'From someone *very* close to her.'

Virginsky frowned, as if the idea of someone very close to Tatyana Ruslanovna distressed him.

'From Dyavol, no less.' Dolgoruky could not resist making his hints explicit. 'They are very attached to one another.'

'I see.'

'There is no need for jealousy. Both Dyavol and Tanya are new people. Both believe that a woman should be free to love wherever her heart leads her. Such old-fashioned notions as fidelity, and therefore infidelity, do not trouble them. If Tanya takes it into her head to give herself to you, Dyavol will not stand in her way.'

'But he might write a nasty article about me in ten years' time.'

'It would be more Dyavol's style to get you to write it yourself.'

'You make it sound as though he can get anyone to do anything.'

'I believe he can.' Dolgoruky's smile took on a particular quality. 'He can make you leave this apartment. Today. Right this minute, in fact.'

Virginsky angled his head sceptically.

'You want to meet him, don't you?' teased Dolgoruky.

'You said that was out of the question.'

'Nothing is out of the question, as far as Dyavol is concerned. Come with me, and I will take you to him.'

A white radiance, a sudden spill of spring, momentarily filled the apartment, cascading in from all the windows at once. Virginsky felt it enter his heart, emptying it of its anxieties, expanding it with light and levity. In that moment, he made his decision. 'Very well.'

The all-encompassing flare faded as quickly as it had arrived. In its passing, Virginsky saw the particular quality he had noticed in Dolgoruky's smile intensify. There seemed in it something malevolent and heartless that was directed entirely at Virginsky. It was unmistakably personal.

30

A cleansing solution

A crowded omnibus ground its way lugubriously down the centre of the broad avenue, the horses' hooves clashing angrily with the cobbles. It was like a giant, round-shouldered beetle trudging unthinkingly along a predetermined path. Lighter, more limber vehicles – carriages, cabs and carts – passed either side of it in both directions, mayflies speeding off towards their destinies. Pedestrians dodged between the traffic: fashionable women in pairs, nursemaids with their infant charges, young bucks in military uniforms, cooks and housekeepers engrossed in the day's marketing. A tradesman in cap and apron cleared the deposits of manure from the road in front of his store.

The sky above Nevsky Prospect was filled with magnified brilliance. The promise Virginsky had glimpsed on the walls and floor of the apartment was fulfilled a thousand times over. The street was wide and long and inhumanly straight, but the sky was touched with infinity. The strings of buildings along either side were silhouetted into insignificance, the relentless stuccoed façades drained of detail.

'This is insane. The police will be looking for me.'

'And you may be assured that this is the one place they will not look! Indeed, have we not passed three policemen already, and not one of them gave you a second glance?'

'You're enjoying this, aren't you, Dolgoruky?'

'Why would I not?'

'Because it's dangerous. It may end badly, for you, as well as for me.'

Dolgoruky grinned. 'Come now, what's the point of being alive if one cannot take a stroll along Nevsky Prospect?'

'I have always found it to be an overrated activity.'

Dolgoruky suddenly turned and ran out into the middle of the road, racing after the omnibus, which was heading back the way they had come. After a moment of reluctance, during which he considered the prospect of his abandonment, Virginsky gave chase.

But it was enlivening to haul himself onto the moving tail-board. A clog of passengers was getting ready to disembark at the next stop. They viewed Dolgoruky and Virginsky with disapproval. But Virginsky was immune to their animosity. He was in possession of a rare privilege, the privilege earned through audacity. He felt himself exalted. Imbued with a sense of his own superiority, he deigned to pity them their pinched faces and mundane concerns.

The Prince bounded up the iron steps to the 'Imperial Deck'. Virginsky felt the tremor of passage in his legs as he worked his way down the narrow aisle to take the seat next to Dolgoruky. He had to admit that it felt good to be raised as high as possible in the open day, and to be moving forward in it too.

But then he remembered that they had been walking in the opposite direction. 'We're going back on ourselves,' he observed.

Dolgoruky gave a frown of irritation. 'What of it?'

'It rather suggests that you have no particular destination in mind, but are simply leading me a merry dance.'

'Did you see anyone else get on the omnibus at the same time as us?'

Virginsky cast a nervous glance behind, before turning to reassess the man next to him. The speed with which they had changed direction, dodged through traffic, and leapt onto a moving omnibus was evidence not of his mad unpredictability, but of a carefully worked-out plan to lay a false trail.

Dolgoruky gave the signal to get up as they approached Znamenskaya Square. Virginsky felt the drub of manageable panic in his heart, followed by a strange hilarity. The Nikaelovsky Station was at Znamenskaya Square, terminus for trains to Moscow.

'Where are we going?'

But Dolgoruky would not answer. Virginsky realised that he was utterly in the other man's hands, incapable of acting without his direction.

From Znamenskaya Square, they walked deep into the Rozhdestvenskaya District, at the eastern edge of St Petersburg, bounded by the Neva. It was a largely industrial area, and one which Virginsky knew well enough from a recent case. It occurred to him that he might be recognised, by one person at least, although the chances were admittedly remote. To his knowledge, Maria Petrovna Verkhotseva still had her school in the area.

The unlikely possibility of encountering Maria Petrovna quickly transformed itself in his mind into a fixed certainty. And now, far from dreading it, he almost welcomed it. Let her see what he had become! Let her see the company he kept now! The clothes he wore. The hunted, dangerous look in his eyes.

Dolgoruky led him along Kalashnikovsky Prospect, as the old Malookhtinsky Prospect was now known. They could smell the river's proximity, though they turned down a muddy side street before they reached the embankment.

They had entered a light-industrial zone, small brick workshops that gave every impression of being hurriedly thrown up, as if shame had been the driving force to their construction. The yards around them merged together into one formless wasteland, churned up and littered with all kinds of detritus: rusting machinery, charred furniture, decomposing organic matter. It was an undefined area, the city's edge petering away.

Dolgoruky seemed to pick one at random. He stooped over his hand as it rapped out the now familiar rhythm on the rough plank door. After a moment, a bolt shifted inside and the door was opened a crack. Dolgoruky was careful to position himself in front of Virginsky, so that only he would be seen by the doorkeeper. As the door began to open wider, he pushed himself into it, holding it so that Virginsky could come round him. As soon as they were both inside, he slammed the door to and replaced the bolt.

It was dim in the workshop, after the glare of the day. There were no lamps lit, Virginsky noted. It was several degrees cooler inside the workshop than out. Something chemical and corrosive in the chill air clawed at his corneas, drawing tears. The smell that came with it was like a punch expanding behind his nose. The light from outside was filtered through a few small, grubby panes high up in the walls. Virginsky blinked away his tears. His eyes were slow to adapt to the gloom, due to the pungent sting in the air. Gradually the featureless shadow who had admitted them became recognisable as Totsky, the young journalist from *Affair*, whom Porfiry had teased by calling 'Bazarov.' Virginsky sensed another presence, revealed in the sigh of shifting silk somewhere behind the journalist.

The young man stood awkwardly, one hand in the pocket of a threadbare tweed jacket, the other splayed tensely as if in readiness for a fight. He glared with undisguised hostility back at Virginsky. 'Why have you brought him here?' he demanded of Dolgoruky.

Virginsky turned to Dolgoruky in confusion. 'Is he – ?'

'Dyavol? No.' Dolgoruky chuckled at the absurdity of the idea.

The presence that Virginsky had sensed earlier stepped out of shadows. The bell-like shape of the figure confirmed it was a woman. The voice confirmed it was Tatyana Ruslanovna: 'You were told to remain in the apartment!' There was a harsh, unforgiving edge to her voice that was new to Virginsky. It filled him with despondency.

'I . . . that is to say, Konstantin Arsenevich thought . . .' Virginsky felt foolish and cowardly for trying to shift the blame onto Dolgoruky.

'What Konstantin Arsenevich thought is immaterial. You do not take orders from Konstantin Arsenevich. You take orders from the central committee. Your instructions were clear.'

'Come now, Tatyana Ruslanovna,' began Dolgoruky smoothly. 'You yourself know I am impossible to resist! Don't be too hard on the boy.'

'He is *not* a boy. He should not be behaving like a child. He is old enough to take responsibility for his own actions. This does not bode well at all.'

'But you must realise this is devastating for him to hear. After all, you know he only shot his friend to get you into bed!'

Virginsky felt the heat rise to his face. To his surprise, Tatyana

Ruslanovna did not react to Dolgoruky's words with equal force. In fact, she merely laughed: the lewd, broken laugh he remembered from an earlier time, an earlier Tatyana Ruslanovna.

'The poor fool was going mad from boredom in that apartment. I mean, look at him. He'd taken to *dressing up* to amuse himself.' Dolgoruky's laughter was disproportionate, bordering on manic.

Tatyana Ruslanovna shook her head. 'This will not do, Dolgoruky.'

The Prince's face snapped into an expression of exaggerated solemnity. 'But he is one of our people now. Surely?' Dolgoruky seemed suddenly abashed. He added hurriedly, addressing the floor, 'I promised to introduce him to Dyavol.'

'You had no right to make such a promise,' said Totsky.

Dolgoruky straightened up and gave Totsky a defiant look. 'Dyavol and I, we have our own relationship. It exists without reference to you.'

Totsky turned to Tatyana Ruslanovna. 'Once again, this man proves himself to be reckless and ill disciplined. There can be no place for him, and his kind, in the movement.'

But all Tatyana Ruslanovna said was, 'Dyavol is not here.'

'Pity,' said Dolgoruky. 'I will have to settle for showing him the next best thing.'

'Which is?' wondered Virginsky.

'Dyavol's toys.'

'No,' said Totsky quickly. 'For one thing, they are not toys. This is not a game, Dolgoruky.'

Virginsky made out several workbenches and tables arranged about the place. A number of glass phials and bottles were laid out on one table, together with a range of laboratory equipment, such as retorts and beakers. Elsewhere, he noticed a poised and sprung machine, which he identified as a small printing press; it confronted him with its circular platen, moon-faced and disconsolate.

'This is where you print the manifestos,' he observed.

'Oh, we do more than that, my friend!' Dolgoruky inhaled deeply. 'Do you smell that? Do you know what it is?'

Virginsky sniffed but the smell seemed to burn the membranes of his nostrils. He started to cough, and placed a hand over his nose and mouth to protect his vital organs from the vicious air.

'That's how the world will smell when it has been burnt clean by us. This is where we make the ultimate cleansing solution, my friend. More powerful than carbolic acid. It will clean away the accumulated layers of filth that have clogged up our society for centuries. Burn and clean.'

'Enough, Dolgoruky,' warned Totsky.

Dolgoruky took a step towards the table. Totsky's hand – the one that had been concealed in his jacket pocket – flashed up. In it, Virginsky saw a revolver. His heart beat sternly.

'Halt!'

Dolgoruky turned towards the shouted command and saw the gun levelled at him. He stopped in his tracks. 'Now, now. We are all friends.'

'Back away from the table.'

'I only want to show him – our newest recruit – what's there. I believe it will strengthen his resolve and bind him more firmly to the cause.'

'You are a dangerous fool.'

'But you would not shoot me, old fellow.'

'Oh, but I would, and with pleasure. I know you have your protectors, those who think you will be useful to the cause.' Totsky flashed a resentful glower towards Tatyana Ruslanovna. 'But as far as I am concerned, you are part of the order that must be wiped away.'

Dolgoruky took another step towards the table. 'On second thoughts, perhaps it would be for the best if you shot me. It is strange how the organism's first craven instinct is to cling on to life at all costs. But it is only now that I consider the full implications of what you are threatening, that I find it does not frighten me at all. In fact, I welcome it.' His hand darted out and he grabbed one of the small phials, the dense brown glass like a congealing of negativity. 'So shoot me! Shoot me now, and let us see what happens.'

'Put it down. Carefully. You don't know how to handle it.'

Dolgoruky grinned back at Totsky. 'You will not shoot me? I find I have no more appetite for life.'

Totsky's hand trembled, it seemed with the effort of preventing himself from squeezing the trigger. 'Now is not the time or place.'

Dolgoruky's grin became triumphant. He lifted the phial and held it high above his head.

'What is it?' murmured Virginsky.

'Death,' said Dolgoruky, with an exalted gleam in his eye. 'This little bottle is enough to kill us all. And all I have to do is cast it to the ground. Is that not so, Totsky?'

'Stop playing games, Dolgoruky. That is valuable materiel. We cannot afford to waste it.' Still he kept the gun pointed at Dolgoruky, though his hand was shaking so badly now that it was far from certain that he would hit his target.

'You are making bombs here?' Virginsky's voice brimmed with awe.

'We are making the future, Magistrate.'

'Enough!' Tatyana Ruslanovna's intervention was delayed but decisive. Virginsky had the feeling that this was often the case. He sensed that she enjoyed waiting to see how far a situation could progress in the direction of chaos, before deciding whether to help it on its way or return it from the brink. She stepped between the two men. 'Totsky, put down the gun. You know you are not going to shoot him. And you are certainly not going to shoot me.'

Tatyana Ruslanovna watched him do as she had ordered: he placed the hand holding the gun back in his jacket pocket. She then turned to face Dolgoruky. Her hand became an extension of her tender gaze, laid softly on his cheek. 'My dear, it is good that you are ready to die. But Totsky is right. Now is not the time or the place. It would be a waste of your death. A waste of you. There will come a time when we will call upon you to lay down your life. And rest assured that your death will be glorious and noble – and more than anything, useful.'

Still Dolgoruky did not lower the phial. 'But he is outside *now*! If I do it now, I will destroy him too.'

'Who is outside?'

Dolgoruky shook his head violently, refusing to answer.

'Is there ever a time when he is not near you?'

'Never!' cried Dolgoruky, desperation straining his face.

'Then you will have another opportunity to destroy him. We will choose the occasion carefully. There will be others destroyed. The oppressor and his agents. I urge you to save your death for that!'

Her hand was still on his face. But it was as if he noticed it for the first time only now.

Perhaps he saw her gesture as a reminder of a tenderness that had once existed between them, or the promise of one to come. He lowered the phial and gave it to Tatyana Ruslanovna.

With a nod to Totsky, she placed it carefully on the table.

There was a groan from Dolgoruky. He moved towards the door and drew open the bolt. His look back to the room before he slipped out was defeated, spent.

Virginsky felt torn. He did not want to let Totsky and Tatyana Ruslanovna out of his sight. He had been puzzled by their presence in the workshop when he and Dolgoruky arrived. More than puzzled: he acknowledged the stirring of an obscure jealousy. He wanted to know what they had been doing there together, what they had been talking about. But he realised that these were things he would never be able to get to the bottom of. And so the next best thing was to watch them closely from now on. At the same time, Dolgoruky's sudden departure left him feeling unusually anxious, almost desolate.

Something unwelcoming in Totsky's eyes, coupled with the nervous twitch of his concealed hand, impelled Virginsky to run after Dolgoruky.

31

Desecration

Virginsky caught up with Dolgoruky as he turned into Kalash-nikovsky Prospect, heading towards the river. 'What is the situation with Tatyana Ruslanovna and Totsky? Surely they are not –?'

'My dear fellow, I fear you are rather too fascinated with the sexual side of things. When the new social order is established, such matters will be taken care of openly, rationally, hygienically – and without the slightest hint of prudery or shame.'

They reached the embankment. The wide river stretched out in front of them, a low black shifting void that, like a vacuum, ultimately drew everything to it. Virginsky thought of Pseldonimov.

'Was that the printing press he used to print your confession?'

'What's that, Magistrate?'

'Pseldonimov. He was a printer.'

'You found that out, did you?'

'Yes. He stole a printing press from his employer. Was that it, the one in the workshop?'

'Why are you so anxious to know, Magistrate?'

'Did you kill Pseldonimov?'

'What does it matter to you now? You are not a magistrate any more, Magistrate.'

Dolgoruky's glance was distracted, mildly irritated, as he scanned the quayside. A cluster of boats was moored around a wooden jetty projecting from the end of Kalashnikovsky Prospect. They bobbed and clattered reassuringly in the gently lapping water. A couple of stevedores tossed sacks of grain carelessly from a barge. They took a moment to straighten and take in Virginsky, but seemed unable to make sense of him. With a sullen glower, they turned to grapple with the remainder of the sacks.

There was a small squat church set back a little from the riverfront, tucked between two vast warehouses. For some reason it reminded Virginsky of Porfiry Petrovich, with its central dome raised like a bald head above rounded shoulders.

Dolgoruky suddenly set off towards the church with a purposeful step. He crossed himself and went in.

Virginsky caught the closing door and followed him in. A high, silvered glamour hung in the air, a weightless pallor that could have been taken for something numinous. Virginsky was not so simple-minded; he saw it was just an effect of the light, alive with spinning dust, not divinity.

The place was crowded out with icons, in heavy encrusted frames. There were those on the iconostasis, the doors of which were closed of course. The walls too were covered with religious luminaries, the static, two-dimensional figures seeming to rush towards him, as if they had been waiting all eternity for someone to oppress.

Virginsky instinctively spoke in hushed tones: 'Wait. A moment! Dolgoruky! Let's talk.'

Dolgoruky felt no such inhibitions. His voice ruptured the hallowed silence like tearing fabric. 'He will not follow me in here!'

'Is that really why you came in here? To escape your demon?'

'You may put it like that if you wish.'

'But you cannot spend the rest of your life in here. You must go out at some point.'

'Must I? What if I end my life in here?'

'Commit suicide in a church? That would be . . .'

'Don't say sacrilegious! Now you are one of us, you shouldn't care about things like that.'

'I wasn't going to say that. You may commit any blasphemy you like as far as I am concerned. I was merely remembering what Tatyana Ruslanovna said.'

'Tatyana Ruslanovna! It is always Tatyana Ruslanovna with you!'

Virginsky didn't know quite how to take this outburst. 'But it's true. It would be a waste. You must use your death more carefully, not squander it.' He watched the prince carefully, as if he believed that if he took his eyes off him for one moment, he would go through with his threat. 'But tell me, do you really have the means to kill yourself now?'

Dolgoruky cast about frantically. 'There is always the means.'

'No. You will not do it,' said Virginsky decisively, more for his own benefit than Dolgoruky's.

Dolgoruky seemed to take this as a challenge. 'Won't I?'

'Perhaps you came in here to pray.' Virginsky's tone was mocking.

Dolgoruky's answer was swift and unexpected. He lifted an immense *manoualia*, one of several candle-stands arranged on the floor around the altar. As tall as a child, it appeared to be solid silver with gold chasing. From the strenuous groan he let out, it must have been heavy. The fat beeswax candle fell to the floor as he hefted the *manoualia* over his head. He ran towards the iconostasis and thrust the stand forwards and down, as if he were wielding a club, or a battering ram into Heaven. The flimsy panel exploded into splinters. Dolgoruky pulled his hands away from the candle-stand, leaving it hanging out of the ruptured iconostasis. The saints around it continued in their frozen, mute benediction, undisturbed by the violent intrusion.

Virginsky looked around nervously, expecting a priest to come out from behind the iconostasis to investigate. But it seemed they really were alone in the church. 'Why did you feel the need to do that?'

'It was intolerable that it should not be done. Did you not feel that?'

'Botkin's manifesto calls for such acts, I suppose.'

'Botkin has a manifesto?'

' "God the Nihilist". Is that not his?'

'Botkin leaves the writing of manifestos to others. His chosen medium is fire.'

'Did he start the fire at Kozodavlev's apartment?'

'Really, Magistrate, you must get out of this habit of asking questions! It is likely to invite suspicion.'

Virginsky dipped his head in embarrassment. To recover, he affected a bantering tone: 'Well, then. Why stop at smashing one icon? Should you not destroy them all?'

'That is a very good idea. But you must help me.' Dolgoruky retracted the *manoualia* from the shattered icon and offered it to Virginsky.

'That is senseless. It serves no purpose.'

'You are wrong, Magistrate. This is my medium. Destruction. Vandalism. The message is clear enough. Take it.'

Virginsky obeyed. The candle-stand was not as heavy as he had expected it to be. 'Your medium. It is not mine.'

'You baulk at smashing an icon, but you happily take potshots at your colleague.'

'I see no need to run unnecessary risks. If someone were to come in . . .'

'I'll leave it to you to take care of them. You are the cold-blooded assassin, after all.'

'I did what I was called upon to do, for the cause. You are simply breaking things to make yourself feel better.'

Dolgoruky gave an ugly, venomous scowl.

'There is some strange craving for perversity in you,' continued Virginsky, at last placing the *manoualia* down. 'The demon you imagine hounding you is simply a projection of that. Your tragedy is that you are not half the criminal you imagine yourself to be. This . . .' Virginsky gestured to the gaping hole in the icon panel. 'This is just a petulant child smashing up his toys.'

'A projection? I understand what you mean by that. Some kind of hallucination. But no. It is not a projection. It is real. *Corporeal!*' Dolgoruky shouted the last word. As its echo died, he looked around the church defiantly. 'Is there no priest here? Why does the priest not come out?'

Virginsky at last understood: 'That's why you smashed the icon! You wanted to draw out the priest.'

Dolgoruky's look was abashed.

'You want to be exorcised, is that it? You want a priest to cast out your demon?'

Dolgoruky seemed to buckle under Virginsky's questions, as if he could not bear to have his intentions made explicit.

'You don't need a priest, Dolgoruky. You need someone who will understand you. A kindred spirit.'

'Do you imagine yourself to be such a one?'

'I too have committed a crime. I may yet turn out to be a murderer. This morning you asked me why I shot Porfiry Petrovich.

373

Perhaps the true reason, the most honest reason, is that I did it to fulfil my destiny. To become the man I am meant to be.'

'And then what? What happens when you have fulfilled your destiny?'

'I don't know,' confessed Virginsky heavily. 'I suppose once a man has fulfilled his destiny, there is nothing left for him to do but die.'

'Do you want to die now? Here?'

'Not particularly. It's harder than you think to fulfil your destiny.'

Dolgoruky's hand delved into a pocket and came out holding a penknife. He peeled open a blade that caught the hanging light, glinting like a new-forged idea.

'You would kill me with a pocket knife?' Virginsky's voice quivered. It seemed that he was more outraged at the proposed weapon than at the prospect of being murdered.

Dolgoruky shook his head, a smile flexing briefly in a spasm of irony. 'I am not going to kill you. I am going to show you something that may make you want to kill me. You may even use this knife if you wish.'

Dolgoruky began to unpick the lining of his coat, skilfully nicking the stitches with the tip of the blade. He teased out a small sheet of paper from the hole he had created and handed it to Virginsky.

'What is this?'

'My confession.'

'Are you sure you want me to read it?'

Dolgoruky closed his eyes. His head dipped in an almost imperceptible gesture of assent.

32

Dolgoruky's confession

Virginsky's hands were shaking when he held the sheet back to Dolgoruky. Dolgoruky was slumped on the floor, his back against the iconostasis. He looked up but made no move to take the manifesto.

'Do you understand now?' Dolgoruky's voice was a rasping whisper.

'Yes.'

'Can you tell me what I should do?'

'It is not for me to say.'

'This was not the end of it, you know.'

'I know. You killed Pseldonimov because he printed this for you. You could not bear that he knew your secret.'

'Do you think I would care about that? Why would I have it printed if I cared who saw it?'

'A change of heart? Your original intention was to distribute the confession to all and sundry, but when the documentation of your crimes was there in front of you, you lost your nerve. More than that, you panicked.'

'It was not like that.'

'But you did kill Pseldonimov?'

'What is this, Magistrate? Have I not confessed to enough crimes for your liking?'

'You said this was not the end of it. I am merely trying to find out what you meant by that.'

'The girl . . . the child . . . I raped. You read that part?'

Virginsky swallowed, it seemed with great difficulty, as if the process of swallowing was entirely unnatural to him, something he had to force himself to do. 'Yes, of course.'

'She . . . she killed herself.' Dolgoruky watched Virginsky closely to see how he absorbed this information. His own face seemed to mirror the revulsion he imagined Virginsky was feeling. 'And I knew. I knew that was what she was going to do. I saw it in her eyes. She said she was going to the storeroom. But I knew she was going to hang herself. And I did nothing to prevent it.'

'Of course you didn't. There was nothing you could do. You had already killed her when you . . .' Virginsky released his grip on the printed confession. It fell with a swooping, distraught flutter. There was hatred in Dolgoruky's eye as he tracked its descent. '. . . did this,' completed Virginsky.

'I thought you were a kindred spirit,' said Dolgoruky, his voice laden with bitter disappointment.

'Why did you not put the child's suicide in your confession?'

'I . . . *could not!*' Dolgoruky began to sob.

'Yes, of course. There is a limit to what we are able to face up to in ourselves. But tell me, did you really show this document to Marfa Timofyevna?'

Dolgoruky nodded, wincing at the memory.

'Ah! There you have it. You wanted her to think badly of you, but not so badly as all that! You censored the account for her consumption.'

'You don't know what it cost me to show her even this. And is *this* not bad enough, Magistrate? It does not require a great leap of the imagination to go from this to the child's suicide. What else was left for her? What else is left for me?'

Virginsky looked away, deliberately evading Dolgoruky's final question. 'Why did you show it to her?'

'She loved me!' cried Dolgoruky. 'At least, she said she loved me. But she didn't know who I was.'

'In the end, she could not believe you capable of this. That is a sign of her love, is it not?'

'But it is a false love, based on falsity.'

'And you would rather have her hatred, so long as it is based on truth?'

'I would rather have her love, based on truth. But it seems that is not possible.'

Virginsky stared intently at the discarded handbill. 'What kind of woman could love a man capable of *that*?' The question escaped without thought. But they had passed the point where tact was necessary or even possible.

Dolgoruky gave a bitter laugh. 'Tatyana Ruslanovna, perhaps.'

Virginsky declined to answer. He suddenly felt an overwhelming revulsion for Dolgoruky, who appeared to him like an insect, deserving only to be crushed. He imagined himself picking up the *manoualia* once more, this time bringing it down on Dolgoruky's head. His feelings were entirely without pity now. He would do this, he imagined, purely to rid himself of Dolgoruky's existence, which had become suddenly intolerable to him. Instead, he satisfied himself with humiliating Dolgoruky: 'One speaks of a woman's ruin. Certainly, you brought about the ruin of that child. But it seems to me that you have also caused your own ruin, Dolgoruky.' He paused before finally answering the question Dolgoruky had asked earlier: 'There is nothing left for you.'

Dolgoruky drew his head up with a perverse pride. 'Thank you.' It seemed that he had reached a decision. Virginsky felt strangely reticent to discover what it was. He turned from the Prince and walked out of the church.

As he headed back along Kalashnikovsky Prospect, Virginsky felt, for the first time that day, exposed. More than that, he felt bereft. It was as if Dolgoruky's presence had acted like a talisman, and although he could not bear to be in the man's company any longer, he missed the strange invulnerability that the Prince inspired. A sudden ache of loneliness and longing came over him. He realised he was tiring of these people, tiring of the position in which he had placed himself. He looked down the muddy lane where the workshop was located. Should he go back in there? What would he find if he did? Totsky and Tatyana Ruslanovna locked in a filthy embrace? It was absurd. He could not imagine anything more unlikely in that chill shed. And yet, her broken laugh, and Dolgoruky's suggestion that she was capable of loving a man such as him, a child-rapist, no less, not to mention all the rest of his insinuations . . . But Totsky? Surely she would draw the line at Totsky?

He had seen all that he needed to see, he decided. It was now a matter of urgency to get back to the apartment building in Moskovskaya District.

*

The man Virginsky had noticed before was back in place, just at the entrance to the courtyard. They confronted one another with a complicated and confused exchange of panic. Virginsky was afraid that the man might say something to him, or, even worse, that he might say something to the man. The other shook out a brief, sharp warning. This annoyed Virginsky, who felt that if anyone had the right to toss his head in warning, it was he. He glared at the man and moved on.

So, that is how things stand! thought Virginsky as he climbed the stairs.

Varvara Alexeevna let him in. 'Where have you been?' Her eyes tracked down and took in his workman's clothes. A flicker of amusement undermined her attempt at severity.

'Dolgoruky came for me.'

'How did you get out?'

'Dolgoruky had a key. He said the apartment is really his.'

'That's a lie. If he has a key he must have stolen it.'

'I suppose that is entirely possible, knowing Dolgoruky.'

'And how were you going to get back in if I had not been here? He locked the door behind you, did he not?'

Virgkinsky frowned and blushed in quick succession.

Varvara Alexeevna shook her head dismissively. 'Foolish man!'

'I had no choice. I had to go with him. He said Dyavol wanted to see me.' Virginsky felt a tingle of self-consciousness at the lie.

'You saw Dyavol?'

'No. It turns out that Dolgoruky lied to me. I only saw Totsky. And Tatyana Ruslanovna.'

'Still and all, you should not have gone out.'

Something about her use of the expression 'still and all' prompted Virginsky to ask: 'Who is Dyavol, do you know?'

'No one has ever met him, apart from Dolgoruky, and Botkin, and maybe a few others.'

'Tatyana Ruslanovna?'

'Perhaps.'

'Pseldonimov?'

'Why do you ask about Pseldonimov?'

'Did you know him?'

'He was one of our people, I know that.'

'And now he is dead. What about Kozodavlev? Had he ever met Dyavol?'

'Why are you asking me these questions? Like a . . . like a magistrate!'

'Forgive me. It is an unpleasant habit of mine. I used to be a magistrate. Until very recently, in fact. I still have the magistrate's instincts. I can't help myself.'

'It is a habit you had better get out of. It will not stand you in good stead with our people.'

'Yes, of course.' And although he tried to, he could not resist another question. Indeed, he was not even aware of asking it: 'Where is Kirill Kirillovich?'

'He will not be back for another hour or so. Now, if you will forgive me, I wish to rest until Kirill Kirillovich's return.' Varvara Alexeevna did not look at him as she said this. Neither did she wait for his courteous bow, before disappearing into the bedroom. He heard the scratch of the hook slotting into its eye, locking the door.

Virginsky moved along the hallway. The light in the apartment was more diffuse now, the flaring panels of sunlight gone. He wondered how long he had spent chasing around after Dolgoruky. His grumbling stomach told him it must have been the best part of the day.

As he entered the main room he saw his service uniform draped over the sofa, almost as if there was a man – a strange two-dimensional, headless man – sitting there. It seemed that

Varvara Alexeevna must have arranged the clothes like this deliberately, perhaps to give him a shock when he came in. Or perhaps her motives were more subtle and psychological: the bottle-green frock coat with the polished brass buttons was a reminder of the man he had once been; it could also be intended to serve as a warning of the powers aligned against him now.

But really, he had to smile at Varvara Alexeevna's stupidity. What if someone had come in and searched the apartment while they were out? He thought about knocking on her door and pretending to be angry about it. While he was at it, he would ask her about food.

But then a furtive embarrassment came over him as he tried to remember where he had left the clothes when he had changed out of them. On the floor in the couple's bedroom, he surmised. He remembered her rebuke of 'Foolish man!' He realised that her displaying the uniform in that manner was just another way of saying the same thing.

So must he hide them, or even destroy them? The simplest and most effective way to achieve the latter would be to burn the clothes, feeding them into the couple's stove. But the idea repelled him in a way he could not fathom. He bundled the clothes up hurriedly and stowed them beneath the table. It was hardly a permanent solution but somehow it freed him to concentrate on what he needed to do.

He crossed to the window, or rather to the wall beside the window, doing his best to keep out of sight of anyone watching the apartment. The room was on the same side of the corridor as the bedroom, so that its window also overlooked the courtyard. Virginsky peered down. The man was still there.

There was a small escritoire in the corner of the room. Virginsky found writing paper and pens in the drawer and drafted his initial report, which he made sure fitted onto one side of paper. He folded the sheet into a paper dart, with the plain side out.

This time Virginsky stood in full view of the window. The man in the courtyard bristled to attention. They exchanged minute nods, understanding one another's gestures perfectly despite the distance between them. There was no one else in the courtyard. Virginsky opened the casement window, wincing at the creak of its hinges, and threw out the dart.

The man in the courtyard seemed determined to disregard the missile. As soon as it began its twisting descent, he looked sharply away from it, and continued to ignore it after it had landed. A terrible thought struck Virginsky: what if the fellow was not the man he had taken him to be? That is to say, what if he was exactly what he appeared to be, an idle loiterer, or even a burglar in waiting? Worse still, what if he was wholly and dangerously mistaken about him; that is to say, he was not a police agent, but one of 'our people,' watching the apartment for any slips on his part, a slip of precisely the kind he had just committed.

At last, as if in response to a signal, the man began to walk across the courtyard, though without looking down at the paper dart on the ground. Even so, he was walking straight towards it.

Virginsky's heart was pounding hard. Surely he had not been mistaken? Porfiry Petrovich had promised him that there would be a man in place, through whom he would be able to communicate. This fellow had to be that man. But if he were not, Virginsky had just, in all probability, written his own death warrant.

The man stooped and retrieved the dart, moving on without opening it. He glanced up at the window. Virginsky tried to interpret his look, for he felt that it must contain the secret of his own fate. But the look was all too brief and utterly inscrutable.

Virginsky turned to the mantelpiece to consult the ormolu clock, wondering how much longer he would have to wait for something to eat. But he saw that Varvara Alexeevna had removed it. Its absence struck him as pointed, and yet he felt a strange sense of injustice at this. After all, it was Botkin who had threatened to smash the clock, not him. Whatever else she might think of him, she had no reason to believe he was a vandal, or a thief.

*

In the adjoining room, Varvara Alexeevna lay on top of the bed, overwhelmed by the sensation of her heartbeats resonating throughout her body. She felt as though her core had been drained from her, leaving a vacuum that seemed to be expanding all the time, pressing up against her epiglottis. It was as if she was on the brink of regurgitating her soul, or what her soul had become now that she no longer believed in it.

She had delivered four babies that day, the first to a merchant's wife in Vasilevsky Island, the second to a clerk's wife in Narvskaya District, the third to a prostitute in Kazanskaya District, and the fourth to the wife of a factory worker, who already had six other children, huddled together in a damp cellar in Spasskaya District. Perhaps the strange physical sensations she was experiencing were symptoms of a kind of elation. She ought to be at least satisfied with a good day's work. The babies had all been born alive, although she could not vouchsafe how long they would remain so. The mothers too had survived the trauma of childbirth. And yet she could not shake off the sense that she was helping to bring children into a terrible world, and therefore she was complicit in fashioning the joyless, loveless destinies that awaited them; in their oppression, in other words. Many of the babies she delivered were unwanted. They would grow up – if they survived infancy – experiencing only hardship and misery. In all likelihood, the girls would become prostitutes; the boys, drunken brutes, fathering more unwanted children. And so it went on. Ignorance breeding ignorance.

She relied on two consolations to bring herself out of these depressive states: the first was her commitment to the revolution, her determination to do what she could to create a better world for the four babies she had delivered that day to grow up in; the second was her enjoyment of the small collection of fine objects she had managed to accumulate over the years. She was aware of the contradiction inherent in these positions. It had been pointed out to her enough times by Kirill Kirillovich and his friends. But as far as she was concerned, both were essential to her, and therefore she saw no difficulty.

At times, however, the latter consolation, that of beautiful objects, was more compelling than the allure of a distant, unachieved future. There was so much uncertainty on the way to a better society, so much debate and disagreement, about methods and means, not to mention objectives, that it was hard to maintain her commitment to the cause at every minute of every day. The present was dominated by sacrifice, as the immediate future would be. There was the very real possibility that she herself would not live to enjoy the rewards that would one day come. In the meantime, all that was left to her was to obey unquestioningly whatever was asked of her by the central committee. But she had to confess, she found this harder than she might have hoped. For example, she had been called upon to harbour the man in the next room. She did not like him. She did not trust him. But it seemed that he was a hero of the revolution, or on the verge of becoming one. And so she must share her apartment, and her food, with him.

It was hard to bear. And what was worse, her husband had left her alone with the interloper. The creak of the window opening in the next room reminded her forcefully of his presence. She sat up and turned her head, to indulge in the second of her consolations, which in this instance meant gazing across at the ormolu clock she had retrieved from the living room, now placed on her rococo dressing table.

It was almost six o'clock. Kirill Kirillovich should be home soon. Varvara Alexeevna rose from her bed and crossed to the window to look out for him. As she reached the window, she noticed a paper dart drift down towards the courtyard. She instinctively pulled back. A man was standing near the entrance to the courtyard. At first, there seemed to be no connection between this man and the paper dart, which he seemed determined to ignore. Indeed, it was his insistence on not looking at the dart, or at the window from which it had been thrown, that convinced her he was linked to it in some way. At last, the man began to walk casually across the muddy space, pausing only to pick up the paper dart, which he pocketed without reading.

33

'The ruse'

Porfiry Petrovich was sitting up in bed, a selection of newspapers spread out over him, as if the hospital had run out of linen and had resorted to these grubby paper sheets instead. He seemed unusually chipper, particularly for someone who had apparently been shot at close range. A small gauze dressing was fixed to his cheek with adhesive tape. His face around the dressing appeared tender and swollen. The room, of which he was the sole occupant, smelt of carbolic acid.

A *polizyeisky* positioned outside his door had been authorised to admit only Nikodim Fomich and Dr Pervoyedov. Indeed, the *polizyeisky* himself had been forbidden from entering the room, although there was nothing to prevent him, other than his un-questioning instinct for obedience. The man had been chosen for his singular lack of imagination and curiosity.

Porfiry looked up as the door opened and Dr Pervoyedov came in. The doctor's expression had settled over the past day or so into one of determined, seemingly unshakeable resentment. The raw, heart-punching fear he had felt the day before, when he had first walked into Porfiry's chambers to see his friend leaching blood from a chest wound, was still with him, a spur to his anger now. Confused and alarmed by Zamyotov's panic, by his garbled talk of gunshot and blood, it had at first been impossible for Dr Pervoye-dov to take in what Porfiry was saying to him: that there was no need to worry; that he was not hurt; that Virginsky had not really shot him. That it was all a ruse.

'A *ruse*?'

'Yes, a ruse!' How infuriatingly pleased with himself Porfiry Petrovich seemed when he shared his secret. Only just released from the anxiety of thinking his friend injured, Dr Pervoyedov felt a powerful urge to inflict the pain he had imagined Porfiry to be suffering. In the event, his adherence to the Hippocratic Oath prevailed. That was when he first noticed the nick on Porfiry's cheek.

'Pavel Pavlovich discharged a blank cartridge!' hissed Porfiry, between delighted wheezing gasps of laughter.

'He did what?'

'We plugged the cartridge with a wad of paper. This,' said Porfiry, holding up the hand that had apparently been staunching his wound, 'is pig's blood!'

Dr Pervoyedov's face contorted into an expression of distaste at the memory, though all the pig's blood had by now been cleaned up. His distaste was at the part he had been forced to play in the deception. It was all very well for Porfiry Petrovich to indulge in these pranks, but to involve others, such as himself and Pavel Pavlovich Virginsky – well, that was going too far.

Of course, Porfiry Petrovich had insisted that it was not a prank. He preferred the word 'ruse', and had asserted that it was entirely necessary, if Virginsky was to be accepted as a committed revolutionist.

At that point, Dr Pervoyedov had given vent to his feelings by indulging in a spate of unscientific language, briefly summarised by the question, 'Have you any idea of the danger to which you are exposing that boy?'

'But the whole thing was Pavel Pavlovich's idea!' declared Porfiry, as if that justified everything.

Dr Pervoyedov had shaken his head in exasperation. His anger at Porfiry's recklessness – how could an intelligent man be so stupid? – distracted him from whatever duty of professional care he might have owed as a doctor. For although he had noticed the nick, and realised it was a genuine abrasion, he did nothing about it. In his defence, it appeared extremely minor. (But was there a desire to punish Porfiry in this trivial act of neglect? If so, the doctor never admitted it.) He ought perhaps to have intervened when Porfiry carelessly rubbed the graze with the hand that was stained with pig's blood, but at the time he had been in full abusive flow. He had scarcely noticed the movement. Furthermore, he had been so caught up with Porfiry's definition of the event as a 'ruse', which implied something harmless and even amusing, that it was almost as if he had developed a professional blind-spot.

It was only later, when Porfiry was installed in the room at the Obukhovksy Hospital, that Dr Pervoyedov had remembered, and attended to, the cut on his face, at last cleaning away the blood, a mixture of Porfiry's own and that of the unknown pig. He had rinsed the wound with a solution of carbolic acid, in keeping with the best advice of the renowned Edinburgh surgeon, Joseph Lister. 'There must have been something lodged in the barrel, or perhaps it was a piece of the cartridge shell that broke off.' He could find nothing of the kind in the wound now. Whatever had caused the injury was long gone.

'It's nothing,' Porfiry had protested.

'Tell me, did he really point the gun at your head?'

'But it was loaded with a blank cartridge. There was no danger.'

'Could he not just as easily have fired into the air?'

'He had to make it convincing.'

'But there was no one else in the room with you at the time. And your door was closed. Who was there to be convinced?'

'Someone might have come in just as he was firing the gun.'

'In which case, your ruse most certainly would have backfired. Pavel Pavlovich would have been detained.'

Porfiry had pursed his lips as he thought about Dr Pervoyedov's objections. 'Perhaps he needed to convince himself.'

Now, a day after 'the ruse', Dr Pervoyedov was less than happy with what that graze was turning into. The skin around the wound was red, the flesh swollen, and sore, judging by Porfiry's winces when Dr Pervoyedov probed it. The wound itself was tiny. But it was moist and gaping, like the mouth of a small bloodthirsty fish.

Porfiry himself, however, seemed little troubled by it, and so the doctor affected to be equally unconcerned. 'I'll just take a look at that cut,' he said, avoiding Porfiry's eyes, and still maintaining his pinched, resentful expression.

'Stop fussing. It's nothing, I tell you. It's the way you keep pulling off that dressing that's made it sore.'

At Dr Pervoyedov's smile as he studied the minuscule wound, Porfiry wondered if he had at last been forgiven. But the smile was a mask. The truth was that Dr Pervoyedov did not like what he saw at all. The flesh was angry and more inflamed than ever. And in the lips of the little fish, he saw morsels of yellow pus.

The doctor felt a weight of shame and grief, his conscience pounding his memory with the sight of Porfiry's pig-bloodied hand touching his face. He knew very well what they might expect if the infection took hold in earnest.

And so his resentment vanished – what a trifling thing it

turned out to be, after all! – and he was restored to Porfiry as the smiling friend of old. If Porfiry was suspicious at the speed of this transformation, he kept it to himself.

As Dr Pervoyedov cleaned out the wound now, Porfiry's winces were more deeply felt and longer lasting than they had been.

*

Porfiry let out a small wimper of protest as he slumbered, waking himself up with a start. His arms felt down the bed and pulled a sheet of newspaper up to read. He quickly tired of the paper and let it fall to the floor, casting a glance towards Dr Pervoyedov. 'What are you doing still here? Don't you have proper patients to see to?'

For some reason, Dr Pervoyedov was grinning in a most unconvincing manner, affecting an insouciance that he clearly did not feel. 'Oh, I have completed my rounds. I was just passing, and so I thought I would look in on you.'

There was a diffident knock at the door. Porfiry looked up to see Nikodim Fomich enter.

'How is our *patient*?' Nikodim Fomich gave the last word an ironic emphasis. His face wrinkled with pleasure. He had never shared Dr Pervoyedov's disapproval of 'the ruse', and had in fact given his secret assent to Virginsky's mission beforehand.

'The wound is not healing as cleanly as I might have hoped,' said Dr Pervoyedov, who seemed to be irritated by Nikodim Fomich's joviality.

'Wound? But I understood the weapon was loaded with blanks?'

'The good doctor has rather made a mess of my face with all his fussing,' said Porfiry.

'I . . . !' But Dr Pervoyedov decided against articulating his protest further.

'Exercise more care, Pervoyedov! We must look after this man. He is the jewel in our crown.' Nikodim Fomich patted Porfiry's leg solicitously. 'Now then, what do you think of this? We have received a message. From Pavel Pavlovich, our man in the field. The system you set up has worked, Porfiry Petrovich!'

Porfiry waved away the compliment.

Nikodim Fomich handed a much-folded sheet of paper to Porfiry. Porfiry looked briefly at the note but handed it back to Nikodim Fomich almost immediately. 'Read it to me.' His hands fell heavily when the note was taken from him and he closed his eyes.

Nikodim Fomich frowned distractedly at this unexpected reaction but did as Porfiry directed. 'Have read Dolgoruky's printed confession. He confesses rape of child. Child subsequently killed self. Dolgoruky makes no mention of suicide in confession. I believe this provides Dolgoruky with motive to kill Pseldonimov: to suppress the confession that he came to regret. Printing press at workshop off Kalashnikovsky Prospect. Also serves as bomb-making factory. Dolgoruky promised to introduce me to 1 known as "Dyavol." Failed. I believe Dyavol head of cell including Pseldonimov, Rakitin, Dolgoruky, Kozodavlev and three others. My first contact, Botkin. Totsky = "Bazarov" from *Affair*. And Tatyana Ruslanovna Vakhrameva! (Remember?) If I can meet Dyavol, will find out more. Dyavol is key to it all. We could arrest Dolgoruky for child rape. He will confess. But if he remains at liberty for present he may lead me to Dyavol. Cell is planning major atrocity involving explosives. I need to infiltrate cell further find out what. Some suspicion (of me) by revolutionists. They would be more convinced if P.P. had died! (Consider announcement to that effect? Staged funeral?) If I am discovered, they will kill me. Botkin ruthless, Dolgoruky mad. Totsky angry. Vakhrameva damaged. Dyavol? Worst of all? I sincerely hope that I am not mistaken in the man I have chosen to deliver this message. (However, advise you change man as he is becoming conspicuous.)

'P.S.: Tatiscev lied. Did know Kozodavlev. "Stole" K's wife many years ago.' Nikodim Fomich directed his attention expectantly onto Porfiry.

'Pavel Pavlovich has done well,' declared Porfiry without opening his eyes.

'Shall we raid the workshop?' asked Nikodim Fomich. 'Seize the illegal printing press and whatever materiel is there? Virginsky has very helpfully drawn a map of the location.'

'If we do that now, the members of the cell will without doubt vanish into the night. We must allow Pavel Pavlovich to continue his operation.'

'With all respect, Porfiry Petrovich,' began Dr Pervoyedov, ominously. The doctor had a tendency to formality when agitated. 'With all respect, I say, would it not be wiser to extract him now before he comes to any harm?'

'Extracting Pavel Pavlovich prematurely will only have the same effect. The terrorists will realise they have had an agent in their midst and, once again, disappear without trace. And so, we have no choice but to ensure Pavel Pavlovich's further advancement in the movement.'

'You are not thinking – I hope to God you are not thinking this! – you are not thinking of taking up his preposterous suggestion?'

'It may be possible to make an announcement along the lines that he has suggested.'

'You would announce your own death? And would you also stage a funeral? Surely even you would hesitate to perpetrate a prank as tasteless as *that*.'

'If it were merely a prank, then of course I would have nothing to do with it. And, with any luck, it will not come to that. However, if we time our announcements well, Pavel Pavlovich's progression within the inner cabal will have reached its conclusion before there is need to go through with any such display.'

'And what will that conclusion be, I wonder? His death?'

'You may not believe this, Dr Pervoyedov, but I tried to talk him out of it, to no avail. I could see that he was determined to get mixed up with these people, with or without my support. I felt it better to put in place a channel of communication, should he need to contact us in an emergency.' Porfiry's eyes were still closed as he spoke. His weariness was such that it seemed as if the conversation, rather than his injury, was taking its toll on him.

'You could have forbidden him.'

'In which case, I would have lost him entirely. I fear that I may have half-lost him as it is.'

'Oh? And what do you mean by that?' said Nikodim Fomich.

At last Porfiry opened his eyes to look at Nikodim Fomich. 'I mean that Pavel Pavlovich's loyalties are, at the best of times, difficult to pin down. The poor boy is deeply conflicted, and fluctuates dangerously in his convictions. If I had forbidden him from proceeding with his plan, I fear that he would have joined the revolutionists in earnest – out of petulance, as it were. He is quite often

393

capable of acting in such an immature way. I sometimes think the only way to understand Pavel Pavlovich is in the light of the difficult relationship he has with his father. He is torn between the desire to assert his independence – in other words, to break free from authority – and his craving for authority's approval. We may be sure that the same complex medley of emotions is present in the relationships he is forging with the revolutionists. That is to say, he will want to destroy them at the same time as wishing to be accepted by them. That is how he looks on everything – including the department, including me.'

'If what you have said is true, then he is the least suitable individual imaginable to send on such a mission,' said Dr Pervoyedov.

'I think you will find that similarly contradictory feelings exist in the hearts of us all. Some of us may gravitate to one pole, rather than the other, but the attraction may be transposed at any time – as in a magnet – because the potential for the opposite continues to reside within us. It is good news that Pavel Pavlovich has chosen to communicate with us. Something, I think, must have prompted him to incline to our side in this struggle. I only hope that nothing else occurs to reverse the polarity of his loyalties.' Porfiry grimaced, as if the idea was physically painful to him. He sank back on his pillows. His eyelids fluttered characteristically and then closed again.

Dr Pervoyedov saw the beads of sweat forming on Porfiry's brow. It was clear that the pain the magistrate was feeling now was not intellectual.

'I think we had better leave,' he whispered to Nikodim Fomich.

The chief of police frowned. 'I don't understand. This is a ruse, is it not? He was not really shot by Virginsky.'

There was a grunt from the bed, which could have been of contradiction or agreement. However, Porfiry did not open his eyes.

Dr Pervoyedov placed a hand on Porfiry's forehead, frowning at the heat that met his touch. Porfiry murmured incoherently in response.

Turning from the bed, the doctor ushered Nikodim Fomich out of the room with an urgent gesture.

As they came out, the *polizyeisky* at Porfiry's door tensed his face into an expression of self-conscious alertness, snapping himself upright in his seat. Nikodim Fomich acknowledged his exemplary watchfulness with an appreciative nod. The policeman stared straight ahead, straining to see enemies of the state in the empty hospital corridor. At any rate, he seemed determined to make it clear that he had no interest in eavesdropping on the conversation of his superiors.

'Nikodim Fomich, I am very concerned about Porfiry Petrovich's wound.'

'What wound?' Remembering himself, Nikodim Fomich glanced at the police guard and dropped his voice: 'There is no wound, doctor.'

'Something extraneous was discharged by the gun. It appears to have grazed his face.'

'Oh yes, that. But why on earth are you worrying about a tiny graze?'

'Because I fear it may have become infected. If the infection spreads to his blood, the consequences may be very grave indeed.'

'What do you mean?'

'His condition has deteriorated rapidly. The beads of perspiration. The exhaustion. He is becoming feverish.'

'So, he will have a little fever. He will get over it.'

'With all respect, Nikodim Fomich, as a physician, I find it impossible to speak with such absolute confidence.'

'Surely you don't think he will die?'

Dr Pervoyedov spoke in an urgent, angry whisper: 'The next twenty-four hours will prove critical. His body may well succeed in fighting off the infection. I don't wish to be unduly pessimistic. It was simply my intention to warn you that the situation is not perhaps as straightforward as you might think. Porfiry Petrovich is not as young as he once was, or as strong. His addiction to tobacco has weakened his constitution over the years. His chest is far from robust. To succeed in overcoming a general infection, an organism needs to be in the utmost good health.' Dr Pervoyedov's voice rose uncontrollably: 'This reckless plan! What were you thinking?'

Nikodim Fomich avoided the doctor's gaze, abashed. 'I certainly did not think there was any danger to Porfiry Petrovich.'

The doctor's eyes widened incredulously, but before he could answer, they heard Porfiry cry out. 'Nikodim Fomich! Where is Nikodim Fomich?'

The two men exchanged glances complicated by anxiety and recrimination, before going back inside.

34

Dolgoruky at peace

The following day, Virginsky noticed a new quality in Varvara Alexeevna's reserve towards him. It no longer seemed that she was afraid of him. Now he believed he noticed something like contempt in her demeanour towards him. She regarded him, he felt, as one might a marked man. Her replies to his mostly innocent questions concerning household matters were tinged with a mocking tone that seemed to say: *Just you wait, my lad. Just you wait.*

Kirill Kirillovich lingered over breakfast, and indeed both of them today seemed reluctant to leave him alone in the apartment, so that all three of them were at home when the first visitor of the day called. What struck Virginsky was that whoever it was failed to use the coded knock. The urgent, formless hammering set their hearts racing: What could it mean? Who could it be?

They were somehow shocked to discover that it was Alyosha Afanasevich Botkin, in a state of supreme agitation. The reason for his excitement was quickly revealed: 'Dolgoruky is dead.'

Varvara Alexeevna, who had revealed her fondness for the Prince – for all his faults – at her husband's name day, let out a small yelp of horror.

'Hanged himself,' continued Botkin ruthlessly. 'Here. He left this.' Botkin thrust out a piece of paper which Virginsky recognised as Dolgoruky's printed confession. There was a handwritten addendum scribbled at the bottom.

Varvara Alexeevna was the first to snatch the sheet. She read it with ferocious concentration. When she had finished, she glared at Virginsky. The contempt he had sensed before had now hardened to hatred. She thrust the confession in his hand. He read: *My thanks to the Magistrate-Slayer, who told me what I must do. By the time you read this, I will be at peace. Prince Konstantin Arsenevich Dolgoruky.*

'I don't know what he means. You know Dolgoruky is a liar. He is lying even in this. I can tell you for certain that this confession omits an important detail of one of his crimes. The child he raped killed herself. That is what drove him to suicide. Nothing that I said to him.'

'How do you know this?' asked Kirill Kirillovich.

'He told me. He showed me this yesterday.'

'This man,' began Varvara Alexeevna slowly, 'is not what he seems. He is a police agent. An infiltrator. I saw him pass a note to a spy who was watching the apartment.'

'That's not true!' But Virginsky's childish blush betrayed him.

'He threw a paper dart from the window and it was picked up by the spy. In addition to that, he continues to ask questions like a magistrate. And he acts without any caution, as if he is not afraid of getting caught. Yesterday he went out with the Prince. And he simply left his service uniform out for anyone to see. A man who was really in hiding would not be so careless.'

'But how can this be?' wondered Botkin. 'He shot his superior.'

'The man survived the attack!' said Varvara Alexeevna. 'All I can say is he did not try very hard to kill him.'

Kirill Kirillovich turned a look of sour distrust on Virginsky. Botkin's expression was one of utter disillusionment.

'I confess,' began Virginsky, 'that my attack on Porfiry Petrovich was intended to be symbolic, rather than necessarily fatal. As I think I have already explained, it didn't matter to me whether he lived or died. To have shot him in his chambers was enough. My own experience, as an investigator, of gunshot wounds is that death is not always immediate. He may not be dead yet, but that does not mean he will not die soon. As far as I could tell, he lost a lot of blood. For a man of his age and physique and general health, it will be difficult for him to get over that. It is ironic that Dolgoruky yesterday proposed that we should go to the Obukhovsky Hospital to finish him off. I should have agreed. But I was concerned that we had no authorisation from the central committee. If it is so very important to you that Porfiry Petrovich die, I will go there today and make sure of it.'

'You won't be able to get within a *vershok* of him,' said Kirill Kirillovich. 'As you well know! For another thing, we do not intend to let you out of our sight. Not until we have heard from the central committee what they want us to do with you.'

'But what is this about a note?' demanded Botkin, struggling to process Varvara Alexeevna's allegations. 'Who was the man you passed the note to?'

Virginsky looked from one face to another. He saw nothing in any of them that offered hope. 'It's true. The man I passed a note to is a spy. And I am an infiltrator. But we are not working on behalf of the police. We are part of another revolutionary grouping. We found out about your group's activities and it was decided that we ought to investigate. Believe it or not, there are two central committees and it seems that they have nothing to do with one another. Certainly, this is how the situation appears to the foot soldiers on the ground. I have been sent in to infiltrate your people to discover whether you can be trusted, with a view to bringing our groups together and co-ordinating our activities. I must confess that Tatyana Ruslanovna's belief that there is already a police agent in your midst concerned me greatly, as did Dolgoruky's erratic behaviour. I communicated as much to my people.'

'Why did your group not approach us directly?' demanded Kirill Kirillovich.

'It is not wise to do anything directly. One simply does not know who to trust. I admit my clandestine behaviour may have backfired. I regret that I was not more open with you, Alyosha Afanasevich, but you must understand that I was obeying the commands of my own central committee.'

'This is all a lie!' cried Varvara Alexeevna wildly.

'One thing will prove I am telling the truth. The death of Porfiry Petrovich. I sincerely believe it is only a question of time. I urge you to await more news on that front before you dismiss me as a police spy.'

'You seem certain, now, that he will die. You did not before,' observed Botkin warily.

'In all honesty, I don't know how he has survived this long.'

'We must consult with the central committee,' advised Kirill Kirillovich. '*Our* central committee. They will decide what your fate should be. I would not hold out too much hope, if I were you. Even if your story proves to be true, they will not be favourably impressed by the deception you have used.'

'You must take me to see Dyavol. I will talk to him directly and put myself at his mercy. I have things to tell him that I cannot disclose to anyone else. I believe I know who the spy in your midst is.'

A startled energy transmitted itself between Botkin, Kirill Kirillovich and Varvara Alexeevna. It was Varvara Alexeevna who spoke for them all: 'You are accusing one of us! Oh, you are very clever, but you will come unstuck! The truth will come out in the end. We'll wind in the pail and discover it cracked.'

'Naturally, we will communicate what you have said to the central committee,' said Botkin. 'They will decide what is to become of you. I warn you, they do not look kindly on those who would betray the cause.'

'Do what you must do,' said Virginsky. 'I have nothing to fear.'

Botkin nodded sharply and deeply, his head scything the air like an executioner's blade.

*

Kirill Kirillovich stayed with him for the rest of that day, refusing, however, to enter into conversation of any kind. All Virginsky's questions – 'When will Botkin be back?' 'Has he gone to consult with the central committee?' 'How long will it take them to come to a decision?' And even, 'Is this how it was with Pseldonimov?' – were met with resolute silence. There was an element of punishment to this, of course. But Virginsky also got the impression that the other man did not quite trust himself. Either he was afraid that he would give away something that might be useful to a potential enemy of the cause, or that he would be swayed by Virginsky's persuasive arguments.

Virginsky expected the central committee to act swiftly. That is to say, he expected the end at any moment. But the hours dragged on, even without Varvara Alexeevna's ormolu clock to mark them out.

When Varvara Alexeevna herself returned at the end of her working day, she gave Virginsky a new look. Her usual suspicion was shadowed, for the first time, by something Virginsky recognised as doubt, the source of which seemed to be the copy of the *Police Gazette* she was clutching. She took Kirill Kirillovich into the bedroom for an urgent conference.

Soon after this, Botkin returned. The three of them came together into the main room, bearing down on Virginsky with the angry glowers of wolves that had been cheated of their prey. 'It seems you have been granted a reprieve,' said Botkin. 'According to the late edition of the *Police Gazette*, your magistrate's condition has deteriorated sharply. The central committee has decided to await the outcome of your attack before determining your fate. If he dies, you will be hailed as a hero of the revolution.'

'And if he lives?'

'If I were you, I would pray that he dies. And that his death is verifiable.'

'And in the meantime, I am to be treated like a convict?'

'Of course. Or, to be more exact, like a condemned man who has received a stay of execution.' The old sarcastic smile settled once more on Botkin's lips, like an animal that had been driven from its lair at last returning.

35

'What will it be like to die?'

He had the sense of someone standing over him.

Give up the fight, my dear! It's time to give up the fight.

It was his father's voice, but where was his father? Did his father exist now just as a voice?

Release your grip! Let go!

'Papa?'

I am inside you. The pain – that pain that you feel – you do feel it, don't you? That pain is me.

'You can heal me!' cried Porfiry. He opened his eyes. And opening his eyes was like throwing open the shutters of a window in a Swiss chalet. In fact, that was what he was doing. He was in the bedroom of a Swiss chalet, throwing open the shutters. A blinding light rushed in, with the eagerness of a sniffing hound. The initial fierceness of the light settled into an amber glow on the planks of the chalet's cladding.

Porfiry turned to where the voice of his father had come from. He had the sense that it had been located in the corner of the room. But his father had said that he was inside him. Did that mean that his father had lied?

The man standing in the corner of the room was not his father. It was Prince Dolgoruky but somehow Porfiry confused him with another prince. He remembered a question that had been on his mind, one that he very much wanted to ask the Prince for whom he mistook Dolgoruky. 'Did you find him?'

'He's not here,' said Dolgoruky, as if he too mistook himself for someone else.

'No,' said Porfiry, as if he had expected this answer. Another question occurred to him. 'Where are we? In Switzerland?'

'Not exactly,' said Prince Dolgoruky.

'What will it be like to die?' asked Porfiry.

Give up the fight, my dear! You must give up the fight.

Porfiry looked up. It seemed to him that his father's voice came from above.

A terrible weight was pushing down on him now. He was lying on his back, pinned to the ground by an enormous stone. It seemed to be a stone, but he couldn't be sure. All he knew was that he had to push it off him. Otherwise it would crush him.

Give up the fight!

His father's voice was in the stone now. His father's voice was crushing him.

'Heal me!' pleaded Porfiry with the weight of the stone.

Don't you think if I could, I would have healed myself?

'But God?' implored Porfiry. 'There is a God?'

His father's answering laughter was devastating.

It is not so difficult. Simply decide that you will give up the fight, and lo!

His father's voice seemed to be answering a question that Porfiry had asked earlier.

'Why can't I see you?'

You must give up the fight if you want to see me.

Porfiry closed his eyes and pushed with both hands. The great weight suddenly became nothing. He looked down to see that he

404

was holding a painted egg in his hands. And somehow, he was standing again.

He heard children's laughter. The five Prokharchin children circled him, arms outstretched, hands linked. They moved around him with half-dancing, half-skipping steps.

Porfiry was overjoyed to see them. 'You did not die after all! It was all a ruse!'

The children giggled back at him. There was a mindless, empty quality to their laughter that began to unsettle Porfiry. He decided that he wanted no part of it. 'That's enough now, children.'

But the children's dance continued and in fact grew faster, until they were whirling around him at an impossible speed. Their faces blurred into a streak of flesh encircling him, their laughter merging into a single scream.

The fleshy blur shrank like an elastic band contracting, tightening around his head. He felt it against his face, filmy, acrid with the taste of burning. The film was unspeakably revolting, as if it were a spider's web, or the web woven by something more repulsive than a spider. He pulled at the web with his fingers.

'Death,' said Porfiry. And the web that clung to his face rushed into his mouth as soon as he opened it to speak. Once it had gained admittance to his mouth it began to expand. He knew that this did not bode well. The more it expanded, the harder it was for him to breathe. It was suffocating him.

Give up the fight, my dear! It's time to give up the fight.

His father's voice was suddenly overwhelmingly comforting. He knew that if he relaxed his being, as his father urged, everything would be all right.

He knew that his father would never lie to him.

He knew that he must do as his father said.

405

He felt the tension go from him. The first thing that happened was that he swallowed the clump of sticky webbing that had entered his mouth.

There was a sound like the wind chasing itself through a tunnel. The window shutters banged against the outside of the chalet.

Flakes of snow came in through the window, quickly building to a swirling blizzard that obliterated the interior. The blizzard became denser and darker. He had a sense of it as something infinite. The bedroom no longer existed, nor the chalet. There was only the ever-darkening snowstorm.

There was the sound of the unseen shutters slamming to. And then all was darkness.

36

Dyavol

It seemed he was not to be left alone from now on. The next day, Botkin sat with him in the morning. Unlike Kirill Kirillovich, he was confident enough of his own revolutionary commitment to engage Virginsky in conversation. 'Where has she put the clock?'

'She moved it into the bedroom. I think she was afraid I would carry out your threat to smash it.'

'That doesn't make sense.'

'Perhaps not.'

'I am glad she's moved it. If it were still here, I would destroy it.'

'A rather pointless act of vandalism.'

'There is no such thing. Vandalism is always to the point.'

'Alyosha Afanasevich, there is no reason now why we may not be completely frank with one another. My fate is already sealed. Either I am to be afforded the revolutionist's equivalent of can-onisation, or I am to be executed. Therefore, you may tell me . . . anything . . . and everything. It can make no difference now.'

'I don't know what you're getting at.'

'When we met, on Easter Sunday night, at the warehouse blaze . . .' Virginsky watched the other man closely, looking for an answer to a question he hadn't asked in the angle of Botkin's defiance.

'What of it?'

'Did you set the fire?'

A crack opened in Botkin's face. From it emerged that sound that Virginsky remembered from the night they met, an axe hacking into soft wood, his laughter. 'What harm can it do now? Yes, I was the *pétroleur* that night.'

'And the fire that destroyed Kozodavlev's apartment?'

Botkin shrugged. 'I know nothing about that.'

'Truly?'

'Truly. Why would I lie to you?'

'Because of the children. The children who died.'

'Ah, my friend, I see you do not understand me. Neither do you understand the nature of the struggle in which we are engaged.'

'What are you saying? That you don't care about the children?'

Botkin sighed, as if he were suddenly bored of the conversation. 'You realise that you have just betrayed yourself?'

'What do you mean?'

'A true assassin would never ask such a ridiculous question.'

'But children!'

'Many more may have to die before the revolution is accomplished.'

Virginsky nodded. Botkin clearly would have had no compunction admitting the crime if he had committed it. 'But can we be sure these children died in the furtherance of the revolution? That is far from clear.'

'Kozodavlev had become unreliable. Such considerations as you just voiced were distracting him from the cause. He was on the verge of betraying us. The central committee was right to instigate his termination. In this instance, they did *not* call upon me to execute their orders. Had they done, I would have willingly answered the call.'

'Whom did they call upon?'

'That doesn't matter. In truth, I don't know. Naturally. That is the way the central committee works.'

'Totsky?'

'There are others. There are many. From time to time, the central committee employs all manner of individuals to do its bidding. Not all are especially motivated by political convictions. Some carry out such deeds for money. Others simply because it is in their natures to destroy – the central committee finds a way to direct their destructive tendencies. There have been common criminals, escaped convicts, used in this way. My guess is that this was the case with Kozodavlev.'

'And Pseldonimov?'

'Pseldonimov was different.'

'In what way?'

'Pseldonimov died ... so that the group might become stronger. It was not true that he was a threat to us. At least I do not believe so. Dyavol had become tired of him – that certainly was true. We needed him to get the printing press. But once that was acquired, we no longer needed him. Of course, there was a danger that he might betray us. There is always that danger, with every one of us. But it was rather the case that Dyavol saw that he would be more useful to the group dead than alive.'

'I don't understand.'

'He would serve to bring the group together. To bind us to one another.'

'In what way?'

'Because we would all have a part in killing him. No one man – or woman – could be said to be responsible for his death. We were all equally culpable. One enticed him. One put him at his ease. One held him. One tied the ropes. One tightened the gag.

One kept lookout. One shot him. All conspired to dispose of the body. And now we all have this hold over one another. And it is our mutual fear and suspicion that binds us together. Rather brilliant, don't you think?'

Virginsky thought back to Pseldonimov's body on Dr Pervoyedov's trestle table. 'He was a Jew. Did that make it easier?'

Botkin shrugged, as if the question was of no importance.

'You said woman? There was a woman involved?'

'Of course.'

'Tatyana Ruslanovna?'

'Of course.'

'Who else?'

'You can work it out, can't you?'

'You. Dolgoruky. Totsky. Kozodavlev?'

'Correct. So far. But you are forgetting someone.'

'Dyavol.'

'Of course.'

'Sometimes it seems to me that Dyavol *is* the central committee. That everything you do is decided by this individual. Are you sure this is wise? It certainly does not seem democratic, no more democratic than the Tsar.'

'Men like Dyavol are necessary.'

'Unlike Pseldonimov.'

'Pseldonimov served his purpose.'

'Who is Dyavol?'

'Ah, *that* you shall not know. Unless Dyavol himself wishes you to.'

'But *you* know his identity? *You* have met him?'

One side of Botkin's mouth shot up and his eyelids fluttered closed in an expression of serene complacency. 'I have been granted that privilege.' He now fixed Virginsky with a look charged with contempt, which was possibly as close as Botkin was capable of approaching pity.

*

Virginsky lost all track of the days. It was not simply that the newspapers were kept from him. Ever since he had fled Porfiry's chambers, he had felt himself severed from the ordinary flux of time that ruled his fellow men, giving direction to their lives and binding them one to another on the diurnal treadmill. He had entered another realm, where the moments were measured by the throbbing of his pulse, by the flickering processions of his snatched and anxious dreams and by the infinitely slow growth of his beard. There was a fisheye looking glass in the room. One day he looked up at it and saw a man he did not recognise staring back at him. He knew then that a considerable number of days must have passed.

At times he was beset by a quaking terror, convinced that Botkin would come for him at any moment, taking him to a desolate spot on the edge of the city, some blasted wasteland strewn with rubbish, overgrown with dingy weeds. And there, alone, weeping like a girl, begging shamelessly for his life, revealing himself at last to be the coward he had always known he was, he would stare down the barrel of his killer's gun.

Some days Kirill Kirillovich sat with him, some days Totsky. He was never left alone with Botkin again, who perhaps now regretted all that he had divulged to Virginsky. There was also the possibility that others had decided that Botkin could not be trusted.

·

Neither Totsky nor Kirill Kirillovich addressed a word to him, or responded in any way to the questions he asked.

Even when he shouted into Totsky's face, 'Surely this must be driving you insane!' the young radical barely blinked. Virginsky was driven to torturing himself by making speculative remarks about Totsky's relationship with Tatyana Ruslanovna. He felt sure that they must be lovers. He was inhibited from stating his fears so baldly by the possibility that they might prove founded. Totsky's silence was infuriating, but in this case it was possibly better than a definite answer. At one time, Virginsky imagined he saw confirmation of one of his more daring insinuations in the curling of a lip and the flood of colour to the cheeks. He was tortured then by jealousy and despair, at which point the realisation hit him that he was in fact in love with Tatyana Ruslanovna. He reeled, as if from a physical blow. The realisation was not a happy one. If anything, he was more devastated after it struck him than before. It was more than likely that Tatyana Ruslanovna was one of those conspiring to kill him. To say that he was afraid his feelings would not be reciprocated was an understatement. On the other hand, it was perhaps equally true that he was conspiring in her arrest. At this moment, however, none of that seemed to matter anymore. All that he wanted was to live, and to be with her. He would have sworn allegiance to any cause, and meant it, to make that possible.

Now it was even harder for him to keep his bearings amid the staggering past of the hours. Varvara Alexeevna came and went; when she was not in the stagnant apartment, she was bringing new life into the teeming world. Food was prepared, and he was allowed to share in it. The curtains were kept closed at all times, to prevent him from communicating with anyone in the courtyard, even by looks and gestures.

And so he could not say with any certainty when it was, or how long after that momentous day when he had levelled a gun at Porfiry Petrovich, that Tatyana Ruslanovna came into the apartment and relieved Kirill Kirillovich from the unrewarding task of watching him. He noticed that she was wearing coarse peasant clothes that did not seem to fit her properly, as if they belonged to someone else. In all likelihood, she wore them to look more like one of the people. However, the ill-fitting clothes only emphasised her individuality, at the same time distancing her from the class she sought to assimilate. To Virginsky, she looked like a child dressing up. He found the effect of her clothes inexpressibly touching.

'They will not speak to me,' he said, as soon as they were alone.

But she did not speak to him either. She pulled him to her and closed her lips around his, just as he was forming the first of the questions floating into his consciousness. The breath went from him, so completely that it seemed she must have sucked it out of him. His heart was in spasm; he felt it thrashing like a fish stranded on the bank.

He gasped for air as she released him. Her gaze shone with admiration and – dare he say it? – love. His own gaze back was questioning.

'He's dead!' she explained. 'Your magistrate died. They published an obituary in the paper. And a date has been announced for his funeral. It seems you really killed him.'

'Dead? Really? Let me see!'

'There will be time for that later. Now.' Her hands were on him again, exploring, guiding, compelling. Pulling away at the fastenings of his clothes. His hands were quick to reciprocate. It seemed an immense privilege to touch those coarse peasant clothes, as if

413

he was being allowed to share in something deeply personal to her, as if his fingers were alighting on her mind. If he had been moved at the sight of the clothes, his feelings now, as he probed and peeled away their layers, were almost too much for him to bear.

And then the fact of her beauty – her complete beauty, revealed to him without shame or affectation, simple, absolute – was overwhelming. Most affecting of all was the trust that it implied. When he had been denied so much, to be granted this – the tears rose to his eyes. He dared not touch her naked beauty. She had to take his hands and guide him.

She pulled him down onto her, onto the sofa, into her, and the release from all his suffering came immediately, and he was shaking with tears of gratitude and fear, sobbing himself into her, a sobbing that came from the deepest part of him. And she held him and soothed him and stroked his hair.

She was more experienced than him, and her experience frightened him. But she put him at his ease and her hands resumed their exploration of his body, and he felt himself want her again, but without the desperate urgency of before: more calmly, more completely, knowing somehow that they had all the time in the world, and that she wouldn't be taken from him, and that they were not just lovers but also equals in their love.

Once more, time meant nothing to him. A lifetime was lived, and everything that could be said or done in a lifetime was said and done.

At the end of that lifetime, she began to get dressed. He watched her in silence, and a strange, appalling grief gripped his heart, as if every item of clothing that she put on removed a part of her from him for ever. At the end of her dressing, she turned to

414

him with a tender smile. 'Come. You must get dressed too. Dyavol will see you now!'

'Dyavol?'

'Yes, of course! You have proven yourself. You killed Porfiry Petrovich.'

It was as if the words she spoke were true. The grief took him over completely now. He wept.

'My God, you're crying like a baby! If this is how you are when you get what you desire! Don't worry, my darling, everything has worked out perfectly. I always had absolute faith in you. Dyavol is very eager to meet you. The central committee . . .'

'I don't care about that.'

'Oh, please don't look at me like that!'

'Hold me, Tanya.'

'There is no time. We must not keep Dyavol waiting.'

'You and Totsky – did you? What we have just done – have you done it with him?'

A pinch of displeasure constricted Tatyana Ruslanovna's face. 'I will not lie to you. Therefore, I beg you, do not ask me such questions.'

Virginsky began to dress with quick stabbing movements, his face an angry, raw pink above his full beard.

*

Even so, despite his unhappiness, he could not resist going with her, silent and resentful at her side. To his surprise, he discovered that she had hired a closed carriage, which was waiting outside. It was an undemocratic luxury perhaps, but she considered it warranted, given that the death of Porfiry Petrovich would rekindle the authorities' efforts to capture him. Naturally, Virginsky did not believe in that death. But even if he had felt like talking, he could say nothing to disabuse her.

For her part, Tatyana Ruslanovna seemed determined to make it up to Virginsky. She repeatedly referred to him as a hero of the cause, saying that he, more than anyone, deserved to ride in such a carriage. She clung onto his arm as if she believed it was in danger of being snatched away by thieves. Virginsky tried half-heartedly to wrest himself from her, his body tense with the contortions of his misery. But she pulled him back to her, with confident ease, nestling her head on his shoulder.

The carriage drew up on the Admiralty Quay. The Bolshaya Neva was freely flowing now, a vein of glistening darkness glutted with boats of every size. Across the water, the narrow end of the long university building was visible. He knew from his days as a student that a ferry left from where they had pulled up, and crossed directly to the University Quay on the other side, before heading onwards downstream past the Strelka.

Virginsky looked questioningly into Tatyana Ruslanovna's eyes. Her gaze offered no answer and so he made to get out. She pulled him back. 'No. You are to stay here. I will get out. But before I leave you, there is something I am obliged to do.' There was a mischievous, almost cruel quality to her smile now. Virginsky felt a sudden pounding dread. She produced from her reticule a strip of black cloth. 'You are to meet Dyavol,' she explained. 'But you are not to see him.' The mischief in her smile softened, and he was no longer afraid. The renewed tenderness of her smile was the last thing he saw before the blindfold went on.

He heard the creak of the door and felt the bounce in the carriage's springs as she got out. A moment later, the bounce was repeated, though this time it was deeper and more prolonged. The presence in the carriage beside him settled back. The door clicked to as the carriage was sealed.

'*Good day, Pavel Pavlovich.*' The greeting was whispered, a breath away from inaudibility, rendering impossible any attempt to identify the speaker. Even so, Virginsky had the impression he had heard that voice before.

'Dyavol?'

Virginsky felt the jolt of the carriage pulling away.

'You are to be congratulated,' continued the whisper. At least that was what Virginsky thought he heard; with the steady cascade of hooves in the background, it was even harder to make out what was being said.

'This is ridiculous,' said Virginsky. 'I can barely hear you! Why must I wear this blindfold?' His hands went up to loosen the cloth, but were restrained.

'We must still take precautions. For your benefit, as much as mine.' The man spoke more clearly now, though it seemed he was disguising his natural voice. 'If you are caught, the less you know, the less you can give away. Still and all, we must do all we can to ensure that you are not caught. We will get you out of the country. Switzerland. Our people there will look after you.'

'*Still and all?* Is it you, Botkin?'

Dyavol laughed. His laughter was the ordinary laughter of an ordinary man, unexpectedly amused. 'Please, don't insult me!'

'You said "still and all". That is one of Botkin's characteristic phrases.'

'I believe it is a common enough phrase. Besides, all our people have come under my influence, sometimes unconsciously.'

'Yes, I heard Varvara Alexeevna use it once.'

'There! I hope you will not accuse me of being Varvara Alexeevna!'

'No. You are not Varvara Alexeevna.' Virginsky waited a moment before committing himself: 'You are Alexander Glebovich Tatiscev.'

'Ah, my friend. I do wish you hadn't said that.' There was a note of sadness in the voice, but it was undisguised now, and clearly recognisable as that of Virginsky's old professor.

'May I not remove the blindfold?'

'No. There are others here whom it would be better you did not see.'

'Others?'

'One other, let us say. A witness to our conversation, who will remain silent and report back to the central committee. I do not act on my own, you know. I am accountable.'

'I thought you *were* the central committee,' said Virginsky. More wistfully, he added, 'At least now we may talk to one another naturally.'

'Yes.'

'But are you really Dyavol?'

'Would it be so terrible to you if I were?'

'Terrible, no. It's just that I don't understand. Dolgoruky told me that it was Dyavol's idea for Kozodavlev to write the articles against you. In which case, you yourself urged Kozodavlev to attack you! Why would you do that?'

'Politically, Kozodavlev and I were close allies. And yet, in our personal lives, enemies. The enmity was not on my side, you understand. I had nothing against him. Indeed, I only ever wished him well, for so long as he was loyal to the cause. But Kozodavlev nurtured a deep and bitter resentment. It was all very well for him to declare himself a new man and to say that he would not stand in the way of his wife's happiness. However, in reality, he could not get past the fact of his hatred for me. I knew that deep in his heart Kozodavlev wished to kill me, and certainly would have betrayed me at the first opportunity. No matter how much we talked things over as new men, and vowed allegiance to the cause, always rankling deep inside him was his hatred for me. I suggested that he write the articles as a way of exorcising his negative feelings, so that we could go on together in the work that really mattered. I urged him to make the attacks as vitriolic and personal as he could.'

'But . . . what did you have to gain by his attacking you?'

'My reasons were psychological rather than political.'

'What about Lebezyatnikov? Why did you have Kozodavlev lampoon him?'

'Oh, that was not my idea. It was Dolgoruky who suggested that.'

'Dolgoruky? He wanted his old tutor to be publicly ridiculed?'

'That is the kind of man Dolgoruky was. The central committee were happy to go along with it as it drew attention away from our people. Lebezyatnikov really was a straw man. I was something a little more subtle. I was . . . well, I was a leader of the revolution pretending to be a straw man!'

'But did it not make life difficult for you?'

'You forget. I am a respected professor of jurisprudence, with friends in the Ministry of Justice. Some of whom were my former students. Besides, there was nothing of substance in the attacks. The authorities were quick to see that. And I was very careful.'

'Careful? What about Pseldonimov? Was *that* careful?'

'That was necessary. Necessity always drives us harder than caution.'

'According to Botkin, Pseldonimov was killed to bind the group together.'

'That is correct. In particular, we wished to secure Kozodavlev's loyalty. My earlier . . . stratagem had not worked. He had poured out his vitriol – without inhibition – but still he hated me. I rather think it was the fact that I approved of what he was doing that undermined the exercise. He needed to hurt me – really hurt me. The problem was, if he hurt me, he hurt the cause. We could not allow that. And so, we needed to secure his loyalty another way. By binding him to the group in mutual guilt.'

'But that didn't work either, did it?'

'Kozodavlev was not cut out for such deeds. When Pseldonimov's body came to light, he panicked. He revealed to Dolgoruky that he was intending to inform. Of course, Dolgoruky passed on that information to me.'

'Therefore Kozodavlev had to die?'

'He had been warned. They had all been warned.'

'Ah yes! You're talking about *Swine*! Dolgoruky told me you wrote it as a warning. Most people took it as a warning to society. But in fact it was written for a very select group of men. A pity that Kozodavlev chose to ignore it.'

'What you must understand is that up until that moment I had nothing but the highest esteem for Demyan Antonovich.'

'That didn't prevent you from seducing his wife, or ordering his death.'

'Come, come. As for the former, what makes you so certain it was a question of my seducing her? We were both adults, and she was in a relationship which, in theory at least, allowed her

420

absolute freedom as far as the dictates of her heart were concerned. Neither of us did what we did in order to hurt Demyan Antonovich. We did it rather to please ourselves than to hurt another. And as for the latter point, his death was approved by the central committee. It was not a question of my ordering it.'

Blindfolded as he was, Virginsky had the sense that all that Tatiscev's words contained was being trampled and churned in the ceaseless rotation of hooves. 'What happened to her?'

Tatiscev hesitated a moment before answering: 'She died. Her death seemed to unhinge Kozodavlev. He became unreliable. I felt – the central committee felt – that he was becoming a liability. His hatred towards me was getting out of hand. It seemed he held me responsible for her death, and for all manner of other evils. He had come to believe the propaganda he had written.'

'And *were* you?'

'I beg your pardon?'

'Responsible for her death?'

'Not at all,' Tatiscev answered calmly, as though it were a perfectly reasonable question, and perfectly reasonable that he might have been. 'She died of consumption. We were no longer in contact. I had not seen her for many years. It was Kozodavlev who informed me of her death. I had moved on from my relationship with her; Demyan Antonovich had been unable to do so, it seemed.'

'A sad story.'

'Yes.'

'But his death was in no way connected to your affair with his wife,' stated Virginsky, as if to reassure himself on that point. He continued: 'In this case, your reasons were political rather than psychological.'

421

Tatiscev seemed to take offence at Virginsky's need to clarify this. 'Of course. How could it be otherwise?' A note of icy restraint entered his voice.

'Well, it's just that he must have embarrassed you, as cuckolds embarrass us all. And his enduring love for the woman you had taken from him and then callously abandoned . . . Perhaps you saw it as a reproach? One that you could not bear.'

'You're a young man. Stupidly romantic. The fact of the matter is more prosaic. He had become unreliable. The central committee makes these decisions. Not I.'

'Tell me, who set the fire? It was not Botkin. Or you?'

'Of course not. We used an escaped convict called Rodya, a semi-literate and easily manipulated fellow. He had got hold of certain of our manifestos and believed that he was helping to initiate the revolution every time he shat inside a church. He was not averse to committing murder on our behalf, and did not need a very compelling reason to do so. A few roubles usually did the trick. Surprisingly few.'

'Where is he now?'

'We have had neither sight nor sound of him since the fire. Perhaps, considering the deaths of the children, he considered it wise to go to ground.'

Virginsky felt that the supposed death of Porfiry Petrovich gave him licence to ask anything. 'What is your attitude to their deaths?'

'Regrettable. But unavoidable.'

'I wonder, is there any point in regretting that which is unavoidable?' Virginsky was perhaps a little carried away by the idea of Porfiry's death.

'You sound like Botkin! I can see how you were able to shoot your colleague. Didn't that cause *you* some regret?'

'I take no particular pleasure from Porfiry Petrovich's death.' It was a statement Virginsky could only make believing Porfiry Petrovich to be still alive. 'However, an act such as this was necessary to initiate the next stage of our great task.'

'Ah yes, the next stage. Rest assured that everything is in place to capitalise on your singular deed.'

'You intend to perpetrate an atrocity?'

'I am not in a position to share details with you. In the meantime, the central committee has decided that it would be best if you were moved.'

'I see.'

'Now that the magistrate has died, there will be a renewed effort to track you down. Your presence in a married couple's apartment can only attract suspicion. We have found a new apartment for you. You will live there with Tatyana Ruslanovna as man and wife. You will be provided with forged papers. I trust that will be agreeable to you?'

'It will be a satisfactory arrangement.'

'You are to have no further communication with the other grouping. Do you understand? You are ours now. We are claiming you as one of our people.'

'You will not talk to them at all?' Virginsky's heart pounded. It was a dangerous gambit, considering the grouping did not in fact exist.

'There is only one central committee. Ours. These people you were mixed up in, it is best that you forget them.'

'Very well.'

The carriage slowed and stopped. Virginsky heard the door

open and felt the bounce of the springs as Tatiscev got out. The door slammed shut once more. But he sensed that he was not alone. 'May I take off my blindfold now?'

There was no answer. He raised his hands to the blindfold. No other hands restrained him. When he slipped the blindfold off, he saw Tatyana Ruslanovna sitting opposite him, her smile sealed with secret irony. 'A *satisfactory* arrangement?' Her words were charged with mock outrage.

'You were there?'

'All the time.'

'You lied to me.'

Her eyebrows bobbed upwards. *Better get used to it*, the gesture seemed to indicate.

37

Husband and wife

He had never seen the city so empty. Yes, there were people about, but they moved like ghosts, solitary and without substance, sealed off from one another, their faces drained of emotion and hope. They seemed to breathe desolation; it was the element in which they moved. For the first time, he realised that everything in this city was too big: vast squares and avenues of vertiginous breadth that could never be filled except with countless regiments of parading soldiers, as if the whole point of raising an army was to ward off this terrible sense of desolation. Even the sprawling palaces and tenements could not fill the emptiness, but simply section it. They stood like aspirations, shell-like structures that overwhelmed the merely human, that were in fact hostile to it. Virginsky was reminded that it was a city that had been built on nothing, or almost nothing – on marshland. It had been dreamt into existence, an act of will, one man's vision which could only demoralise those who came to live in it, as it had destroyed so many of those who had built it. The premeditation of the place sapped the life from its inhabitants. One was presented everywhere with straight lines and purpose, universal direction imposed by the city's first planner, still dictating their lives even after his death. It was no wonder that most people chose to keep off the streets. Virginsky imagined them cowering in basements, huddled together as far as possible from the excessive scale and expanse outside. But he could not be sure of their presence even there, so great was the sense of abandonment he felt.

He looked across at the woman facing him in the moving carriage. The space that had opened up between them was equal in vastness to any outside. And he was as alone here as he was anywhere in St Petersburg.

*

The driver must have been paid in advance, or was perhaps one of 'our people.' At any rate, he didn't ask for money, and none was offered. The carriage pulled away with a disconsolate lurch. Virginsky looked around to get his bearings but did not recognise the deserted lane they had been left in. The district was poor, and his sense was that it was far from the centre. He had been too distracted to follow consciously the route they had taken. A strange reticence prevented him from looking at Tatyana Ruslanovna, though she was the cause of his distraction. Tongue-tied, he waited for her to take the lead.

But it seemed that she was affected by an equal shyness. When at last he dared to glance at her, he saw that she had her eyes fixed on the ground. He tried to think of something to say to set her at her ease. But all that came to mind was, 'Where do we go?' Even to his own ear his voice sounded harsh and unforgiving.

She looked up, her glance still shy. 'They have taken rooms for us in a tenement building around the corner from here. I did not think it would be advisable for us to be seen arriving by carriage. We are to pose as a poor working couple.'

He understood now her peasant clothes. Somehow they lost

their charm for him, striking him as suddenly calculating. He almost hated her for them.

They began to walk. An unbroachable space was maintained between them, the result of a magnetic repulsion that kept them from touching. More to the point, there was an equal space between the couple they were now and the couple they had been that morning. At that moment, it was unimaginable that she would ever appear naked to him again, or that he would ever know again her clinging embrace around his quaking flesh.

Somehow, he had fallen from grace. Perhaps it was because he had asked her about Totsky. Something like rage rose up in him. No – he was not to blame, or at least not solely. She had acted deceitfully to him. Not only that, she had shrugged off the lie in which she had been caught.

Their position, he realised, was entirely false, and that was what had changed between them. To be thrown together by the central committee in this sham marriage pre-empted whatever natural feelings might have developed. Furthermore, Tatyana Ruslanovna must have known of the central committee's intentions when she gave herself to him, as was proven by the clothes she came to him wearing. Besides which, she was a member of the central committee. It was evidence of further deceit on her part. He couldn't fathom what she had meant by that act but felt that there must have been more to it than he had first thought. It was not, in other words, a simple declaration of love, and there was no trust implied in it at all.

And then it struck him: she had wanted him simply because she believed he had killed a man. It was curiosity rather than love that had driven her, and now that her curiosity had been satisfied, there was no possibility of the act being repeated.

Had she been disappointed in the experience? Or had she simply got all that she wanted from him?

She must have noticed the unhappiness in his expression. 'What is wrong, Pavel Pavlovich?'

Her question provoked him. 'How long are we to remain living this lie?'

'Until the central committee decides –'

He cut her off with an anguished, derisive cry.

'Until the central committee decides,' she resumed patiently, 'that it is safe for you to be removed from Petersburg.'

'So we must wait for the central committee to decide our fate?'

'It is not a question of that. You placed yourself in their hands when you killed your colleague and declared it a revolutionary act.'

'What do you mean? Of course it was a revolutionary act. What else could it be?'

'Perhaps you had other reasons for wanting him dead. Please don't take offence. It doesn't matter. None of that matters. You must trust the central committee.' After a moment she added, 'You must trust me.'

They came to a broad avenue, again unknown to Virginsky. The street was muddy, and occupied mostly by manufacturing premises and cheap restaurants. She led him across it to another narrow lane, overshadowed on both sides by the looming black walls of vast tenement buildings.

He followed her into the yard. The ground was swimming in waste matter. The yardkeeper, who had the physique of a young man, but the face of someone much older, was busy shovelling the filthy mud away to the sides. But it always seemed to settle back, covering the area he had just cleared. At the sight of the yardkeeper's prematurely aged face, Tatyana Ruslanovna gripped Virginsky's arm and pulled him to her. He felt the sinews of his heart ripple, as his misery slipped from him. It no longer mattered that it was a lie. All that mattered was that she was holding on to him.

*

The 'rooms' that had been taken for them turned out to be one room on the fourth floor. To be more precise, it was a partitioned area within a larger room, which was subdivided into four small rooms in total. But at least they had a door, and therefore the possibility of privacy. The room was surprisingly clean, although sparsely furnished. There was a narrow bed, a deal table with two chairs and a small wardrobe. One half of a large, ugly stove butted through the partition, like a prurient intruder. The only other items were an icon of a grey-bearded saint and the icon lamp before it.

The occupants of the other rooms, the tenants from whom the central committee had rented Virginsky and Tatyana Ruslanovna's lodging, were a couple of the merchant class. The husband – if indeed they were married – was much older than his wife, who had a submissive demeanour, as if she were in constant expectation of a beating. They greeted Virginsky and Tatyana Ruslanovna in silence, only bowing to them and averting their eyes immediately. The couple kept a servant, an ancient hunchbacked woman who spent all her time slumbering on the massive stove. It seemed to be to everyone's relief when Virginsky and Tatyana Ruslanovna took themselves into their room.

Tatyana Ruslanovna opened the wardrobe, and closed the door on its emptiness immediately. Virginsky looked up at the icon.

'How appropriate,' said Tatyana.

Virginsky frowned.

'St Nikolai. He is my favourite saint.'

'I am surprised to hear that you have a favourite saint.'

'Of course, it is all nonsense,' said Tatyana, almost regretfully. 'But as a child, a very young child, I was always attracted to St Nikolai. I was taken in by the stories, I suppose. The idea of his giving up his parents' wealth and devoting his life to the poor and the sick struck a chord with me. It appealed to my undeveloped instincts for social justice.' Tatyana Ruslanovna frowned. 'Since then, I have learnt that the Church conspires in the oppression of the people and therefore no symbol or representative of the Church can truly stand for social justice. Still and all . . .' She smiled self-consciously and blushed as she met his gaze. 'Yes, *still and all*, it is hard to shake off these childhood associations. The movement must learn to make use of them, I believe. It is the only way to bring the people with us.'

There was the smell of cooking from the next room. Virginsky found himself distracted by it. 'Have they provided any food for us?'

'The old woman will cook for us.'

He nodded tersely. 'You knew all about this, this morning . . .'

'Yes, I knew. Does it matter?'

Virginsky shook his head, though without conviction. It was more as if he was shaking off his resentment than answering her. 'All that matters is the cause,' he said.

He looked down and saw that she was sitting on the bed, reaching out to him with both hands. 'It's not all that matters,' she said.

There was a knock at the door. He turned from her open arms. It was the young merchant woman, who was now nestling a tiny baby, virtually a newborn, in the crook of one arm. Virginsky was disproportionately shocked by the sudden appearance of the baby, although the simple explanation must have been that it was sleeping out of sight when they arrived. He understood in a flash that the old man was not the girl's husband, and indeed that their relationship and the existence of their child was in some way deeply problematic. He saw all this in the way her eyes steadfastly avoided his, and also in the uneasy, complicated gaze she bestowed on her child. 'We are about to eat. Will you join us?' Her voice trembled. It was almost as if she questioned her own right to speak.

Virginsky deferred to Tatyana Ruslanovna, her hands now folded demurely across her lap, apparently incapable of reaching out in longing to any man. Her nod was barely perceptible.

A meal of cabbage soup, beef and *pirogi* was laid out on a table in the main room. Virginsky and Tatyana Ruslanovna murmured appreciative comments, which were ignored by the old merchant and seemed to pain the young woman, who gave a small wince whenever she was addressed. And so the company quickly lapsed into silence.

Virginsky watched the baby grope the air, fascinated by its perfect fingers and minuscule fingernails. The young mother seemed strangely unwilling to engage with her child. The gently curving hands restlessly sought out something to grip, and it would have been natural for her to slip a maternal finger into their reach. It was an inclination she resisted. The baby's innocent animation was in contrast to the adults' stiff constraint and seemed almost to offend the old man. When it began to cry, the merchant set down his cutlery with a disapproving clatter and looked sharply up into the corner of the room, averting his gaze as far as possible from the sound. The child's mother took this as her cue to sweep the child away from the table, carrying it off into the couple's bedroom. The old man continued his meal as if the child, and its mother, had never existed.

*

In the night she answered all his fears with wordless consolations. And although their position was fraught with difficulties and deception, there was honesty in what they gave to one another in the darkness. And what they gave had a voice, a bleating presence ratcheting the infinite night, pulling it tighter around them, making a black blanket of the void.

Afterwards, he realised that the sound he had heard was the baby crying in the next room. He realised too that Tatyana Ruslanovna was also crying. He held her and was shocked by the tremors of her weeping, her tears damp on his chest. 'What is it? What's the matter, my darling Tanya?'

'I'm afraid.' Her voice was so small it was almost not there at all.

'Don't worry. I'm here. Nothing can hurt you.' His eyes were wide open as he lied.

'I'm afraid,' she repeated. 'What if . . . what if we are wrong?'

The bleating of the baby had become something inhuman and incomprehensible. The old man shouted something that Virginsky could not make out. 'What do you mean?' His murmur was for Tatyana Ruslanovna.

'I was thinking of the children who died.'

He thought of the answer he ought to give, the argument of social utility, of a price that has to be paid, of sacrifices that have to be made.

It was almost as if she had heard his thoughts: 'Oh, I know what Botkin would say. But what if Botkin is wrong? Men like Botkin frighten me.' For a moment, she allowed the child's cries to speak for her. 'Men like you frighten me.'

'I?'

'It frightens me that we need murderers. Somehow it seems to undermine every argument we make that we must have men of blood to put them forward for us.'

Virginsky tensed. He felt a reciprocal tensing in her body. Beads of sweat began to break out between them. 'But surely I don't frighten you?'

She did not answer. He frowned in the darkness, his brows compressing around the idea that it was fear that had prompted her to give herself to him; that the sexual act was, for her, a way of overcoming her fear.

'You know what they are planning next?' she continued.

'An atrocity of some kind?'

He felt her head move in anguished confirmation. 'What if other innocents die?'

A shudder of revulsion was the only answer he could give.

'Sometimes,' she went on, 'I cannot understand how it came to be that I am involved with such men.' She clung onto him, and the feel of her nakedness and need against him was enthralling. It empowered him.

'But you were in Paris, in the Commune?'

'Yes, I was there. And what I saw terrified me. And what I did – what I saw I was capable of – terrified me even more.' Her body shook with what could have been laughter, the bitterest. 'I sometimes think the only reason I was there was to shock my parents. It was an act of childish rebellion. And look where it has got me!'

'*With me?*' His whispered consolation lacked conviction.

'In the arms of a murderer. And now, you will betray me to the others. You will tell them of my fears, that I am losing heart, that I cannot be trusted. And so it will begin. They will come for me . . .' She seemed to see her comrades closing in on her. Her voice brimmed with terror.

'No,' he said. 'You need not be frightened of me. I am not like them. I am not a murderer.'

'But you killed Porfiry Petrovich.'

He shook his head. 'It was staged. I . . . I fired a blank cartridge. Porfiry is not dead.'

'But they announced his death in the paper.'

'Porfiry Petrovich has always been a great prankster.'

He sensed her relax in his arms. He had the impression that she fell asleep. He was alone with the crying of the baby, and the occasional incomprehensible barks of rage from the old man.

*

She was no longer in his arms when he awoke. It was morning. She was dressed and had opened the one low window to air the room, as if she wanted to dispel all trace of what had happened in the night. She seemed stubbornly reluctant to face him.

434

38

Virginsky's destiny

The intimacy of the first night was never repeated.

He dreamt one night that the merchant couple's baby was dead. When he looked down, he saw that one of his hands was over the baby's face. An atmosphere of unspeakable guilt pervaded the dream.

When he woke in the morning after the dream, he strained to listen for the baby's cries. Instead he heard voices in the room outside. He sat up and pulled on his trousers, throwing the blankets onto the bed. Almost as soon as he had done so, there was a violent knocking on the door. Tatyana Ruslanovna admitted Botkin, Totsky and, to Virginsky's surprise, Professor Tatiscev. Totsky was carrying a small suitcase made of polished steel, which he seemed reluctant to let out of his hands. The room was cramped with five people in it, and Botkin's customary stench, of petrol and masculinity, was a sixth unwelcome presence, crowding them out.

Totsky and Virginsky remained standing, confronting one another across their rivalry for Tatyana Ruslanovna. Botkin pushed one of the chairs against the door and sat on it. Tatiscev took the other chair and Tatyana Ruslanovna sat on the bed.

'Are you sure this is wise?' began Virginsky. He glanced nervously towards Tatyana Ruslanovna, whose expression had become peculiarly set. 'All of us here like this?'

'Don't you worry about that,' said Tatiscev quickly.

For a moment, no one spoke. Virginsky found the brisk determination of the men ominous; he picked up subtly unnerving signals in the glances that passed between them. He felt that he ought to have been frightened on Tatyana Ruslanovna's behalf, but a strange fixity had come over her face that was more chilling than anything he saw on the men's. She was the first to speak, and the flitting of her eye just before she did so told him that he would do better to be frightened on his own account.

'It's as we suspected. It was all a pretence.' She tilted her head dismissively towards Virginsky. '*He* fired a blank cartridge. He is here to spy on us.'

Virginsky felt as if a cannonball had dropped inside him, forcing the wind out as it bounced into his solar plexus. She turned to face him with a look of brazen contempt.

Tatiscev merely nodded. Nothing Tatyana Ruslanovna had said seemed to surprise him.

Botkin leant forward in his chair, his heavy axe-shaped head looming towards Virginsky dangerously, as if even his consideration was something to be afraid of.

Totsky's face lost what small amount of colour it had. His mouth was pinched into a disapproving dot. His hand tightened around the handle of his steel suitcase.

Tatiscev produced a small glass bottle from the inside of his jacket. He handed it to Botkin, who looked into it with an unseemly hunger, flashing a mocking grin towards Virginsky. 'Come now, take your medicine like a good boy.' Botkin took the stopper out and rose to his feet.

There was nowhere for Virginsky to go. Botkin was coming towards him, blocking the only way out. He climbed onto the bed.

Botkin climbed up next to him. The mattress dipped and bounced like a stretch of river ice on the brink of cracking.

Tatyana Ruslanovna looked up at him. Her look was poised and finely balanced: some ravaged, pathetic part of him thought he detected a residue of love; but, of course, quite opposite emotions were also evident. Her expression seemed to fluctuate between one that believed in him and one that held him in utter contempt. He could not say in which manifestation she appeared more beautiful. All he knew was that her contempt cut him like a long blade driven beneath his fingernails.

He tried to struggle against Botkin's grip but the man's hand was locked around the back of his head, pulling him forward to the open bottle. The fumes rushed into him like wolves breaking cover. His head was the prey they ripped apart, tossing sloppy gobbets of his consciousness around the room. An expanding nothingness took over his insides. His limbs evaporated.

*

The emptiness inside him was being tightened, squeezed so much that it solidified into pain. His sides ached. His chest ached. Even his head ached, though there was no tightness there, just the dull pounding of a hangover. He did not want to be where the pain was. Perhaps if he opened his eyes he would escape it, but he could not be sure. There was always the possibility that he would open his eyes to even more pain.

He could hear voices, murmuring.

The voices sickened him. If he opened his eyes, he would have to face the voices. The more he listened to them, the more nauseated he felt. If he opened his eyes, he would be sick. The voices

437

would draw the vomit out of him. Out of his eyes and his ears, as well as his mouth. He imagined the vomit pouring out of every opening in his body, so pervasive was his nausea.

Now it became important to him to keep his eyes closed.

But the voices were saying his name, calling his name. And one of the voices was hers.

He squeezed his eyes tightly, forcing back the nausea. Then, without realising that he would, he simply opened his eyes. So easy was it, in the end, to pass from one mode of being to another.

He saw the face of his old professor frowning at him. He felt inordinately saddened because it seemed that he had disappointed Professor Tatiscev. But then he heard a voice that matched the face say, 'Good.' The word seemed to come to him from far away, reverberating through an endless corridor that reminded him of his university days. The association brought with it an idiotic happiness that swept over him and lifted him to his feet.

It surprised him how far away his feet were, so far away that looking down at them brought on a wave of vertigo. He was surprised also to see that he was now fully dressed. He did not remember putting on the unbelted *kosovorotka* shirt he was wearing.

'Steady,' said another voice. He noticed for the first time that he was being held up by hands that didn't seem to belong to anyone. 'You have to be careful now. You must avoid any sudden movements or jolts – until we get you in the church. On no account must you fall over until you are inside the church.' He had thought this man his enemy, and yet he was showing such solicitude towards him. It seemed he had misjudged him. He wanted to embrace the man, whose name had been swallowed up in the sweeping nothingness, to kiss him even. But the man seemed to be holding him at arm's length.

He was aware of his mouth opening, and wondered if he was going to be sick. Instead, he heard something that surprised him: 'Church?'

'Yes. We're going to church.'

For some reason, he found the idea extremely funny and began to shake with uncontrolled hilarity.

'You must calm down.' The man's voice was intensely serious.

Virginsky wanted to apologise. But all that came out was an incoherent slurring. He tried to concentrate. He tried to stop the bubbles of hilarity breaking out. He wanted these people to think well of him. He wanted to know whose hands were holding him up. He made a great effort of will to match the seriousness around him. But every time he thought he had got the better of his giddiness, another explosion of hiccup-like laughter shook him.

'This is hopeless,' said the man whose name he could not remember. 'If he keeps this up, he will blow us all up before we get him out of the building.'

His old professor leaned into his face. The gesture cowed Virginsky into silence. 'This will not do. We expect better of you. Tatyana Ruslanovna expects better of you. This is your destiny. You must face it like a man.'

Virginsky gasped at the rebuke. He felt on the verge of tears.

'That's better,' said Professor Tatiscev.

A wave of relief crashed over him.

'Now you must go with Totsky. You must do whatever Totsky tells you.'

Totsky! That was the man's name. Virginsky grinned with delight. 'Tot-skeeee!'

'Enough!' continued the voice of his old professor. 'If you do not do as you are told, the baby will die. The only way to ensure that the baby lives is to do everything that Totsky tells you. Is that clear?'

Virginsky nodded. Solemnity had entered his bones like a chill. 'Baby?'

'The baby here. It has been decided that Botkin will kill it if you do not do as you are told. So, as you see, it is essential that you do as you are told.'

The hands under his arms guided him towards the door. The moment the hands released him, he swayed on his feet. Other hands shot out to steady him, those of the man called Totsky. Virginsky felt better knowing whose hands were holding him up. He remembered that Totsky had been carrying a steel suitcase, but saw that he wasn't any more. He noticed the steel suitcase lying open on the floor, empty. He breathed in deeply, his chest expanding against the constriction he had felt earlier. He realised that it had a physical cause, that he was wearing something that was tightly bound around his torso, like a corset. He did not remember putting a corset on.

At the last moment, Tatyana Ruslanovna rose from the bed. 'I will go with them.'

'You do not trust *me*?' demanded Totsky.

Virginsky missed the subtleties of the look that was her response. By then it was all he could do to keep his caw down. And from now on he knew that this would be the whole focus of his being.

*

He was supported between Totsky and Tatyana Ruslanovna. His legs seemed to be executing a movement that approximated walking, though it could just as easily have been dancing. But it did not seem that they had anything to do with the forward motion of his body. He wanted to make a joke about it but could not quite think of the right words, so simply giggled to himself.

'That will do,' said Tatyana Ruslanovna sternly.

What he had wanted to say came to him: 'Is this the way the new people walk?' But he no longer thought of it as a joke.

Tatyana Ruslanovna and Totsky ignored Virginsky's question. They began to talk about him as if he wasn't there.

'He inhaled too much ether,' said Totsky.

'At least we can move him,' said Tatyana Ruslanovna.

'Like this, he's dangerous. He will attract attention.'

'He looks like a drunk. A common enough sight in Russia.'

'If we weren't holding him up he would fall over. Which would be fatal.'

'The ether will wear off,' said Tatyana Ruslanovna.

'Then we will have the opposite problem,' warned Totsky.

'May I remind you this whole adventure was your idea, Totsky.'

'And still it may succeed,' said Totsky, after a momentary pause. 'Provided we exercise due caution at all times.'

Tatyana Ruslanovna began to laugh. Virginsky felt the shards of her laughter spike his soul, a thousand exquisite impalements. 'I wonder, what is the correct amount of caution due when one is escorting a human bomb to an atrocity?' she asked.

'It is all very well for you to laugh,' said Totsky. He looked at Tatyana Ruslanovna as if he had paid for her laughter with his blood. 'You know that I am doing this for you.'

'Then you are a fool. That is the worst conceivable reason to go to your death. For a woman such as me.'

'No. Not for a woman such as you. For you.'

'You should be doing it for the cause. For the people.'

'Fine words. They mean nothing to me. I do this only to earn your admiration. I know I cannot hope for your love.'

It seemed to Virginsky that Totsky was speaking on his behalf, saying to Tatyana Ruslanovna precisely the words he wished to say, but was unable to.

'What does it matter whether I admire you or not?' said Tatyana Ruslanovna.

And Virginsky felt every bit as devastated as Totsky must have, as if her stinging words had been directed at him.

39

The inexplicable corpse

He began to feel as though he was trapped in an ambulatory prison. He could not say with any certainty how long he had been confined between his captors, but there were moments when it was hard for him to remember a time before this forced march, and impossible to imagine it coming to an end. He had entered eternity and it was exhausting.

Tatyana Ruslanovna and Totsky handled him with a combination of extreme solicitude and utter disregard. The slightest trip on his part provoked the most anxious ministrations, and a tightening of their fingers around his upper arm. And yet they steadfastly refused to address any remarks to him directly.

'What am I wearing?' he ventured to ask at one point. But they would not answer his question. 'I can feel something around my torso, like a corset. Why have you put a corset on me?'

They took him along the back streets, cutting through a network of connected courtyards, the secret spaces at the hollow heart of vast buildings, the chain that linked a hidden city. His progress through this private, inner St Petersburg corresponded to his return to a functioning consciousness. The streets began to appear more familiar to him, at the same time as the nausea lifted and he felt his feet connect more solidly with the ground. He felt the strain on his arms where Tatyana Ruslanovna and Totsky were holding him, as the anaesthetic effect of the ether wore off.

There was a return, too, of his imaginative capacity to put himself in the place of others: he wondered at the tense ache they must have been experiencing in their locked hands. His sympathy for his tormentors at that moment struck him as absurdly inappropriate, and he was all at once overwhelmed by self-disgust. But the implications of his predicament were too much for him to take in. If anything, his headache increased in intensity.

'What did you mean by that remark? When you said something about escorting a human bomb? How can I be a human bomb? Is it something to do with the corset?'

'Silence! Remember the baby. Do as you are told or the baby will die,' ordered Tatyana Ruslanovna.

He felt a soft explosion of emotion in his chest. It was not anger; it was the most tender, affectionate pity. It seemed he had become severed from himself. This fate, this inescapable death, was both his and not his. The part of him that would not suffer it, that would survive it, was able to look with pity – and, yes, love – on the part that would be inevitably destroyed. This was the soul's pity for the body, he realised. Of course, such a realisation went against the whole tenor of his professed convictions, which until this moment had been unshakeably materialistic. He had not until now believed in the soul, or, rather, he had not known that he had. He did not feel confused by this, or angry. He felt no resentment for the years that had been taken from him. He felt at peace, elated almost.

He looked up to see the Church of the Assumption of the Virgin Mary towering over him.

And then he understood that all that he had just experienced was the last trace of ether disintegrating in his blood. His ruthless clarity returned to him. He was about to die. There was no soul.

Nothing would survive the imminent incineration of his body. He was, in effect, already dead.

The elation left him. His body went into spasm. He became a flimsy marionette whose strings were being jerked by an angry puppet master. He slipped out of the grip of his escorts, and even threw one clenched hand into Tatyana Ruslanovna's face.

'Hold onto him!' shouted Totsky.

It was surprise that had shaken him out of their hands, and a momentary rush of strength. His fingers pulled at the *kosovorotka*, lifting the bottom hem up over his head. With his free hand he felt what seemed to be rows of glass capsules sewn into the unfamiliar undergarment into which he had been bound.

'No!' Tatyana Ruslanovna's imperious tone stayed his hand, for the moment at least. He released the hem of the shirt and it fell back into place.

'If you take that off, you know what Botkin will do,' continued Tatyana Ruslanovna. 'Will you condemn that baby to death?'

As Virginsky struggled to take in what she had said, Totsky's hand came up towards his face. He expected Totsky to strike him, but his hand fell short of a blow. Then Virginsky noticed the vitreous flash of the bottle the other man was clutching, and he felt once again the wolf-like fumes devour the membranes of his nostrils. He staggered back, arms flailing the suddenly viscous air.

'It's alright! He's had too much to drink!' Tatyana Ruslanovna shouted excitedly into the godless void in front of the church. 'Grief. He was very close to the deceased, you see.'

Their hands were on him again. 'Deceased?' cried Virginsky. 'Who is deceased?'

'Someone you killed, that's all,' answered Tatyana Ruslanovna.

'Porfiry Petrovich, do you mean? But he isn't really dead. You know that. He wouldn't go through with this!'

Tatyana Ruslanovna tilted her head back, in an expression of high disdain. Apart from a slight spasm at the corner of the mouth, it was the only answer she volunteered.

*

He had never seen so many candles. The tiny glimmering flames seemed to form a sea of light out of which the congregation was rising. And then he realised that each member of the congregation was holding a candle in front of them. He wanted more than anything to have a candle of his own but the service had already begun. And Tatyana Ruslanovna and Totsky hurried him into the church as if there was no time for that.

In his confusion, he connected the glow of the candles with the sound of chanting, as if the burning of wicks suspended in wax produced an auditory effect, as well as a visual one. Then he realised that it was the people holding the candles who were producing the sounds, which truly were as beautiful and soothing to his ears as the candlelight was to his eyes. A slowly soaring melody ranged over the upper registers of his emotions like a high majestic bird riding eddies; beneath it, a deep bass drone persisted, its beauty sombre, powerful and enduring. There could be no arguing with that bass. It vibrated viscerally, physically, taking hold not just of his internal organs but of the frame that contained them.

The solemnity of the sound made a deep impression on him. And yet something about it struck him as inappropriate, almost ludicrous.

He glanced to either side of him and noticed that Tatyana Ruslanovna was no longer holding onto him. In fact, she was backing away towards the door. Totsky was still there by his side, gripping his upper arm tightly.

'Where is she going?' cried Virginsky to his one remaining captor. His shout went off like a firecracker. It drew disapproving frowns from those around him.

'Pavel Pavlovich? Is that you?' The voice hissed from just in front of him.

Virginsky turned to see the familiar face of Nikodim Fomich, which seemed to float out of the sea of candle flames. The apparition acted on him like an emotional lodestone. His eager, deprived gaze latched onto it. Feelings that he was not aware of harbouring surged out from the core of his being to its surface. He searched for reassurance and succour in insignificant details. And yet there was something that jarred in the Chief of Police's face, an inexplicable hostility squeezing his mouth into an uncharacteristically sour pucker.

Virginsky felt the hand around his arm tighten. Totsky was looking nervously over his shoulder at Tatyana Ruslanovna, who was lurking by the door, ready to make a break for it when the time came. Virginsky could not be sure whether it was Tatyana Ruslanovna's imminent flight, rather than Nikodim Fomich's intervention, that had prompted Totsky to increase his grip.

Certainly Nikodim Fomich's appearance had the effect of sobering Virginsky, of concentrating his mind. There was now a danger, he realised, that Totsky would panic, that he would be pushed into acting precipitously. He had to think – and act – quickly. The vital thing was to remain on his feet for as long as possible, and to keep out of the press of the congregation. He felt himself to be remarkably in control of his actions. He shook his head warningly to Nikodim Fomich.

At that moment the priest began to lead the congregation in the Kontakion to the Departed: '*With the saints give rest, O Christ, to the soul of Thy servant . . .*'

The words of the Kontakion continued to reverberate in the vast sounding box of the cathedral, voices overlapping with voices to create a rising bed of sound on which the meaning was borne up, as if to Heaven: '*. . . where sickness and sorrow are no more, neither sighing, but life everlasting.*'

Now Nikodim Fomich shook his head, in a grave, slow, momentous sweep. The gesture was imbued with unexpected pity, and therefore left no room for hope.

Virginsky yanked himself free of Totsky's hold. And if he had thought about it, he might have been surprised by how easily his freedom was achieved. But he was beyond that now. He did not even care that he was jostled as he pushed his way through the crowd of standing mourners to the front of the church.

Around the coffin were placed four great *manoualias*, each densely packed with fine candles giving a thick cluster of flames. The candle-stands were arranged one at the head, one at the foot of the coffin, and one on either side, forming the branches of a flaming cross. Virginsky could not yet bring himself to confront what lay within. His eye went instead to the memorial table nearby, on which were placed the dish of *koliva* that the mourners would eat after the service. He understood the symbolism well enough. Although he was an atheist, he was still a Russian. The wheat of the *koliva* represented rebirth through death. The grain had to fall to the ground before it could give forth fruit, just as the faithful had to die before the eternal life of the soul could come into being.

But Virginsky saw only a glutinous mound of cold boiled wheat. As food it was unappetising; as a religious symbol it repelled him. The burning tapers – small fragments of the greater flame – that projected from it were like the cheap tricks of a bad stage conjuror. Had Porfiry really invested the core of his being in such counterfeit props? Virginsky had never given much thought to his superior's faith. It was something he had taken for granted; out of respect, he had held himself back from challenging it. At the same time, he had not taken it entirely seriously either. He had thought of it as another of Porfiry's eccentricities, almost as an affectation. But now, for the first time, it struck him that his faith was the one thing of which Porfiry would never have made light. It was inconceivable that he would have deceived the church authorities into conducting a bogus funeral, and equally inconceivable that they would have gone along with such a charade.

He turned, at last, from the memorial table to the coffin, as if to demand an answer. And in the moment of turning his head to make that confrontation, he thought of all the other confrontations with death that Porfiry Petrovich had forced on him: heads severed from their bodies, naked corpses laid out on slabs, and most recently the drenched and partly saponified corpse of Pseldonimov.

At first, he could not understand what he saw. The body in the coffin was that of a woman, a tiny, old woman, as frail as the long stems of the roses with which it was strewn. Virginsky laughed out loud once in savage delight. He turned to the congregation, to see if they were in on the joke. From the stern faces that met his gaze, it seemed that they were not.

449

Virginsky shook his head in amazement. Surely they had noticed that the body in the coffin was not that of Porfiry Petrovich? And then it occurred to him: he was the only one there who had expected it to be Porfiry.

Virginsky looked down at the old woman again. She was dressed like a doll in a costume that was too big for her, and which appeared never to have been worn before. Her tiny body was swamped by an elaborate gown of the kind worn by ladies of the Court, encrusted with braiding and padded with quilting. Banks of pearls concealed her neck. As if to draw attention away from the deep wrinkles of her face, her head was adorned with a high, crescent-shaped *kokoshnik* headdress, so that her head seemed massive in comparison to the rest of her body. Virginsky's eye was drawn to the paper crown that had been placed beneath the *kokoshnik*. On it were written the words of the Trisagion: *Holy God, Holy and Mighty, Holy and Immortal, have mercy on us.*

For the first time, he wondered who she was. Something about her extraordinarily diminutive structure seemed familiar. He thought of Tatyana Ruslanovna's words to him just before they entered the church: *Someone you killed, that's all.*

Had she said it simply to make him think of Porfiry Petrovich? She knew as well as he did that Porfiry was not really dead, and that therefore Virginsky could not in any way be said to have killed him.

Indeed, there was no one whose death could be laid at his door. *Unless one counted Dolgoruky.*

Of course. Now he recognised the woman in the coffin as Princess Dolgorukaya, Dolgoruky's mother. So Princess Dolgorukaya had died. But how could he be held responsible for her death?

The chanting had come to a stop. Virginsky turned to face the sea of candle flame. Without the auditory accompaniment, the light seemed wan and almost incomplete. The faces of the mourners were turned towards him, in anxious expectation. He saw a number of men in police and gendarme uniforms assembled at the front, forming a kind of human barricade around one part of the congregation. The officers shifted nervously. Among them he recognised Major Verkhotsev, whose expression was wary, although again Virginsky noticed the unmistakable presence of pity. Verkhotsev was standing at the head of the bank of men; immediately next to him, to Virginsky's surprise, was Totsky. If it was not such an absurd idea, he might have thought the two of them had just been in conference.

Virginsky cast a glance towards the back of the cathedral, seeking out Tatyana Ruslanovna, as if the sight of her face would explain everything. But instead of an explanation, he saw only contempt.

He turned back to the cordon of tense, bristling uniforms. They seemed to be closing in on him, by slow, measured steps. In the shift and bob of the men, he caught sight of the one man who was truly responsible for the terrible predicament he found himself in, the Tsar whose jealous retention of autocratic powers had driven 'our people' to the only reasonable course of action open to them: revolution. Everything followed from that, including his own infiltration of the movement, and the ruse that had been required to make that possible.

For the first time he saw that everything that men like Botkin and Tatiscev had argued was not only right, it was also necessary. There could be no justice without social revolution. And the new society could not be founded until the old one had been destroyed. The troubling duality of his conflicted morality was all at once resolved. His convictions clarified. He remembered watching the fire on Alexandrovsky Prospect, and how he had come close to welcoming his own annihilation.

He was a dead man already. He saw now that he had been betrayed by Totsky, who had no doubt informed on him to ensure his destruction.

As always with Virginsky, there was something inescapably personal in this too. Again he looked for Tatyana Ruslanovna. The look of contempt was still in place. She gave a nod that was charged with challenge and mockery. Perhaps that was all it came down to, in the end: her nod propelled him.

He took one step towards the cluster of uniforms. He was aware that his movement seemed to provoke an agitated stir.

A second step, and there was a shout. He had the sense of a mass of blue rushing at him, a wave of twill that hit him with a shocking force. He landed heavily, his head thrown back, his eyes open on the highest tier of the iconostasis, the symbol of the entrance to Heaven. His skull hit the ground with a sickening crack. He felt the glass phials pocketed around his body pop and crumple, heard their brittle splintering, felt here and there the points of their tiny shards prick him through the material of the corset.

He braced himself for the end. But the explosion did not come. Above the screams of havoc filling the church, he thought he heard the sound of broken laughter.

40

A room in Fontanka, 16

The room that Virginsky was taken to resembled a well-appointed drawing room. He was not held under any kind of restraint but was treated with the utmost civility by Major Verkhotsev and his subordinates. He was given tea, which made him realise how hungry he was, and so he was also brought a meal of cabbage soup, sturgeon and potatoes, accompanied by a palatable French wine. He was rather given the impression that whatever he asked for would be provided.

'Where is Porfiry Petrovich?' asked Virginsky, pushing his empty plate away from him. 'I insist on Porfiry Petrovich being present during my . . . interview.'

Major Verkhotsev rolled a waxed moustache between thumb and forefinger. 'I am afraid that won't be possible. There was an accident, you see. Your little prank backfired.'

'What are you talking about?'

'The prank you and Porfiry cooked up between you. It was a very stupid thing you did, you know. And dangerous. To discharge a gun at close range.'

'But the cartridge was stuffed with a wad of paper. Porfiry prepared it himself.'

'Something went wrong. There must have been a foreign particle lodged in the chamber. Porfiry Petrovich sustained a slight graze.'

'A graze!'

'Which became infected. The infection took hold.'

'What are you saying? He is not dead? Not really?'

Major Verkhotsev blinked once before continuing: 'It has not come to that. Yet. However, I warn you, his doctor, Dr Pervoyedov, is far from hopeful. He advises us to prepare for the worst.'

'No! Porfiry is as strong as a bear. He will not succumb to a *graze*!' Virginsky was on his feet. 'I must go to him.'

'There will be time for that. First, we need to have a little chat. Please, sit down. You will be taken to see him in due course.'

Virginsky sank back into his seat. 'Taken? Am I to consider myself under arrest?'

'One cannot simply overlook the fact that you tried to assassinate the Tsar.'

'Did I?'

'That's certainly how it seems.'

'But I did not even know that the Tsar was in the church. He was concealed by your men.' Virginsky hurriedly asserted his lie, the desperation rising in his voice.

'The deceased was a distant relative of a dear friend of the Tsar's, and had been a courtier. It was therefore natural that the Tsar should attend her funeral.'

'A dear friend? You are talking about his mistress?'

'Please, you must not pay attention to scandal-mongers.'

'I saw Totsky talking to you,' said Virginsky abruptly.

'Yes. Totsky was our agent.'

'Then you will know from him what happened. Unless he is lying to cover his own duplicity.'

'That fellow saved your life, you know. If it hadn't been for the fact that he had rendered the nitroglycerine in your corset inert, you would have blown yourself up and taken God knows how many innocent souls with you. Mine included.'

Virginsky overlooked the Major's appropriation of innocence. 'I was drugged. They put the corset on me without my knowledge or consent – of course. I was acting under duress. They said that they would kill the baby if I didn't obey.'

'Baby?'

'There is a baby. They said that they would kill it.'

Major Verkhotsev smiled. 'It is unlikely that they ever intended to kill it. Even these people have some compunction. It was enough to hold out the prospect of infanticide to ensure your compliance. You have to hand it to them. They are astute psychologists.'

'Have you arrested Tatiscev?'

'It seems that Professor Tatiscev has gone to ground. He has not been seen at the university, or at any of his other usual haunts.'

'And Tatyana Ruslanovna?'

'From what Totsky says, wherever Tatiscev is, Tatyana Ruslanovna will not be far away. You knew of course that they were lovers?'

'Totsky and Tatyana?'

'No. Tatiscev and Tatyana.'

'I see,' said Virginsky, as if it made no difference to him. 'What about the others? Kirill Kirillovich and Varvara Alexeevna? Botkin?'

'Oh, we have *them*. So that is something, eh?'

There was a momentary silence. The animal pacification that Virginsky had experienced at the satisfaction of his immediate bodily needs gave way to a dull depression. 'Tell me, was Porfiry Petrovich's death ever announced?'

'His death? No. Of course not. He has not died.'

'No, I meant as a ruse. To convince the terrorists to trust me.'

'There were bulletins about the seriousness of his condition and his decline in health. But naturally we would not release such egregiously false information. No matter what plans you and Porfiry had hatched.'

'She lied to me. She told me that his obituary had appeared in the papers.'

Major Verkhotsev shook his head. 'They played a ruse of their own, it seems.'

'And Princess Dolgorukaya? That *was* Princess Dolgorukaya in the coffin?'

'Yes.'

'How did she die?'

'She suffered a heart attack.'

Virginsky let out an involuntary laugh.

Major Verkhotsev raised a quizzical eyebrow.

'It was something Tatyana Ruslanovna said,' explained Virginsky. 'She implied that I had killed her.'

'Unless you were responsible for her son's death, you did not. Princess Dolgorukaya's fatal heart attack was brought on by the news of Prince Dolgoruky's suicide. The old princess was deeply religious, you see. As far as she was concerned, he would go straight to Hell. It broke her heart.'

Virginsky placed a hand over his eyes.

'Yes, it's all been a terrible strain for you, I'm sure. The tragedy is that none of this was necessary. If you had come to us, we would have told you that we already had a man in there. This distrust between the Department of Justice and the Third Section is most regrettable, you know. It helps neither of us.'

456

'It is hard to trust people who employ such methods as you do.'

'My dear fellow! What a thing to say! After all this!'

Virginsky removed his hand from his eyes and stared accusingly at Major Verkhotsev. 'Rakitin.'

'Rakitin?'

'The witness you took from us.'

'We have no record of ever receiving anyone by that name. And neither do you, by the way.' The remark was made lightly, almost cheerfully. There was no sense of threat in it.

Major Verkhotsev seemed to be aware of the difficulty this would cause Virginsky. He sensed the need for explanation: 'It may surprise you to learn this, but I am considered a liberal, you know.'

Virginsky gave a cynical shrug.

'Ask my daughter.'

Virginsky bristled at the mention of Maria Petrovna.

Major Verkhotsev smiled with satisfaction at the effect his last sally produced. 'Yes, Maria Petrovna and I are as one on many issues.'

'She does not condone the murder of state witnesses.'

'No one has been murdered. Whatever wild conclusions you have leapt to concerning the fate of this – what did you say his name was?'

'Rakitin. You know full well.'

'Yes. Rakitin. Rest assured that, as so often, it is not as you imagine. Perhaps Mr Rakitin wished to disappear. And perhaps we aided him in the accomplishment of his wishes. Perhaps he found himself superfluous to events, and so took himself off. One simply does not know.'

'You know.'

Major Verkhotsev tapped an index finger impatiently on the table. 'Yes, I am quite the liberal,' he continued, as if they had not talked about Rakitin at all. 'I keep up with all the liberal papers, and even some of the radical ones.'

'I'm sure you do.'

'Oh no. It's not like that. I don't do it to keep an eye on them, if that's what you're suggesting. I read them because they interest me. Genuinely. I find myself sympathetic to many of the views expressed.' Verkhotsev crossed to another table at the side of the room, on which a number of newspapers and journals were laid out. 'Take this, for example. In this week's *Spark*.'

Prayer for an Investigating Magistrate

Knowledge of the worst that men can do
Opened your eyes to the best in them.
Zones of darkness you dared to enter,
Observing with an eye informed by ruth.
Dwelling there you saw not monsters but brothers;
A light you shone into their souls, discovering
Virtue lives alongside vice; hope neighbours hate;
Love beds down with lust; joy succumbs to fear's embrace.
Eternal God, the judge of all, we beseech you,
View with equal compassion our brother's soul.

'Of course, it's just a bit of doggerel by someone who never knew him. And it reads rather too much like an epitaph, for my liking. Still and all, it is rather affecting. I wonder who wrote it,' said Major Verkhotsev. 'It is not credited to anyone. But quite an extraordinary stance for such a radical-leaning publication to take, do you not think? I was particularly struck by the overtly religious tone. A prayer indeed! And when you consider that most radicals believe that Porfiry Petrovich was the victim of a justifiable revolutionary attack . . .'

'Kozodavlev,' said Virginsky. There was a sense of wonder in his voice.

'I beg your pardon?'

'Kozodavlev wrote it. If you look at the first letter of each line.'

Major Verkhotsev retrieved the paper and scanned the lines of the poem eagerly. 'Good Heavens! But I thought he died in the fire?'

'Yes, that is what he wanted us to think. But, obviously, it was the man they sent to kill him who died.' Virginsky shook his head in begrudging admiration. '*What Is to Be Done?*'

'Well, of course, we will make enquiries with the newspaper.'

'No. I meant the book. *What Is to Be Done?* by Chernyshevsky. Have you never read it?'

'Of course, Lopukhov's hat! Well I never. But this is not quite the same, is it? I mean, in *What Is to Be Done?* a deception was perpetrated, but no one died. Lopukhov's hat was fished out of the water with a bullet hole in it and from that the authorities concluded he had committed suicide. By the by, I always objected to the stupidity of that episode. It is highly implausible on so many counts. But here, five children perished, as well as the unknown individual found in Kozodavlev's apartment.'

'Yes, although in Kozodavlev's defence, it is probably fair to say that he was desperate in the extreme. This man intended to kill him. Somehow, he managed to get the better of him, but he knew that Dyavol would never let it rest there. He would send another assassin, and another, if necessary. He saw an opportunity to make his enemy believe that he was the one who had perished in the fire, which was after all what Dyavol was expecting to hear. And so, in order to render the dead man unidentifiable, he set the fire, disguising himself as his attacker to make his escape.'

'Dyavol? The Devil is involved in this?'

'I mean Tatiscev. That was what our people called him.'

Major Verkhotsev laid down the paper and rolled one of his moustaches thoughtfully. 'You know, we are always on the lookout for clever young men here in the Third Section. If it should prove problematic for you to return to the Department of Justice, our door is open. I imagine it will not be the same working there without Porfiry Petrovich.'

'He is not dead yet!'

'You do not have to make a decision now. Think about it. In the meantime, my wife and I – and Maria Petrovna, of course – would be delighted to see you at one of our at-homes soon. If you have a moment, I shall find you a card.'

'You mean I am free to go?'

'Of course. You have given a satisfactory account of yourself.'

Virginsky seemed stunned. 'But what if I were to tell you that I really did wish the Tsar dead?'

Major Verkhotsev had found the card with the address of his family residence. He held it out to Virginsky. 'There you are. We are at home every Thursday.'

'Did you not hear what I said?'

Major Verkhotsev smiled. 'Evidently not.' He held out a hand to Virginsky. 'Until we meet again, Pavel Pavlovich, goodbye.'

'Will I be safe? From Dyavol?'

'You mean Tatiscev?'

'I don't know. Dolgoruky claimed that he was haunted by a devil. Perhaps the same will happen to me now. They blamed me for Dolgoruky's death, you know. Which means I must also be responsible for his mother's. And if Porfiry dies . . .'

'You have nothing to fear from Tatiscev. His main concern now will be to flee the country.'

'And from the Devil?'

'My dear fellow, you're one of the new generation. A rationalist. A young man with a scientific outlook. You must simply tell yourself that devils do not exist.'

Virginsky ran a hand over his face. 'I will try.'

Major Verkhotsev nodded encouragingly. 'That's the spirit. Now, I imagine you wish to go straight to see Porfiry Petrovich? He is at the Obukhovksy Hospital. I will have you taken there.'

'If it is permitted, I would rather walk. Alone.'

'Yes, of course. But, please, don't do anything silly on the way. I don't want to be fishing your hat out of the river.'

'I'm not wearing a hat.'

Major Verkhotsev smiled. 'Just as well.'

*

The Fontanka river stretched out in front of him between parallel embankments, unnaturally straight, like a vast bolt of fabric unrolled. It was a shimmering cloth, made up of many subtle colours. In the peaks of its rippling surface, an incarnadine glow danced over oily depths. The river seemed somehow wider than he remembered it, as if the quality of distance had changed in the period of his strange confinement. Everything now was further away, it seemed; in particular, the barriers that divided the city

461

had increased. And at its heart, of course, the city was emptier now, immeasurably emptier.

Across the river he saw the peculiar pseudo-medieval construction of the Mikhailovsky Castle, now the School of Engineering. He thought of the sons sent there by their fathers to acquire a useful profession, imprisoned in that red fortress by vicarious ambition. And yet, somehow, he envied them the certainty and security that such a start in life promised. He wondered if there was a young man standing at one of its windows, viewing him with an equal but opposite envy.

The day was mercilessly bright, spring asserting itself with the insensitivity of the eternally recurring. The sun knew nothing of his suffering. He wondered vaguely how many days had passed since it had all begun. All he could decide with any confidence was that it must be May.

The shriek of a solitary gull ripped the sky. It was a plangent sound, bearing hope away, as if it were a fish snatched from the Bay of Finland.

He thought of Major Verkhotsev's last words to him. The prospect of disappearing from his life held an undeniable allure at that moment. But the river's expanse did not tempt him to suicide. No, what appealed to him was the idea of leaving a hat on the ground, with a suitable note tucked into the band, and slipping away to start a new life, with a new name, somewhere far from where he was standing now. But the trouble was that he would always want to be far from wherever he was standing.

The city's emptiness poured into him, inexplicably weighing him down. He could not understand how the core of him could feel so heavy when he knew it contained only an expanding vacuum.

It was at that moment that he first had the sense of someone, or something, standing behind him, watching him. He did not turn round. If there was someone there, the chances were that it was a Third Section spy. *But surely Verkhotsev would not be as unsubtle as that?* he thought. Or perhaps that was the essence of his subtlety, to order a surveillance operation so implausibly unsubtle that Virginsky was bound not to believe in it? At any rate, if it was a spy, Virginsky judged it best not to reveal that he knew he was under surveillance. He would retain the advantage if he led the other to believe that his presence was not suspected.

In fact, Virginsky's instinct was that his watcher had not come from Fontanka, 16. Indeed, he found it hard to admit where he thought it had come from, or what he thought it was. But his thoughts were accumulating around the conversation he had had with Dolgoruky about a demon. And now Virginsky's refusal to turn round came not from cunning, but from fear.

He turned to his left and started walking along the Fontanka Embankment in the direction of the Obukhovsky Hospital. He heard no footsteps, but he was dogged by the sense of another following him. The further he progressed, the more real that sense became.

He counted his steps, straining to hear an echo of his own footfall that would confirm the reality of the entity tracking him. But if there was a man behind him, his steps were perfectly synchronised with Virginsky's.

At the tenth step, he halted, and of course there was only silence. He set off again, and halted again, this time after a further thirteen steps. Again, silence. His follower was either able to guess exactly when he was going to stop, or made no sound as he tracked Virginsky. But the sense that he was being tracked did not diminish.

*

Porfiry's breathing was shallow and uneven. Each breath when it came seemed like an epic victory. It left him as wearied as if he had wrestled an angel to the earth.

His eyes were closed, bulging blindly in dark sockets. The change in his physical form since the last time Virginsky had seen him was shocking. His cheeks, one of which was padded with a thick dressing, were sunken. Silver stubble over his face added twenty years to his age, or perhaps revealed his true age for the first time. The hair on his head grew in white wispy clumps, exaggerating the irregular shape of his skull, its strange protuberances seemingly forced out by the peculiar ratiocinations that occurred within. As for the rest of the body, it was hard to believe that the shrunken form beneath the covers had ever once been Porfiry Petrovich. There was nothing left of his considerable paunch. It seemed to have melted away in a fever along with the muscles of his arms and legs.

Virginsky began to shake. He fell to his knees and clasped one of Porfiry's hands in both of his, squeezing the clammy flesh as if he thought he was sealing the life in. 'Forgive me.' He lifted the hand and pressed it against his forehead.

He sensed movement on the bed. Porfiry's eyes were open now. Something like a smile flickered weakly over his lips. 'Pavel Pavlovich?'

'Yes. It is I.'

'Good.'

'I . . . did this to you.'

'No.'

'*Forgive me*,' insisted Virginsky.

With heroic effort, Porfiry swung his other hand over to lay it over Virginsky's with a reassuring pat. It took an equal effort for Porfiry to swallow. 'Pray for me. For my soul.'

'You are not going to die!'

Virginsky felt the squeeze of Porfiry's grip. It was surprisingly strong.

'Pray for me,' repeated Porfiry.

'I . . .' He was about to say that he could not, that he did not believe in prayer, or the soul. This once, he exercised tact when it came to expressing his convictions to Porfiry Petrovich.

But Porfiry seemed to have sensed what was on his mind: 'My father . . . was a non-believer too. And yet, God gave him the gift of healing. *Pray for me.*' The entreaty was charged with an urgency that even Virginsky could not escape.

He closed his eyes. He tried to remember the words of Kozodavlev's prayer. '*Eternal God, the judge of all, look with compassion on this our brother.*'

Porfiry lifted his head from the pillow. 'I don't know that prayer.'

'I'm sorry. It's not a proper prayer. The words just came to me.'

'God gave you the words.'

'No, I don't think so. I read it somewhere.'

'No matter.'

Porfiry's head fell back against the pillow. There was a flurry of blinking as his eyelids settled over the bulbs of his eyes. His breathing settled into a deep, regular pattern. His hand relaxed.

Virginsky placed it onto the sleeping man's rising and falling abdomen.

*

He stayed by the bedside all night, dozing in an armchair that was found for him. He dreamt again of the merchant couple's baby but also of his own father. In this dream, the baby was alive, although his father was dead. He shook his head sharply when he woke from it, as if to deny the subconscious wish his dreaming mind had voiced.

In the morning, Dr Pervoyedov expressed himself satisfied with Porfiry's condition; indeed he described himself as more satisfied than he had been for days. He told Virginsky to go home and sleep.

Virginsky found himself on the Fontanka Embankment again. He walked alongside the gently lapping river and thought of the much smaller river that ran through his father's estate. In fact, the river ran through a birch coppice that his father had recently sold. The sale had been the cause of some tension between them at the time. His father had believed that Virginsky's anger derived from seeing his inheritance sold off, but there had been more to it than that, as Virginsky now realised, perhaps for the first time. The river was part of his childhood. It seemed that his whole childhood had been spent running breathless through that coppice; that childhood was a silver lattice made from threaded shafts of summer. But his brightest, happiest memory was of one rare afternoon sitting on the riverbank beside his father, the two of them lazily teasing the water with lines dangled from simple rods. He had looked up at his father, and in his father's gentle smile, happiness dwelt. It was the betrayal of that memory, he realised, that had provoked his anger at the sale of the coppice, not any resentment at the reduction of the estate he stood to inherit.

He crossed the Fontanka by the Semyenovsky Bridge, and it was as if he was walking over the memory of that day. He felt a renewal of the anger he had once entertained against his father, but almost as soon as it had come upon him, he was newly aware of the same unseen presence dogging his steps that he had experienced the day before. But, unlike then, he now had the unmistakable sense that the presence was benign. Whatever it was, he was no longer afraid of it.

Forgive him! The words arrived in his consciousness as an urgent plea. At the same moment, Virginsky realised that if he forgave his father he too would be forgiven.

He would go straight home, as Dr Pervoyedov had advised. In his mind, he began to draft the letter he would write to his father as soon as he had reached his lodgings.

Acknowledgements

My greatest debt is to Fyodor Mikhailovich Dostoevsky. Porfiry Petrovich is his character, of course, not mine. If this book encourages even one reader to turn to Dostoevsky's great novel *Crime and Punishment* for a brush with the original Porfiry, then perhaps I will be forgiven for my shameless purloining.

I'd like to thank Rachel Yarham, Daniela de Gregorio and Mike Jacob for intervening at a crucial moment and preventing me from doing something stupid. Thanks also to Liz Yarham for giving me my first corpse.